D0167146

Acclaim from readers:

"I love this book. Colyer showed the masculine and feminine shadow without apology." **-Anje Waters** (Grass Valley, California)

"Wow, hard hitting, especially for us men. . ." **-Bill Blackwell** (Gallup, New Mexico)

"The book was impossible to put down. The prospects of healing abound." **-Joanne Reatterford** (Ojai, California)

". . .left me wanting more! . . .can't wait for number three." **-Ken Bether** (Brookings, Oregon)

"What an inspiration. My husband and I had our best talk ever after we read your book." **-Sylvia Wolfe** (Fort Collins, Colorado)

"Nik has an ability to capture the perceptions of both sexes. . . Everyone should read this book." **-John Bennett** (Jackson Hole, Wyoming)

"Very powerful message, yet adventurous and playful. Good combination." **-Lynn Barton** (Phoenix, Arizona)

"I want more! Both Biker Bob's have a lot to say, and I like that it's all placed on a Harley." **-Bill Richards** (New York, New York)

"Colyer's gone where no other fiction writer has gone. He's breaking new ground." **-Dusty Heaton** (Seattle, Washington)

"These novels have something important to say and we need to hear it." **-Chris Turner** (Vancouver, Canada)

"Great story! Number two was even better than the first book." **-Bo Sanfield** (Babylon, New York)

". . .really said something about men's work here. Keep it up!" **-Clark Barton** (Houston, Texas)

"Couldn't help myself. Read it straight through." **-Tom Chaffin** (Reno, Nevada)

South

The compass direction South symbolizes the element fire, metal copper and the season summer. South brings us life force, joy, and the noonday sun. The South rules energy, passion, spirit, heat, maturity, blood, healing, flame, destruction, bitterness, watching and laughing. South symbolizes the deserts and active volcanoes. Its color is red.

Copyright © 2002 by Nik C. Colyer -First Edition-

All rights reserved under International and Pan-American copyright conventions. No part of this book may be reproduced or transmitted in any form or by any means, electronic or mechanical, including photocopying, recording, or by any information storage and retrieval system, without written permission from the Henrioulle Publishing Group, 228 Commercial St. #173 Nevada City, California. (530) 470-8739

Publisher's Cataloging-in-publication
(Provided by Quality Books, Inc.)

Colyer, Nik C.
Channeling Biker Bob : Lover's Embrace, the second in a four part series / by Nik C. Colyer. -- 1st ed.
p. cm.
LCCN 2002117344
ISBN 0-9708163-1-6

1. Men—Life skills guide--Fiction. 2. Men—Psychology--Fiction. 3.Man-woman relationships—Fiction. 4. Harley-Davidson motorcycle—Fiction. 5.Alcoholism—Fiction. 6. Spiritual life—Fiction.
I. Title

PS3603.O584C43 2003 813'.6
QB133-994

This novel is a work of fiction. It does not intend to represent any person, living or dead.

Thanks to my editors Bobbie Christmas, Anne-Marie Henrioulle, Kate Henrioulle, Diane Newby, Melissa Marosy, Shera Banbury, Rachelle Hall, and Marie Hatton.

Thanks also to Robert Bly, Michael Meade, Gordon Clay, and many other less visible members of the men's movement.
Printed in the United States of America.
10 9 8 7 6 5 4 3 2 1

To my wife Barbara.
Without her valuable input, I would
look like a chauvinist jerk.

To Lynn and Charlie

Channeling Biker Bob 2

Lover's Embrace

CONTENTS

Author's Note

We live in a volatile world. It's difficult to remain calm when an increased level of tension pervades our environment.

Is it possible that the daily struggle I see in the news reflects my own inner turmoil? Do the people I demonize have more in common with my own private monsters than I care to admit? It was my quest for answers to these questions that led me to the current landscape of *Channeling Biker Bob: Lover's Embrace.*

I wrote in the forward to *Channeling Biker Bob: Heart of a Warrior,* that the feminists had broken new ground for both men and women. Many of us men who were aware during the 70's and 80's, in an attempt to be more "user-friendly", learned to conceal our unpopular masculinity until it was eventually lost altogether.

In *Heart of a Warrior*, it was easier to speak about the lost male. We are so soft and compliant, even if we might be passive-aggressive as hell.

Consider the man who couldn't hide his aggressive behavior, and acted out in an attempt to control his environment. How about the belligerent male who drank too much, spoke too loudly, took over conversations, and stepped over the line in so many ways? What would Biker Bob have to say about him? Although we look at this man and point our fingers in dismay, isn't his blatant and harsh attitude, in reality, a part of us that we keep under wraps?

Could the journey with this unlikely hero also have positive repercussions in our lives? Is it possible that if we actually looked our shadow in the eye, we wouldn't be so quick to judge or force anyone to carry it for us?

During this last year, while I wrote *Lover's Embrace,* these questions walked with me. As the plot unfolded, there were times when I was terrified of how you, my reader, would respond, and I still am. While I sat in front of my keyboard each morning before dawn, I realized that the characters I conjured up may be too much for our sheltered natures to handle. Yet, here the story is, my earnest attempt to attend to a part of humanity uncomfortable to us all.

There is a piece of me in this story, as you will find that there is also a piece of you. It's something that we, you and I, prefer not to look at, but it is a part after all, and don't we need to understand and heal that which haunts us and drags us away from those we love?

Once again, Biker Bob mentored me through this project, and I followed his lead. Still, I am the writer, damn it, and you are the revered reader. In the end, *Channeling Biker Bob Lover's Embrace* never forgets its birthright: misplaced manhood, marriage on the rocks and motorcycles over easy.

Nik January 2003

Channeling Biker Bob 2

Lover's Embrace

The second in a four part series by: Nik C. Colyer

Heart of a Warrior

Lover's Embrace

Magician's Spell

Wisdom of the King

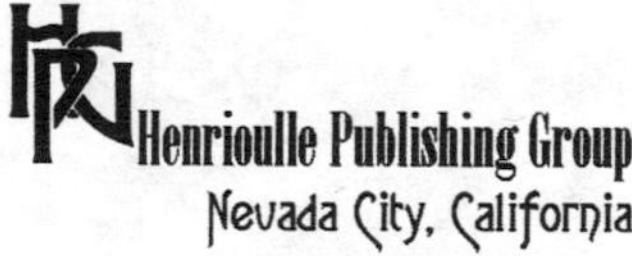

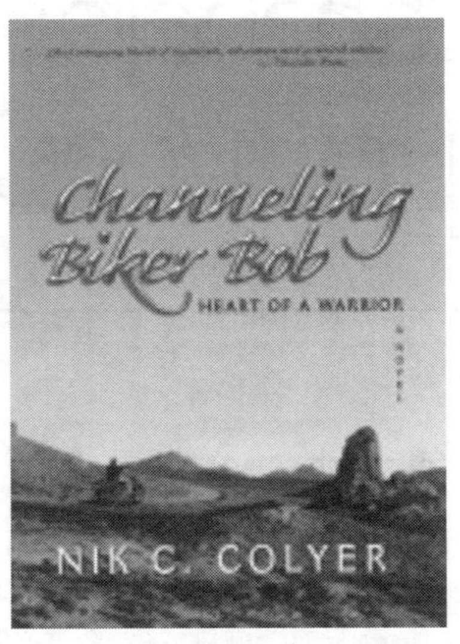

Although as a novel

Channeling Biker Bob 2, Lover's Embrace

stands on its own,

the author intended this four

part series to be read consecutively

with

Channeling Biker Bob 1, Heart of a Warrior

as the first book.

Available through your local bookstore for $13.95

(Ask for: ISBN # 0-9708163-0-8)

or

www.ChannelingBikerBob.com

Chapter 1

Busted

From the shade of a royal palm under the Bill's Big Boy Burgers sign, I observe three dirtbags converge in a parking lot across the street at Waley's bar. It's a known meeting place for outlaws and drug dealers. If I'm patient, they'll slip up and show their true natures. With my thick forearm, I wipe sweat from my face, then grab my borrowed police-issue field camera. I focus on the short one wearing black leather. He's known as Bucky. I snap the shutter. My mouth salivates with the anticipation of busting this crew. The angular face of Tazz, my real quarry, has a rare smile. I can't wait to wipe that grin off his mug.

I zoom out while all three go into a short group hug. I search through the lens for some kind of secret handoff. One of those sleezebags is making a delivery; all I need to do is capture it on film. The electronic bug I installed on the light pole three days ago shouts through my earphones. Lucky for me, they parked close to it.

When they come out of their hug, Tazz who stands a foot taller than the other two, pulls stringy brown hair out of his eyes, and says, “Hey, Buck, how you been?”

“I don’t know,” the little one replies while pulling off his ridiculous fingerless black gloves; a chrome stud on each knuckle. “Things have been strange with Jessica and me.”

Tazz rubs sweat from his ruddy cheek. “Man, I told ya’, when you started with her that you were taking on a big load.”

Bucky folds both gloves and puts them in his back pocket. “She doesn’t let up. I try to keep up with her, but man, it ain’t easy.”

My recorder is on. No need to interpret their code. I can go over the information later. I’m fed up with this gang of thieves and misfits. If it was up to me, I’d plant some shit on ‘em, make an arrest and get it over with. They’re dirty as hell, I just can’t prove it yet.

The longer this thing goes on, the more I want to kick some ass. Last month my Lieutenant, Leonard goddamn puckerface McKerney, took me off the case. He said I was too involved. I’m doing surveillance on my own time. I’ve screwed up so much lately, this bust might be my last chance before I’m back driving a patrol car. I’m not messing this one up. I won’t start any fights. Not one cross word, until I have the goods on them. When I bust them, they’ll know how it feels to fuck with Thomas Goreman.

“Did you get it?” the third guy, a pudgy pecker-brain, asks.

I haven’t seen him before. Maybe he’s an out of town connection. Both Bucky and Tazz look around, a sure sign that something big is about to go down. I lick my chapped lips, drag my arm across my forehead again and pull the focus back to see what their hands are doing.

Tazz says, “Yeah, we got it, but it won’t help.”

The new guy’s jaw drops. I focus in on his dumpy face, and I see an expression of disappointment. “What do you mean?”

"It ain't what's wrong," answers Tazz, as he takes two steps to his old Ford pickup and pulls out a square box the size of a block of ice.

Oh, Sweet Jesus, it's a kilo of grass. Better yet, maybe a few pounds of coke or heroin. Man, old puckerface would shit some bricks if I handed him a kilo of heroin and these three on a platter.

Tazz hands the box over, then does a strange thing. He pulls out a pocketknife, slits a plastic film on top of the box and removes a slip of paper.

It's a ruse.

I've been given explicit orders to leave them alone, but a kilo of heroin doesn't come around that often in a cop's life. Except for the DEA bastards, a big bust is almost non-existent for a regular cop. How many chances does a guy get?

I pull my service revolver, swing open the cylinder and double check that the gun is loaded. After I replace my pistol in the shoulder holster, I set my camera on the floor, squeeze out of my compact car and stroll toward the three sleezeballs.

I step off the asphalt of Peseo Del Oro drive and walk across the crappy parking lot. I don't get it, I'm big as a house and less than twenty yards from them, and they don't see me. It's like I'm invisible. I'm almost to the front door of Waley's Bar as I sidestep a pothole, five yards from my bust. My service revolver is up and I scream, "This is the police. On the ground, face down."

Bucky's hand is in his pocket as he turns toward me. He's known for sharp knives. Out of self-preservation, I lay a quick swipe across his head with the butt of my gun. He drops like a sack of potatoes. I point my pistol at the other two. "On the ground, now!"

They drop. My cuffs are out, and I have Tazz hog-tied in a second. From my back pocket, I pull two heavy zip ties, draw the hands of Tubby together and strap him up. Bucky moans while he lies on the hot pavement. He's the last to get trussed. I kick Tazz on the side of his leg. "Turn over."

He turns toward me with an icy glare. In any normal situation he looks dangerous, but cuffed, he's just another dick trying to push drugs in my town, and I don't put up with that kind of shit.

I look at Tazz with a satisfied grin and say in a sarcastic tone, "What's in the box?" I pick it up, heft it, and yes, it weighs a couple of pounds.

He doesn't say a word.

I glare.

I've hated this guy ever since I saw his ugly face. I know he's a player, I just couldn't prove it till now. What's it been, three months? Today will change everything. Ol' fat-ass Leonard will have a little more respect for Detective Thomas Goreman.

"I asked you a question."

Although I might outweigh the skinny bastard by a hundred pounds, he's always worried me.

I reach down and pull open one flap of the box. A small bundle of bubble wrap flops out, and I yank at the material. My big heroin bust shrinks as the wrap unravels. Oh well, I've got a pound of hash or coke instead of a kilo. A pound is good. I unwrap it further, then look at Tazz.

His steel blue-eyes glare, but his face has turned back into a stupid grin. "Today, Twig, you busted the wrong people."

I scream, "Don't ever call me that name!"

I can't hold back any longer. I swing my right foot at him. My kick moves fast. I'm sure I've caught him square, but he turns at the last second. His leg comes up and grabs my waist, knocking me to the ground. My gun and the box slip from my hands. I'm on my back, floundering for my revolver, when somehow that skinny bastard has me pinned.

What I thought would be a day to remember, a bust to get me out of hot water with Leonard, has turned to shit. My own handcuffs snake around my head and pull tight on my windpipe. I have no idea how, but he's choking me while his hands are cuffed behind his back.

My air restricts, as I buck hard against his weight. Thank Jesus, the tension relaxes. I buck again, flip Tazz off, and look for my gun. With his hands still behind his back, the tubby guy points my pistol at my nose.

I put my hands out, fingers splayed. "You're resisting arrest from a Las Vegas police officer."

Tubby turns to get a better position. "You have no manners."

No manners? What the hell is he worried about?

I say, "I'm a police officer, and if you know what is good for you, you'll give my gun back. You give it back now and I'll forget this whole incident."

Tazz comes up from behind me. "Give me keys to the cuffs, and we'll forget you ever walked over here."

Trussed up with my cuffs, he's still more dangerous looking than ten men.

"Right vest pocket," I say.

"Get it!"

I produce the key.

"Unlock me."

I do as I'm told. I hope a black and white drives by. Where's a cop when you need one?

When he's free, he gives me a frozen glower, pulls his knife and opens it. Oh, sweet Jesus, he's going to gut me right here in the parking lot.

With one swipe of the blade, he slashes the plastic tie holding Tubby's hands together. He walks over to Bucky and repeats the move. Bucky rolls over, and a rivulet of blood runs down his cheek. He pulls himself to his feet and leans against his yellow Harley for support.

Tazz picks up the box of contraband, reaches in and pulls the contents out. He gives me a thin-lipped smile. "Let's see, Twig, you were busting us for this?" He unravels the packing, and a small steel object falls out. "I suggest you look up the laws. Last time I checked, a 1937 Harley oil pump ain't illegal. Rare, yes; expensive, definitely; but not illegal."

In a quick flash, one side of my handcuffs wrap around my thick wrist. With an effort, Tazz latches them. "Now Mr. I'm-a-Las-Vegas-police-officer, step over to the light pole, please."

"No, you wouldn't." He's going to cuff me to the pole and pistol-whip me with my own gun. Now that the tables have turned, I'll be lucky to get out of this alive.

I wrap my arms around a rusted thirty-foot-tall steel pole and feel the second half of my cuffs bind around my other wrist. I prepare myself to be beaten when Tazz grabs my service revolver from Tubbo.

How many times will it take for me to learn I'm not John Wayne? I'm not Humphrey Bogart. I can't go off half-cocked and expect everything to turn out. I think of the reaming that I'll get from McKerney once I get out of the hospital. Hell, if I get out at all.

I wait for the first blow. Instead, Tazz steps in front of me. He opens the gun and drops six shells at my feet.

"I hate guns," he says and slams the pistol hard to the pavement. The barrel digs a deep hole in the asphalt. My six hundred dollar Smith and Wesson is ruined. He takes his heavy motorcycle boot and smashes it. The open cylinder breaks away from my favorite gun. It rolls across the pavement and stops ten feet away. He continues to stomp his boot repeatedly into the body of my trashed pistol. He's in a total meltdown and crushes the gun into hot pavement until it's half-buried.

He looks at me with a sneer. "I feel better."

"Yeah, well who's going to pay for my gun?"

He helps his little buddy to his truck and opens the door. Once Bucky is in the truck, Tazz turns to me. "We'll take Buck to the hospital now, because you ain't got a clue how to deal with your anger. Get a grip on your life, Twig and stop buggin' us."

"Don't call me that name."

He shakes his head. "We don't deal drugs. Hell, Twig, haven't you noticed, we don't have anything to do with drugs?"

Tubby mounts Bucky's yellow Harley and kick-starts it into life. With a thunder, it and the pickup drive away, leaving me in the blazing sun, cuffed to a light pole. Halfway across the parking lot, Tazz's truck makes a sudden turn and swings back toward me. Maybe he's changed his mind. Is he going to ram me? I swing around behind the pole, my only protection.

His truck swerves and stops with the driver door beside me. Tazz pokes his head out the window. "You don't deserve this."

***

I ask Shorty to leave his car and follow on Bucky's bike while I help my bud into the truck. We drive across the lot, and before we pull out into traffic, I swerve back toward Goreman. I point at the open glove box and say to Buck, "Give me that bottle of water."

Buck has found a wad of napkins in an abandoned Burger King bag on the floorboard. He holds it up to the gash on his forehead. "Just ram the son of a bitch, and put him out of his misery."

I steer for the light pole, stop next to Twig and look at Bucky. "No matter what kind of asshole he is, we can't leave him without water on a day like this."

"Let him sweat it out. He'll flag someone down soon enough."

I don't say another word, but hold out my hand and snap my fingers twice.

Bucky huffs, reaches in the glovebox and pulls out a bottle of water. Before he hands it over, he says, "It would serve him right."

"Come on, Buck, I remember when you were just as angry and didn't know it either. I don't know why, but Bob has plans for him."

Buck hands over the bottle, shifts his bloody napkin and looks at me. "Biker Bob?"

"Yeah, go figure. Bob came to me last night and told me to keep an eye on Twig."

Buck snorts. "What the hell for?"

I shrug. "You know how mysterious Bob is."

I poke my head out, scowl and toss the bottle at Twig. It bounces on the hot pavement. "You don't deserve this."

When I drive away, Bucky rotates, looks out the back window and flips Twig the bird.

I grin. "That ain't gonna' help a thing."

He turns back and faces the windshield. "It helped me."

I merge into traffic and shift to second gear. "We better get you to a hospital."

"Hey, fuck a hospital," Bucky holds pressure on the bloody bunch of napkins. "I haven't got any money for hospitals."

"I don't know, Buck, he opened up a pretty big gash above your eye. You're going to need a couple of stitches."

"Can't we just put a few butterfly bandages across it?"

I turn my rear view mirror toward him. "Have a look for yourself, Pal. Twig didn't hold back. It's opened pretty wide."

"Look, Tazz, I don't have any money. Maybe we could go over to Doc Winter. He's retired now, but he owes me a favors. I'm sure he could throw a few stitches in me without much fuss."

I look at him and back at a long string of slow moving cars. "I don't know, Buck, Winter is across town, and traffic is pretty heavy. It'll take an hour to get there. Hell, you might lose a lot of blood by then."

"I'll be okay."

I change lanes and say, "It's only been five minutes, and already you don't look too good. I got medical insurance from work. Maybe we could pass you off as me."

"Shit Tazz, you're way over six feet, and I'm down here at five-five. How do you think we could pull that off?"

I grin and make a left onto a side street, headed toward Sunrise hospital. "Maybe they don't check."

Buck pulls the napkin away from his forehead. "Hey, man, the bleeding has slowed. Why don't we go to Winter's place. He'll button me up, and I'll be on my way."

I spin a U-turn, drive into a gas station lot and wave Shorty forward. I look at Bucky. "You know, you're one stubborn son of a bitch."

Shorty pulls up and kills the engine. "What's up?"

I turn to Buck. "You want him to take your bike to his house?"

"Yeah, I guess. I really wanted to go for a ride today."

"Man, in an hour you're going to have a headache that won't quit. I think riding is out for the next couple of days."

Bucky huffs in disgust and waves his hand. "Okay."

I turn to Shorty. "Take his bike to your house. He'll pick it up when he's feeling better."

Shorty lifts off the seat and looks in the window. "Hey, Bucky, I like the attention your bike gets."

Bucky puts the napkin back on his forehead and glares at Shorty. "Don't get too used to it. You and my bike are going to be a one-night fling."

Shorty grins. "I love one-nighters."

Buck flips him the bird.

Shorty gets a serious look. "I'll keep good care of your machine, man. Let me know when you're feeling better."

He cranks the bike, kicks it into gear and turns into traffic.

***

I sit in the hot sun for ten minutes before a couple comes out of the bar and walks across the blistered pavement. They both have a noticeable stagger.

I lift my handcuffed arms and say, "Hey, call the police for me."

The guy, a squat, sausage-legged biker, looks at me. "Call the cops yourself, Twig. Serves you right for spying on us."

"Don' t call me that name."

He saunters by, and his roundish girlfriend rotates her head after they pass. They get into an old beater Dodge with sun-peeled paint.

I yell, "I' ll be back to arrest you for drunk driving."

He starts his reluctant engine. When his car pulls away, he flips me off.

I have the bottle of water half-finished before I see a black-and-white cruiser along the main drag. I' m on my feet yelling and banging on the steel pole with my handcuffs. At the last second, the car swings into a dirt lot next to the bar, then pulls around and up to me.

The window rolls down, and that punk kid, Sandy Harvey, pokes his head out. "What' re you doing, Sarge?"

"Oh, shut up," I scream. "Unlock these cuffs."

"Sure enough, Sarge," he says with a cackle. "But, you gotta' tell me how you got cuffed to the pole in the first place."

I glare.

He and his partner get out. Sandy fumbles for his key and unlocks my wrists. Without a word, I gather up my gun parts and storm off straight for my car on the far side of the boulevard.

"Hey, Sarge," he yells as I cross the parking lot. "Least you could do is thank me."

I get to my car, and my borrowed three-thousand-dollar camera is gone. Oh, God, I didn't exactly tell anyone at work that I'd taken it.

I start the car. I'd better have a few beers to calm myself before I go home. I don't want any problems with Georgina. It wouldn't take much for me to go off on her. She doesn't deserve it, and I don't need any more screwups. It hasn't been a great day. Hell, it hasn't been a great month. A cloud of disaster has followed me, and I'm exhausted.

Sammy's Sports Bar is around the corner, but all of the guys hang out there. I drive along the strip for a mile and pull into a back-alley dive called Wizard's Corner. When I want to get away, this is the place.

I get out of my car, and a blast of desert heat stings my already raw nose. Being cuffed to a light pole in this inferno ruined any chance of my sinuses healing from spring pollen; one more reason why I'm determined to get those biker pricks.

I walk across the parking lot and up to the door as it swings open. A weasel-faced guy barges out. In a half-inebriated drawl, he apologizes and walks toward the cars. I enter the dark, cool building and sit at the bar.

A heavy guy, with a salesman look, sits three stools to my left. His red tie is loose under a cheap, wrinkled suit that stretches too tight across his back. He takes a long pull from a dark ale.

A dozen stools to my right, a washed-out blonde stares into her Manhattan. A couple murmurs at a corner table. They're too far away for me to hear. In a sense, I have the place to myself, exactly what I need after this disaster of a day.

A kid with spiked hair steps over. "What'll ya have?"

"White Russian double and a Coors."

"Kind of a dangerous combo, don't you think?"

"Just pour it and don't analyze my choice."

The kid shrugs. "Hey, it's your life, I'm only the bartender."

He turns and mixes my drink. Through a wall-length mirror, I watch the blonde pull her gaze from her glass and glance in my direction. All I need a middle-aged broad to talk my ear off. To my relief, she drops her attention back to her glass and finishes the drink.

My Russian is set on the bar, and I down half of it. My beer shows up at the right moment, and I chase the milky concoction with a long draw from the amber bottle.

I've finished my drink and order another when the door bursts inward. A heavy-shouldered football-player type saunters in. He sits two seats away from me. It's obvious he's not a quiet drinker. I don't want any trouble, so I look the other way. When my second Russian appears, I take it, my half-finished bottle of beer, slide off my stool and walk across a postage stamp sized dance floor toward a little table in the corner.

The big guy rotates on his stool and looks at me. "What, I'm not good enough? Is that it?"

I know where this'll go. I say nothing and sip my beer. I look toward the blonde, who hasn't brought her stare out of her new drink in five minutes.

He won't get a rise from me. I want a quiet place with no trouble, certainly not with this overheated bull.

I don't look at him, because if I do, he'll be over here, and it won't take long before someone throws a first punch. I'm relieved to see his attention has shifted from me to Blondie. He moves two stools closer to her. "Hi, honey, I'm Frank Bonnin." He has a different tone, but it's still loud and demands attention.

She doesn't stir.

"Leave the lady alone," the kid says. "She's married."

Mr. Trouble spins his head back to the bartender. "Did I ask your advice?"

The kid throws up his hands and backs off.

Despite his belligerent response, the guy settles into his bourbon on ice.

It goes that way for a relaxing fifteen, maybe twenty minutes, long enough for him to down three drinks.

When he slugs his third and orders another, his attention returns to Blondie. He moves one more stool toward her. "If you're married, how come you don't wear a ring? I mean, every woman who's married wears a ring."

She doesn't reply, but looks up at the skinny kid behind the bar. "Another Manhattan, please," she says without a single glance toward Mr. Bull-in-a-china-shop.

The kid shrugs apologetically and mixes her drink.

"Why don't you wear a ring?" he demands in his boom of a voice. He pulls over one more stool, leaving four between them.

All it takes is one jerk to ruin a perfect end to this fucked up day. The way things have gone, I should have expected it.

He stares a hole in what little chest she has. I imagine slather dribbling down his chin.

If he moves one seat closer, I'll say something, but not until then.

Her complete disregard of his advance slows him down. He takes a long draw from his drink, slams the empty glass on the bar, demands another, then gets up and lumbers towards the restroom. When he passes, I see he's much bigger than I first estimated. He must be two inches taller and outweighs me by twenty pounds and not an ounce of him looks like fat.

While he's in the restroom, the bar returns to its nonchalant atmosphere. I finish my third Russian, and for a minute feel the knot loosen on a noose that's been around my neck for a week. In my mind, I'm transported back to a time when I lived on a commune in the hills above Sacramento. Those wonderful unencumbered, stress-free days. It's where I met Georgina. Sweet Jesus, how long ago was it, fifteen years?

Things seemed much easier: just drop out of society and disappear into the woods. Was I there only a single year? It felt like three. What happened? How did I end up in Vegas, of all places? How did I end up a cop and not a very good one, at that?

The silence ends when Mr. Lugnuts bursts out of the bathroom and pushes his way across the bar. He goes out of his way to make a special path by me.

When he sits back at the bar, he perches one stool closer to Blondie and pulls his fresh drink over with him.

I won't say anything unless he starts to bug her.

I've already guessed that he can't leave her alone. He's one of those men who can't help but cause trouble.

He takes one short slug from his drink, leans toward her and in a decided slur, like he's become Tom Cruise, says, "Hey Babe, you want some company?"

"Leave her alone," I growl from my table.

He spins on his stool and glares at me. "Fuck off!"

"She doesn't want to be bothered."

He leaps off his stool and lands on both feet. When he walks toward me, I'm inclined to jump up, but I stay seated. When he arrives at my table, he towers over me. "You got more to say?"

I'm in my element. I want him to take a swing. All I have to say is anything other than an apology, and a battle is sure to begin. Maybe it's the very one I've looked for all day, ever since I was turned down for sex this morning. I look across at the barkeep. He's taken a spectator's stance. If it were his bar he would never condone this, because when the two of us bulls get started, the bar will be a shambles.

Hulk towers over me.

My empty beer bottle is in my fist. I say in a quiet tone, "Leave her--" My last word, "alone," never leaves my lips.

His right fist comes from around his back. It bears down on my nose. It's a fast swing. He means to shatter every bone in my face, but he's not quick enough. I lift my bottle butt first to meet his freight train of a fist. When it connects, the bottle doesn't break, but I hear a number of bones crunch. I feel the impact;

my arm is pushed toward my face. The bottle and his bone-shattered fist graze my forehead. I slide down in my chair, and my knee finds his crotch. He writhes on the floor and tries to catch his breath. I'm on my feet and take my first satisfactory kick to his midsection. It'll take any wind he has left. My second punt is to his thigh, which hobbles any chance of him getting up. I've kicked four or five times before the barkeep arrives to pry me off of the bastard.

"Come on buddy." He pulls at my right shoulder. "You got him. That's enough. Stop before you kill him."

I land one last bone-crunching kick to his chest and allow the kid to pull me away. I'm hyped and ready to take on the world.

The kid yanks me back from the groaning lump on the floor. "Hey, man, that's enough. No need to kill him."

I pull myself away from his grip and turn on him, fist in the air, ready to let it fly on my next victim. Bring 'em on. I'll take all comers.

Blondie steps into my line of vision. "Thank you, stranger," she says in a soft voice. "You can stop now."

As usual, a woman's voice, any woman's voice, puts the brakes on me and my good time. The pitch of her voice, not frantic, not worried, but calm and matter-of-fact, takes the punch out of my frenzy. When she touches my arm, the very arm ready to swing on the kid, my strength drains. My hand falls limp to my side. I feel a childish quiver on my lower lip. I want to reach out to her, bury my head between her breasts and blubber for three hours. I want her to caress my hair and tell me everything will be all right. Tears well up in my eyes, but quickly get replaced with anger. My body tightens. I yank my arm away from her and spit out my next few words. "Don't fuck with me."

I turn and walk out of the bar, ashamed at myself for feeling little again.

When I stomp across the parking lot, the faces of those bikers come back to me. Not faces of anger, even after I'd handcuffed them and conked their buddy for nothing. Not faces of drugged-out bikers, but expressions of calmness. Once they'd turned the tables on me, and I was attached to the pole with my own cuffs, they didn't take their frustration out on me, and not because they were frightened that I was a cop either. The only anger I saw came from Tazz when he killed my gun and Bucky, when he flipped me the bird.

I reach my car, unlock the door and get into an oven. When I start my engine, the air conditioner cools things a little. I pull out into molasses-slow traffic. The ride home gives me time to recover and put my anger monster away.

When I pull into my double car garage, I'm calm. I'm the epitome of calmness; a Buddhist monk. The bikers aren't the only ones who can do this. I get out of my car and walk into the house.

"What the hell is going on?" I yell as I enter the stifling kitchen. "How come the air conditioner isn't on?"

When I step over to the thermostat and turn its dial, I don't hear the familiar click of the heat pump or its blower.

"Georgina," I scream, "what's going on?" Damn, my Buddha calmness is gone.

"Georgina?"

I get no response.

I walk out of the kitchen and up the stairs toward our three bedrooms. Halfway up the stairs, I call out again.

I hear her familiar timid voice from the patio, "I'm out here."

I'm downstairs and walking fast toward the sliding glass door. I'm a patient man, but when I see her, I bark, "What the hell is going on?"

She cringes in one of those crappy plastic lawn chairs she bought last month. Before she can answer, I'm looming over her. I don't know why she flinches, I've never hit her; at least I've never meant to hit her.

When she pulls back, I take a breath, drag over a plastic chair and try to sit in it carefully to keep it from collapsing. Why she wastes money on cheap garbage like these chairs, I have no idea.

After my deep breath, I calm and ask again with a strain in my voice. "Honey, how come the air conditioner isn't on?"

Her voice quavers. She's nervous. "It's broken."

"What?" I snarl.

She pulls back.

"What do you mean?" I ask again in a controlled effort to not snap her head off.

"It broke this morning. I didn't know what to do."

"Sweet Jesus, you call a repairman before I get home."

"Yes, honey, I'll call him now, but I didn't think we could afford it."

"Now won't help. I can't believe you don't know how to take care of a single thing without my intervention. You're about as hopeless as. . ." I catch myself and let the sentence fade.

She asks, "Can I get you a glass of lemonade?"

"Get me a beer."

She scrambles to her feet and rushes back into our oven of a house. She returns moments later with my beer.

"Warm beer?" I shout. "What the hell will I do with warm beer?"

She takes the bottle and feels it. "It's not warm. I put it in the fridge an hour ago."

"Obviously, an hour isn't long enough."

She grimaces and moves toward the kitchen.

I grab it. "Never goddamn mind. There's no use in putting it back, you already opened it."

She goes into a familiar deer-caught-in-the-headlights look and freezes into position. She stands for a moment before speaking. When she does, her voice breaks. She can't get a sentence to come out in an intelligible manner.

I'm fed up with her stumbling around. I bark. "Sit down and say what you want to say."

She gets a determined look. Her sentence is loud, too loud. "I can't take it any more, Thomas; I'm leaving."

Oh right, how many times has she said that?

She spins away from me and walks through the sliding glass doors into the house.

I leap to my feet and follow. "What do you mean?" It's obvious she's headed for the front door. I pour on speed, round my leather couch and block the door. When she sees me, she turns and sprints for the back door. I run to catch her and take a short cut through the kitchen. She's a sly one and doubles back to the front door again. She opens it, runs through and bangs it behind her. I'm pissed. I grab the lever handle, pull down harder than I want and rip it off the door.

She's halfway down the walk before I grab the collar of her blouse and yank her backwards. She slips and falls hard on her hip. I haul her back to her feet, grab her hand and pull her ten yards back into the house. Before I close my front door, I look out at the other ticky-tack houses. Their manicured lawns and trimmed hedges make me sick. I search for anyone peering out of a window or walking along the sidewalks. I see no one. No one ever is outside in our cemetery of a neighborhood. Before I spin back to face the nasty bit of business Georgina started, I notice nosy Mrs. Frunder's front window blinds snap back into position. I pay her no attention, push the front door closed and march Georgina into the living room. I sit her down on our couch. She puts her hands up for protection.

"I won't hit you, if that's what you're afraid of." I sit on the arm of my favorite lounge chair. "Now what were your plans?"

It takes her a month to form a single word, and I get impatient.

"What?" I shout.

She flinches, then with a determined face says, "I can't stand it, Thomas. You're not reasonable anymore."

On what I already thought was one of the worst days of my life, reasonable is not what I'm left with. I'll be demoted over borrowing the camera alone. I must live with the embarrassment of being found by loud-mouth Sandy, the twerp in the black and white. Tazz smashed my service revolver. I may have charges filed against me from the guy I beat up in the bar. Certainly, there'll be property damage for the busted bar furniture. I should have paid off the bartender.

After everything, a broken air conditioner does not leave me in a mellow state of mind.

I bellow, "What do you mean you're leaving?"

Convenient tears spill down her cheeks. She whimpers.

I'm on my feet and tower over her, "What the fuck do you mean?"

She cowers into the couch and says nothing. I calm myself and return to my original position on the arm of the chair.

I want to be patient. I know she must cry herself out before I can get another word out of her. I'm not sure, does she want to go to her mother's for a weekend? Maybe she's planning a California visit to her women's-lib sister. I hate her sister. She puts dangerous ideas into Georgina's head.

Five minutes of sobs, and I get more edgy, but I hold my tongue and wait. After another minute of sniffles, she's quiet.

I want to be reasonable. I'm ready to be friendly, but I feel my rage monster. I ask in a controlled, monotone voice. "What do you mean, you want to leave?"

She has her face buried in her hands. She looks up. "I can't take it anymore. You're too angry."

"You mean you want to take a break for a while?"

"No, Thomas, I'm leaving for good."

I'm on my feet, pacing the room. I turn to her and shout, "What the fuck do you mean?"

"You frighten me. I can't live with you any longer."

I'm confused. In a thousand years I couldn't have guessed she would ever leave. She's talked about leaving, but never looked this serious. She's always been mousy, unable to do anything for herself. How could it be that the first decisive act she attempts is to abandon me?

I flop in my chair and plead, "You can't leave, Georgina. You can't just walk out. I know I've been aggressive lately, but I'll change, I swear I will."

I'm sure my pleading voice gives her courage. "How could you change, Thomas? Your meanness runs deep. Even if you did start to change right now, it would take years for you to get this poison out of your system."

"I'll quit my job," I promise, knowing I may already be fired for the missing camera.

She looks at me with tears in her eyes. Her mouth quivers. "If I could only believe you. How many times have you made this promise? How many times have you agreed to go to a therapist with me? Have you gone once? I have too many bruised wrists and twisted elbows from you manhandling me. My sister told me to leave a year ago. I've waited for you to show good faith and make some changes, but you haven't. I'm leaving. You must let me go."

I sit stunned. She's leaving me on the worst day of my life.

She gets up, turns and starts for the front door. I let her go. I should be sad. I should bawl my eyes out, but all I feel is numb. All I see is a dismal future of being alone and with no job. Without thinking, I jump to my feet and rush for the door. By the time I open it, Georgina has made her way to the sidewalk. She turns, sees me and sprints for her car; the one I bought for her three years ago. I reach for the handle as she locks the door. She fumbles her keys into the ignition. I yank on the locked door, go into a black fury and smash my fist through the window. I don't care about glass. She won't make a fool out of me, not on this disaster of a day.

My fist shatters the glass. A thousand shards spray over her and the front seat. I open the door, grab her hand and pull her up the walkway. If I can get her inside, where peering eyes can't see, we can have a serious talk about her plans. I'll convince her to stay.

On the porch she makes an unexpected twist. I stumble sideways toward the concrete and release my grip to break the fall. Before I land, she wriggles away. As I right myself, she's on her feet and runs toward the car.

"Don't do it," I yell. "Don't get in the car, or I'll. . ." I can't finish my sentence, because I'm not sure what I'll do. I round the back of her car as the door closes. The engine is still running. I have only a second before she pulls the shift lever down and drives away. Her hand grabs the lever and pulls toward her lap. In a last ditch effort, without thinking about what I'm doing, my right arm makes a wide arc, and I fling it through the opening where a window used to be. I'm going for the key, but she leans forward at the same second, and I accidentally catch her hard below the ear. Her whole body jerks. The car lurches forward and drags me with it. Her head falls forward. The horn blares as her car trundles across the street. I can't stop it. I run along, reach inside, grab the steering wheel and direct the car toward the middle of the street. I sprint in an attempt to keep up with it. I try for the gearshift, but miss. The car lurches to a speed I can't maintain on foot. I lean in the window, feet in the air and grab the shift lever. I pull it up, out of gear and accidentally put it into reverse. Tires squeal, as the car suddenly reverses direction and rolls backward. I'm ripped from the window and land flat on hot pavement. My arm is almost torn out of its socket. I sit up as her Toyota rolls diagonally across the street and crashes into the left headlight of a Las Vegas black and white. Georgina's car idles fast, pushes against the big cruiser, but doesn't move.

Mike Sands, a veteran uniform, gets out and sprints for her Toyota. He reaches inside the window and turns off the key. Her car relaxes and rolls away from the black and white. Before it can go much farther, Mike shifts into park. I hear the familiar ratchet of an emergency brake.

I sit in the middle of the street rubbing my injured arm.

My ex-partner, Frank Henderman, gets out. "What the hell's going on, Thomas?"

"Hey, Frank," Mike says, "you'd better call an ambulance. This one's got problems."

I'm on my feet, still rubbing my sore arm as Frank leans inside his cruiser to call in. He turns to me. "What happened?" His tone isn't friendly.

I think fast, then tell a convincing story about my wife passing out at the wheel and how I had to break a window to save her from crashing. My story looks good, and I have the two cops persuaded, when Mrs. Frunders comes into view.

She points at me. "I don't know what he's telling you, but I've watched him manhandle his wife for years. This time he went way over the line. I'm the one who called."

While Mike attends to Georgina, Frank pulls out his lined pocket notebook and a pencil. "What happened?"

She steps closer to Frank and looks at the notebook as he writes. "As I said, he's been abusing his wife for years. I happened to look out my window and I saw. . ." She goes on for ten minutes before the two cops turn to me.

Frank asks, "How much of this is true?"

If I deny, I have problems. If I confess, I go to jail. I lean against his crumpled cruiser and cross my arms in front of me. "Who you going to believe, this nosy old biddy or a fellow cop?"

An ambulance rolls up, and paramedics take care of Georgina. They put a neck brace on, load her into the vehicle and drive away.

Had I been anyone else, I'd be handcuffed and hauled down to the station for questioning. I'm a fellow cop. Once they finish with Mrs. Nosy, they help me hand push the crumpled Toyota back into a parking place, then a tow truck hauls them and their car off.

I walk into my house for another beer. At this point, even a warm beer will taste good. I need to lie low and get through this day without any more trouble. On a day like today, it won't be easy. If I stick around home in front of the TV, maybe nothing else will happen. I'll visit Georgina later. For now, I'll stay put before anything else turns to shit.

At seven the next morning, I awake to the blare of my phone. Without a hello, Lieutenant Leonard yells in my ear. "What the fuck do you think you're doing?"

I don't say a word.

"She's your wife, for God sakes. How could you beat up your own wife?"

My end of the line is silent.

"Goreman, I don't know what to do with you."

"Sir, I can explain."

"There's nothing to explain. You're on temporary suspension until we get this whole thing figured out. I've known all along you were a dick, but I can't believe you'd take it out on your wife. You're an embarrassment to the force."

My phone goes dead, and I awake again at nine-thirty. This time a woman is on the line. "Mr. Goreman?"

"Yes." My voice is groggy.

"I'm Doctor Maribeth Soranto, at the station."

"Yes." It's all I can think to say.

"Because of recent circumstances, I'll need to meet with you at one o'clock today."

She doesn't request a meeting and I hate women ordering me around. She is the station shrink, though, and all I can say is, "Okay."

I despise shrink types. They always have smug smiles, like they know everything. But, if there's any chance to keep my job, I'd better show up.

At ten, after showering, I hear a knock at my door. I'm supposed to be at work and Georgina is normally at home. Is that her lover at the door? Although I've never caught her, lately I've been suspicious that she's seeing someone on the side. I step to the door and look through the peephole. It's an LVPD uniform. Has she been seeing that dork Delivan? I swing open the door, ready to confront the home wrecker bastard. I'm curious what he'll say.

He and I face off. I look at his surprised face. His partner stands behind him. I can never remember the guy's name.

Has Georgina been fucking both of them?

"Thomas Goreman?" Delivan says in a dramatic official voice.

"Yeah, sure, Sam, you know me. What's up?"

"You're under arrest." His partner steps out with a pair of cuffs and proceeds to force one side over my thick wrist. He turns me around and pulls my hurt arm up. With mechanical indifference, Delivan reads my rights.

"Why are you arresting me?" I protest. "I didn't do anything."

"Look, Thomas, this morning I was given the worst kind of duty. I was sent to arrest a fellow officer, and that's what I have to do."

"What for?" I say. "If it was the fight in the bar last night, it was self-defense. I've got a whole bar full of witnesses to back me up."

Delivan looks embarrassed. "The State of Nevada has filed a complaint for your wife."

The second cuff is on, and the two cops lead me down my walkway. "My wife? That was an accident."

"I don't know, Thomas. I'm just doing my job."

"She was leaving in such an all-fired hurry, she banged her head. She's the--"

"Thomas," he yells.

I stop.

In a quieter tone, as he opens the back door of his car, he says, "Save it for the judge."

He helps me into the cruiser. I give a last protest and go silent.

The two men get in front and drive a well-known route to the station.

I sit in a cell for two hours, and not one cop checks in on me. For the first time in my life, I'm led to a courtroom and seated with six other defendants, all from a familiar walk of life I despise.

The first is arraigned on burglary, a second on six speeding tickets that went to warrants, the third is charged with drunk and disorderly, then it's my turn. My attorney, a little pudgy guy I've just met, steps up with me.

"Thomas Goreman," the judge says, "you are being charged with felony assault and battery, disorderly conduct for an officer and spousal abuse. How do you plead?"

"Felony battery, your honor?"

My attorney nudges me.

"Yes, sir. Your wife is being treated for head contusions, a broken jaw and a concussion."

"She hit her head getting into the car."

The judge glares. "Sir, I'm presiding over an arraignment. Tell me how you plead."

I take a moment to assimilate the charges, then remember my nosy neighbor and the police who took her statement.

My attorney pulls at my jacket sleeve and mouths the words.

"Not guilty, Your Honor," I say.

He looks at the bailiff. "Bail to be set at fifteen thousand dollars."

He turns to me. "Mr. Goreman, Mrs. Georgina Goreman and the State of Nevada have filed a temporary restraining order against you. Bailiff, please give Mr. Goreman a copy. You're not allowed. . ."

I hear his words, but the message doesn't sink in. In automatic response, I say, "Yes, Sir."

He bangs the gavel. "Next case."

Fifteen thousand? How could such a small squabble between spouses be such a big deal?

I'm back in a cell and waiting for bail. I think about the beginning of that horrendous day: surveillance on the biker guys and how it turned out; the lost camera; a brawl in the bar and finally, my fight with Georgina. Was she really going to leave? I remember how the bikers responded to me with restraint and how they're unlike any other bikers I've ever seen. Considering my current situation, I guess I could use some of that kind of self-control.

I sit thirty minutes in the holding cell. It's time enough to think a lot about where things went awry. It was an all around bad day made much worse by my hostility. I mean, hell, isn't it why I work alone, because no one wants to partner up with me? Isn't it why my lieutenant put me on shit details, ones that needed no second, because of my temper?

Lots of time to think before the cell door opens, and I'm led down a long hall to Receiving and my bondsman.

Once papers are signed and a check written, I walk out of a building I've walked out of every day for twelve years. Instead of being a cop with respect, I walk out on the other side of the fence. I feel tarnished, unclean. All I want to do is go home and take a shower, but I need to see Georgina, to change her mind.

The day is blazing hot by the time I get to my car. I pull out onto the city streets and head south toward University Medical Center.

Sweat drips off of my brow as I walk into the cool, acidic air of the hospital. The woman at Information gives me Georgina's room number. I take an elevator to the third floor and walk toward her room. At the nurse's station I'm greeted by a glowering male nurse the size of a basketball court.

"I'm sorry, Sir, Mrs. Goreman can't accept visitors."

"It's okay," I say, "I'm family." I turn away and walk toward her room.

Quick as an ally cat, he's out from behind his desk and heads me off. "Please, sir, no visitors for now."

I stop and stare at him. "I'm her husband, for God sakes."

"Please, Sir, come back to the station desk, and let me show you the paperwork."

It's obvious that short of a physical confrontation he isn't going to let me walk down the hall. I'm a little put out, but I want to be reasonable. I turn and walk back to the nurse's station. He follows.

After a bit of shuffling, he hands me a document.

"A restraining order?" I bellow.

In my confusion and embarrassment, I stand warily on my side of the desk. I mutter some unintelligible remarks and have a vague memory of the judge saying something, but a restraining order? In a trance I walk to the elevator, go to the ground floor. Still dazed, I exit the building.

I'm out in the heat without noticing, until I sit in my oven of a car. The heat is nothing, compared to the familiar fury building inside my chest.

Without thinking, I find my car homing in on the nearest bar, three blocks away. I swing into a parking space, pull my fingers through my short black hair and take a constrained breath. I get out and step across hot pavement to the front door. Refrigerated air chills me. I walk across the room and sit at an almost-empty bar. One old guy is at a table engrossed in a baseball game.

The barkeep steps over and nods. It irks me that he doesn't greet me, but this isn't the Holiday Inn, and being welcomed isn't the reason why I'm here. "Double White Russian," I say, as I grab for some mini pretzels in a bowl on the counter. I turn and with my back to the bar, try to watch the game on TV. The day's events distract me, and I can't get excited, even when Mark McGuire grand slams another in a long string of homers.

When my drink comes, it's gone in one long gulp.

My glass is back on the bar and over my shoulder I order another.

Twenty minutes later, on the second-most rotten day of my life, my outlook has shifted. Although my concentration on the game lacks its normal vitality, I go through the motions and yell in all the right places, make comments at appropriate moments.

By five, I've sipped my way through four doubles. The bar fills, and it's my cue to vacate. In the inebriated and dangerous mood I'm in, I'll only find trouble in this gathering of working stiffs unwinding from a hot day. It isn't my crowd and I know it.

I unravel myself from my barstool, drift across the room and plow my way through the front door. In my altered state I don't feel the heat. There's no feeling in my fingertips or toes.

My drive home is tenuous at best, but I manage to steer the vehicle into my garage without a scratch. I stumble into the house and discover the air conditioner still doesn't work. I remind myself to call a repairman when I recover.

In a sweaty heap, I fall onto my unmade bed and pass out.

Chapter 2

Losing it

"What the fuck do you think you're up to?" a voice from the deepest corner of my dream echoes out.

"Up to? What do you mean?"

"Don't give me that crap, just answer my question."

I search the dark mist. "Who are you?"

"Answer my question."

I know what his question means, but I don't have an answer, so I stall. It's my only alternative.

"Where are you?"

"Never you fucking mind, just answer my question. Even if you don't have an answer, give it your best shot."

A lanky man steps into sight with a cocky confidence. His biker leathers and long blue/black ponytail remind me of the bastards who cuffed me to the light pole.

"Who are you?"

"Never mind for now. Consider what you're doing with your life, Twig."

"Don't call me that. I hate that name."

"I hate being stalled, so answer the question."

"What are you talking about? This is my dream. I decide what questions I want to answer and which ones I don't. Who are you to tell me--"

"Answer my fucking question, Twig, before I'm forced to do something you'll regret."

"Don't call me that name, and what could you possibly do in my dream?"

In a flash, I'm out of the vague darkness and standing over Georgina's hospital bed. Her jaw is wired, and one whole side of her face is plum colored.

"Sweet Jesus, did I do this?" I say to her, forgetting I'm in this weird dream. Her closed eyes flash open. She looks like the little girl in "The Exorcist". "Yes, you did, you violent son of a bitch. Did you think it would be fun to take your anger out on your wife?"

"Georgina, I didn't mean to hurt you."

"Georgina," she mocks in a sarcastic voice. "I didn't mean to hurt you. You never mean to hurt me, you stupid ox, but you've hit me for the last time."

I've never heard her be so hostile.

"What do you mean?" I ask.

"The restraining order isn't temporary. I'll keep that order in place for the rest of your natural life. The District Attorney filed charges and promised me you'll be convicted."

"Convicted of what? I love you."

She's quiet and shakes her head. "You don't get it, do you? Can't you see anything different about me? Can't you comprehend that you hurt people everywhere you go? You're a walking disaster to anyone who gets in your way. Listen up, pal. You're not getting away with it this time."

I feel a ball of emotion rise from deep in my guts. It's the very sentiment that always leaves me vulnerable. I hate feeling small. I stuff it, and my old friend anger reappears. "Now you listen to me, Georgina. I have--"

"You have nothing, Thomas," she shouts through her wired teeth. "Unless you find a way to let your emotions come to the surface without getting violent, you will be a raging dick for the rest of your life. You can't suppress it, then take it out on innocent bystanders like me."

Her demeanor shifts from anger to pity. I hate her pity. "I'm sorry I won't be around to see you make the shift, but you've hit me for the last time. I know that my weakness allowed your brute to run the show. It's time for both of us to get help. It's too late for us to be together." Her face shifts into a sad expression. "Good-bye, Thomas."

My emotional ball rises again. It's much too big to deal with. My wife's left, and she isn't coming back.

"I'm sorry, Georgina," I wail. "I'll never hit you again."

I cry, maybe for the first time in ten years. I'm on my knees; my hands cover my face; I'm bawling like a little baby. I can't help it. I can't get control.

I shift from a kneeling position to lying on my oven-hot bed in one choking second. My emotional outburst never happened. My tears, thank Jesus, were all left in that horrible nightmare. A streetlight throws a dancing shadow of the acacia tree across my bedroom wall. Georgina and I planted that tree when we bought the house. Its branches are tossed by stiff desert gusts. The wind chimes she hung from our front porch, tinkle out a sorrowful melody.

I don't cry and that's all that counts. I get up, tear off yesterday's clothes and go into the bathroom to relieve myself. On the way back into my bedroom, I flip on an overhead light for a second to get my bearings. On the edge of my bed is that guy again.

I'm enraged and move forward in a threatening way. "Why are you in my house?"

He points and mocks me. "Have you forgotten, you're stark naked?"

I stop my forward movement and look down.

He says, "Will you answer my question, or do we take another trip down memory lane?"

"How did you get in here?"

"Don't worry about the particulars, Twig, just answer me."

"Why are you calling me that name?"

"It's your name, isn't it? Didn't dear old Dad call you by that name?"

I awake again with the tree still whipping shadows across the far wall. The tinkle of Georgina's wind chimes makes an eerie melody in the night, and I have yet to go to the bathroom. I get up and stumble to the toilet.

When I return, my desk lamp is on, and the goateed guy is still here. He sits in a chair reading a book. He looks up with golden eyes, gives me an all-knowing grin and closes the book. "Interesting reading. Do you have much time for pleasure reading?"

"It's my wife's."

"Ex-wife," he says.

"What do you mean?"

"As of yesterday, when you beat her unconscious, she's your ex-wife."

"That was an accident," I say. "She'll come back."

"I wouldn't be so cocksure of yourself, buddy. If you check with your wife-beating meter, you went way over the line, and not only will she not be back, but soon you'll be moving out of your house, because she'll own it."

"What?"

He gives me a comical grin, stands, pulls closer and glares into my eyes. I swear I see fire and mini lightning bolts flashing from around both irises. When he speaks, it's with a deep satanic baritone, like in a horror movie. "She'll own everything, Dipshit."

I awake to a sweltering room. My clothes are soaked with sweat. No desert wind, no tinkle of wind chimes, and I still have to pee.

I get up, stagger to the bathroom and empty my bladder, then come back into my bedroom with caution, because I'm sure the goateed string bean is still here. When I peek around the door and turn on the overhead light, I'm relieved that no one is around. I go to the kitchen. It looks the same: the blender, the toaster, her ugly little frog collection on the windowsill. It's all here. I open the fridge and see life still has some kind of normalcy. The shelves are full of bags of vegetables, a selection of cheeses, two cartons of milk and three frosty beers. I grab one, twist the top and throw the cap toward a garbage bag in the far corner. It thunks against the cabinet, clatters to the floor and hides behind the bag.

I take a long pull from the bottle, and in an instant, two things happen. The cool liquid relieves my overheated body, and the alcohol tickles my screaming monster. It leaves him with a taste of fulfilled desire, but not even close to satisfied.

My second swig quiets him. A third and fourth finishes the bottle. I want another, but I'm not some alcoholic. I'll stop at one and go back to bed.

Morning arrives, and the blasting heat has not subsided. If it was a hundred and eight last night at nine o'clock, then it must still be a hundred.

My head pounds as my stomach churns. My mouth tastes like a ten-year-old chicken coop. I can't stay in my sweat-soaked bed, but I don't have any energy to get up. I don't have a job to go to anyhow, so what's the point?

A rise in the morning temperature forces me to my feet. A cold shower is my only relief from another desert summer day.

While a dull razor scratches off yesterday's stubble, I remember the dream and how real it seemed. I remember what Georgina said and how she said it. She's normally so meek. Her attitude didn't fit. Lucky it was a dream.

By noon, I toss together some breakfast, which includes my second of the three beers, and drive downtown to the hospital.

On the third floor, the same basketball guy greets me with a grimace and is calling security as I step up to the counter. When he refuses me, I want to make a scene, but I turn and take a single step toward the elevator. I have no idea what motivates me anymore. I spin and bring my fist into his gut. I don't hit him hard enough for any real damage, just enough to render him incapacitated. I just want to talk to my wife for a second.

Up the hall, a little round nurse yells for me to stop. I move quickly along the hall to room three-thirteen and turn left. In the bed closest to the window I see the eyes of my wife, though the rest of her face I can't recognize. I see fear, and I try to reassure her. "Hi, Honey, how are you doing?"

Her eyes get larger.

"I came to apologize. I don't know what gets into me. I promise, if you come home, I'll never hit you again."

With a frightened look, she shakes her head.

"Georgina, I love you, Honey. Come home and things will be like they've always been. I miss you already."

She sits up in bed with her black-and-blue face and wired jaw and pulls the covers up to her neck, like covers will protect her.

My anger flares, though I keep it under wraps. "Why not?" I plead.

She can't answer. She looks at me.

Two security geeks step into the room.

I turn to face them.

The bigger of them speaks in a wary voice, "Mr. Goreman, you'll need to vacate this room. We have explicit orders to maint--"

He doesn't complete his sentence before my anger has found a target. I spin and throw my fist in that soft place just under his ribcage; a sure bet to disable anyone. I hit a solid wall of muscle. My arm bounces back impotent and crumpled. Before I get another stance, before I can take another jab, my world goes black. I fall toward the floor, then swim in a dark void. On the way down, I hear another voice. It must be the second guy. "He won't cause any more trouble today."

Far off in the distance, I hear a response from Mr. Iron Gut. "You didn't have to hit him that hard, Fred. Those night sticks aren't soft."

I'm in a void, floating far beyond my body, until I notice a flickering light in the distance. I come closer and see people sitting around a campfire. It's a group of men, and I'm certain they're waiting for me. I float to the scene and onto a stump of wood. One of the men talks about his problems at home.

I look around the circle and can't believe my eyes. The motorcycle dicks that cuffed me to the light pole sit across from me. That bastard Tazz started this whole disaster.

A voice wafts from across the circle. "Why do you think Tazz is to blame?"

I look up. It's the goateed guy standing opposite me.

"Because he started everything," I say in my defense, though I don't feel like I have voiced my statement at all, just thought it.

All eyes are on me. All attention is focused in my direction.

"How do you figure that Tazz is the cause of your recent troubles, Twig?"

There's that name again. I spring to my feet, then remember it's probably another one of those weird dreams. I got conked, and the two security guys are probably dragging me down the hall by my pant cuffs.

My aggravation is temporarily shelved. "Who are you, anyhow?"

"Did you see that, men?" he mocks. "He can shift out of anger after all."

I look around as the men grunt in approval and nod.

I turn back. "Who are you?"

He steps forward and walks through the fire without harm. When he gets within three feet of me, he puts out his right hand. "I'm Biker Bob. We've been watching you for some time, Twig."

I don't reach out, because my fury flares again. "Don't call me that name; I hate it."

"And why do you hate your name?"

I growl, "I don't need to have a reason."

"No problem, Twig."

Snickers rise up from around the fire. I pull my right fist up to catch the smart-ass in his jaw. I've surprised him. My fist heads for teeth. My punch lands, and I swear I feel the impact, but my arm, my fist, my entire body spins out of control. I'm splayed on the dirt, face down, sucking a cloud of dust.

I scramble to my feet and prepare for an onslaught of punches and kicks. Nothing happens. Back into a defensive stance, I look at his goateed face and he giggles. The others are having fun at my expense, too. Restrained chuckles drift out into the darkness.

The lanky fucker tosses his head back and howls at the moon. It's an easy cool punch to his belly. He'll be on the ground. I aim my fist into his mid-section. He won't be able to move at the last second this time.

Since he hasn't attempted to protect himself, my fist goes forward. The full weight of my body is behind it. I watch it land. His soft belly muscles collapse. I feel a satisfying gush as his guts buckle, then I stumble through the full force of my swing. I try to catch myself, but lose balance and topple toward the fire. In a last attempt to keep from falling face forward into the blaze, I spin and succeed in rotating my body. I drop, back first, on the burning logs. When I land, sparks flare and disappear into the night sky. Charcoal logs crunch under my weight. I flip away with my shirt on fire. I roll on the ground, pulling at my cotton shirt. No one helps. When I have it off, I feel no heat, no singed skin, nothing. I stand in dumbfounded silence, look at my shirt and pants. There's no hint of ash or dirt, much less the smoldering rags I expected.

I look, as Goatee smirks. "The name's Biker Bob."

The second missed punch leaves me winded and unwilling to try another. He's some kind of Houdini to move that fast. Because no one's trying to attack me, I take a break.

He says, "Okay, now that you've given it your best shot, Twig, maybe you can sit back in our circle and we can get on with the meeting."

I'm completely off guard. I don't know how to respond. In a last-ditch effort to restore my dignity, I stumble back and drop into position in the circle. There's a moment of silence. Every eye is on me. Expectation permeates the night air. Am I supposed to say something? The silence stretches into an interminable two minutes, and no one moves.

"What the fuck am I supposed to say?" I blurt out. "What do you want?"

Silence.

In a long shot, I grab for something, really the first thing on my mind. "My wife left yesterday, and I don't think she's coming back."

Still not a word is spoken, but a bunch of nods and grunts drift around the fire, then float off with the weightless embers.

A deep-seated knot gurgles up and doesn't stop. It bubbles past my throat and comes out in a wracking sob. In seconds, I'm doubled over bawling. My long-held-back dam overflows.

After five minutes, the strange bout of grief subsides.

A hand touches my shoulder. "This is the appropriate emotion for your grief," the voice says. "Held back tears turn us into enraged and violent men."

I look up, and it's the goateed guy. He says, "Feel the fear of Georgina leaving, the uncertainty of losing your job, the onslaught of a legal battle, not only with your wife, but also with the prosecuting attorney." His words bring on another onslaught of sobbing.

My tear-soaked eyes can't see them, but I feel support from the other men. I want to say something to Goatee, but I'm beyond words. I'm past anything but releasing long-pent-up emotion.

"Remember, Thomas, this is the healthy response to pain and suffering. Sadness and grief is nothing to be ashamed of. A mature man experiences all of his emotions, including the ones that frighten and embarrass him most."

With his last word, I awaken, bound to a hospital gurney. I try to pull myself free, but I'm cuffed to each rail. I struggle, then give up and float into my thoughts. Blackness surrounds me once again. The fire isn't there. Goatee doesn't stand over me. I'm alone in my thoughts and must face the facts of my screwed up life. Have I made a mess of things or what? Do I deserve a medal for raw stupidity?

A thin voice comes through the darkness. It's the tenor of Goatee?

"Admitting you've made a mess of things is your first step, Twig. You have a lot to think about, but you'll have a lot of time. Take stock of your life while you have the opportunity."

His voice fades, and I'm left to float in a void. I get a vague awareness of someone putting stitches in the back of my head, then I float again. When I awaken, I find myself in a ward with heavy-screened windows and a big uniformed guard at the door.

It takes five minutes to realize I'm in some kind of hospital lockup. At least the cuffs are off. I reach up, feel a sore spot on the back of my head and remember the nightstick incident. Although I haven't murdered anyone, my troubles are of a similar proportion. Georgina has left. The cops are no longer on my side, and I have a lot of explaining to do, mostly to myself.

I lie in a black funk for three hours before a nurse approaches my bed. Her middle-aged graying blondness and wide hips have a matronly beauty. Her wry smile shows straight teeth with a slight hint of lip-gloss. Her face is calm and friendly.

Before she gets close, she asks, "We won't have any trouble will we, Mr. Goreman?"

I shake my head.

She moves closer. "I need to have a look at your stitches. You won't hurt me?"

I shake my head again, afraid to say a word. I'm ashamed that someone even has to ask. Jesus, how did this happen?

She steps up to my bed and has me roll to one side. She peels back the gauze and lets out a quiet whistle. "Five stitches? I guess Fred hit you pretty hard." She redresses the wound without another word. When she finishes and sets her tray aside, she hands me a small paper cup with a blue pill, then pats my shoulder. "Take this. It'll help your pain. We'll keep it nice and quiet. I'm sure you have a whopper of a headache."

I hadn't felt it before she said anything, but now my throbbing head comes to the forefront. "How long have I been out?"

She steps to the end of my bed, picks up a clipboard and studies it. "Two days. Fred must have really whacked you. He's got a mean streak, you know."

"He's not the only one," I whisper.

She gives me her movie-star smile. "Guess you racked up some points in the violence category yourself."

I grimace and growl, "What do you mean?"

She picks up her tray, gives me a worried look. "Oh, nothing." She turns and exits.

My head throbs. Any loud noise, especially from myself, feels like I'm detonating explosives.

I ease back on my pillow and concentrate on being calm until the pill kicks in. I repeat a phrase in my thoughts. "I'm not violent. I'm a normal man in reaction to an abnormal situation."

For another day, I'm poked, prodded, bandaged and rebandaged, until I can't stand another moment. On the morning of the third day, I get my first visitor. It's not my mother, who lives in Florida, not my sister, who lives in the next county. It's not even my supposed best friend, Adam. During the time in bed, I'm forced to come to terms with certain facts and one of them is that I have no friends.

Christmas bells jangle from far down the hall, and I wonder who let Santa Claus on the ward in August. I expect to hear him bellow, "Ho, ho, ho, Merry Christmas." The chimes get closer. Although my headache hurts, I turn and crane my neck to see who's coming.

When the jangle gets so loud I'm certain an entire reindeer team is sliding down the hall, a thick-shouldered, black-leather-vested, key-rattling biker-type walks into view, looks up to check the number on my room, then steps in. He walks to the end of my bed. "Biker Bob told me to look you up."

Black leather fingerless gloves reveal callused fingertips with caked grease under short nails. He says, "I'm Nick Brown." He steps to the side of my bed and pulls up a chair. "You've harassed my buds for three months, and I can't figure out why."

"How did you get in here?"

He smiles, comes in close and whispers, "I told them I was your brother from New Mexico."

I'm ready to press my buzzer, but this guy intrigues me.

"Why are you here?"

"I told you, Bob sent me."

"Bob who?"

He leans back and spreads both hands, fingers splayed. "Why have you been harassing my buds?"

I know what he's talking about, but I feign ignorance. "Who might that be?"

"Come on, man, don't fuck with me. We both know who you've been tailing. I want to know why?"

I give him a sarcastic grin. "Police business."

"I don't get it, because most of the time you tailed Tazz on your days off. That doesn't sound like police business to me."

"I'm a detective. I work odd hours."

He pulls off his gloves, sets them on the table, then cracks his knuckles. "Sounds to me like some kind of obsession."

"I'm a cop, what can I say."

He gets a serious look. "We got some people in your department, and word is you screwed up one too many times. Your lieutenant might be finding a way to get rid of you."

I don't respond, but my face tightens.

The biker locks his hands behind his head. I'm not sure if it's to gloat or relax.

"Look, Twig, I didn't come to mess up your day. I'm here because Bob sent me."

"Stop calling me that name."

He ignores my outburst. "Bob came to me last night. He told me to talk to you about your violence."

"What the hell is all this talk about violence? I don't have a violent bone in my body. I wouldn't hurt a fly."

He grins.

"What?" I say in an irritated tone.

"Bob said you would say those exact words. I'm amazed at how accurate he is."

"Who the fuck is Bob?"

"You remember, he was in your dream."

I have a flood of images and a distinct memory of the goateed guy in a series of disturbing dreams. I pale and in a more quiet voice than I mean to, I say, "Bob is the guy with the goatee?"

"The very one. You've been blessed to have him look in on you. Not many of us get direct visits."

"What do you mean?"

"Come on, man, Bob's a ghost."

"Bullshit!"

"It's no bull. Bob died in the fifties and you're one of the lucky few. For some reason, he likes you."

My room is silent for a long time before I speak. "You're not here to tell me I've been visited by some spook, are you?"

"No," he says. "Bob sent me to talk to you about your violence. He said you need support. Your station psychologist will visit today. She can help, if you want. Don't chase her off like you do most people."

"I don't chase people off."

"Don't fuck with me, Twig. I didn't make this up, I'm simply delivering a message."

"Don't call me that name."

"Sorry, pal, Bob also told me to call you Twig. He knows what's going on, and I've learned to follow his lead."

"You follow some ghost?"

He ignores my question. "I guess Bob has his sights on you. I'm sure you'll get to know him soon enough. Until then, relax, and don't sweat the small stuff."

"Hey, who are you to tell me--"

"Come on, man, your red face tells me your blood pressure is off the scale. Although you're flat in bed, you're ready to take me out, and you say you're not violent?"

The biker gets up and bends over my bed. He puts out a hand for me to shake, and I sneer at him.

"Look," he says, "far as I can tell, your friends aren't standing in line to visit you. I'm here because Bob sent me. I'd say you need some help getting through this transition. The One Percent of One Percent bikers might be your last hope. We don't usually take in dicks like you, but I guess at one time or another we've all been in your position. Bob's interested, so I'll cut you some slack."

He reaches into a top pocket of his greasy vest and pulls a glossy black business card with gold block letters. He hands it to me, but I don't give him the satisfaction of looking.

"When you get out," he says, "call me. I'll introduce you to the others."

When he sticks out his hand to shake again, I grasp without thinking. In a fast swipe, quicker than I have time to react to, he swings his hand past my outstretched fingers and slaps my fingertips with his.

He pivots and jangles toward the exit. In the doorway, he turns back. "Give me a call, Twig, and we'll talk."

After he disappears, though it hurts my head, I yell, "I don't like that name." My last two words fade off. "You bastard."

An hour later I eat a horrible tasting lunch; the one thing edible is an overly sugared tapioca pudding. I rest in an attempt to digest the gooey mess and fall asleep. I'm awakened when a woman in a blue tweed business suit steps through my door. She carries a black attaché, which she sets on the floor next to the visitor's chair. She settles into the chair and crosses her meaty legs. "Mr. Goreman, I was sent by your department. My name is Doctor Maribeth Soranto. I'm a clinical psychologist."

"My department?"

"Standard procedure. When any kind of physical violence takes place inside of the department, we're called in to assess." She removes a pen and notepad from her briefcase. "Can you tell me what happened?"

"I came to visit my wife and two goons jumped me."

She scribbles for a second, then looks up. "Could you be more specific?"

"No," I say. "I can't be more specific. Get your story from the police report. I'm sure someone filed a report."

She looks up with a patient smile. "My job is to get the story from you. If you give me your version, I can get out of here and leave you to nap."

"How about you forget my story and just get out of here."

She jots a quick note, cocks her head at an odd angle and looks at me. "Mr. Goreman, you've been accused of unacceptable violent behavior. If I leave now with what I've found so far, I'm afraid you might have some big problems. Get my point?"

My face reddens and not from embarrassment. No female has ever talked to me this way.

"Look, lady, take your report and stick--"

A tingling sensation starts at my fingertips. In a second, the sensation turns to numbness, climbs both my arms, then fills my entire body. Am I paralyzed?

A booming voice goes off inside my head. "Tell her what the fuck is going on, Twig." I look around to see if Ms. Tweed heard it, but she still sits awaiting my response.

"Who is this?" I think back at the voice. There is no answer. As suddenly as it began, my numbness dissipates, and I'm back to normal.

I take a moment to think about the command.

When she returns her pen and notepad to her case, I blurt out a single phrase, "It's been a bad week."

Once the dam opens, all the frustrations and fears of my entire life pour out. I'm a walking ball of emotion. I choke up when I tell her about hitting my wife and how sorry I am. She looks up from her notepad, then continues to write. My mouth has gone on a verbal marathon down memory lane. I can't stop. I talk about my childhood and the hardship I had to endure. Even more surprising, I tell her about Mom and how fucked up my life was after Dad died. I'm crying and angry while the stories leap out of me. Emotion froths from my body, spews forth from my eyes, nose and mouth. She scribbles for thirty minutes; hell it could've been an hour. I make a final run for the finish.

Exhausted, I drop my head on the pillow. I've said too much to a department shrink. My job is dead meat. With the admissions I've made, especially all of the abuse I showered on Georgina, I may as well quit.

After a moment of silence, I say, "I didn't mean to say all that."

She gives me a composed smile. "Mr. Goreman, what you've told me is your first step in a long road to recovery. It took guts to go deep into your life story in this first session."

"You don't understand," I say. "I didn't mean to say a word. Something happened, and I couldn't help myself."

She stops writing, crosses her hands on her lap and looks at me. "Something happened all right. Now that this burden is off your back, look inside, and tell me how you feel."

"You don't understand. Something made me tell you all--"

"Go inside, Mr. Goreman."

It's obvious she doesn't understand how the thundering voice forced me to turn into a human talking machine. I do what she asks and turn my attention first to my stress, which is something that strangles me every day. It's gone. Secondly, I check my heart rate, which has been an ever-growing battle to lower. It, too, has dropped for the first time in six months. "I guess I feel better," I say.

She scribbles another quick note, then glances up from her pad. "You look better. Your color has improved. I wish I had a mirror so you could see yourself. When I walked in you were beet red. I actually see flesh tones breaking through."

I look at my arm. "No kidding?"

"Do you know why you're calmer?"

It takes a while to answer with a shrug.

"Because, Mr. Goreman, you may have relieved yourself of some ghosts you've carried for years. Sharing with me has taken some of the pressure off." She pulls out a business card and writes a quick note on the card face. "Call me when you get out of here. I'll set up a date for you to come in and talk."

"I don't want to talk," I try to say, but the words never form. She slides the notepad in her case, closes it, unfolds those thick legs and gets to her feet. "I'll see you soon, Mr. Goreman." She grabs the case, turns and steps out of my room.

I drop back onto my pillow. "I don't want to talk," I whisper, long after she's gone. I hear a distant voice in my head. It has a familiar tone, an insistent quality. "You must talk, Twig."

"I hate that name," I murmur. Exhausted from the effort, I fall into a deep slumber.

In a dream, Bob steps into the light and gives me a toothy grin. "How did it feel?"

"How did what feel?" I already know what he's referring to.

He shows more of his large teeth, but says nothing.

I stammer and eventually answer. "I haven't cried in years. I forgot how frightening it is."

He tugs on his goatee. "Frightened or not, how'd you feel after?"

"Relieved, I guess."

"Yes, relieved is one part, but I want to bring something else to your attention."

I take some time to think about what else I felt. I can't come up with anything other than relief.

Bob is patient.

I shrug. "I don't know. What do you have in mind?"

He clicks his tongue, like Mom used to and rolls his eyes back to the whites.

"What? Please tell me, because I don't have a clue."

"Clueless, are we?" he snipes. "Don't think to get the answer. It's in your body, not your brain."

I check my body and yell, "Less tension. I feel lighter, like I don't have any worries."

"Bingo! You got it, Twig."

He blinks out of existence before I have time to tell him how much I hate that name. Deep inside my chest I feel pressure, no, more like a longing.

Before I awake, his voice returns. "Be aware of how different you feel when I call you 'Twig'."

I check in, and my body has tightened again. Well, of course it has; I hate the name.

"Think about your two different body feelings," he says, "and see how fast the tightness returns once you're awake."

My eyes open, and I stare at the ugly green ceiling of my hospital room. An imaginary steel band is already snug around my chest and neck. Jeez, I can't believe I live with this constriction every day.

After the morning feeding, because with this hospital food that's all one can call it, a nurse checks my stitches, and my doctor prods my appendages.

At one o'clock, a small man walks in with a wrinkled brown suit and a neon red tie. He carries a black leather briefcase. "Mr. Goreman?"

I nod.

He walks over to the chair, lifts his case to my small, metal cabinet and unsnaps two clasps. When he opens it and pulls out papers, he fingers through ten or twelve sheets. "Mr. Goreman, you've gotten yourself into trouble a number of times before. It won't fare well in your hearing."

I interrupt what sounds like a long list of reasons why I'm a bad person. "First, who the hell are you, and how do you fit into this scenario?"

His pale skin turns three shades of pink. "I'm sorry," he says, "I assumed you knew I was coming. I'm Fallwick, your lawyer. Don't you remember? I was at your arraignment."

In a continued awareness of my body tension, I feel more bands tighten.

"I don't need a lawyer."

The little guy shuffles papers, pulls one from the stack and puts on some reading glasses. "Let's see, disturbing the peace is an easy way to start." He looks up. "We can go on down the list."

I nod and close my eyes.

"You're charged with destruction of property, willful misuse of your status as a police officer and disorderly conduct. The state has charged you with assault and battery concerning Mrs. Goreman, violating a restraining order and the altercations with both Mr. Harding, the day nurse and Mr. Felps at the bar."

My eyes flash open. "That was self-defense."

He looks up from his paper, then continues. "We have two automobiles your wife's car sideswiped after you broke her jaw. On top of everything, you're on suspension for misappropriation of police property, while The Board decides whether or not to terminate you altogether." He flips a sheet over and continues. "Last but not least, there's a charge of willful destruction of your police revolver. I'd say you have great need of a lawyer, Mr. Goreman. Maybe you don't want me. Frankly, I'd be relieved to not handle your case, but you'll need someone with you at your second arraignment and also in front of the Police Board. Right now, your future looks pretty shaky."

"I didn't break my gun. That biker bastard stomped it into the pavement."

The little guy smiles, folds the sheets back into his briefcase and closes the lid. He looks over his glasses. "Then I'd come up with some plausible explanation as to why the biker had your gun in the first place."

He stands, grabs his case and turns toward the door.

I bellow, "Don't go!"

He turns to face me. "Mr. Goreman, I'm not interested in messing around with a bunch of excuses. You promise to put a cap on your attitude, and I'll stay for a while to see what we can work out."

"Okay," I say. "Please stay. I need some help."

He sits, places his case on the cabinet again and says, "We have a lot to do before court."

***

"Shit, Tazz," I say. "Why'd he try to arrest us in the parking lot, anyhow?"

Tazz's chiseled face makes a grimace. "The guy's a walking time bomb, Buck, and he's obsessed with busting us. Although Bob has plans for him, we've got to be careful. I wouldn't put it past the jerk to plant some shit on us."

I take a sip of my mineral water. "Careful how? We've done nothing wrong."

He lifts his soda and takes a long drink.

The music comes alive, and my favorite oldie blasts from the jukebox. Except for two guys in the back, playing pool and Martha, who nearly lives in Waley's, the bar is almost empty.

Over loud music, I yell, "Bob told me to go look him up."

Tazz looks at me. "No kidding, me too. What do you think he has in mind?"

"I don't know, but everything Bob's ever told me has worked out pretty well. I guess we're supposed to go see him. You know where he's at?"

Tazz takes another drink and looks toward the pool players. "The other day I went to his house. An old woman across the street said he and his wife are at University Medical Center."

I shrug and motion Baby Face Joe over. "Maybe the music could be lower?"

He walks over to the volume control and cranks it up. He turns to me, smiles, waits five seconds, then brings it down to a lower volume.

I flip him the bird. "Hey, while you're at it, could you get Tazz a Pepsi and me another water?"

When he steps over, he says, "Waley isn't making any money off you jerkoffs. I don't know why I put up with you."

I flip my thumb toward the front door. "Yeah, well, shove it. We're paying customers and it looks like soon to be your only customers." A blast of afternoon sun engulfs the two guys who were at the pool table.

"A Pepsi and a fizz water. Man, that isn't even paying the cost of washing our glasses. What happened to the days when you guys would pack away a sixer with vodka chasers, and we'd roll you out at closing?"

Tazz says, "Shit happens. Hell, you still got plenty of bikers to kick out at the end of the night. In another few hours this place'll be jumping, and you won't have time to piss and moan about a couple of teetotalers."

His cherub face breaks into a grin. He leans closer toward us. "Don't tell Waley, but I like you guys better this way."

I smile. "Your secret's mine."

He turns, reaches under the bar, pulls out a Pepsi and my water. He twists the caps off both and slides them down the bar toward us. When he steps toward Martha, I say, "He's okay. How come he don't join up with us?"

Tazz takes a sip. "For one, if you remember, he has two kids and a wife instead of a Harley."

"All the more reason for him to come to our circles. You ever invite him?"

Tazz puts both hands together and pops his knuckles. "Over the months, two or three times. He always has something else to do."

"Well hell, you can't force anyone."

"Yeah, only Bob can do that."

I reach for my spiked gloves and slide them on. "So, you want to ride over together and pay a visit to that dick, Twig?"

Tazz downs the Pepsi in one long pull, bangs it on the counter and lets out a gigantic belch. Martha and Joe look up. Tazz raises his arms and splays his fingers in a winner's stance.

I slip from my seat. "Let's get in the wind."

We wave to Joe and Martha, push through the padded door and walk out into the inferno.

As usual, I kickstart my '59 Panhead ten times before it roars to life. I return the distributor to running position and sit on my little leather seat. My springer front end is extended seven inches and the frame is kicked out to accommodate the extra length. Maneuvering my bike while moving slow is difficult, but once we're rolling it's fine. When I get the bike turned around and in position, Tazz starts his gold chopper, and we're off.

We roll into afternoon traffic and point our bikes down the wide boulevard past the big casinos. By the time we get to the hospital, the sun has baked my helmet and cooked my brain. We step inside the coolness of the lobby and walk up to the information booth. I ask for Thomas Goreman's room.

The candy striper looks at a computer screen. "Room six-fifteen," she says in a squeak of a voice, "I'm not sure you'll be able to visit. He's under police lockup."

"What'd he do?"

She gives us a nervous smile. "I'm not supposed to say."

We go around a corner and take an elevator to the sixth floor. When the door opens, a large uniformed officer steps up. "Who are you here to visit?"

"Thomas Goreman," I say.

He writes entries onto a clipboard. "Step through the security gate. Please remove any metal objects and put them in the tray."

When we're through the gate, he gives us back our keys and change then has us sign in. He points down the hall. "Fifth door on your left."

We step into Twig's room just as he bites into a banana.

"What are you two doing here?" I sense fear in his voice.

I pull up the single chair and sit. Tazz stands at the foot of Twig's bed.

"Bob sent us," I say. "Otherwise I'd be somewhere else for sure."

"Shit, this Bob guy has you all dancing. Another guy was in here yesterday. He said the same thing."

I look at Twig, then back at Tazz and ask, "Who was it?"

"I don't remember, someone that jingled like a Christmas sleigh."

Tazz leans his elbows on the end of Twig's bed. "Gotta' be Nick."

"Yeah, that was his name."

After an awkward silence, Twig asks, "What do you want?"

I say, "I don't know why we're here. Bob didn't say what to do, just to get here."

"What makes Bob so special that grown men do his bidding?"

Tazz pulls a wild lock of hair out of his face. "You'll find out soon enough. Maybe you have some questions?"

"Other than how you distribute drugs right under the eyes of us cops and never get caught, I have no questions."

"Shove it, pal," I say. "I already told you, we don't use drugs anymore, and we don't sell drugs."

Tazz says, "Why do you insist that we're dealers, Twig? Can't you see how insulting you are?"

"Don't call me that name."

I say, "It's what Bob wants us to call you."

"Why?"

Tazz sits on the edge of the bed. "If we knew the why of what Bob does, we would be mystics, not bikers. Answer my question. Why do you insist that we're drug dealers?"

"My lieutenant got some strong information that drugs were being dealt out of Waley's bar," Twig points at Tazz, "and you were the leader."

"Well shit, Twig, do I look like a leader? I can hardly lace my own boots."

Twig looks over the edge of the bed. "Your boots don't have laces."

Tazz throws up his hands. "No laces, and I still can't do it."

Twig grins.

There is another moment of silence. He takes another bite of banana and looks at us. There is a shift in his attitude. He gets a guilty look. "I guess I have a problem with anger. Some guy came to me in a dream the other night. He said I was out of control. I guess it's why I'm in lockup."

Tazz leans on the rail with one elbow. "Well shit, that's the last thing I expected you to say. The question is, what are you going to do about it?"

"I don't know," Twig says, "I just found out yesterday."

"Yesterday?" I snort. "You whacked me with your pistol in Waley's parking lot for no reason, and you don't know you have an anger problem?"

"Hey, Buck," Tazz says. "That ain't helpful."

I stand, glare at Tazz, and my voice rises. "It helps me a lot to say it. He's been tailing us how many months? He pistol-whips the fuck out of me, and you say it isn't helpful?" I point at my forehead and yell, "You haven't got a fuckin' gash in your head."

A round, middle-aged nurse steps in the room. "This is a hospital, mister. If you can't keep it down, I'll ask you to leave."

"Sorry," I say, feeling an embarrassed flush.

She turns and exits.

Tazz whispers. "I don't care what she says, that was good."

I beam and nod. "You think so?"

"Yeah, man, lots of expression."

Twig says, "What do you mean it was good?"

Tazz stands and stretches. "He expressed his anger when it happened, and he did it without hurting anyone. I'd say, for a guy like Bucky, that's damn good."

I smile and look at Twig. “Like you, I’m a recovering man of violence. I used to beat up everyone around me, including my ex-wife.”

Twig’s eyebrows rise. “You admit this to a perfect stranger?”

“Not right off,” I say. “It’s taken a year or two and help from the One-on-One guys. The more I speak about it, and express things when they happen, the less tendency I have to strike out and hurt someone.”

Twig asks, “One-on-One?”

Tazz reaches in his leather vest pocket. “One Percent of One Percent. It’s what we call our group.”

Twig asks, “What does it mean?”

We talk about the One on One group for a minute, until I stand and put on my gloves. “Our job as men is to get our anger out in appropriate ways, the second it comes up, and not let it build up. For sure the One Percent of One Percent guys have helped.”

Tazz turns and walks toward the door. I follow. Before he exits, he looks back at Twig. “When you get out, look us up. If Bob wants you at our meetings, I guess I’m the one to take you.”

***

I’m lying in my hospital bed while two greasy bikers talk about anger and how they can help each other get through it. Tazz reaches into his vest pocket and pulls out a glossy black business card with gold block letters.

I look at the card. “The other guy gave me one of these. What does it mean?”

“One percent of the American population are bikers,” Bucky says with a choked pride in his voice, “and one percent of them are like us, willing to do the necessary emotional work to become more human.”

The two men walk to the door and turn. Tazz says, "Look us up when you get out. If Bob wants you at our meetings, Twig, I guess I'm the one to take you."

I yell, as they disappear down the hall, "Why does Bob want you to call me that name?"

They don't stop or answer. I'm left with one big question, and a new view of two men I thought were low-lifes. It looks like I was wrong.

The day drags on, and night allows me some sleep. In the morning, I dress and get released into the custody of Sergeant Hansen and his partner. They cuff me and take me down to the station, where they put me in another holding cell. Before Hansen closes the door, he looks at me. "We'll be back in a while to take you to court."

When I appear in front of the judge, I say, "Not guilty, Your Honor." This time the judge imposes a ten-thousand-dollar bail. Thirty minutes later, after writing another bond check for a thousand, I'm back out on the sidewalk.

Hansen steps up behind me while I prepare for a hike and bus trip across town to get my car.

"Hey, Tom, the lieutenant wants me to give you a ride to your car." I follow him in silence along the sidewalk and under the shade of a three-story parking structure.

As Hansen maneuvers through the last traffic light, he asks, "You doing all right?"

I look at him. "What do you mean?"

"The restraining order and everything?"

"Everything?"

He stops at my car without answering.

When I open the car door, I want to go see Georgina, but I've had enough trouble. I get into my car and drive to the Santana Club, anything but a cop watering hole.

Four doubles later, I drive the last three miles to my house.

Inside the sweltering inferno, I pass out on my couch and find myself following a gang of thieves and motorcycle misfits. At first I think I'm in my car, but soon realize I'm on a Harley, riding with them. I've transformed from my law-abiding police role into one of them. The worst part of it is, I like it. Hell, I love it!

A bike pulls up beside me. I look across at the driver, then realize it's that Bob character. "Think about your violent streak," he says. "Does it serve you?"

I'm no longer on a Harley, but floating in a steamy void. The blackness breaks up. I see a green mist, then bright shimmering lights, and my eyes open. I'm staring at my avocado colored couch. Sweat pours down my back. My clothes are soggy. I sit up in a single startled movement, stand, strip off my sticky clothes and drop them on my way to a cold shower. I've got to get that damn air conditioner fixed.

The shower cascades over my head and cools me, when I recall my bike dream. I remember riding a Harley, the feeling of open sky and raw power at a twist of the throttle.

Once my shower is over, I put on fresh clothes, shave and step out to a blazing early afternoon.

On my way back to Santana's, I think about the Harley ride. On a whim, I make a left turn and drive to the run-down bar called Waley's. Maybe I'll talk to someone about Harleys.

I pull in the crappy parking lot and turn off my engine, but stay in my refrigerated car. Seven bikes are lined up by the front door, with ten or twelve cars scattered around the lot.

I'm known in this bar and not in a positive way. If I go in, I'm certain to get into some kind of trouble, but something compels me.

I get out into the heat, and hear an old Boz Skaggs song thump through the faded green stucco. I step around to the front door and push. As if my entrance were timed, Skaggs comes to a soulful finish. I walk into the cool darkness of the building.

twenty people turn in unison and glare. I swagger across a concrete floor and step up to the bar. The room is pin-drop silent. I hear the jukebox switch records. I climb on a seat with empty stools on either side of me and feel twenty sets of eyes bore holes in my back.

The baby-faced bartender stands dead center of the bar. He doesn't move an inch in my direction. When I say my first word in a White Russian order, a raucous country song fills the air. In the same second, Babyface reaches back behind the ancient chrome cash register, and the sound of Merle Haggard or Johnny Cash, I never can tell the difference, dies into nothingness. The only noise left is a hidden refrigeration unit somewhere under the bar.

Babyface turns back to me, but still hasn't moved.

"I'll have a White Russian," I say.

He shakes his head. "Sorry, pal, can't serve you."

Is this my first battle? I love it. I don't even get past the bartender, and I've already got my hackles up.

I make my order again, pronouncing the words in a slow careful manner.

"How come you're here?" he asks.

"I just want a Russian."

The exchange goes back and forth several times. I'm patient, but I'm getting irritated. The room behind me is silent. Even the pool players stand at attention. I'm ready to leap over the bar and push Babyface's nose into the container of maraschino cherries. If he gives me one more negative response, I will.

"Just give me a Russian, and I won't cause any trouble."

After a long pause, he reaches under the bar and pulls out a wooden baseball bat. He rests on it like a cane. "You caused trouble when you came in here. Now I'll ask you nice to leave."

A voice stretches across the silence. "Give him the Russian, Joe. He's with me."

I turn and can't believe my eyes; it's Tazz.

"I'm not givin' this asshole nothin'," Babyface growls.

Tazz steps up, and leans against the bar. He moves close to the barkeep. "He's the guy Bob sent."

Babyface's grimace shifts to confusion. "Bob sent him?"

"Pretty fucking crazy, huh? Bob came to me last night. Twig's the guy I've been waiting for."

Babyface rolls his eyes and sighs. "Bob sent him? Well, whatever."

I growl, "Don't call me that name."

Tazz turns to me. "It's the name Bob gave you, and it's the name I'll use. You want your Russian or not?"

I nod.

"Once you get it, come over to our table in the back. We got shit to talk about."

"I don't have anything to say to you."

Tazz grins. "I don't much like your ugly face, either, but if Bob says we got something to talk about, we got something to talk about."

A Russian slides toward me. I pay, take a sip and follow Tazz across the length of the building. He sits among three other bikers I know from my months of observation. He kicks a chair out into the aisle. "Take a load off."

I swing the chair around, sit and rest my arms on the back.

Tazz shakes his head. "You're such an asshole, Twig. I'd love to have left you to Joe. He would have made mincemeat out of you. The one problem, though, is that Bob came to me two nights in a row and we talked about you. He wants me to put you through a kind of training. Tell you the truth, I don't know why. He thinks you've got potential."

"Training?" I ask. "What the fuck do you mean?"

"I won't explain it, because I don't understand myself. All I know is Bob wants it."

"You do everything this Bob wants you to do?" I ask with a sneer. I have my wits about me again. I can hold my own with these guys.

Bucky, who sits on my right, chimes in. "When Bob says something, for sure it's good for all of us. I'd listen."

"Who is Bob?"

The four men look at one another and smile. Tazz says, "He's the goateed guy in your dreams."

Wham! A rug is pulled out from under me. I feel myself short of breath, but I show nothing. I wouldn't give them the satisfaction.

I snicker. "You follow a person from a dream?"

Bucky's eyes narrow. His rat face scrunches.

Tazz reaches a hand over and grasps Bucky's shoulder. "Hang in there, Buck. He ain't got a clue. Remember how you reacted when you first found out. Let out a scream or two for now, but don't make a move."

Bucky's voice takes a two-octave leap. He lets out an ear-shattering yell, which lasts for five seconds.

When he's composed again, his face relaxes. "I'm okay now," he says.

Tazz pats him on the shoulder, then points at my jacket pocket, "I gave you a card the other day. You give me a call when you're ready."

I reach in the pocket and damn, the black and gold card is there. I glance at the inscription: One Percent of One Percent.

Under its lettering also in gold, is the name Tazz Lankerman and a phone number.

"Don't hold your breath." I crumple the card and toss it on the table.

In a slow, methodical movement, Tazz picks up the card, unwrinkles it and inserts it back in my chest pocket. He pats the pocket. "Man, you got an anger problem. When you want to work on it, call me. I'll be around."

He gets up, and his three buddies rise. I leap to my feet, and knock my chair over in the process. I'm in a defensive position long before any of them can begin to move.

Bucky shakes his head. "Hey, man, chill out. We're not here to go to the mat with you. If we were, you'd already be down. We came because Bob says you have potential. I don't get it, but I trust Bob."

I'm still in my stance while they file around the far side of the table. They saunter across the barroom and out the front door. The second the door closes behind them, the Moody Blues blasts through the jukebox. I'm left with my Russian on the table and a bunch of eyes staring at my back.

I sit, sip my drink, and notice for the first time that all four men drank sodas.

When I order my second drink, the bartender refuses. I'm much too dazed to make it much of an issue. I stumble out of the bar, not because I have had too much to drink, more like I've had too much to think.

If the goateed dude leads these bikers around, why has he come into my life? Why has Tazz offered to train me? Train me for what? He has a right to beat me to a pulp after the pistol whipping I gave his buddy. Will a beating be part of this friggin' training?

The heat brings me around. Heat does that. It wakes me up and forces me to deal with the moment. I get into my car and pull out into traffic. I want to go home. Home is my safe haven. It's a place where I can relax and take stock of my situation.

I drive through town in sweltering heat and make my familiar left into Fairview Park, a housing tract of five hundred flat-top, two stories, built in the late fifties. They're not ugly, but their plainness gets monotonous after the first block. I make a number of left and right turns, winding my way into the center of the tract. When I turn onto my block, two obvious differences assail my view. A Las Vegas black and white is parked in a standard fashion, askew in my driveway, and an air conditioning repair truck sits on the street in front of my house.

I pull up, stop my car on the street and get out. I look at the patrol unit to see if I recognize the cops who drove it.

I walk up the concrete path I poured eight years ago. A tall, slender cop opens my front door. From his nervous demeanor, it doesn't look like he's been on the force more than a week. His smile at the same time disarms and demands. "Mr. Goreman?"

"Yes."

He has a bundle of papers in his hand. He lifts his long arm and holds the paperwork out to me. I take it.

"You already know about your restraining order."

I look at him with a blank stare.

"We're here to escort you into the house to get some of your personal belongings, but you must promise not to attempt to speak to Mrs. Goreman."

I look into his worried face long enough for him to repeat himself. "Sir, we aren't going to have any trouble here, are we?"

I've heard his words, but I'm unable to respond. I stand slack jawed and look from him to the papers, then back. I repeat my movement I don't know how many times before he places his bony right hand on my left shoulder. My immediate response is to knock his hand away.

The bitch has locked me out of my own house, and she got some punk kid cop to do her bidding. My one place of rest and peace is off limits.

A burly repairman opens the door and steps onto my porch. He turns, reaches back and grabs two toolboxes. Before he closes the door and steps around the punk cop and me, I feel a sweet breath of cool air waft out of the front door. I hear an air conditioner hum.

"We won't have any trouble, will we?" The officer repeats. His worried demeanor turns to a more prepared stance. He has a hand on his club, though he has yet to pull it.

"Mr. Goreman, I need your promise. We go in together, you get some personal items, and we leave without any problems; otherwise I can't allow you in the house."

Mark Howard, a beat cop from my early days on the force, steps through the door and closes it behind him. "How are you doing, Thomas?"

"She took my house, Mark."

"She didn't take it. She's only using it for the moment while you two get things worked out. The judge will decide."

"Where will I go?"

"Get a room in a hotel. You can get a more permanent place in a week or so. For now, go to one of the casinos and get a room."

"I hate casinos."

There's a silent moment until Mark says, "We're here to help you get your stuff without any problems. You must agree to behave yourself or we can't let you in."

"Is she in there?"

The kid butts in, "We can't say."

"Can I see her? I'll talk some sense into her."

Mark gets a worried look. "You're a cop, Thomas. You know you can't see or talk to her."

I feel deflated, no, defeated. I sit down on a brick planter I built four years ago. "What am I going to do?" I mutter more to myself than anyone else.

"If you want some of your stuff, we'll have no trouble when we go inside. After, you'll find yourself a place to stay somewhere else. Do you agree?"

The two cops ask the same question a dozen times, but I haven't answered. I finally say, "I don't want to cause any trouble."

"Okay," Mark says. I hear relief in his voice. "You want to go in and get your stuff?"

"Yeah, sure, whatever." I stand and follow them into my air-conditioned living room. The house is more pleasant with cool air. Why didn't I get that fucking thing fixed?

They lead me up to the master bedroom. Two suitcases have been laid out on my bed, which is made for the first time since all of this happened.

I open my dresser drawer, scoop out necessities and dump them into my luggage. I grab my favorite photo of Georgina and me. We'd been in Los Angeles and booked an afternoon on a sailboat to Catalina. It was the most romantic day I can remember. I take a long look at the photo. Why didn't we do more of those sorts of things? I add it to one of the trunks and close them both.

When I grab the handles, I hear a noise in the second bedroom. "Georgina," I yell. "Is that you, Honey? Come in and talk to me, will you?"

The cops tense, and Mark steps in front of the door. "Hey, Thomas, you promised no trouble."

"Yeah, yeah, I know. I thought she might want to talk."

"For one, her jaw is wired, and she can't talk."

"Georgina," I yell. "Come on, Honey. Come in here."

My anger bubble almost spills over. I want to take these two guys down, then go in and talk some sense to her. I want to tell her it's my house, and she has no right to kick me out.

I want to do many things and some of them aren't too pretty, but Mark stands in my way. He's always been a good guy, and I wouldn't want to fuck up his friendship, though I've had little contact with him for four or five years. It rubs against every fiber of my being, but I do a subservient walk out of the bedroom and down the stairs. In the living room, I stop. "What about my moose head? Can I take the moose head I got in Alaska?"

"It's for the judge to decide, Thomas. Those things come later. For now, only personal stuff."

I'm out of the cool house and standing on the burning sidewalk. I turn, look back, and see a curtain close. It's her, I know it's her.

I slam the suitcases into the back seat and get in my car. I could fry an egg on the seats alone. I drive away from my house and don't come back to full consciousness until I've tried six hotels. Each tells me there's a computer convention in town and all rooms are booked solid for a week. In a blistered haze, I happen to pass a motel on the old highway south of town. It faces open desert. A sign says, "air conditioned", but it's so dilapidated, I'm not sure I believe it.

I get out and walk into a smoke-filled office. The door closes behind me and trips a buzzer that summons the manager. He walks through an inner door, wearing a stained tank top over a belly the size of Las Vegas proper. His wide pudgy face cracks a smile. He says hello through the butt of a nasty smelling cigar.

"You got a single with air?"

"You're in luck pal, we got one left."

"Can I look at it?"

His smile turns to a pout. His eyes glaze over and without a word, he turns. With sausage fingers, he grabs a single key from an almost empty rack and tosses it on the counter like he's done the same maneuver a million times.

I look at the key attached to a thick brass plate. It reads, "Happy Honeymoon Motel". I turn it over and read the number twenty-three.

"Upstairs and to the right," he says. "It's at the end of the balcony."

When I open the door of the room, heat blasts me like a furnace. My first move is to turn on the piddly window air conditioner and wait for cool air to pump. I'm not sure if the unit will ever cool my room, but it's the only room available in a city filled with motels and hotels. I leave the air conditioner to blast, close the door behind me and walk to the office.

Ten minutes later, I schlep all of my worldly possessions up the steps to my room. The inside temperature has dropped a degree or two, but it's obvious many hours will pass before my new home is bearable.

Without unpacking the suitcases, I turn, exit my room, walk down the ugly concrete steps and get into my car. I'm on the southern end of town and unfamiliar with the bars, so it takes a while to find a neighborhood lounge and park my car. I promise myself no trouble and spend the next three hours in cool darkness, drinking myself into oblivion. How many I drink, I don't know. I lose count at four during the first hour. By the time I'm ready to go, the bartender insists on calling me a cab. After a small verbal skirmish, I hand the cabby my brass key ring, and I'm poured into the back seat.

The cabby helps me upstairs and into my room. I give him an extra ten for his effort.

Before I lie on my bed and pass out, I turn on the TV.

Somewhere in the middle of the night, after a hideous nightmare, I find myself on the back of a Harley. My right hand rests on a shoulder of the goateed guy while we rumble along a dark, flat valley. The road is arrow straight. Once we're in the bowl of the valley, he releases his throttle and coasts to a walking speed along a single strand of barbed wire attached to blanched cottonwood branches. He turns left through an open gate.

The rutted path leads back three hundred yards and past a burnt-out house, before it drops into a twenty-foot wash. At the bottom of the wash, Goatee turns left and rolls toward the base of a distant mound, the only bump in an otherwise featureless valley.

In five minutes we round a turn, and the flicker of a fire illuminates the wash. Another turn reveals a campfire with fifteen bikers standing too close to the flame for such a hot night.

Goatee pulls up, parks his ridiculously long Harley at the front of the line, and we dismount.

He turns to me. "Come over and meet my buds."

I'm compelled to follow.

As we approach the fire, the men get quiet.

"Hey," he says, "this is Twig."

I hear murmurs, all with disagreeable tones.

"I don't like that name," I protest, but no one hears me.

Everyone sits on old tree rounds placed around the blaze. I follow suit.

Goatee removes a perfectly formed, ten-inch-long, unbelievably clear, quartz crystal and hands it to a man on his left. The crystal goes man to man until it stops with a black guy. He tells a short tale about his estranged wife and little boy. He says he wants to talk about it later, then passes the crystal on. It travels around until it stops at a guy with greasy hair who fingers its facets and tells a short rendition about the possibility of going to prison for possession of marijuana. He passes the baton and on it goes four times around the circle, stopping randomly, until every man has contributed to the mix, but me. I pass the crystal on. It continues around, until I have it again. It's obvious the damnable roundabout thing won't end until I say something. When it comes to me, I snort, "My name is Thomas Goreman, not that other name. Has everyone got that?"

The circle is silent. I pass the baton, and it travels around until Goatee has it. He puts the crystal down, stands and turns to me. "Your life is a mess, isn't it?"

"It's none of your business."

"Remember, Twig, it's your dream, too. You can say whatever you want."

"Don't call me that."

"Don't call me Goatee. My name is Bob. It would be Biker Bob to you, for now."

I'm stunned. "How did you know what I was thinking?"

He grins. His gleam is infectious. When he speaks again, he does so with a fatherly tone. "In this setting, your name is Twig."

"I'll make dog meat out of anyone who calls me that name."

"Oh," he says in a mocking tone. "I'm frightened, Twiggy. You going to kick some ass?"

Old angers flare. They're familiar friends. I find myself on my feet. I take a nice clean left jab at Goatee's face. He doesn't have time to move or roll with my punch. This one will land on some of his oversized ivories. My swing is hard enough that it may take some of them out. Goatee may end up looking like some of the other guys in this motley mixture of so-called men.

The very second I make contact, I find myself in bed, slugging my fist into the paper-thin wall. The moment my fist pierces wallboard, I pull back and jump up. I stand bewildered in front of Goatee. My arm, with its doubled fist, rests at my side.

Bob says, "Remember, Twig, it's still a dream. Anything can happen in a dream."

I glance at my fist and see gypsum dust on my knuckles. When I look up, I'm back in front of the fire.

"How did you do that?"

"Magic, but it's not why we're here."

A man from the circle chimes in, "We're here to talk about your anger."

"What anger?" I say.

"The same anger that's willing to punch Bob out for calling you Twig. It's the same anger that broke your wife's jaw."

"How do you know?"

Goatee turns back to me. "You could say you've acquired a unique set of guardian angels. I want you to meet some of the card-carrying members of the One Percent of One Percent bikers.

"Tell me how he knew," I demand.

"We all know."

"You all know what?"

"We all know everything about you."

"How do you know?"

Goatee gives me a secret smile. "Let's talk about your anger first."

I'm overwhelmed with his revelation. I sit hard on the stump. When I look up, he says, "First, my name is Biker Bob, not Goatee. Second, ever notice how you blame everyone else for your troubles? Have a close look at how you've created your own problems."

"I'm a victim of circumstances."

"Twig, wake up. Your attitude creates victims. Your wife, the guy in the bar, the male nurse, were all created by your attitude."

"My name isn't Twig."

"It's Twig to me. How about it, everyone? What's his name?"

A resounding yell rises up in the unanimous voice of twenty men, "Twig."

I'm up on my feet again, ready to kick some ass. "Next guy who calls me that will regret it."

In another unified salvo, they all yell, "Twig!"

I grab the vest of a big guy next to me and pull him to his feet. He goes slack, and I find myself picking up a 200-pound load of dead weight. When I drop him, I go to the next guy and the next, until I realize not one of these wimpy bastards will fight. Not one is man enough to stand up to me.

By the time I comprehend that I'm alone in my battle, I turn to Goatee, and he hands me a baseball bat, grip first. "Take the bat and beat the shit out of that tire."

I have no idea where it came from, but the fire is replaced with a threadbare truck tire.

I turn to him. "Why don't I just swing on you?"

"Try it on the tire, Twig."

I take a swing and make a satisfying thud on the tire. I pull up and take another. One more follows, then another. I give the tire all my energy. I hear a steady rhythmic beat in my ear. I pound the tire, swinging my bat down harder than I've ever swung. I don't have to hold back for fear of killing someone. I don't pull my punches. A chant in the background is egging me into more. After ten minutes of killing the tire, I recognize what they chant; "Twig, Twig, Twig. . ."

Beads of sweat pour from my brow, and a nervous chatter repeats itself in my head, "You bad boy, bad boy, bad, bad, bad." Something clicks inside, and a steel band around my chest unravels. It's a tightness I'd forgotten I even had. I drop to my knees, grab the tire, wrap my arms around it and bawl like a newborn. I'm embarrassed, but I can't help myself. It's a tension I've had since I was young. I remember the very moment I began to carry it. My mother found out I had been jacking off in my bedroom. She was appalled. She scrubbed my hands till they bled, then locked me in the closet for the night. I might have been seven.

After what seems an hour, I cry myself out, wipe my eyes on my sleeve and look at Goatee.

He says, "When you wake up, write down your thoughts. Don't wait even five minutes. Write them as if your life depends on it, because it does."

I awaken to a flamingo-colored sky. My window looks out over the Eastern horizon, and a tinge of violet dusts a distant hilltop. I remember Goatee's instruction. On a counter next to the TV sits a pen and pad of legal paper. I grab them, get back into bed and write in a frantic unintelligible scribble.

Three pages are filled before I set the pen down.

One sentence keeps coming back to me. "Find Tazz and take his training."

It's one thing to unleash my inhibitions in a dream, but something else to seek out my enemy and ask for help. Hell, to ask another man for help, even a friend, might be misconstrued.

I've felt relief, no, more like release, since I killed that tire. I get up with an unaccustomed lightness and take a shower. The shower and coolness of the morning air give me a boost. I walk down the concrete steps and into the parking lot. I step under that idiotic stucco arch that sports the faded hotel sign. I turn left, walk across the street and out onto the sand.

Twelve years I've lived in Las Vegas and not once have I walked on pure desert sand. My stroll through loose sand is hard on my calves. A half-mile away from my hotel, I come upon a small wash and climb into the gully where the sand is compacted. I follow the zigzag cut of last winter's water. I haven't walked another hundred yards when I round a sharp bend. Standing next to a ragged truck tire, Tazz holds a wooden baseball bat in his hand. One foot rests on the edge of the tire.

"What are you doing here?" I ask.

"Bob told me to meet you here."

I've stopped long before I'm within range of his bat.

He lifts the bat and points it at me. "Bob said I should start your training."

"What kind of training?"

"You know," he says and taps his bat on an edge of the tire. "You remember last night, don't you?"

"Last night? What do you mean?"

"In the circle."

A cold chill rushes into my flushed face. Something extraordinary is about to happen.

I ask, "You were there?"

"Hell, man, don't you remember?"

Goose bumps build colonies on my arm. "You were in my dream?"

"No, we were all in each other's dream, and Bob sent me this morning to get you started."

Tazz flips his bat in the air, grabs it by the thick end, and points its grip toward me. "Look, Twig, I'd much rather have slept in. I could use the rest. Just like you, it's Bob's insistence that has me here."

I continue to stand five yards away. "You always do what he says?"

"When he tells me to do something, I understand it's for my own good. I have no idea how meeting you is better for me, but Bob has never led me astray."

"I don't understand."

"You don't need to understand, Twig. Just take the fucking bat, and beat on the tire like you did last night."

"I don't think so."

He shakes the bat at me. "I was scared the first time, too."

"I'm not scared."

He continues like I haven't said a word. "The first time I was scared out of my mind." Tazz steps toward me, holding the bat out. "Take it, Twig and beat the tire."

I back up. "I don't want it."

He takes three steps closer. "Take the bat, Twig, and let's get it over with. It'll feel good once you get started."

I back up. "I don't think so."

"You're a stubborn bastard." He takes another two steps closer, and I let him. He's still not close enough that I can't turn and sprint away if he tries anything.

He steps closer. "Bob sent me to help." He stretches his arm and points the handle at me.

I back up the gully.

"Why would I want to pound a bat on a tire?"

"Man, you ain't got a clue. Didn't you get it last night in the dream? The tire is a place to put your anger without hurting anything or anyone."

"Why would I want to--"

He leaps the last few feet and jams the bat into my stomach. It happens so fast and hard that I don't have a chance to tighten my muscles. The bat goes deep into my gut. It pushes a belch of air out. I grab his bat, and my fury leaps to the surface.

Although my wind is gone and I can't breathe, I pull the bat away from his grip and swing it around my head. I stumble forward toward him. He backs up. Is it a smile on his face or a sneer? I want to wipe it off. I want to beat him into the sand. I can't do much, because I'm out of wind. I lurch toward him. In three steps, I falter and take a wild swing with the bat. I miss him by a mile. I pull the bat back and prepare for a home run. I'm running out of air. I need a breath before I move another step. I try, but my muscles are still cramped.

I bend over, and the cramp relaxes. The bat is on my shoulder. I feel like puking.

When my muscles give way to my need for another breath, I take a deep gasp, blow it out, take another, then look up. Tazz stands in front of me, but not close enough where I can swing on him. If I leap at him, I could get one in. He's dead meat, but I need another ragged breath first.

I make a move toward him. He jumps back and taunts me by stopping just out of reach. I take another breath.

The air goes out, and I take another. I'm ready. I think I can make a full-on attack. I might have enough air to run at him.

When I take my first step, he yells and points at the ground. "Hit the tire, Twig. Hit the tire."

I see the tire, but I want nothing to do with it. I look up and ready myself to swing on him. I pull the bat back and take a full muscled swing. He doesn't move. He doesn't take a step back, nor does he raise his arms to protect himself. He stands, ready to take the beating of his life, and I'm ready to accommodate him.

He repeats the same four words. "Hit the tire, Twig."

I'm bent on his destruction. The bat swings around, but something happens. I feel an overwhelming urge to swing down, until, with a force unmatched, I clobber into, and I can't believe it, the fucking tire. Big as the truck tire is, my impact makes it spring into the air and flip over. I swing again, this time harder. The tire leaps again; sand billows out from under it; the bat rings. I pound the tire until I work myself into a lathered sweat.

Five yards to my left, with arms swinging, Tazz yells, "Make a sound."

My first noise is a grunt. Each time I lay into the tire, the noise gets louder until I yell. I scream. I don't feel my injured gut. I don't feel recoil in my arms. I scream at Tazz, and he screams at me. "Beat it, Twig. Whack the fuck out of that son of a bitch."

Spittle flies from my open mouth. Sweat rockets into the air. I'm no longer yelling at Tazz, but at my wife; at fat-assed Leonard, and the laundry woman who is always snippy at me. I scream at my sister; at the fucked-up car I drive; at the judge and my entire situation. I slam the tire, killing it for twenty minutes, when, like a camera flash, a picture comes into my brain. It's clear and real. I stop. I could never hit Mom. Her image is close and intense. I toss the bat aside and fall face first onto the tire. My breath is heavy, and I can't catch my wind. With a picture of Mom filling my vision, I cry. My cry turns to a wail, which turns to a howl. Tears stream down my face and drop onto the sand. My mouth is open. I pound sand with my open hand.

"I was just a kid." I scream between sobs.

Before I reverse the process from grief to an eventual calm acceptance, many images flash before my eyes. I remember after Dad died, Mom constantly screaming that I was a jerk. Once he was gone, Mom was helpless and leaned on me endlessly. Oh shit, just like Georgina. I chose a wife like Mom.

I lie in a quiet, altered state and remember traumas I endured as a child. After ten minutes, I sit up and wipe my puffy face on my shirttail. I look at Tazz, who sits cross-legged on the sand. He grins. "You did good work."

"I feel foolish."

"Don't worry about it, we've all been there."

"What do you mean?"

"Bob has had all of us on our knees, blubbering about our past. It comes with the territory."

I say, "I don't like this particular territory."

"It isn't much fun." He tosses over a legal-size note pad with a pen clipped to the first page. "Bob wants you to write your images. Nothing has to be coherent. Just write, so you don't forget."

I reach for my shirttail to wipe my drippy nose again. "Who is this Bob, and what does he want with me? Why is he so interested in my welfare?"

Tazz looks toward the sun, which is higher in the morning sky than I realize. When he turns back, he has an uncommon radiance in his face. "Bob helped me find myself a few years ago. He's taken an interest in you, which means to me that you're worth the time. Up until this morning, I couldn't imagine why. You've proven once again that Bob knows what he's doing."

"Why me?"

He puts up a hand and raises one eyebrow in a gesture of confusion. "Tell you the truth, I said the same thing when I began. Hang in there, Twig. Bob'll reveal his plan when the time comes. Until then, you've just passed the first test toward becoming a member of the One Percent of One Percent Club."

I turn around and sit on the tire in silence. Tazz continues to sit cross-legged on the sand. "Once you've written your impressions, don't do anything different, and don't show them to anyone. Put the tablet away until tomorrow morning."

"Why?"

He gives me a tortured grin. "Hell, man, if I knew an answer to that question. . ."

After another short silence, Tazz says, "Bob also wants you to notice how you feel after each session. He wants you to have a look at the pressure you've put yourself under."

"What pressure?"

"How does it feel now that some of your self-imposed pressure is off?"

"I don't feel any different."

He holds a hand up, palm out like a school crossing guard. "Don't try to defend yourself. Just notice the differences, and write them down. I'll be back tomorrow at the same time. I'll expect you to be ready to do it again."

"Do it again? What the hell for?"

"For the sake of you, of everyone you run into, and the difficult times you're about to encounter."

"What are you talking about?"

He stands and towers over me. "Make sure you're here. Bob demands it. He has something cooked up for you, and I have no idea what it is. Given who you are, I'm sure it'll be wild."

Tazz turns, takes twenty steps along the gully toward town, and disappears around the first bend. I pick up the yellow pad, pull the pen and start writing. My words are stilted at first, but soon I belch out pages of scribbled notes. Eventually, I write an angry letter to Mom. I've never expressed anger towards her in my entire life.

After my tire thumping session, I feel much lighter than I've felt in years. I find myself whistling while I stroll to a local diner. I feel like I'm on a cloud. For a guy who just got kicked out of his own home, lost his job and has a string of charges against him, I'm surprisingly happy.

It isn't until I'm halfway through a mildly interesting breakfast that I make a connection between my mood and the tire beating session with, of all people, Tazz.

By noon, I find myself on the street again, without a place to go or a reason to be there. My old desperate feelings creep back.

By happy hour, a dark cloud has dropped around my shoulders again, and droplets of despair fog my sunglasses. I find myself bellied up to a familiar leatherette bumper in a neighborhood bar.

Magically, a White Russian rests in front of me, and just as mysteriously, without my knowing what happened, the bartender asks if he can call me a cab.

"It's closing time," he says. "I want to go home."

"I don't need a cab," I say with a slur that surprises even me. "I'm staying at the hotel around the corner. I can walk."

The stool, which feels welded to my numb butt, takes some time to dismount. The front door creates a whole other set of problems. I'm out on the hot sidewalk and walking close to the line of buildings, with only an occasional streetlight to guide me. In my confused drunkenness, one hand feels along for support, first on glass, then stucco, a wooden door, back to glass and stucco, until I weave to the corner.

Although I find my way home, I don't remember how. I left my air conditioner on, and the room is bone chilling. Unable to do much of anything other than find my bed, I collapse and don't awaken until morning. It's comical to have chattering teeth in the middle of a Nevada desert in summer.

Once I've showered and dressed, I'm compelled to walk back out onto the sand and down into the little ravine, then up the gully until I see Tazz with his fucking baseball bat. There's the tire.

The day begins with another tire beating session. I scream at life, cry long, tearful sobs, then whistle a tune while I walk to the restaurant. I stumble back to my room at two-thirty the next morning, then repeat the exact scenario again the next day and next and next, until I've forgotten how many days I've been in my little hovel of a hotel room.

One morning while I shave, I hear four sharp knocks. I open my door.

"Mr. Goreman," the beer-gutted guy says, mumbling around what looks like the same chewed cigar. "You plan on staying another two weeks?"

"What?"

"If you want to stay another two weeks, I'll need it paid in advance."

He doesn't hold his hand out for payment, but I feel immediacy in his voice. "Come to the office and pay for your extra seven days, then for another two weeks if you want our bi-monthly discount."

"How long have I been here?"

"Three weeks tomorrow."

"I'll take care of it when I'm finished shaving."

He gives me a nod, turns and walks along the concrete balcony. I watch long enough for him to go down the stairs and disappear in the direction of his office.

I look at my watch calendar. Three weeks, and other than the tire beating sessions, I don't remember any of it.

After I sign up for another half-month, the manager gives me a curious look. His cigar stub flips to the side of his mouth. "It's no big deal, but I see you walk out onto the desert every morning. What the hell is out there?"

I think fast, because the real truth is embarrassing. "I take a morning stroll. It's good for my health."

His stained-tooth smile tells me I've given him a good answer. "Yeah, sure," he says, "it's a quiet place to walk."

He turns, grabs an envelope from the back counter and hands it to me. "This letter came for you."

I look at the return address. State of Nevada Judicial Court. "Thanks," I say in an absent-minded daze. I walk through the filthy sliding glass door into an early August inferno. I tear open the end of my envelope and pull out a single document.

State of Nevada versus Thomas Goreman.

I scan half of the page of legal jargon until I come to a court date of August sixth, two days from now.

The letter goes in my back pocket as I walk into the desert and along the gully. I see Tazz holding his fifty-two-inch bat. Without saying a word, he hands it to me. I don't take my normal allotment of swings, but lean on the bat. "I got a court date in two days. My police career might be over, and my wife sent me divorce papers."

"I know," he says. "I've waited for you to bring it up."

"What do you mean, you know?"

Tazz backs up to the wall of the gully and sits on a rise in the sand. "Bob keeps me informed."

"Bob again."

Tazz picks up a small stick and snaps it in half. He looks at me. "If you wouldn't get drunk every night, you could remember your meetings with Bob. He has a lot to say, and he can help."

"I don't get drunk. I have two or three, then go home."

"Remember, Twig, we all know what happens. We know how many drinks you down every night and how you stumble home."

I pick up the bat and take a swing at my drunkenness, and another at my inability to control my drinking. I'm off into a bat frenzy, like I have done so many mornings.

After my fury with the bat and an embarrassing emotional breakdown, I sit on the tire, wipe my eyes and look over at Tazz.

"Why are you doing this?" I ask again, for what seems like the hundredth time.

He sits on the embankment, picks another stick from the ground and scribbles figure-eights in the sand. "At first it was only because Bob told me. Believe me, I was reluctant, you being a cop with a violent streak and all." He fingers his jaw. "Now that you have a few weeks of bat work under your belt, I see your potential."

"What potential?" I thump the bat, making small, round divots in the sand. "It's relieved some pressure, is all. It works for an hour or two. By noon, I'm pissed again."

"That's true," he says, "but aren't those few hours glorious?"

A small grin breaks my otherwise somber face. "I guess you're right."

"Now that you've asked, it's time to go to your next step."

My smile turns to a sneer. "What next step?"

"Changes like this are never gigantic leaps. They're more like baby steps. You're unraveling a lifetime of habit."

"What's Bob have in mind now?"

"It's the same thing most of us have had to go through at one time or another. You've got to quit drinking."

I hear a pit bull yammer inside my guts. I feel an immediate snap of jaws from my viscous canine. He wants to tear out my intestines and run through the desert dragging them behind him. Without realizing it, I back up three steps. "Why?"

Tazz puts up a hand. "Look, man, I didn't say you've got to do it now. Just think about it."

"I don't need to think about it. I like alcohol. It's my only way to unwind."

Tazz sits casually on the embankment. Without saying another word, he continues to draw figure-eights. I pace up and down the gully, swing my arms and point at him. "Don't even go there, asshole. I like my life just the way it is."

He stabs the stick in the middle of his figure eight. "If you like your life the way it is, why is it such a mess?"

I stop and glare at him. "Mind your own fucking business." I rush him with my fist drawn.

He continues to sit, unaffected, like I'm not even there. "Get a handle on it, Twig. Grab the bat and whack the tire. Put your anger where it'll do some good."

I glare at him.

"Pick up the bat, Twig, and do the tire, not me."

I rush back, grab the handle and begin another cycle; focused violence, emotional release, then another piece of understanding.

When my clock has run down, my rage monster satisfied, I sit on the tire and look at Tazz. "It's the uncontrolled action I'm most frightened of. I don't know when it'll surface. I never know what to expect. I don't like this part of myself, but I don't know what to do when there is no tire or bat around."

Tazz puts his hands to his mouth. "Hand scream."

"What's a fucking hand scream?"

He puts his callused hands together like he's praying, opens a gap, and places them like a mask over his nose and mouth. A muffled scream comes from deep in his belly. After a moment, he drops his hands. "It's a way to let your energy out without alarming the neighbors. You can go into a restroom and let it all hang out without anyone knowing."

I give it a try and after I seal up the leaks, succeed in a scream without much of a sound.

Tazz says, "That'll help during emergencies."

"How will a scream help?"

"The simple act of finding a private place to scream helps a lot. Screams are a mini version of hits on a tire."

He picks up his stick and continues drawing figure eights. "What do you think, Twig, you want to give the no drinking thing a try sometime?"

"Maybe," I say with a nervous titter. "Just not right now. I got a lot on my plate. One more thing might send me over the edge."

"No problem, man. Whenever you're ready."

Tazz gets to his feet, drops the stick and saunters down the gully. Without turning, he says, "I gotta' get to work. See you tomorrow."

"Yeah, see you."

When he disappears, I pick up my pad and pen, then complete my morning ritual.

Once back in my room, I put on my best suit and drive downtown to my ten o'clock suspension hearing. In the room, four men and a woman pour over my records and ask too many questions.

When they're done at one, we break for lunch.

While eating, I limit myself to two beers. When I come back, my judges look fidgety. "We've considered your record," says the leather-faced woman in her tailored navy-blue suit. She doesn't look up, but reads from an inch-thick folder. "We have decided it would be better all around if your suspension continued for another month." She looks tense and flutters a stack of papers before continuing. "During the month, you're to carry through with evaluations with our staff psychologist." Another group of papers gets shuffled. "We also suggest you seek out an anger management program and join Alcoholics Anonymous."

While they make one suggestion after another, my old friend rage bubbles up an express elevator like a bad fish dinner.

Yes, it's up, but in my brain I visualize the tire and me with the baseball bat. I think about how good it feels to let it all out in the gully with no one around. I concentrate on the tire and don't hear when they excuse me. Someone touches my arm and breaks my trance. When he does, I jerk myself free. I catch myself at the last moment before I double my fist. I must have done something, because he lifts his arms to protect himself.

Before I get myself in any more trouble, I nod, turn and walk out of the room.

I stomp down the long hall, slam the front door hard on its hinges and get into my car. I drive to my hotel, park and walk out into the desert, down into the gully and pick up the bat. It's the first time I've done it without Tazz to oversee things. It's also the first time I break the bat.

After my anger drains, then turns to grief, I write notes to myself. I know what I must do, and it has nothing to do with anger management or Alcoholics Anonymous.

I want my old life back. I remember the uncomplicated life of following orders, doing my job and going home to my wife. After breaking Tazz's bat, I realize my old life is over. Everything I struggled for, if I've attempted anything at all, is finished.

After an hour of sitting on the old tire in the burning sun and writing, I stand and walk back to my motel. I call my lawyer and have him get a court continuance, then I gather up a few worldly goods, pack them into the two suitcases provided by my wife, and carry them to my car. I start the engine and drive out into traffic. I know I must return for court hearings and legal battles, but I point the nose of my car south, headed for what, I don't know.

Chapter 3

Clean

It's long after the blazing sun has set when I pull into the Shady Rest Motel. A tall, older man at the desk signs me in. He gives me a key and points to the rear. "It's around back to your left. You'll see it on the ground floor."

My room is small, pleasant and well cared for. I pay little attention, because I've felt a gnawing grumble in my guts all afternoon. My head feels like a manhandled melon. My hands are shaking, and my nerves are piano-wire tight.

I take a shower and crawl into bed. Although I'm exhausted, sleep evades me like a skittish lover.

I lay for hours alternating between sweats and freezing. I toss my sheets and ten minutes later, pull the covers over my head.

In the middle of my miserable night, someone is in the room. I open my eyes and reach for a bed lamp. When I turn it on, Bob sits with one leg tossed over the padded arm of a chair. He cracks a grin. "Well, Twig, how you doing?"

"Bob?"

"At your service. I've had a hell of a time getting through to you during this last binge. I wondered when you would drop your foolishness and get down to business."

"What business?"

"Life, of course."

"Oh that."

"Not just that, Twig. What you're about to do is big. It's huge. You're looking for a new life."

"I don't want a new life. I want my old life back. I want my wife back and my house."

"Trust me, my man, no matter how good you are, it isn't going to happen. Your woman is done with you. It's time to start fresh, and this is a good way to begin."

He gets up, steps across the room and picks out one of twenty plastic flowers from a vase on the desk. He turns to me. "You've got some important work to do. It's time to prepare."

"What do you have in mind?"

"What you're doing now is the most important thing. Get yourself sober. You'll need a clear head for this next phase." He twists off the long, wired stem and puts the flower in a single button hole of his dirty biker vest. When he has the flower in place, the blossom, which started as a small plastic bud, opens into a full-blown burgundy rose. He points at the flower. "Keep your eyes on the roses."

I awake in the throes of a freezing bout. The covers are over my head. My teeth chatter. I can't get warm. I put on extra socks and a sweatshirt, turn the heat up and get back into bed. In a freezing nightmare, I think about what Biker Bob said. I look at the vase of plastic flowers. The burgundy bud is missing, and a broken plastic stem rests on the counter.

I get up to pee and look out of the bathroom window at a hint of dawn. Without a shower or shave, something I've done every morning since Police Academy, I grab my suitcases, get into my car and head south toward Los Angeles, a destination I'm convinced I will never attain.

By the time I'm back on the old two-lane, dawn is serious. Except for scattered desert willow and a profusion of salt brush, the landscape looks barren and at the same time, beautiful.

I drive for six hours on a southern trek, until I climb over the only hills for a hundred miles. Once through the pass, I look out over another open pan of hot desert and don't see one other car. Five miles into the flatness, something strange happens. It begins to rain, but not water. At first, a few thump against my windshield, then bounce off onto the road. I'm moving fast enough that I think I've hit some stray birds. I look though my mirror and see that they weren't birds after all. When I return my attention to the windshield, a dozen pelt my hood and grill, bouncing off onto the side of the road. I look in my mirror again and see them skipping off the pavement into the sand. My eyes shift back to where I'm going. Fifty or seventy-five thunk, like hailstones, on my hood and roof.

As five hundred or a thousand pummel my car and the highway around me, I brake hard and slow from sixty to thirty. In seconds, a curtain of burgundy completely block my view. I slam my brakes, running over hundreds of them, before I come to a sliding stop, askew in the middle of the highway. I lean forward and look up through my windshield. In an otherwise flawless desert sky, a single, angry-looking, blood-red cloud, floats directly above my car. The burgundy-hailstone-pounding builds in intensity for another fifteen seconds, stacking a pile six inches deep on my hood, obliterating my view. I lean back in my seat in shock or is it wonder? I'm lucky I stopped the car.

As if someone turned off a spigot, the strange, crimson hailstorm stops. A few remaining thunks hit my car, then all is silent. I lean forward, look skyward and the cloud is gone. When I'm sure nothing else will fall from the sky, I carefully open my door and get out, crushing hundreds of them with each step. I look up and see only the brilliant blue sky.

In the middle of nowhere, because there is nothing on this stretch of highway; no cliffs, no buildings, not even a tumbleweed in view, tens of thousands of small, burgundy rose buds cover my hood, stick to the windshield wipers and plaster themselves to my grill. I look back on the road. For five hundred yards, buds cover the dull grayness of asphalt with a thick blanket of blood red. My eyes follow a path of flowers from behind me, that covers my car and goes forward for fifty yards, then turns left onto little more than a one-lane dirt path. For another hundred yards, the buds carpet the sandy-bottomed road. During the five minutes I stand there with my mouth hanging open, the flowers, in clumps of fifty or a hundred at a time, open into full bloom, give off an breathtaking aromatic fragrance, then wither and dry into minuscule knots.

I kneel and pick a woody twig off of the ground. A thorn stabs me. A small droplet of blood leaks from my forefinger onto the stem and the single flower re-blossoms.

Bob said to pay attention to the roses, but I wasn't prepared for anything like this. I look down a dirt road where the roses lead, scrape thorny buds from my windshield, get back into my car and turn left over the bed of thorns.

Any faster than five miles an hour and the washboard riffles will shake me and my car to pieces. A distant rise, ten or fifteen miles away, is the direction the road leads.

For hours I poke along, knowing I'm supposed to be going this way, but not why or what I'll see when I reach my destination. The mound is close, when the road makes a sharp left and dips a hundred feet into a fifty-foot-wide wash. When I reach the bottom and attempt to cross, my car drops axle-deep in soft sand. If it was any other time of year than August, being stuck in the bottom of a gully could be a dangerous place. Any chance of rain in a two-hundred-mile radius is unlikely, but who knows with Bob. Not that I'm free and clear. I'm still buried and hours from any possibility of help.

It's late afternoon, and I'm worn out. I decide to wait until the cool of morning before I attempt to walk out. The remains of my gallon of water won't get me back in this heat.

My car is much too hot to sit in, so I rifle the glovebox and come up with a well-worn copy of "Purple Cane Road" by James Lee Burke, then sit in the shade of a large mesquite, next to a patch of crucifixion thorns.

An hour later the sun drops behind the horizon, and in another hour, darkness envelops my little bivouac.

Before it gets too dark to see, I gather up enough greasewood and mesquite branches to make a small blaze and keep it going until I go to sleep.

On my second day without alcohol, my nerves are ragged. Rest is not easy to find, especially while curled up in the back seat of my car. I use my spare clothes as a pillow and night drags on.

Far off in the distance, sometime before dawn, I hear thunder from the west. Rushing water has a thunder sound to it. I leap from my car and scramble up the dark embankment to safety.

On top of the gully, I look back along the dirt road. A number of bobbing lights come my way.

The sound continues to grow for another half-hour before it comes close enough for me to recognize the rumble of a bevy of Harleys.

As the thunder reaches its logical climax, sixteen bikes pull down into the ravine and stop by my buried car. When the last engine is off, I hear a voice. "Hey Twig, where are you?"

I recognize the voice. "Tazz?" I yell back from the rim.

"Get your ass down here."

It takes a minute to climb down. By the time I'm in the midst of shadowy figures, someone has restarted my embers. Firelight dances on dusty faces. Glistening eyes all turn toward me, greet me with the finger-tip biker handshake.

Tazz moves toward the fire. Each man finds his own position around the circle and sits.

Tazz presents a foot-long stick with a pointed blue stone on one end. He hands it to a gangly redhead on his left. Red passes it to me, and I pass it on. It goes around a quarter of the circle to Bucky. He stands. "When Jessica left, she left a big hole in my life that I can't fill." He goes into a story of his ex-girlfriend I would have never told a soul.

He talks for ten minutes, sets the stick down, then fields some questions. Satisfied with the exchange, he thanks the group, sits down and passes the stick.

It travels through six pairs of hands before it again halts, this time in the grip of a thickset black man. He speaks for ten minutes about his relationship with an overbearing wife, three kids, and a boss who won't leave him alone. He puts the stick down and fields a question-and-answer session.

The stick travels around the circle until it comes again to me. I'm ready to pass on the whole stupid thing, when my mouth begins with a will of its own. "I beat-up my wife, and I have a drinking problem."

The group is silent. I'm embarrassed, revealing this dark part of myself. I want to pass the baton, but I continue to hold it. Something more must be said before I can get out of it, though I can't think of a thing.

"I may have lost my job, and my wife is divorcing me."

Again there is dead silence. I hear crackles from the fire and the ever-present sound of crickets. Not a breath is drawn. I set the stick on the sand.

"What do you want to do about your drinking problem?" A recognizable voice comes from behind the fire.

"I haven't had a drink in two days."

"It's a start." Bob rises from his sitting position. He walks around the fire and towers over me. "What are you doing about it from now on? You can't get yourself lost in the desert forever. You'll have to go to a store sometime. When you do, beer and bourbon will be there. What's your plan?"

"I don't know."

Bob looks wild-eyed when he focuses on me. His horsy grin glistens in the firelight. He spreads sinewy arms, indicating the men. "Learn to lean on others."

"What?"

"You need someone you can call on. These men are people you can trust. Pick two, get their phone numbers and contact them when you're feeling weak."

"I've gotten along pretty well on my own, thank you. Plus, who would want a cop to call them? My guess is no one."

"Each man is ready to be here for you, Twig. If you want to take charge of your drinking problem, you gotta' be able to trust others."

I don't believe it; I've been obsessively spying on most of these men for months now. Why would they want to help?

"Because you ask them," he answers, like I asked my question aloud. "All you have to do is ask, and any of them will be available."

"I don't need anyone."

"It might be better put," Bob says, "that you feel like you don't deserve anyone."

Oh God, he hit the nail right on the head. I wasn't thinking it, but when he says the words, I know he's right. I'm a sleaze of a human being, and I don't deserve anyone. I collapse inward and dive deep inside of my well of self-pity.

"Before you leap headlong into your ever-familiar depression and go find the nearest liquor store, pick two men."

"What?"

Bob sweeps his arm around the circle. "You have a choice. Every man has already said they would be honored to check in on you. All you have to do is choose."

I feel an unreasonable amount of pressure to succumb to Bob's demand. In a panic, I point at Tazz, because I already know him, and across the fire at Bucky, who, though I pistol-whipped, I'm drawn to.

"Done," Bob says. "Now you need to make another choice."

I look over at Bob. "What?"

"Either choice will work," he says. "You're at a crossroads, Twig. Do you want to go back to your old life and try to repair the damage or are you ready for a new one?"

I should think about it, but a clear choice leaps to the forefront in my mind, and my lips follow. "I want a new life."

Bob's large grin spreads. "That's good."

He looks around the circle. "Let's get this dickhead's car out of the sand."

In a flash, the fire is gone, Bob has disappeared, all of the men have vanished, and I wake up in the back seat of my car to the desert pinkness of dawn. A cacophony of birdsong heralds the day. Although my mind reels from the dream, I'm left feeling stronger after being with the men. Yes, it was a dream, but it feels real, and I like it. Too bad something like that doesn't exist in real life.

After fifteen minutes of lying awake on my uncomfortable back seat, I sit up. The early morning colors have vanished, leaving a starkness of bright desert in their path. When I look about to see where I am, a shiver runs through my stomach.

My car sits on solid earth, twenty yards beyond the soft wash where I was stuck. I get out and inspect deep-set footprints in the sand and my tire tracks leading across the ravine. I get back in, start my engine and drive up the far rim of the gully. I stop and look forward on an open pan of desert. The first flicker of another sizzling sun peeks over the far horizon.

Anxiety ties a knot in my throat. There's a big part of me that wants to go back to Vegas, to my job, my wife, and my old life, but nothing is left there except pain and heartache. I sure made a mess of things. I know I must go back for my legal problems, but for now, a new life awaits. I drop my shift lever in drive and pull out to face a rising sun and the unknown. Maybe I can make a clean start.

Chapter 4

Time

"That was seven years ago," I say to Stewart Chance. "A lot has changed since those days, and the One-on-One bikers have helped me every step of the way."

We stand looking over a renegade trash dump above Barstow. A hawk circles overhead making familiar cries.

Stewart pulls back his black hair. "Did they help you stop drinking?"

"Them and twelve-step. I called on Tazz and Bucky countless times during the early years. We had many men's circles to keep me dry. It was hard the first three years, but I haven't had a drink since that last day in Vegas, and I owe much of it to the One-on-Ones."

"What happened to your wife?"

"She got the house, and I got the bills, though I don't regret a minute of it. She met a nice guy, and they're happy in that piece of crap home in the suburbs. She can have it. I was never happy there."

"How did court go?"

"Oh, when the judge saw I was getting help, he slapped some fines on me and forced me into an anger-management group. I did a two-year probation in Victorville. Thank God I got away from Vegas.

"Last year I went back, looked up Georgina and did my ninth step with her."

Stew looks at me with his unusual blue eyes. "What's that?"

"I made amends. It felt good to tie up loose ends."

We look out toward the distant horizon for another minute. The breeze rustles some scrub. The redtail hawk circles overhead in a cloudless desert sky.

I step back and rest sideways on the seat of my bike. "Whatever happened to that redhead who saved you from the fire?"

Stew looks away from the view and gives me an odd grin. "You mean Melinda?"

"Yeah, you heard from her?"

"She called last month and told me she had found some grizzled old codger in Northern California. He knew something about anger and how it connected to her parents. She quit her job in L.A. and has been living closer to him in Cazadero, west of Santa Rosa."

"They lovers?"

He steps back, drops a lanky leg over his bike and sits. "No, he helps her sort out her anger."

"No doubt she's a pistol," I say.

He crosses his long arms and smiles. "Do I detect interest?"

My face reddens. "Guess because I'm not so much of an asshole these days, I'm interested in a woman strong enough to meet me head on."

He gives me his television newscaster smile. "Hell, Twig, you're just as much of an asshole, just a different kind."

"Hey, fuck you."

He looks out over dead refrigerators and rusted car bodies. "Melinda will meet you head on and then some."

We have another moment of silence while the wind kicks up a notch and whips my wiry long hair.

"How's your family?" I ask.

"Renee and the kids are still in Sacramento. I don't think she'll ever move to the desert, though she visits every other week."

Our conversation goes on for another half-hour before we get back on our Harleys and ride off the bluff. In the middle of town, Stewart waves and turns left in the direction of his cabin. I continue through Barstow and onto the highway.

I drive to Victorville, then up Fourth Street to my apartment above old Glen Segal's house. I park my bike in the garage and walk up rickety back steps. When I go to unlock my door, I see it's ajar. My mind goes for the worst. Someone has ripped me off. What could they possibly want? My only real possession is my Harley. Nevertheless, with my index finger I push the door open and peek in. My heart stops. My breath comes up short. My knees go weak. I feel a catch in my voice. I ask my nervous-teenager stupid question of the hour. "What're you doing here?"

I close the door behind me and walk across to my kitchen sink before I hear, "Bob sent me."

I pour two glasses of water, get ice cubes from the fridge and step back into my minuscule living room. I hand one over and sit on the arm of my couch. In an attempt to calm my shaking hand, I down an entire glass of water and chew the ice.

"Bob told me to spend some time with you. I drove in from Santa Rosa and came straight here. Your landlord let me in."

She reaches up, pulls a wild strand of strawberry hair from her face, gives me a Cheshire smile and reaches out a freckled hand. I take her fragile looking fingers in my meat hook and try not to squeeze too hard.

"I'm Melinda Chambers."

"Yeah, I know."

"Heaven's sakes, Twig, how do you know?"

"I've been aware of you since you and Stewy pulled Nick's folks from the fire two years ago."

There is a moment of awkward silence before she says, "Do you have any idea what Bob has in mind?"

I shake my head. "You know Bob."

I get up to pour another glass of water. With my back to her, I say, "I'm kind of hungry. You want to go get somethin' to eat?"

"Thought you'd never ask." She stands to a nice comfortable height of five feet seven without shoes, and grabs her overnight bag. "Let me change into some old jeans before we ride that greasy hawg of yours." She turns and disappears into the bedroom.

In fifteen minutes the sound of my engine thunders off the buildings in town.

That night, she sleeps on my couch. The next, because the couch is uncomfortable, fully covered with flannel snoopy pajamas, she sleeps in my bed. Weeks pass before we approach anything closer than cuddling. I don't mind, because a dream has come true, and I'm a patient man.

A month later, I ride my Harley in the dead of night, down a long slope into a valley. The road is smooth. A cloudless night sky with a half moon, allows me to ride with no lights.

At the bottom of the slope is a small flicker. It's Bob and my buds. I come upon the scene, park and step over to a somber circle of men. Tonight will not be one of those wild parties, but a close-knit camaraderie of men doing men's work; an important part of my new life.

I sit in the sand, in a space saved for me, and warm my hands over the small fire.

"Glad you could join us, Twig," Bob says and rolls up the sleeves of his plaid logger shirt. "We have some work to do tonight." He pulls out his familiar foot-long crystal, hands it to Stewart, and the evening begins with our point man talking about loneliness without his family. When he passes the crystal on, it moves hand to hand, each man speaking for a minute about his life, until it comes to me.

I stand, because it's important for me to be standing. "I'm happy for the first time since I can remember, and I attribute it to these last few months with Melinda."

A number of chuffs and grunts sound from the circle of twenty, but because I hold the crystal, no one speaks.

After a minute long monologue, I sit and put the crystal on the sand.

Bob pulls at his graying goatee. He looks at me and asks the first question. "Are you ready to work out your fury toward women?"

I glare into his arresting golden eyes. "What the fuck do you mean?"

"It's the reason why you two are together. You both have a similar reaction to anger. My question is, are you willing to stick it out and work through your shit with one another?"

"Well," I say, feeling embarrassed, "She's my perfect match. We're like two peas in a pod. I couldn't ask for a more perfect woman to have in my life."

Bob gives me one of his big-toothed smiles. "She's perfect, all right, but not in the same way you're talking about."

"What?"

Bob springs to his feet and leaps over the small blaze like a jack in the box. When he lands in front of me, he does so with a flair, sliding in on one knee, with arms splayed, palms up, fingers outstretched. He pulls back a loose lock of blue/black hair and looks at me. "Are you ready to do the work, buckaroo?"

I hate being on the spot. I look around for some help, but see only stupid grins. No one wants to jump in and take the pressure off.

"It doesn't feel like work with her. She talks about soul mates and how perfect we are for one another. I'm not sure I believe in the soul mate bullshit, but it does seem easy."

Bob's eyes gleam in the firelight. "Soul mates is what I would call it." He turns and faces the fire. "The two of you have a lot of work to do and it'll be here soon. Enjoy the sweetness of your romantic period, but be prepared to go through the fire with this woman."

"What?"

He steps on top of a burning log and turns toward me. A pant leg catches, and I smell scorched cotton.

"Are you ready?" he shouts.

"I guess so."

"Don't guess, Twig. It's your life we're talking about. You've been sober for seven years. It's time to get clean from violence."

A finger of flame creeps up to his knee, consuming a long sliver of denim.

"I haven't been violent once for the past seven years. How could you say I need to deal with violence?"

"Be prepared, my man, because all of your shadows stand at the threshold, and they want back into your life. This woman is your perfect reflection. First, you'll have to battle with your own demons, then make friends with them, because you're on the brink of another discovery."

I smell hair and burnt flesh.

"Are you ready?" he asks.

I spring to my feet and push him out of the fire. I'm ready to roll him in the dirt, but my eyes open to another crimson desert dawn. What a relief; it was another Bob dream. I look at a mass of strawberry curls and roll closer with my swollen manhood to cuddle up to our growing relationship.

Sex with Melinda, though it's better than I've had in years, is missing a segment. A cog slips whenever our sexual frenzy builds. She's ready and willing, but some hidden part of her clicks off, and once that happens, the rest of our encounter is like a well-practiced play or movie. She goes through the motions, but isn't personally involved. I'm in love, so I'm patient.

I lay my left arm over her slender waist, slide my hand up her belly, past her ribcage, and between those delicious fleshy orbs of pleasure. My hand comes to rest, not on one of her expressive exclamation points of flesh, but over the rhythm of her heart.

She slides one of her slender hands up my arm and laces her fingers with mine. She pulls me tighter against her. I feel her body wriggle down, down, down, until her fluffy little triangle targets my engorged appendage. I feel her fur first, then a silky slipperiness as she continues her downward journey. Her arm slips away from my fingers. She reaches back to grab my left thigh, pulling me into her. Sweet Jesus, I'm in heaven.

Dawn has turned into another full-blown autumn day by the time we lie in a familiar awkwardness.

She whispers, "It wasn't very good, was it?"

"Sure it was, Melinda. We're still a little shy with one another, that's all."

"It's not all," she says. "This is a familiar place for me."

"We did just fine."

She turns toward me. "Tell me the truth, Twig."

"It is the truth," I say and begin down a long, winding and treacherous path. We do a number of back-and-forth exchanges. Each one shifts her from the mild-mannered woman I'm familiar with, to the screaming Medusa I've heard about from Stewart and Nick. When her fist clips my jaw with the force of a framing hammer. I'm taken aback, but not surprised.

I vault out of bed and back up until my bare butt hits the wall. She drives hard onto me. I put my arms up to protect myself. She's much quicker than I expect. A fast two hits clobber my nose and above my left eye.

Something snaps inside of me. Some primitive part of me that's been buried for seven years leaps to the forefront. Before I think, my arm swings out, and I backhand her across one shoulder. She flies across the room and lands helter skelter on my bed. My animal instinct pushes me forward, and I rush her with an arm drawn back. What I don't expect is her banshee shriek. She grabs the desk lamp and shatters it across my shoulder.

My collarbone makes a crunch sound. A piercing sharp pain spreads up my neck. She grabs me and pulls me toward her. She scratches my back and bites my chest. To my amazement, I feel her pull me down on top of her, open her legs, and my hardness finds its way to her soft, yielding vessel. The flailing insanity of her, the incredible recklessness unleashed, the wild feral cat of her insatiable body leaves me out of breath and exhausted long before she's finished.

When we're complete and lie in a heap of tangled and bloody sheets, I open my eyes and look at her and she at me. We both see the damage.

She bounds toward the bathroom and returns with a wet towel to sop up a trickle of blood that drips from my shoulder. With dismay, I study a large bruise on her neck and the left side of her face.

I'm horrified and guilty. With an overabundance of apologies, we dress. She drives me to the emergency room for treatment of a broken collarbone and an assortment of cuts and bruises.

We don't say much until we're returning to the apartment. She says, "I don't know, Twig, maybe being together isn't such a good idea. We both have a propensity for violence."

I reach over with my good arm and wrap my sausage fingers around her wrist. "That may be true, but it was the best sex I've ever had."

Without letting her eyes stray from traffic, a winsome smile splits her bruised face. "Me, too, but look at the mess. Neither of us could survive a steady diet of this kind of lovemaking."

"You might be right, but when I'm well, I'd be willing to give it another try."

She makes a left on Fourth and breaks into tears. "That's my point. It's good, but if we talk only from our genitals, can the rest of our bodies afford it?"

I put my good arm out and rest a hand on her shoulder. "I've never met anyone like you, Melinda. I've never been with anyone willing to meet me head on, toe to toe, nose to nose."

She turns into our driveway and parks in front of the garage. With tears still in her eyes, she looks at me. "Fist to fist, too, and that's the part that worries me. I've had an anger problem all of my life. I've tried to work it out, but I don't get anywhere."

I look at my watch. "I've got my men's gathering in an hour." I lift my taped arm and show it to her. "I can't ride my bike; could you give me a lift over to Bucky's?"

"Heaven's sakes, Twig, we spent our entire day in the emergency room. I don't like what's happening to us." She restarts her engine and backs out of the driveway.

As we drive south down Main Street, I say, "I thought I'd left my anger problem behind when I quit booze. It's been a long time since that old rage has come up. Even when my ex-wife raked me over the coals, I got angry, but I didn't get physical. I thought it was alcohol-related, but obviously it isn't."

There is a long silence while she drives to the far end of town. When she speaks, it startles me. "Maybe our tendency for violence is why Bob put us together."

"You might have a point. In my dream last night, Bob told me we had some work to do. I guess this is it."

She drops me at Buck's house, and I ride on the back of his bike in contemplative silence. We go north along Historic Route 66 for ten miles, until we come to a familiar dirt driveway. He turns left and drives past the remains of a burnt out farmhouse. We drop into a gully behind the house and ride along an old wash that hasn't seen water for decades. When the ravine opens, we pull up to an ancient beaver dam. Five bikes are parked in a line, with six men positioned around a cold fire pit.

Bucky parks his bike next to the others on the hardpan, and we dismount. When we sit, the men greet us with the customary fingertip slaps.

A blue Fat Boy pulls up and parks. Stewart looks over at me. "Hey, Twig, you grab onto the business end of a tiger?"

"I don' t think so," Tazz says. "Looks like a freight train."

I give them a shy smile. "Melinda and I got into our first fight."

"Shit, man," Tazz says, "Melinda did all that?"

Stewart steps into the circle. "I told you she was a handful, Twig. What happened to your chest?"

"Broken collar bone."

"Holy shit, man, you two got to be more careful."

"You' re telling me. I got some shit to talk about tonight." I look around the circle. "Hope all of you are ready."

The men nod or give gestures of acknowledgment while Stewart grabs sticks from the old beaver dam, tosses them in a growing pile and finds a comfortable seat on one of the cedar rounds.

During the next ten minutes three more bikes, with five men, show up and add to the circle.

While Bucky opens up the evening' s activities, dusk paints a turquoise and crimson splash across wispy cirrus clouds.

He stands, starts a small fire, thanks everyone for showing up and lights a small sprig of cedar. Using a hawk feather, he walks around the circle, wafts the smoke and invites each man in for the evening. When he sits, he picks up a foot-long ironwood stick with a single feather hanging from its center. He passes the stick and it goes around until it stops at one of the new guys, Charlie, who gives a two-minute check-in about trouble with a particular client, then passes the stick on.

The other new guy, and I always forget his name, stops the stick. He tells a short accounting of his teenager and the boy' s trouble with cops.

There are no comments during check-in, just a chance for each man to speak honestly about his life and be witnessed.

When the baton reaches me, I explain my injury and turn to Bucky, our leader for the evening. "I'll need a half-hour to talk."

Buck nods, and I pass the stick.

It goes around three times before each man has taken an opportunity to speak. Once we're finished, the stick goes back to Buck, and he moves the evening to the next step.

"Let's see, Twig, Charlie, and Stewart have some work to do tonight. Which of you would like to start?"

Stew motions with his hand, grabs the stick, and tells a tale about Renee's latest visit. They argued all weekend. He ends his monologue by saying, "I don't think it's a good idea to fight the whole time with my wife. I'm afraid she won't want to come back."

He stops, sets the stick down, and our circle is silent.

Buck asks, "Do you want comments?"

He spreads his arms, palms up. "I need some help."

Tazz chimes in. "Fightin' with your wife shows that each of you want to be with one another, and both of you have strong wills."

"I don't know about me," Stew says. "Renee is the warrior in our family. You gotta' give it to her for pure spunk."

Everyone snickers.

Bucky speaks out. "At least both of you show up. If you didn't, you wouldn't want to voice your opinion and argue."

"I don't know what to do next. She left Sunday night in a huff, and we haven't talked since. I've called ten times, but she won't answer. What is it, four days now?"

"Do you love her?" Charlie asks.

"Yeah, sure I do."

"Let her know. Send her some flowers with a love note. She'll get the message, then don't pursue her. Give her some time to miss you."

"Yeah, man," Buck says. He sings a short ditty from the seventies, "How can I miss you, if you won't go away?"

The circle laughs.

Charlie says, "If she distances herself from you, give her room to think."

"You mean don't call or try to contact her?"

"Exactly!"

"You drop out of sight, and I'm positive she'll call within a day, if only to find out that you're okay."

Stewart shifts into an introspective huddle. Buck brings him out when he asks, "Are you complete, Stew?"

He raises a hand and flips his wrist twice, as if to say go on without him.

The circle sits in silence. I pick up the stick and everyone focuses on me.

"I think I love her. We have all of the makings of a relationship, but something happened earlier today I don't understand."

I shift position and get on my knees. I put my one free hand to face the warm fire and continue. "As you can see, we got into it, and we hurt one another. She's got a pretty bad bruise. I thought I'd left violence behind when I quit drinking, but it's reared its ugly head once more, and I'm terrified." I talk for another ten minutes and set the stick down for comments.

Nick Brown, who's been silent, even during check in, speaks in a low, frustrated tone. "She's a tiger in bed, but someone has to get hurt to get her fired up."

I turn to him. "Yeah, I found that out, and I don't like it."

Nick gives me a wistful glance and his next few words have venom. "I never met a woman who was so fucked up."

Buck lifts his hand. "Hold on, Nick. No slamming women." Sudden as a summer rainstorm, Nick springs to his feet and goes into a screaming tirade. "That bitch messes up everything she touches. She's the kiss of death."

Charlie speaks over Nick's rant. "Didn't you hear Buck?"

Since he's the leader tonight, Buck holds out one hand and silences Charlie. "Let the man do his work." He nods at Nick, who builds into an unparalleled frenzy.

We all move back to give Nick room to flail his hands and kick sand. His screams match the roar of a Harley. His body makes chaotic, spastic movements, while he yells obscenities at Melinda. He breathes hard and snorts, as he expresses dark, inexhaustible hatred. The devil himself could not be more alarming. When he picks up a bat-sized log and crashes it into the fire, Buck leaps to his feet. "Away from the fire, Pal." Buck herds Nick some ten yards into the darkness. Nick clobbers the base of a cottonwood tree with another branch. He curses her until his rage reaches a climax and he smashes the stick hard. It snaps in two. Breathing fast, he walks back to his place and sits.

Buck says, "Pretty good, Nick. You need to do more?"

Without saying a word, Nick motions for us to continue.

There's a moment of silence before I pick up the crystal again, which indicates that I have something to say and there will be no interruptions, no comments, not even any snorts of approval or disapproval, until I set the stick down.

"Anyhow," I say, like nothing happened with Nick, "Melinda and I have run up against our violence and it frightens me. At the same time, we both know Bob put us together. I need to work on my re-emerging streak and find a way to direct it when it comes up." I set the stick down.

Tazz chimes in. "You still do the baseball bat thing?"

"As you know, I used it for years, and it worked well when I was alone, but I don't think it works with domestic problems. I tried it the other day and it added to my anger instead of relieving it. Put a woman in the mix and the bat doesn't help a bit. There must be another way."

Buck nods. "I get your point." Murmurs of confusion come from around the circle, but no one has an answer.

The circle is quiet. I give the stick to Bucky and say, "I'm complete for now."

He holds the stick up. "The circle is open for another man to talk."

Hours later, when the evening ends, I get on the back of Bucky's Harley. We ride to town in a unified motorcycle amoeba: ten bikes, thirteen men cruising in a thrum of Harley fever. The sound of engines rumbles along under a star-studded sky. A waning harvest moon peeks over the distant horizon. When we come into town, Tazz is the first to pull away from our pack. He turns left. Three bikes turn right at the next light, and five turn right two lights later. Bucky drops me in front of my apartment, and I pat his shoulder while I dismount. "It was a good night," I yell over the engine.

Bucky grins. "Yeah, man, tight, very tight. See you Friday."

"What?"

"The Reno run, Street Vibrations, don't you remember?"

"Sweet Jesus, I forgot."

"You're still with us, aren't you?"

"If my shoulder is better, I'll ride, if not, I may take a car. I'm there either way."

"Cool. See you Friday at dawn." He slips his bike into first with a familiar clank of gears, gives his throttle a short rev and pulls away from the curb.

When the noise of his engine fades, I turn and walk around the house, then along my driveway. Before I go upstairs, I look in on my bike. I sit on the seat for a minute and hope I can drive to Reno.

Chapter 5

Working It

When I open the door, Melinda leans against the sink taking a bite of celery. "Hey, you," she says through a mouth full of crunching. "Did you have a good meeting?"

I nod and step over to the small round table, gently kick out a chair and sit. "I'm worried."

"About what?"

"Us."

She takes another bite. "If we're meant for each other, we'll work through this part."

I stand and grab a glass from the shelf. "I don't want either of us to get hurt in the process."

She says, "I worked with a guy who lived near Santa Rosa. He helped me get in touch with my anger. Maybe we could see him together."

I take two steps to the sink and pour myself a glass of water. "Santa Rosa is kind of a long way."

She bites the celery and chews while she speaks. "That isn't the half of it. He moved to the coast of Oregon when I came down here."

I drink the water and say, "Oregon is three times farther."

"It is, but no one else has helped me get close and believe me, over the years I've tried them all."

"Okay," I say, "when do you want to do it?"

She bites off another noisy crunch and talks while she chews. "Soon as possible, before we kill one another."

We give each other sheepish grins, like we are in on some kind of joke, though it's more serious than either of us wants to admit.

"Look, Twig, Bob put us together for one reason I know of. We need to explore every possibility. I'm ready to go there next week, if you are."

I down the glass of water and say, "After the Reno run."

"Sure." Her lips curl into a sarcastic sneer. "Your precious Reno run is so much more important than what we're working on."

I think fast. "What's wrong with after the run? I'll park my bike at Nick's brother's, and we'll take a train from Reno over to your friend's. We could stay a few days on the coast. It should be fun."

"How are you going to take your bike with one shoulder taped?"

I look at my arm. "I forgot."

Her dark expression shifts. "If we take my car, we could drive from Reno, but how do we pay for such a good time?"

"Hell, Melinda, I got some money saved up for a rainy day and my fucked up job at the rubber band factory owes me some time."

Her face lights. She takes another bite of celery. "You're on."

Thursday afternoon, my doctor says no riding for at least another week. At dawn the next morning, we pack the car and Melinda drives to the Piggly Wiggly; our rendezvous place with the One on One bikers.

As usual, someone has to have a bike that doesn't start. Since Nick isn't here yet, I step over and get the bike running.

Once Nick shows up, Melinda and I follow the caravan in her car. We wind our way through town, out to Highway 395, then north. Thirteen bikes and sixteen people roll for three uninterrupted hours, until we come to a town called Lone Pine and stop for lunch at a little burger joint along the main drag.

Our group takes another break south of Mono Lake, where we pull out onto a sandy bluff and park. When I get out of Melinda's car, I take in deep breaths of crisp air laced with pungent desert sage. Bill's wife comes over. "Hey, Twig, can I ride with you two for a while?" She points at a two-thousand-foot wall of granite on the far side of Mono. "We've got to go over that pass, and I'm already freezing."

"No problem, Sylvia, I'd love to get in the wind for a while. You and Melinda can ride together."

Melinda glares at me. "Your doctor said--"

"Oh, screw the doc, it's only for a few miles, anyhow."

"Heaven's sakes, Twig, it's your shoulder."

I step over to the last of the parked Harleys and talk to Bucky. The two women converse by the car. It isn't thirty seconds before Melinda stomps over, grabs my good arm and spins me around. "What the fuck do you think you're doing making decisions for me? It's my car, and it's my choice who rides with me. You, buster, have no say in the matter."

I look at her with confusion. "I thought you liked Sylvia."

"I do, but that's not the point. You have no right. . ." She rants on for a minute before I can get a word in edgewise.

"Melinda, what's the big deal?"

I guess I said the exact wrong thing. Her face scrunches. In a flash, her little fist takes a swing at me. Luckily, I'm prepared. I move back just in time. She misses my nose by the slightest margin. She continues her swing, and the momentum throws her into a spin. She slams against me. I try to hug her. She wriggles out of my grip and comes back ready to fight.

I say, "Melinda, slow down."

She comes in for another pass. I put up my one good arm and block her punch.

Tazz steps in, takes two solid hits to his chest and says, "Last night, Bob told me this would happen."

Melinda stops. Fists drawn, she waits.

"Bob told me what to do, if you want to try it."

She dances on the balls of her feet like a prizefighter. "What?" She fires the word like a thrown fist.

"Let's go out into the sand," Tazz says. He yells at the milling group. "I'll need eight or ten men to help. Get your bedrolls, fast."

People scramble to unlash sleeping bags and blankets strapped to the backs of their bikes. In a minute, everyone is in place.

Tazz comes over to me and whispers, "Keep her riled up, if you can."

"That shouldn't be too hard."

Tazz lays a tarp on the sand and positions the men in a tight circle around its edge.

I walk over to her. "Melinda, why are you so pissed? I didn't do anything."

With my few words, she's dancing again, fists clenched, head bobbing. "Look, you fat bastard, you have no right to. . ."

I guess I'm doing my part, because she's at me again.

Tazz steps between us and grabs her dangerous fists. He stares at her and growls, "Over there!"

She spits the words. "No one tells me what to do."

He spins her and pushes her hard into the tight circle of men, all holding sleeping bags. Once she's inside, the gap closes, and she can't get out. Her fists swing toward one man, then another, only to hit a sleeping bag or bedroll. She launches into a banshee wail at a pitch that is certain to blow out my eardrums.

Tazz whispers, "Now, Twig, egg her on. I want her to go killer."

He hands me one of two rolled-up bags, and we both slip into the circle without opening an inch of space for her to wriggle through.

"Why are you so upset, Melinda?" I yell over her screams.

Her body slams against sleeping bags with more intensity. The pitch of her yell, which I thought had reached an unknown octave, leaps higher.

"Let me out." She doesn't say the words, more like spits them. "I'll kill you."

Her body smashes, her feet flail. Her kicks at groins and shins land only on padding. She's in a full-blown frenzy when she loses her balance and falls to the tarp.

Tazz motions everyone to close in with our bags in front of us. She doesn't stand, but kicks and swings her fists hard, hitting pads.

Tazz motions me to add a little juice.

"What's your problem, Melinda?" I ask in a sarcastic tone.

Her anger intensifies, and she flails harder at the buffers, screams louder, with a higher pitch.

She's on her back, coming unleashed without constraints for ten minutes before she slows from exhaustion.

Tazz nudges me to do it again. I whisper, "Are you sure? She looks wiped."

"It's what Bob told me to do."

I shrug and add another insult. My sarcastic tone lights her up like a Roman candle. She spins, hurls fists, feet, then head against whatever presents itself, hitting only soft sleeping bags.

As suddenly as her storm came on, her screaming stops.

Tazz speaks a series of fast questions. "What came into your thoughts? What do you feel? How old are you? Don't say a word. Mark it and talk about it later."

"It's my dad," she says, and her words fade off into a blubber of unintelligible garble.

With eleven men over her, ready with sleeping bags, Melinda opens her feelings. Her emotional dam overflows.

These are people she obviously trusts, or it would never have gotten this far. The One on One bikers make me proud. These men hold a critical place for Melinda. They witness her unraveling with tears in their eyes, and even the hardest of us has softness in his face.

It takes another fifteen minutes before Melinda is calm and sits up on the tarp. The men, including me, kneel on the tarp's edge, sleeping bags still ready, but not quite as on guard as before.

When she stands, tears stream down her face. "I can't believe what you all did for me." She breaks into a long wracking sob, reaches out and hugs each person.

When she's gone around our entire circle and thanked each person, she comes to me. "Oh, Twig," she cries. "Maybe we're meant for each other after all." Her tears spill over again. She wraps her arms around my neck and pulls me close. I'm in an awkward position as she pulls me down. I roll over her and lie flat on the tarp. She squeezes me, unwilling to let go, and forces me to lie there until she's finished.

When she's done, she sits up and looks around. She gets a comical expression. "I don't feel like having sex."

All sixteen people who sit and stand in witness to her, roar with laughter.

When things get quieter, Tazz says, "Let Sylvia drive and write all of your impressions while you were on the tarp."

She nods.

Sylvia slips in and puts a hand on her shoulder. "I don't have to ride with you."

Melinda breaks into a fresh bout of tears. "No, Sylvia, None of this had anything to do with you. I'd love it if you rode with me. I need to talk. If I get Twig to say more than ten words at any given time, I'm lucky. I need another woman around to talk these feelings out with."

She grabs my face with both hands and kisses me. While the crowd breaks up and we prepare to get back on the road, Melinda and Sylvia pull into a huddle next to the car. I go to the outdoor bathroom at the edge of the parking lot, bundle up in long johns and leather, then get on the back of Bucky's lean, yellow machine. He pulls out onto the highway beside Nick. I look back and see Melinda and Sylvia yammering up a storm. Melinda nods her head while Sylvia drives. I'm glad not to be in the car, because hours will go by before those two will slow down to a pace I could bear.

Although the ride is exhilarating, my shoulder doesn't like the cold, and I'm forced to get back into her car after an hour.

By late afternoon, we roll through Carson City, and a half-hour later the two-lane Highway 395 turns into a freeway. The gleam of Reno comes into view.

Groups of fifty and a hundred bikes roar past us. Bikes are parked in restaurants and gas stations, along streets, and in parking lots. Bikes are everywhere.

As we get within shouting distance of downtown, the throngs of Harleys are deafening. Tazz leads our group along Virginia Street through the city, over a freeway, to a small motel a mile north of town. In red paint, with a familiar scrawl, a hand-lettered sign stretches for ten feet along a steel rail balcony of the cheesy two-story motel. I know I'm home when I read the words, "Welcome One on One bikers."

Sylvia manages to find a parking place in the lot, while the riders back up to a concrete wall of a closed bank next door. We wait while Tazz confirms reservations and gets keys to our rooms. I get out of the car, and a distant rumble of Harleys permeates the air. A roar of bikes passes on the freeway, then the lone sound of a gunned engine thunders in the distance.

I lift my arm into the air and scream, “It’s Hawg heaven.”

Melinda sidles up to me, puts her arms around my waist, and gives me a hug. “It’s noisy,” she says.

“That’s the point of this whole thing. Why would we be here if it weren’t for the sound of Harleys, lots of ‘em?”

She says, “I’m starved. Let’s stash our gear in our rooms, then get something to eat.”

“All in due time. Get yourself a snack over at the 7-Eleven for now, because it may take a while for everyone to get settled.”

She releases my waist, pulls her head back and looks up at me. “I thought maybe you and I could sneak off for a nice romantic meal.”

“Jesus, Melinda, I can’t leave my buds. We came together, and we stick together.”

One more time it’s the wrong thing to say. She pulls back a yard and glares at me. Without a word, she turns and speaks to Sylvia.

Once again, I’ve stepped in the ol’ proverbial dog shit. I’m in for some major trouble; but hasn’t trouble been with me ever since I met her? Haven’t I been the recipient of one angry remark after another for months? I’m tired of the constant barrage of femininity and all the demands that come with it. I turn my back on Melinda and talk with Stewart.

Bucky nudges me and points across the lot. “Where’s she going?”

I look up and see the taillights of Melinda’s car pulling out into traffic.

“Shit, I don’t know. Do you ever know what makes a woman tick?”

Snickers arise from our small circle of leather-clad bikers. They sound apprehensive, coming from men who have faced the fire and withstood the heat, reluctant to step back into the inferno unless absolutely necessary.

I've already crossed the line. I'll face her fire soon enough and I'd better be well fed first. Who knows when I'll get another chance for a meal?

Tazz walks out of the office and divides keys among us. He says, "I'm hungry. Let's meet back here in ten minutes and go eat."

"Hey, Tazz," I say. "Who came up with the sign?"

He shrugs and gives me a confused look. "Ain't got a clue. Thought it was you." We all look at one another.

"Well, shit, if none of us did it, then who?"

Stewart steps closer and studies the sign. "I saw script like this once on a bathroom wall."

I step next to him and put my hand on his shoulder. "What do you mean?"

"Maybe Bob hung it."

Tazz walks up next to us. "Why would Bob--"

Stewart turns to him. "Maybe there's some kind of hidden message."

I look again at the sign. "Christ, Stewart, plain as day it says 'welcome'. Put your mumbo-jumbo bullshit away; there's nothing hidden."

"Maybe we better look closer."

Nick steps up. "I'm hungry. I say we get settled, then follow Melinda's lead and get somethin' to eat."

We unload our bikes and take the stuff to our rooms.

In ten minutes, Nick opens my door. "Come on, man, you better be ready, 'cause I'm starved."

I pull on my black leather "One on One" vest and step out into the warm evening. We walk along a concrete deck and roust our people from each room, working toward the bikes.

Engines start, and I get on the back of Stew's Fat Boy. We're a well-polished unit of steel and leather. Our thirteen bikes pull onto the street and roar up toward the center of town.

There are so many bikes rumbling through the cruise, the drive through downtown takes thirty minutes. When we find an agreeable Mexican restaurant, we pull into its lot and park in a single line, backed up to a short concrete retaining wall.

Unlike many situations when a bunch of bikers step into a restaurant and the staff cringes, this time the manager meets us at the door with a smile and a welcome handshake. Red carpet treatment feels good, for a change.

The staff pulls three big tables together, and we sit in a long oval. A round of drinks is ordered, mostly nonalcoholic, including one margarita for Nick and a mineral water for me.

"What?" Nick says after the waitress leaves, "Are you all AA now?"

No one looks sheepish or unsure. No one is embarrassed when I say, "I got to be. My life is a mess if I drink."

"Come on, Twig, you, I understand. The rest of these assholes, it don't make sense."

Bucky takes a long gulp from his water and sets it down. "I can't drink and drive. It don't work for me."

Stewart adds, "I never did drink."

After we order and our waitress has gone, Stewart pulls in close. "What do you think about the sign?"

"Jesus Fucking H. Christ, Stewart," I say. "Will you let it go for a moment? We got other fish to fry. Tonight I'm ready to cruise, and I won't be spinning off on no Biker Bob wild goose chase."

"Yeah, that's fine," he says. "I was just wondering out loud. I mean what--"

Five wadded up napkins arc through the air and cut off his sentence. Buck laughs. "Stop with the speculation Stew. Tonight we have fun lookin' cool on the strip."

Our drinks arrive, along with chips and salsa, and I start the evening with a toast. I raise my water high, and extra loud, say, "To a killer weekend in Hawg heaven."

I get a shit load of agreement and glasses clink. We dig into the chips.

An hour later, we're cruising with a thousand other bikes of all sizes and shapes. The thump of Harley engines fills every extra decibel, overpowering even the roar of jets overhead.

Reno is alive with black leather, heavy boots, wild women wearing spike heels and more chrome than I've ever seen.

Those who are not riding, walk or sit on lawn chairs along the sidewalk. Some reel with drunkenness, while the overly sweet smell of pot permeates the air. Of course there are T-shirt hawkers, key-chain sellers and emblem scalpers.

The cruise is slow, with lots of stops, which don't help our overheated air-cooled engines.

Halfway down the long street, in front of the bright lights of a casino, I notice a hollow-jawed "Soldier for Jesus". How can I not notice? He stands wrapped in a dirty white cloth and labors under a ten-foot wooden cross, rough cut from heavy beams. A circle of barbed wire is wrapped around his blood-spattered skull. Bent low from the weight, he makes his way along the sidewalk yelling unintelligible sentences, I assume scripture warnings of death for sinners. He looks the type. With so many sideshows going on, no one pays the ghost of a man much attention.

Ahead of us, a long line of Harleys sits at a full stop waiting for a distant light to change to green. Sidewalks are packed. I sit in comfort on Stewart's fat boy back seat and notice a stunning brunette in skin-tight cutoffs. I tap him on the shoulder and point. She prances out into the middle of the street and pulls off her already skimpy halter-top. When she drops it over Bucky's head, who sits on the bike in front of us, her ample breasts bob around like overly-ripe papayas. Every man within view of the scene stares with open-mouthed wonder.

As Bucky struggles to pull her top off his head, she climbs on the back of his bike. A cheer bounces off the concrete casino walls. Applause fills the air, equaling the sound of a thousand Harley engines.

In the next second, she reaches around Bucky's waist and pulls herself in close to his back. I wish I were driving Bucky's bike. We're all men. We all wish.

Far ahead, the stoplight changes to green.

Before traffic resumes, the cross-bearing scarecrow steps in front of Stewart's bike. Up close, his face is a frightening mass of pimples and blackheads. His lips are chapped beyond repair. His bare feet are split and bleeding. He looks like he's dragged his ten-foot tall cross over the Utah salt flats, one step at a time.

The blood, dry on his forehead, has dripped from each stab of barbed wire wrapped twice around his head. The guy's a walking martyr.

With hollow-eyed sockets, he stares at us with solid black eyes; his pupils are dilated beyond any normal human.

He shifts the weight of his cross, looks at me, and says, "Have another look at the sign, Twig. Do it now, before it's too late."

"What the fuck?" I scream, much louder than necessary.

Bucky, with his topless woman on the back, is already far down the street before our screwball-for-Christ turns away and drags his cross back to the sidewalk. Stewart guns his engine and pulls away.

When he catches up with Bucky, he turns to me. "What did that guy say?"

"Something about a sign." I feign ignorance, because I don't want to stop cruising. I know what he said.

We come to another stoplight and, behind Bucky again, I see he's picked up a wildcat who's almost having her way with him right on the street. Stewart turns his head around to me again. "Twig, what did he say?"

"Will you stop with the hocus-pocus crap?"

"Twig."

I roll my eyes, then say in a monotone voice, "he wanted me to have another look at the sign, and he called me by name, like he knew me. Something about doing it now."

Stewart pulls out of formation, jumps a curb and guns his engine along the center divider to the front of our line. He motions Nick to follow, drops off the divider on Fourth Street and turns left, away from the throng of riders and onlookers. When we leave the crowds, he drives two blocks into a fast-food parking lot, circles around a light pole and kills his engine.

"Jesus, Stewart, must you make a federal case out of it? He was just some lunatic."

One at a time, the other bikes pull up and kill their engines. Stewart steps off and stretches. He looks at me. "You mean to tell me a total stranger steps up to you and calls you by name. He tells you to do something, and you blow it off like nothing happened?"

"Why not?"

He shakes his head. "Holy shit, Twig, we aren't here just for fun, you know." He looks at Bucky, who barely holds his own with the brunette. Stewart turns back to me. "Well, most of us."

"We came because Bob told each of us to come. You think he made that suggestion for us to cavort around like a bunch of assholes?"

Nick pats Stew on the back. "Hey, Stewart, you really got a handle on the cussing thing."

Tazz laughs and points across the dark lot at Buck. "He's occupied, though I'm not sure if he's trying to undo her pants or extricate himself from her grip."

"What's up?" Bill asks, and we all jump when a huge explosion rocks downtown. All of us turn and look the two blocks toward Virginia Street. A large burst of fire mushrooms up between the canyon walls of the casinos.

"What the hell?" I murmur.

"Son of a bitch," Tazz says.

The explosion is loud enough that Bucky and his new playmate stop and turn toward downtown.

We're all shocked into silence.

Stewart turns to me. "Now do you see, Twig? That guy saved us. We would've been right there had we not turned. Tell me exactly what he said."

"Fuck that guy, Stewart, where's Melinda?"

"She was in a car, man. No way she'd be anywhere near the explosion. The traffic was snarled for miles."

"I got to find her."

Stew grabs my arm. "Tell me what the guy said first."

I glare at him. "He told me to have another look at the sign, and his emphasis was on the word 'now'."

"We can assume," Stewart says, "that he meant our mystery sign. I suggest we go back to the motel. I'm sure Melinda will be there."

Sirens converge on what's left of the Street Vibrations event. We start our engines and pull onto Fourth, then take a roundabout route back to our motel.

When all thirteen bikes pull into the parking lot, it's obvious the sign doesn't say welcome any longer. The letters are much smaller. From our parking place, I can't read the words. We get off of the bikes, and Tazz runs up the steps, pulling out his knife. He cuts the canvas away from its string hangers. The sign floats to our feet.

Stewart picks it up and spreads its ten feet of cloth on the pavement. After a moment, he says, "What do you make of it?"

I look at him. "I don't know."

Bucky's new girlfriend steps into our tight circle. Her halter top has returned to its original position, a good move in the somber moment. She points at the sign. "The letters are backwards. Turn it over, and let's see what's bled through."

Stewart lifts the cloth and flips it on its face. Nothing is revealed. We stare at a blank piece of frayed canvas.

Stew says, "Maybe hold it up to light?"

He picks up one end while Tazz grabs the other, and we stretch it in front of Bucky's headlight.

A strange, red-line sketch of a castle and dragon, with intertwined letters, spells out, "Sattley in the morning."

"Sattley," I say. "What is Sattley?"

Stewart looks. "Maybe it's a town. We better get a map."

Melinda and Sylvia pull into the parking lot. Melinda gets out of her car, and we run toward each other. She throws her arms around my neck as I lift her off the ground. We're laughing and hugging at the same time. "Twig, you okay? Oh God, I was frantic. Something exploded downtown. We thought you were there."

"We were, but Bob got us out in time."

"Bob?"

She stretches her arms around my waist and hugs me. Her head is sideways on my chest and she says, "We were paying our bill at the restaurant when it happened. The windows almost shattered."

Stewart points at the sign. "Look what we found."

The two women examine the canvas. Sylvia asks, "What is Sattley?"

I saunter over to Melinda's car and open the shotgun door. "We think it might be a town." I bend down and open her glove box. A map of California sits under gas receipts, reading glasses, and a handful of old registration forms. I pull the map out, open it and walk back to the crowd. In the light of Bucky's bike, with Stewart holding two edges, Melinda studies the legend. She says, "There is a town called Sattley, and it's close." Her fingers trace the lines until they converge. "Sattley must be small, because I don't see it. No, wait, here it is." She traces her finger across the map. "Forty miles north of Truckee."

Tazz says, "Where's Truckee?"

"Thirty miles west of here."

Bucky jumps in with an attitude. "So, we goin' off on another of Bob's wild goose chases, this time seventy miles farther north? Remember, we got to turn around and ride seventy back when we're ready to go home."

Melinda gives him one of her disgusted glares. "Heaven's sakes, Buck, why are you so negative about Bob? He's done only good for us."

As usual, Melinda's nailed him. He stands in the glare of the light, gives her a dangerous sharp-eyed stare, and opens his mouth to say something. After a second or two, he closes it. When he opens his mouth again, he says, "You all follow Bob around like a bunch of lost children. I'm not going." He grabs the hand of his new girlfriend and pulls her two steps before she stops him. She turns to us with a frightened look. "I had a dream last night, which is why I was waiting on the corner." She looks at Bucky. "The dream told me to follow a guy with a cross and do what he said. Just before you guys pulled up, the guy turned to me and told me to get on the back of your bike." She turns to Melinda in an apologetic tone. "I've never done this kind of thing before."

Bucky tugs at her with impatience. "Shit happens, but I'm tired of hearing about Bob. Let's go upstairs."

She gives Melinda one last look, smiles, looks back at Bucky, and follows him up the cement steps. At the top, he turns left and leads her along the deck. After they disappear into the room, Melinda says, "A little testy, aren't we?"

"I don't know about anyone else," I say, "but Bob's got us this far. What the fuck, I'm not stoppin' now."

Tazz pulls at the map, folds it, and hands it to Melinda. "Sattley, here we come."

"Morning," Melinda says. "The sign says in the morning."

"Shitfire." Nick says. "No point in freezing our butts riding tonight, anyhow."

Stewy rolls the sign into a tight bundle. "I don't know about anyone else, but I'm beat." He looks at his watch. "It's only nine thirty, but I don't think I could make another ten minutes without being horizontal. I'm off to bed. See you jackoffs tomorrow."

Tazz reaches over and pulls Buck's keys from his ignition. The killed headlight drops the parking lot back into its normal semidarkness of streetlights and traffic.

I slip my first two fingers into Melinda's hand, and she looks at me. "You still like me?" I mouth the words; our little ritual of confirmation. With a glisten in her eyes, she nods and squeezes.

As the group dissipates, we walk upstairs to our room at the end of the landing.

I unlock our door, flip a light switch, enter the room and flop backwards on the king-sized bed. It's still a few inches short for my length. All beds are too short.

She goes into the bathroom and speaks through the half-open door. "I didn't get a chance to tell you what happened back at Mono Lake."

"I wondered what you came up with."

She flushes the toilet, leans against the sink to look in the mirror, then digs through her overnight bag. "Once I was on the ground kicking the sleeping bags, an old memory came to me."

I'm always in awe when watching a woman apply her layers of special soaps and oils, just to get ready for bed.

She scrubs her face and rinses in tap water. "I didn't remember until I was on my back."

She towels her face and grabs a tube of pale yellow salve, squirts a dab into her palm, rubs her two hands together, and scrubs it into her face. "When I was a baby, Dad and Mom used to get into horrendous fights."

Another layer of a white salve from a jar gets dabbed onto the outer edges of her eyes and around her mouth. Once she's applied the goo, she continues. "Their fights always ended after someone got hit, and if I remember, it was Dad who got hit more than Mom."

One more bit of pale lotion is applied to the lids of her eyes before she reaches for toothpaste. I'm familiar with her nightly ritual. I'm glad she leaves the door open, because it's an intimate part of sharing her life with me.

Before she jams the toothbrush into her mouth, she looks through the door. "After they fought and someone got hurt, they were always passionate. I don't recall much, because I was five when Dad died, but when I look back from my adult perspective, I remember that they disappeared into the bedroom and left me with a loud TV."

She scrubs and a minute later comes up for air. After she spits and rinses, she walks back into the room. "Once someone got hurt, passion was sure to follow. I must have been pretty small when I learned to equate violence with sex."

I say, "Quite a revelation."

"Yes, and it didn't stop there. After Dad died, Mom married the same kind of guy, except they did their passion even more openly. They all but screwed one another right in front of me. Sometimes they would rip off each other's clothes before Mom would finally drag him into the bedroom."

She steps back into the bathroom, unzips her Levi's and drops them to the floor. She pulls her tan blouse over her head, reaches around back and unsnaps her bra, then drops it into a growing pile. She slides her ever-surprising lace panties first down off one hip, then the other. Her underpants discarded, she turns off the bathroom light and steps into the room. She stands unaware of my growing attention on her shapely nakedness; her carrot-colored triangle; those ever-so-lovely breasts, each with its own personality, its own expression of a nipple. I want to leap on her and take her, but she's still talking.

"The thing is, everyone was held hostage by their tension for weeks before the big blowup. When the eruption turned to sex, our little existence was back to lovey-dovey sweetness for a period, until tensions built again. It was crazy making."

She looks down at me. "What do you think, Twig? Pretty big, huh?"

"It might be the key to your violence."

"I think this is just the beginning. I sense more layers, but I can't get to them yet."

She steps over to the bed and gives me a patient smile. "Does it make you more excited to have sex with your biker clothes on? Don't get me wrong; I can do it, if it turns you on, but it may be a bit scratchy."

"Oh," I say, and get off the bed. In moments, I've stripped. I move for the bathroom to take a quick shower. A day of riding is fine for hanging with my buds, but not much for intimate closeness, especially with this goddess.

Deep into the early hours of morning, I ride a machine with tall "Ape-hanger" handlebars. I'm forced to lift my arms high to reach its grips. A pre-dawn crescent moon lights the long gentle slope of a desert valley. The road, a narrow one-lane, is smooth and flat, not a typical desert highway. I float over unfamiliar terrain, feeling the rumble of my engine under me. I'm riding in biker bliss, when I'm aware of another bike beside me. I don't see it coming or hear the engine. It simply appears. Only one biker could just appear like that. I look over at the long front end, with its impossibly slender front wheel. When I shift my gaze from the bike to its rider, a big-toothed grin greets me in the pale moonlight.

I nod.

With a nod of his head, he directs me to pull into the parking lot of a small roadside grocery.

After two downshifts, a left turn and going up a flat curb, I park under a light pole that strikes a ghostly iridescence.

Bob turns off his engine and unfurls his kickstand. I follow suit. When we step off our bikes, I don't feel the typical vibrations my body usually feels after riding.

My hearing adjusts to the silence of early morning hours. A buzzing vapor lamp overhead is the only sound.

"Hey, Twig, how you doing?" Bob sits sidesaddle on his skinny seat. He crosses his arms.

"Okay, how 'bout you?"

His grin widens. "Oh, shit, you know; life's a bitch, then you die. Death's a bitch, too."

I ask, "Where you been? It's been a while since I've seen you."

He raises his arms and shrugs. "Around."

"Yeah, me too."

A bat cruises around the light, picking moths and other night insects out of the air with an aerial display of twists and dives.

"You and Melinda okay?"

"It's not easy. Last week I was about to dump her."

"Yeah, I know. Considering that she's so difficult, it would be easy to do."

I look away from the bat's aerial antics. "Why do I sense a 'but' in your sentence?"

"Because both of you need each other to get to the next stage."

"What's that mean?"

"Stick it out with her and in a few months, you'll answer your own question."

"But she's so much trouble."

"Hey, Twig, you ever look in a mirror? You aren't the easiest person to live with, either."

I give him an embarrassed smile. "You might be right, but I'm easy to live with, compared to her."

He ignores my statement. "Next time she gets angry. . ." He lays out a simple game plan. It sounds ridiculous, but Bob's never been wrong. I tuck it away in my memory, ready to pull it out when needed.

After another fifteen minutes of jabbering about bikes and the ride to Sattley, although he says nothing about what'll happen, we get back on our bikes, pull onto the smooth highway and roll toward a wispy flamingo pink dawn.

One moment I ride with Bob at my right and the next I'm alone in a black void. My eyes open to the same brilliant pink dawn, though I look out the window at Reno's sky, with a noisy freeway and the sound of Harleys, even this early in the morning. Melinda lies next to me.

I slide one of my arms over and lay my sandpaper paw on her soft back. I feel her breathing and heartbeat. Bob or no Bob, though I'm scared shitless, I want to stay with her.

***

"It wasn't easy, sleeping alone," I say to Twig the next morning when we walk into a corner restaurant for breakfast.

"What'd you expect, Tazz? It's what you get for leaving your wife home with the kids."

"You want to take two screaming kids on the back of your bike? Donna and I made a deal. I get my weekend with the boys, and she goes to a workshop in three weeks with her girlfriend. It's a pretty good deal."

"With your kids, I'd agree. You got a duo of spitfires."

As our group is seated, I ask, "Where's Bucky?"

Melinda sits next to me and says, "He and that bimbo haven't come up for air."

"Good for him. He could use it."

"Use what?"

I study the plastic-coated menu. "He needed to get laid. The guy's been living like a Buddhist monk since Cindy dumped him and what's it been, a year?"

Melinda shakes her head. "You men think sex is a cure to all world problems. All a guy needs is to get laid and everything'll be okay."

"Most of the time," I say, while I set my menu down, "it is all a guy needs to straighten things out."

She shakes her head. "Don't you see how chauvinistic you sound?"

"Chauvinistic or not, it's true."

Melinda snorts and picks up her menu.

Stewart leans forward. "If you figure a guy has the capacity of producing 20 million little sperms in a single day, sperm cells whose job it is to get out and go find an egg, think how they might affect a man who holds back and doesn't go along with the program. Add in a lot of pain from a lost relationship, some anger because of the way she left, which in Buck's case was pretty bad, and you might understand why the guy's so uptight."

Melinda says, "Your sperm theory is just an excuse."

Stewart scans his menu. "Oh, yeah? Well if it's such an excuse, then I guess those certain days of a woman's monthly cycle when she's more edgy than normal is an excuse too."

She glares at him.

He replaces the menu in the stack. "I'm not saying a woman's cycle isn't real, but if menses is a natural, valid process, why does a man's experience get discounted?"

Sylvia says, "Because a woman has a real cycle. Guys will use any excuse to get laid."

Stew takes a sip of water. "If we all live under the same tidal effects and the same moon cycles, then it stands to reason men would also be affected in similar ways by the same natural rhythms."

Melinda says, "So, men have cycles, too?"

"Yes."

Twig slips in. "They're not as apparent as a woman's, but I'm sure they exist. I don't like to admit it, but there are times of the month when I get all teary-eyed at the slightest provocation. Those same times, I'm just as easily upset and cranky."

Melinda looks at him. "At times you're one cranky son of a bitch."

Stewart puts his menu down. "If we kept a moon calendar, I bet we could track cycles, too."

"Sorry Stewy," Twig says. "It'd be too weird for me. I'd be embarrassed to bring anyone around who might see it."

"I didn't say to keep one, you macho dick, just if we did, what would it look like?"

Stewart unleashes his last sentence, as a mousy blond waitress steps up to our table. "You guys got to keep the cussing down. This is a family restaurant."

Stewart turns the color of Melinda's hair and shrinks into his seat.

"Okay, what's everyone ordering?" She turns to Stew and poses her pencil on the order pad. "Let's start with you, blue eyes."

He says in a sheepish tone. "Eggs over easy, country fries and wheat toast."

She says, "Will that be all?"

Something in him changes. He sits up, pulls himself to his full height, lifts a hand and draws a strand of longish black hair out of his eyes. In a low voice, he says, "Fuckin' A."

She shoots him a nasty glare. I'm expecting her to stab him with the pencil. Instead, she points it at me. "What do you want?"

"French toast with strawberries."

She goes around the table taking orders, turns and give's Stewart one last glare. "Just keep it down."

I lift off my seat, lean across the table, extend one hand, fingers up, toward Stewy. Our two hands smack together. "You're gettin' the cussing thing down, Stew."

When we're in our seats, Melinda jumps back onto the former subject. "I'd love to see Twig's moon chart. We could hang it up right next to mine."

"Don't hold your breath," Twig says.

After a moment of silence, Melinda, never at a loss for words, says, "What does it all have to do with twenty million sperm cells supposedly making a guy uptight from being trapped in his scrotum?"

Stew says, "I don't think the cycle thing has anything to do with it. A man has to open his floodgates and let his little guys out on a regular basis or he gets uptight. It's just how things go."

"Why does it have to be physical? Why can't you admit that intimacy is what you long for, not just getting laid?"

I say, "Intimacy is a good secondary factor, but even when I have sex with myself, I feel a lot better."

Melinda looks at me with an exasperated glare. "Oh, God, Tazz. "Stick your little wickets in anywhere and you'll be happy. Is that all it takes?"

All of us men look at one another and nod. I say, "Pretty much."

She shoots me a glare. "What about intimacy, Tazz?"

I set my coffee cup on the table. "That's good too, but only after ol' one eye has done his part."

"That's not true," Melinda says. "Once ol' one eye is done, all Twig does is snore."

Twig's face turns red. "It's because by the time you're done, I'm exhausted."

Everyone sitting around the table moans.

"Now, children," I say. "Let's be nice. We have a long day ahead of us, and I don't want any murders or maiming."

Melinda already looks like a murder might be what the doctor ordered. Maybe a long, slow dismemberment, involving a couple of jewels and not the gem kind, either.

The tension is broken when our waitress steps up with an arm full of platters. "Who has pigs in a blanket?"

She sets the plates in front of us and rushes off. When she brings a second set of dishes, she also refills our coffee.

Melinda has a first bite of pancake on her fork. She lifts it half to her mouth, then looks at me. "If getting laid is all it takes for a guy to be happy, why hang around us women at all? It's well known that we're irrational, inconsistent, moody, even bitchy at times."

Buck bounces up to our table, pulling his new flame along in his wake. He says, "Because you're all so very sexy."

When the woman catches up to him, he introduces her in a formal tone, "Everybody, this is Bridgette." He pulls out a chair in an exaggerated gentlemanly manner and seats her. When he sits next to her, he reaches over to hold her hand.

I'm astonished. He's bright and cheerful, even pleasant to be with. It's a rare occurrence during this last year.

I hold out my hand. "I'm Tazz." The woman slips her milk-white palm into mine, grips hard and we shake.

"Pleased to meet you," she says with a nervous titter.

Introductions are made around the table as our waitress drops two menus in front of them. Bridgette tells Buck what she wants and excuses herself to go to the restroom.

Melinda looks at Bucky and says, "So, Buck, you feel better?"

He looks at her with confusion.

We all focus on our food, anything to not get in the middle of her awkward question.

"I wondered, because we've been talking about. . ." Melinda goes on to explain in close detail all of the little nuances of our conversation.

Buck glares. "It's none of your business," he says, as the waitress and Bridgette steps up at the same time.

The waitress' manner is gruff. "What do you two want?"

The second she finishes with the order and steps away, Bucky says, "Are we going to Sattley after breakfast?"

"I thought you weren't going," Melinda says and before she can say another word, Bucky interrupts. "I changed my mind and Bridgette's riding with me." He looks over at Twig. "Sorry, pal."

Twig finishes his orange juice and sets the glass on the table. "Nothing to be sorry about. You look happier than I've seen you in a year."

I fork a piece of my eggs, then look at Bridgette. "Where are you from?"

She nervously takes a sip of water, then says, "Riverside, in the L.A. area."

"Hey, we all live east of there."

"I know," she says. "Buck told me last night."

Melinda wedges herself in. "I'm sure it isn't all he told you last night."

Twig scowls at her. "Look, Melinda, just because you're mad at me, don't take it out on everyone around you. You got something to say, let's go outside and get it out."

"I got nothing to say to you, asshole."

He spreads both hands in a gesture of surrender and says, "When you're ready to work it through, I'm here, but don't let it spill out on the rest of them."

"I do what I please."

"Melinda," I say, though I know I'm opening myself to trouble for getting in the middle of their conflict.

She spins her head. "What do you want, Tazz?"

I know I'm overreacting, but I must get her attention. "Work it out or put a lid on it."

She springs to her feet fast enough for her chair to fall back. At the top of her voice, she screams, "Well, fuck you too, Tazz."

She turns, gives Twig a scowl and leaves the restaurant.

Twig is on his feet and ready to chase her down, when I put my hand on his arm.

"Let her cool off, Twig. She needs time. If you go out there now, you're sure to get into a battle."

He moves to go. I grab his leather vest and pull him back to his seat. "Come on, man, finish your breakfast. We've got a long day ahead of us and you need to eat."

He succumbs to my insistence and sits. He speaks into the awkward silence that permeates the group. "What did I do? How can I possibly fix it?"

***

I don't know why I'm pissed. I let Twig have it with both barrels when I made my snide comment about him falling asleep. I guess I'm not used to him coming back so quickly. Sex is a sore spot in our relationship, and he went right to the core in front of everyone. I despise him for that, and I hate him for being a man and saying it. Yes, I like to take my time with sex, but I have yet to meet a man who shares my feelings.

I stomp out of the restaurant and up a noisy street without knowing which way I'm going. Three blocks from our argument, I slow down and look around. I'm in front of the cordoned off area of last night's explosion. Maybe because I look determined enough to cross any line set up by a man, even a police line, a city cop moves over to me. "You can't pass through, Miss."

I look around at smoke-charred buildings. "I heard the explosion last night. What happened?"

His determined cop look softens, and he points in the direction of the casinos. "Propane sprung a leak inside a parked RV and exploded."

"Did anyone get hurt?"

"A bunch of people got burned, one pretty bad, but everyone will survive."

"Guess I was lucky not to be here."

"Me, too," he says. "Walk back to the corner and up two blocks to get through. We've got this area closed off."

"It's okay, I'll go back. Will the 'Street Vibrations' be canceled?"

He points behind me. "We moved it over three blocks. It'll be up and running tonight."

My talk with the cop calms me. The realization that all of us might have been in a hospital or worse sobers me.

I thank the cop, turn and walk back toward the restaurant. It's easy to enjoy the morning sun and cool desert air without Twig to think about. As a steady stream of bikers roar past, I even wave back at revved engines and wolf whistles.

At the restaurant, I hesitate to go in and face the aftermath of my outburst. I'm determined to be nice and not bite Twig's head off. I open the door and walk to my seat in a friendly posture. When I sit down and eat my cold breakfast, the table is quiet.

With a bite of toast chewed and swallowed, I look at Twig. "When I'm finished, we got to talk."

"Whenever you're ready," he says in his familiar sickly way. He's trying his hardest to be agreeable, which irritates me. I'm ready to jump across the table and grab him by the collar. I restrain myself and eat.

When I take the last bite of eggs and finish my cold coffee, Tazz says, "How about we go back and pack, then head out to find this town of Sattley?"

Everyone at the table awkwardly gets up and steps over to the cashier. Twig remains.

I turn to him. "What, you're not going with them?"

He looks nervous. "I'm with you, Melinda. Through thick and thin, I'm with you."

He couldn't have found better words to redeem himself, but he won't get off the hook so easily. I ask, "How come you had to say that in front of everyone?" I want to be demanding and strong. I don't mean to sound plaintive, but my words come out whiny.

His protective posture relaxes. "I thought we were sparring, like we normally do. I answered to your last jab. You have to admit, I did pretty well."

"It hurt my feelings."

"That's obvious."

I want to slide my hand around two of his big fingers, like I usually do, but I don't. "Let's not beat a dead horse here," I say. "I'm ready to drop the whole subject, if you can grant me one request."

His bushy eyebrows rise, but he says nothing.

"It's an casy one."

He asks, "Yes?"

"Apologize for hurting my feelings, and let's go on like it never happened."

His demeanor changes. I see a twitch in his eye, one that tells me more is on the way. It's not over after all.

In a second, his twitch disappears, and his face relaxes. "Because you were first to throw insults, it's only fair that you apologize first. I'll follow."

My blood pressure rises. My breakfast almost comes up. All of my muscles tighten, like I'm ready to tear his eyes out. My fists clench, and it takes every ounce of effort not to vault over the table and smash his nose. I see him prepare to protect himself. I see dread in his eyes, and it's the only thing that stops me. I settle down, which takes ten seconds and whisper a monotone sentence, "Not on your life, asshole."

He leans back, still guarded, but says nothing.

Tazz steps over to our table. "You two want to come with us, or are you just going to glare at one another all day?"

I look at Tazz, then at Twig. “You’re not riding in my car.”

“Fine,” Twig says. “It’s your car.”

I get up and head for the front door. Once out of the restaurant, I walk ahead of the crowd.

Sylvia catches up. “You okay, Melinda?”

“No.”

“If you want, I’ll ride with you, and we can talk about it.”

I look over at her concerned face. “Yeah, okay, if you want, but it won’t be fun.”

“It isn’t always fun being friends, but you’ve been around when I had trouble. It’s what friends are all about, isn’t it?”

We step across the street to the parking lot, when I notice another bike added to our row of machines. It has a long front end, with a huge slender front wheel. I think I recognize the bike, but can’t place its owner until I’m upon him. He sits comfortably, hands behind his head, resting against his three-foot-tall chrome sissy bar. His body is molded to the seat. His feet are kicked up and crossed, resting on the crux of his ludicrous “ape-hanger” handlebars.

I feel a cold shiver as I step toward him. His image fades. When I blink, it’s in clear focus again.

I take another step forward, lifting one hand to shade my eyes from the morning sun. “What are you doing here?”

“Wouldn’t miss the fun.” He flashes his pearly whites, flips his long legs off the handlebars, makes a short spin as his feet drop to the pavement. His body lifts to a sitting position.

I say, “You’re not supposed to be here. This isn’t a dream.”

I glance back, and not one person has taken a step closer.

He swings one hand in front of his face and blinks repeatedly. “As you can see, I’m not exactly all here.”

As if to prove his point, he fades again, then comes back into clear focus.

I step back. “But--”

"But nothing," he says. "I wouldn't miss this ride in a million years."

"What?"

He licks his forefinger and rubs a small speck off his flame painted peanut tank. "The ride to Sattley, of course."

My voice quavers. "But, you're a spirit."

He laughs. "Spirit, schmirit, I'm here aren't I? Doesn't that count for something?"

"What're we supposed to do?"

His laughter builds to a gleeful climax, then eventually dies to a giggle. "I'm here and it was no easy feat."

He turns to the frozen crowd and hollers over the sound of the freeway. "Get your gear ready, and let's ride to Sattley." He reaches over and touches the extreme tip of one handlebar, just the rubber of his grip. The engine comes to life. Over the sound of his idling engine, he shouts to the ogling crew, "What are you waiting for? We got miles to burn, and standing around with your mouths open will only draw flies. Get your asses in gear, and let's ride."

As if his words are commands from a Marine drill sergeant, everyone rushes up the stairs to get their things. When only Bob and I are left on the asphalt together, I ask, "We're in a dream, right?"

He touches his throttle grip again, and his engine dies. In the relative silence he says, "More like I'm dreaming. I figured out how to step through the veil. Who knows how long I can maintain this image? It takes an incredible amount of energy. While I'm here, I want to ride. I've wanted to ride for far too long. Get your gear, and let's get in the wind."

I point up to my room and say, "I packed everything before we went to breakfast."

"Your makeup bag is still in the bathroom."

He's right, and I sprint upstairs.

Twig's rolling his extra clothes into a sleeping bag. He looks at me with a pasty stare. "Is it really him?"

I go into the bathroom and grab my makeup kit. "I think so."

As I walk back into the room, Twig finishes tying his bag. "Why is he here?"

"He says he wants to ride."

Twig gives the room a quick search. "Holy shit, we'll be riding with a ghost."

"Not just any ghost, it's Bob."

He hoists the bedroll and grabs his leather jacket. "It's easy to ride with Bob in my dreams. I already pinched myself and this isn't a dream." He gives me one last look, pulls down his riding sunglasses and says, "I'll ride with Stewart. You okay with that?"

I nod and give him a scowl.

Twig turns, opens the door, and the cheap building trembles as he walks along the concrete platform.

I pull a string on my net makeup bag and sling it over my left shoulder. When I leave the room, I also look around for anything we forgot, and I pick up my silver barrette from the floor. I dropped it last night as I was getting into bed. It's more proof that I'm not in a dream. I step through the front door and close it behind me.

All the riders awkwardly stand next to their bikes. No one talks to Bob, who leans against his machine, arms folded, sunglasses in place. At the bottom of the stairs, I open my car, toss my makeup bag in the back seat and walk over to Bob. "If we aren't in a dream, why do I get a sneaking suspicion something is different?"

He lifts his glasses, rests them on his forehead and looks at me. "Which is more real, the dream world or the awake world?"

I ponder his question, sure there's some kind of catch. "The awake world."

"Are you sure, because I've existed in the dream world for a long time, and your awake world seems vague."

I stamp my foot on the pavement. "Feels pretty solid to me."

"Yes, objects are solid. Everything else is slippery."

"Like what?"

"Emotion is a good example." He strikes one black boot on the asphalt. "In my dream world, emotion is solid. We know what's happening and how to deal with it. In your so-called real world, emotion is almost invisible."

"You might have a point. In your dream-world gatherings, emotion is much more accessible."

When a bike starts, I look toward the sound. Bucky's bike is always the hardest to get started on cold mornings. When we all travel together, his bike must be first, or we could sit around burning gas, waiting for him to kick the beast into life.

A number of other engines fire, then Bob touches his rubber grip. His bike rumbles and drops to an idle.

"You want to ride with me?" he says. "It'll be a ride you won't forget."

"You aren't going to disappear and leave me to slide to a stop on the pavement, are you?"

He grins. "I wouldn't do that."

I look back as Sylvia climbs into the passenger position of my car. I run over, poke my head in the window and give her a kiss on her cheek. "You drive; I'm riding with Bob."

"He's a ghost, Melinda. How do you ride with a ghost?" I give her a wild-eyed grin. "I don't know. All I know is he invited me and said nothing bad will happen. I can't pass it up."

She lifts her eyebrows. "We'll have our talk later."

All of the Harleys are running. Riders are in their seats. I climb on the back of Bob's bike and lean against his tall sissy bar. He guns his engine, shifts into first gear and pulls away from the pack. When he turns left, I feel a flutter of fear and awe in the pit of my stomach. I turn and see the other bikes following. Something is blurry about them.

Bob drives along the street, turns right, makes a quick left, then climbs an on-ramp going west on Interstate 80. The other bikes are close behind. When he cranks his throttle, I sense a surge of power unlike any other Harley I've ridden and there have been plenty. We're not rolling on broken pavement, but floating two inches above the asphalt. His engine winds up, as I look over Bob's shoulder at his speedometer. At eighty, he levels off, and we float down the ribbon of a four-lane in a dance of Harleys I have never experienced.

I look back and thirteen bikes follow. Far behind us, Sylvia brings up the rear in my car.

When I look forward, everything gets hazy, like we've pierced a fog bank. The hills are blurred, pulled in close, compressed into little mounds inches from the bike. I'm miniaturized, riding down a freeway created in a model-railroad scene. The bikes behind me are fuzzy images.

The world shifts, and I'm in the air alone without a bike, without Bob, without a body. I'm high above the model-railroad scene, floating through the canyon. I drift left, right, then weave in and out of the gorge walls, never making contact, but come close.

I'm back on Bob's bike in the real world, vibrating with bumps in the road and wind whipping under my helmet. The fog has lifted and the bright sun strikes a golden glow over a mountain peak, splashing me with warmth.

Chapter 6

Sattley Cash Store

Stew and I are second in line behind Melinda and Bob. I put my right arm over his shoulder, point and yell, "Look at that."

Stewart turns his head toward me and shouts back, "Dang, Twig, they completely disappeared that time."

The bike and its two passengers reappear and continue to roll out freeway miles like nothing happened. We pass a truck inspection station and drive over an open, high desert plateau. A line of stunted pine trees to the left heralds a forest that leads up a mountain pass and over to Lake Tahoe. In ten minutes we come to the Highway 89 turnoff. Bob bleeds off his speed, leans into the on-ramp and coasts to a halt. We follow. When we turn right, Bob's phantom bike makes another slow fade, disappears and winks back into sharp focus.

I tap Stewart on the shoulder and point ahead.

"Yeah, I see it," he yells.

Highway 89 is a biker's dream: a fast, smooth road, with long sloping turns. It rises over tree-studded peaks and drops into deep canyons, with a view of endless ancient forests and meadows to die for.

After a half-hour of riding heaven, we come to a one-street micro town. The green city limit sign reads Sierraville, elevation 4,984 feet, population 345. Twenty or thirty houses pepper both sides of the road, with five or six on the hillside behind them. We pass a schoolhouse, church, then come to the center of town and a single stop sign. When Bob turns left, I glance right at seven or ten small businesses: a restaurant, ancient hotel, fire station and small grocery, then we're out of town, crossing a lush, low-slung valley surrounded by majestic high mountain passes. The cattle look healthy, horses happy, with a sprinkling of white tail deer. A dozen clapboard and tin roofed farm houses dot the landscape along the way. It's a perfect country scene.

We make eight or ten twists in the road and in five miles, pass another faded green sign: Sattley, elevation, 4,989, population, 27. Two hundred yards later, we follow Bob to a corner and a single story building that doubles as a grocery store and post office. On an upper wall, below the high peak of its roof, a hand-painted white sign with black block letters reads, "Sattley Cash Store".

Bob's bike makes a long sweeping arc, and he parks in front of the small verandah, with his front wheel facing the road. I get off, and Stewy backs in next to Bob, then Bucky, Tazz, and the others. Eventually, a long, neat row of bikes lines the dirt and broken pavement in front of the gold-rush era, building.

When all engines are off, Stew steps over to Bob. "What are we doing here?"

Bob points at the sign above the store. "This is Sattley."

Stew says, "I gathered that, but why here?"

Bob grins and says nothing.

Stew points away from the building toward open meadows. "There isn't a thing for miles and it looks like the store is closed."

"The store is always closed," Bob says.

I point at a clucking bird pecking and scratching the hard-packed earth. "Nothing here but us chickens."

Bob turns to Stewart. "Relax, Stewy. We got shit to do here, but all in good time."

I step over to Melinda while Stew continues to question Bob. I whisper, "You okay?"

She steadies herself by putting one hand on Bob's tall sissy bar. There's an edge in her voice. "Sure, I'm okay."

"You look gray."

"I had the ride of my life, and all you can say is I look gray."

"I was worried because you and Bob kept fading."

Her hand still grips the chrome sissy bar. With a sarcastic manner, she says, "No kidding?"

I know from experience not to pursue my question when she has an edge to her voice, but curiosity gets the best of me, and I push on. "Where did you go?"

"I was on the back of Bob's bike. I went the same place you did. What do you think?"

"I mean when you disappeared."

"Disappeared?" she says.

"Three or four times, you and Bob faded completely away and a minute later, you'd reappear."

"I don't know what you're talking about."

Without another word, she walks twenty feet away and plants her butt against her car next to Sylvia. I'm left with a seed of anger. I hate being dismissed.

Bob raises one hand up to his ear and says in a loud voice, "Now that the bikes are off, listen. We're in one of those rare moments of being alive. It's nature at its best. Pay attention."

I listen, then say, "I don't hear anything."

Bob twists, looks at me, and puts one index finger high in the air. "Exactly!"

"What do you mean?"

"It's silent: no cars, no sirens, no city sounds at all. Listen to the music of birds, the scratch of this chicken, and the distant sound of the breeze. Isn't it wonderful?"

I look around. "Jesus, Bob, you sound like Mary Poppins."

I get a few snickers, but everyone is silent.

For twenty minutes, we are taken on a guided nature walk led by Bob. I half expect him to do something fantastic, but no magic tricks, no lectures, no men's talk, nothing. We wander a half-mile into the meadow, and it's so quiet, I still hear clucks from the chicken at the store. I listen to the breeze, an occasional moo from cows, meadowlarks calling one another and the buzz of insects. We stop and look back at the curious store in the almost nonexistent little town of Sattley.

After a long, quiet stroll back to the road, across the street from the store, Bob stops. I ask, "Why are we here?"

Bob turns to me and points at the building. "You're here, Twig, to go through that door."

I look at a battered screen door with the words, "Rainbow Bread" painted diagonally on the screen. Without turning back to Bob, I say, "The store is closed."

"All the better."

I nod at Stew. "I thought he was our point man. Shouldn't he be first?"

"Not this time, pal, you're first."

I look at the door. "You want me to break into a closed store?"

He says, "Go through the door, but you won't be going into the store."

"What?"

Bob breaks into one of his famous grins. "Something else will happen. It's all I can tell you."

In a bolt of understanding, I find my hands trembling. My forehead breaks into a cold sweat. My voice flutters, "Why?"

"Because it's your turn, Twig. We'll wait here while you step through the door."

As if I have no choice in the matter, I jerk away from the crowd and walk in a machine-like manner across the street to the store. I step up onto the porch. When I put my hand out to grasp the ancient purple glass knob, I turn and look back at Bob.

He lifts one hand and sweeps at me with his fingertips. "Go ahead, Twig, get to it."

The air around me is charged, like I'll be struck by lightning any second. I look at my compadres, who only stare. We all know something out of the ordinary is about to happen, and this time it's me on the receiving end.

I turn back to the violet glass knob. I stretch out a sweaty hand. I double my fist, stretch my fingers and reach closer, inches from the knob. I wipe my hand on my shirt and touch the knob. It disappears. My buddies disappear. Bob vanishes. The Sattley store is gone. All of creation winks out of existence. I float in darkness, but the air is alive with expectation.

Out of a black void comes a familiar voice. I haven't heard this voice since a car hit him on a Los Angeles freeway.

"Dad," I yell, but hear no answer.

There's a speck of light coming at me out of the darkness and it gets larger by each second. In no time it's a grapefruit, a basketball, then the size of a compact car. With the speed of a desert storm, the light envelops me. I stand inside a bubble of existence I'd forgotten. It was so long ago, it could have been another lifetime.

***

"What happened?"

Bob glances at me, then back at the door. "Don't worry, Melinda, he'll come back a new man."

"But, he blinked out."

Bob puts his hand on my shoulder in a fatherly fashion. "He's got some shit to work out. He'll be back."

I break away from his hand, walk across the narrow street and step onto the porch to have a closer look at the doorknob. It pulsates. With each throb, it changes to a different shade of purple.

I look back at Bob. "Where'd he go?"

Bob steps onto the porch and sits on the two-person wooden bench that faces the street. "Only Twig knows where he is, but don't worry, he'll be back."

I bend low and study the knob. Something swirls inside the single inch of hexagonal glass. Images are vague, if they're images at all.

I reach for the knob. My hand is shaky. My forehead feels damp. I come within a finger length of the grip before I stop. I turn to Bob. "Where did you take him?"

Bob lets out a shrill, nervous, titter. His apprehensive giggle frightens me more than the fluctuating glass and more than the disappearance of Twig. Bob doesn't know what's going to happen, either. For the first time since I have known him, he's worried.

He stretches one arm across the back of the bench and tries to look calm. "I didn't take him anywhere, Melinda. My job was to get all of you here. The rest is up to you."

I put my hand on my hip, the same hand that almost touched the knob. "Do you mean all of us are going where Twig went?"

Bob looks at the crowd, then, with a twitch in his eye, back at me. "I don't know."

Bucky steps onto the creaking porch and leans against a whitewashed post. He crosses his arms high on his chest. "Shit, Bob, what do you know?"

"Not much in this situation. I do know this corner, and particularly that door, has certain inexplicable abilities. There are many converging points on earth that do different things. This one has something to do with memories. It's up to you to go there or not, but only go if you're ready."

Buck nods toward the door. "How did you know Twig was ready?"

He points at me. "Just like Melinda is at this moment, he was drawn to the door like a moth. He was ready."

A grimace crosses Buck's weathered face. "What're we supposed to do, just wait?"

"I think so," Bob says. "I hope Twig reappears soon. Otherwise, we need to get out of here quick."

"What the fuck are you talking about?" yells Buck. "I thought you were looking out for us. We're just going to abandon Twig in this hell hole?"

Bob looks nervous. "Things will get very strange for us if we don't, and we won't be able to get away."

"I can't leave him here."

Bob looks down at his watch, at the purple doorknob, then at me. He points at the knob. "If it starts melting, let me know."

"Melting?" I say. "What's that supposed to mean?"

"You know, like honey."

I look at the knob. Although I see cloudy activity in the interior of the glass, it has yet to change its basic six-sided shape.

"The rest of you get on your bikes and be ready, but don't start your engines yet."

A frantic shuffle follows while people climb on bikes; clanks of metal, shifting distributors, jangling keys. When everyone is ready, we wait in an anxious silence.

A meadowlark warbles in the distance.

I glare at the knob, when sure enough, its deep purple turns to lighter lavender. It shifts color again and loses shape. Before I can say a word, the glass expands and turns into one large dewdrop-shaped drip. As I watch in horror, the entire knob enlarges to the size of a basketball, loses all color and drips, like hot honey, toward the floor.

"Bob," I say with an apprehensive trill. "It's happening."

Bob turns to me, glances at the door, gets quickly to his feet and yells, "Start your engines, and let's get out of here."

As I hear the first roar of Stewart's bike, always the easiest to start, the glass transforms into thin liquid. It drops to the slat board floor and melts over to consume my feet. It glues me to the porch and climbs fast up my calf. I scream while it quickly covers both legs, my thighs, my chest and arms. When it constricts my breath, my panic skyrockets.

The last engine starts, and everyone pulls away, leaving me stuck in violet taffy, unable to move.

"Wait, you bastards!" The thickness covers my mouth and eyes, then I drop into a darkness I have never before witnessed.

I float in the void for minutes or is it hours? Wait, there's a speck of light far away. It gets larger by the second. When the brilliance surrounds me, I stand in my mother's kitchen, though she's been dead seven years, and her house was bulldozed to make way for a convenience store.

***

"Dad," I say again. "It's me, Twig."

My father stands five yards across the broken concrete floor, but doesn't hear me. The single overhead light makes strange shadows on the open stud walls in his dilapidated garage. As he leans on his tool-cluttered workbench, his focus is on a boy of eight or nine who has his back to me.

I'm shocked, when my father, whom I recall as a paragon of gentleness, swings his left hand up and backhands the kid hard across the shoulder. The little guy spins from the blow, falls, legs akimbo, on hard concrete.

I feel the pain and surprise of Dad's random act. I remember the moment and look more carefully at the boy. It's me, thirty years ago. I am the child.

"What did you do that for?" I ask, but no one hears me.

The child rolls into a ball and prepares for more. My current memory does not allow for such violent acts from Dad, but I'm forced to confront the situation. Why didn't my mother protect me?

With a violent explosion, my father rushes over, swings his leg out and kicks the boy in the thigh, spinning the little body in a complete circle. The child pulls close into a ball, moans and prepares for another blow. Had I prepared for blows many times? I don't remember. Yet, it's happening. My father strikes again, and I recall every frightening nuance of the experience. Each time Dad strikes my child body, I feel the pain as an adult.

I want to step forward, because I'm certain another kick is coming. I want to stop it, but I can't move. I scream, but my voice is not heard. All I can do is feel the fear, experience pain, then suffer the shame and humiliation I felt so many years ago.

If my father was a brutal man, why don't I remember him that way? Why do I remember him as gentle and kind?

He takes a step forward and prepares to strike another blow, then says in a tone of gentle instruction, "Get up, Son, and fight."

The boy groans, "No, Dad; I can't."

"Get up, Son or I'll do it again. A boy's got to learn how to stand up and fight, even against all odds."

The boy cries. "I can't, Dad."

"Don't be a sissy, Son. Now get up and face me."

The boy bawls and curls up tighter.

"Get up, Son," my dad says patiently, laying a hard kick into one of the boy's calves. I feel the ache from the blow.

The child scrambles to his feet, backs into a far corner and puts his hands up. "No more, Dad. Please, no more."

"A boy has got to learn to be tough. We don't want no pansies around here." My dad doubles his fists, puts them up, and moves into a fighter's stance. "Now put up your dukes, and let's get to it."

"No, Dad, please; I'm scared."

In a gentle voice, he says, "Come on, Thomas, it's time to take a few and give a few. Be a man and come out fighting."

Oh, my God, he said it. It was my father who first said my ever-present mantra, "Be a man and come out fighting." Even now, thirty years later, the words I never knew the origin of, continue to roll around in my head. It was my Dad all along. He instilled the fighter in me.

With a rush, because only a rush would end the insanity, the little boy leaps toward dear old Dad and throws a single punch at his face.

Back then, I never saw it, but I see clearly now. Dad feigns a protective posture, but leaves himself wide open and lets the punch land on his cheek. It's a wide swing, a glancing blow, the boy's fist grazing his dad's cheek and landing on his nose. Blood spews from Dad's left nostril. My old man reaches out and grabs the boy. Although it looks like he's going to rip the poor kid to shreds, I know why he grabs him. I'm certain what's about to happen next.

With his bloody nose, he pulls little Thomas up into his arms and hugs him. Both father and son cry and my father says, "I'm proud of you, Son. You showed your manliness today. You must never show weakness to anyone. A man never cries and never back down from anyone, not even me."

The boy wraps his arms around his father's neck, and they hold one another until the scene fades. I'm left with goose bumps and barely holding onto reality. I'm in a pitch-blackness I've never before experienced. Wait, there's another pinpoint of light. It gets bigger as the seconds tick by. Something else is about to happen. I double my fists and say, "It's time to be a man and come out fighting." I can't believe my dad started it all.

How old was I when I first heard it? I can't remember for sure, but maybe five or six.

***

As we slow, I pull my bike beside Bob and yell, "We can't leave them back there."

"Don't worry about it Stewy, they'll be all right."

"Melinda didn't look like she was all right when we abandoned her on the porch."

He points toward the little town with his free left hand. "We'll wait here, and when they're done, they'll find us."

We slow to twenty-five and drive into Sierraville. Our bikes weave around a short turn and take a slow rumble along Main Street.

"Shouldn't we have waited? What if they can't--"

"Look, Stew," Bob interrupts, "what could you do if we were to go back?"

Bob pulls up to the tiny general store, arcs his bike around, and backs up to a weather-beaten hitching rail. I follow suit, and twelve bikes line up beside us. When every engine is off, Bob looks over at me. He sits comfortably on his little seat, two small springs between him, the ridged frame of his bike, and bumps in the road. I never understood how anyone could be comfortable on such an unlikely machine.

"Hell, Stewart, if you're so fired up to save them, it's only five miles. Why don't you go back? We'll wait for you."

"Okay, I'll just do that." I reach over, touch the starter button of my bike and roar off toward Sattley. When I drive out of town, I get a feeling Bob's set me up once again. I ignore the thought. When I'm back at the Sattley Cash Store, I pull up, park and step onto the porch. I already know no one is here. When I touch the glass knob like Twig did a half-hour ago, the perfect scene of meadowlarks and mooing cows disappears. What appears is a bubble of existence that surrounds me and traps me in an awe-inspiring scene with my mother.

"Little Stewy," she says to my child. "From now on you'll be the man of our house."

Oh, God, I remember her words, and I remember how much weight was on me after my dad moved out. I hated those words, and yet, when I was seven I took them to heart and tried my best to live up to Mom's demand.

I remember when I stepped into my father's role and was overwhelmed by the sheer magnitude of the task. How angry I was. I was a kid, for God's sake. I also remember carrying the father/hero role until I met Renee. Her strong personality took over, and I was able to relax for the first time since I was a boy. I probably relaxed too much, because I gave the entire mess over to Renee when we got married. For seventeen years she carried the responsibility of our life. No wonder she was angry.

A snapshot of my past comes to me, encircles me, then disappears all in a single moment. I float headlong in a dark void until I see a distant light that I move toward. When I come through the tunnel of darkness and light surrounds me, I plop down on the wooden bench of the Sattley store, legs akimbo, back twisted. I sit up and look around at Twig and Melinda stretched out on the deck.

"What happened?" I ask.

She lifts herself and looks my way. "I don't know, but a huge part of my life came back to me." She looks over at Twig, who sits up and spins around to face us. With tears in her eyes, Melinda, in a series of broken sobs, says to Twig, "I'm terrified I can't have sex without violence and I'll lose another good man because of it."

Twig slides over and puts his good arm around her slender waist. "It's okay, Honey, we'll figure it out together. My violent streak is just as hard to get a handle on."

Her sobs turn to a gut-wrenching wail. I feel like I don't belong here, though I want to talk about my revelation, too. I get up, step off of the deck, and walk along the deserted road for a hundred yards until I can't hear them. I listen to the meadowlarks, a breeze in the trees, my own breath and the ever-present yammer of my thoughts, especially because now I have so much to think about. I miss Renee.

Fifteen minutes go by before Twig and Melinda get up and step off the porch. They walk over to her car, get in and drive off without acknowledging me again.

I walk to the store, get on my bike and follow them to Sierraville.

Once we are all together, Bob leads us south toward Truckee, then east, back in the direction of Reno.

Chapter 7

Awakening Again

Somewhere along the freeway west of Reno, in a weird funnel-like transference from one scene to another, I drive my car in the middle of a thunderous pack of Harleys, then open my eyes and look at the paint-chipped ceiling of our apartment in Victorville.

I close my eyes again, and I'm back in the pack of bikes.

When I open my eyes, I see the ceiling and listen to Twig breathing.

Damn, it's another Bob dream.

I turn in bed and look into the smiling face of Twig. I ask, "You were there, weren't you?"

"Yep," he says, "and it was great. Like it really happened, and we were in two worlds at once. I love being in Bob's dreams."

I ask, "Were we at the Sattley Cash Store together?"

"I got the piece about my father there."

I sit up in bed, pull a pillow behind my back and rest against it. "The dream seemed more real than any of the desert biker parties."

Twig says, "Maybe we actually--"

Our phone rings, and Twig turns to reach for it on the nightstand. "Hello?"

"Hey, Stew."

"Yes, we were there with you. Calm down and get your butt over here. We got shit to talk about."

When he hangs up, I stare at him. "Why did you invite Stewart over? I wanted to spend the morning together, alone."

"You said the dream was more real and we were all in it. We need to talk about it."

"That might be true, but--"

The phone interrupts my sentence. Twig picks it up. "Yeah?"

He waits a second and says, "It's going to take a half-hour for Stew to arrive. You better get over here too."

When he hangs up, I'm more than perturbed. "Do you check with me first or am I chopped liver?"

"Jesus, Melinda, we got some stuff to work out, and I need my people around me to sort out the details. This is important shit, and I don't want to miss a bit of it."

"Don't I get a vote?"

Twig sits up, spins around on the bed with his back to me, reaches down for his pants and pulls them on. "Vote for what?"

"Why, you asshole! You don't have a clue, do you?"

"Look, Melinda, I don't have time to get into an argument right now. We got people coming."

"You son of a bitch! What do you think you're doing?"

He stands and opens his arms, palms up. "What?"

"What?" I say. "You self-centered jackass. You no-account-lowlife worm." I say more, but my words don't come out coherent, only a familiar string of verbal abuse to match his insult. Somewhere in the middle of my barrage, I pick up a pillow. I throw it at him, then see myself in my dream at the Sattley Cash Store. I'm a little girl faced with my father's violence and scared to death. I wanted to protect Mom and Dad from each other. I see all of it, but nothing will stop what's about to happen. It's coming. I can sense hate sizzling from my guts, the unbridled energy ready for action, ready to kill.

The pillow arcs across the room. I could stop, but some bigger part of me wants to have this tantrum. I need to know I'm still alive.

The pillow hits Twig in his chest and falls on the floor. He looks at me puzzled. I'm perplexed, too. The part of me out to destroy takes over while the peaceful me gets pushed into the background. I leap across the bed and come at him with both fists. A left punch lands high on his thick chest while my right clips his chin. I have the element of surprise. Momentum pushes him back until he contacts the wall. The building shakes like last month's earthquake. I keep pushing. I try to get purchase on the polished wood floor. I'm all over him before he has a chance to protect himself.

A flash of red and white stars goes off in my head. The fucker hit me. I was pissed a second before, but now I'm ready for blood. I shake off my dizziness. My nails are out, claws of destruction. I'll rip his eyes out. I'm two inches away from my goal when another whack against my head rings my ears. I'm thrown aside like a rag doll. I roll on the floor and land on my feet. I'm ready for more.

He bellows some childish obscenity and comes at me. He's in a rage. I'm familiar with that voice. His fist is doubled, with white knuckles. He pulls back his right arm for a full swing.

At the last second before his arm flashes down on my head, before my lights are turned out, maybe forever, I drop to my knees and grab the only defense within arm's reach. I yank a pillow up to my face and scream. The blow never lands.

I hear a thump and another male voice, "Twig, stop it. Stop it right now."

Twig returns a volley of cuss words, while I look out from behind my pillow and see the skinny butt of Tazz as he pushes Twig back toward the bed.

"Stop it, Twig!" he yells. "Quit it this second."

When Twig calms and sits, I leap to my feet, bounce five steps to them and clobber his bandaged shoulder.

He bellows in pain.

Tazz's long arms wrap around me and pull me in close, not to hug me, but to restrain me.

"Let me go," I scream and struggle.

His vice hold is unrelenting. My arms are locked in his grip. I try to stamp, but once he lifts me off the ground, my feet find only air.

"Quit it, Melinda."

"I quit nothing a fucking man tells me to quit, you bastard." I continue with another long string of cuss-infested insults for what seems like forever, until, with deep inhalations, I run out of steam. When I calm and relax in his grip, he loosens up, which allows me to take my first full breath in a minute. When I come back to consciousness, back to the side of myself that is rational, I see what I've done. I feel frightened and desperate. A familiar sensation springs up from my stomach and turns me from a raging Medusa to a sex-starved maniac. I want copious amounts of sex, wild, unbridled sex, more sex than three men could satisfy. I want it now, and I won't take no for an answer.

In a normal voice, I say to Tazz, "You can put me down now. I'm okay."

"No more hitting?"

"I promise."

He releases me, and all I feel is desire. I want Twig now, and I must get rid of Tazz.

I turn to Tazz. "Unless you want to witness us having sex, I suggest you leave for an hour, because I'm going to tear the big guy from limb to limb."

I can feel extra saliva in my mouth, a growing tingle between my legs, the wantonness of my libido.

"Get out, Tazz, right now, because I don't think I can wait one more second."

Twig has a happy gleam in his eye. He wants me, too. This'll be a good one, maybe a great one.

I turn and see that Tazz still stands with a puzzled look. "Get the fuck out, Tazz," I scream.

When I turn back to ravage Twig and take him with the same fury with which I fought him, I see something else in his eyes. Twig says, "Don't go, Tazz. I want you to stay."

Okay, I think. What the hell does he want? He wants me to take on both of them? Weird, but I'm ready.

I look at Tazz, then at Twig. Something strange is in Twig's eyes. I don't recognize his look, or is it that I don't want to recognize it? Oh God, is it resolve?

Tazz turns and heads for the door. "If you two have some stuff to work out, I'll wait in the garage."

"No, Tazz," Twig says. "Please stay."

"I don't think so, buddy. I've helped you through a lot, but with this, I don't think you need any help."

Twig says. "I need help in not having sex with her."

"What?" I scream.

"We have to break this cycle of violence and sex addiction. I won't have sex right now because of your aggravated state. The wild creature you've turned into frightens me."

"What the fuck are you talking about?"

"You already know."

"No," I scream. "Not this time. Not now, when it'll be the best I've ever had. I can feel it. It'll be fantastic."

Twig pushes wild tufts of hair away from his eyes. "I already know it'll be great, that's why I'm not doing it."

First, I try to talk him into it, then plead. I kiss him and pull at him, but he stands firm. He pushes my advances away like I'm a leper. Is there nothing I can do to get him to respond? Out of desperation, I turn to Tazz and play out some kind of strange sexual dance with someone I'm not normally attracted to.

He also rejects me, and I bolt for the front door. Twig is already in front of it, and I have no place to go.

I didn't know I had that many cuss words inside me. I go into a long bout of fury, trying to cut them into the wimps they are. I go for five minutes until something clicks deep inside and my desire turns to grief. I'm lost, like all I want to do is crawl up into a hole and die. A single tear dribbles down my face, with rivers to follow. I turn, drop on the bed face down and wail into my pillow.

***

She is a wild thing fresh out of the woods. I know this dance of hers. Sex with her will be the best it can ever be, but it will only serve to feed a wounded part of her. Although I fear I may never be able to have good sex with her again, I also know if we don't break the cycle, I'll find myself in the hospital or dead or I'll do the same to her. When she tells Tazz to leave, I ask him to stay and help. I have no idea what's going to happen. Maybe her wild sexual energy has turned her into a monster. Maybe she'll try to kill me. With that many maybes, I need Tazz's help.

Once she realizes neither of us will satisfy her desire, she comes unglued. I'm not sure Tazz and I together will be able to contain her anger. Medusa reaches her summit of rage, then crashes back into a hole of despondency I've never before witnessed.

I try to console her, but she snaps a string of obscenities and screams for me to get out.

Tazz and I leave her in the bedroom. I let the door rest ajar to keep an eye on her.

I walk into the living room and sit exhausted on the couch, toss my head back and close my eyes.

When he sits, Tazz says, "What's this?"

I open my eyes, but I'm too worn out to tilt my head forward.

"What?"

"You'd better look."

I roll my head in his direction.

He points at the coffee table.

A teal colored, low-slung bowl, slightly larger than a dinner plate, sits on the table. I lean forward and have a closer look. An inch of sand lies smoothed at the bottom of the bowl. Four corks are positioned in a perfect square around the edge in the sand. A single strand of bright, multicolored African style beads lies on the table next to the bowl. An unlit votive candle rests direct center, with a small black feather, which stands upright, stabbed into the sand.

Everything looks strange and expectant, as if something is about to happen. A stick lies across one side of the bowl.

Without picking it up, I bend in and study it closely. "What's this stuff all about?"

"Shit, man," Tazz says. He moves forward. "I ain't got a clue. It's your apartment, not mine."

The stick is a polished desert branch, a half-inch thick, with a slight curve. Its length is divided in the center by ten careful wraps of thin copper wire. The same careful ten circles wrap the other side of center in silver wire. From the junction of the two wraps, a three-inch-long, weather-bleached incisor hangs loosely from a small silver eyelet. Maybe the tooth came from a horse. One end of the stick has the raw edge of an ancient break, while the opposite end has a perfectly formed point made of a halved acorn shell.

"Come on, Tazz, where'd you get it?"

"I'm tellin' you, it ain't mine."

A knock comes at the door. I get up and walk five paces, open it and Stewart steps in. He gives me the biker finger-slap greeting and says, "Hey, Twig, was that dream something or what?" He walks over to Tazz. "You were there, too?"

Tazz slaps fingers with Stew and says, "I was. What do you think it means?"

I step back to my chair and drop, while Stew sits on the couch next to Tazz. He points at the bowl and its decorations, "What's this?"

"I don't know," I say. "It isn't mine."

He lifts the bowl and pulls a small piece of paper out from under it, opens the paper and reads aloud, "This bowl and its contents are to be present at gatherings or used during conflict. Protect it with your life."

Stew looks at me and hands the paper across.

I take the note and study it. "Who would leave such a thing?"

Stewy stares with a wry smile. "We already know who, my question is why?"

"Bob?" Tazz asks.

"Looks like Bob's chicken scratch to me."

I fold the note and hand it over to Tazz. As he studies it, I say, "Are we in another dream? This is too weird to be real. How can he leave these on my coffee table, and us not be in another dream?"

"We could be dreaming," Stewart says, "but I've been in one of Bob's double dreams, and this doesn't feel like one to me."

Tazz glances at the note, bends and carefully studies the bowl, then looks up at Stew. "What do you mean?"

"Things are too real."

"Too real?"

Stewart points at Tazz's feet. "Look at the soda can lying on its side on the floor."

I look next to the coffee table at the can. A dribble of half-dried liquid lies on the worn hardwood floor. I reach down, grab the can and wipe up the dribble with my thumb. "Yeah, a Coke can, so what?"

"In Bob's double dream, everything is perfect. You would never find a spilled can in the first place. I'll bet you remember drinking it."

"Yeah, sure."

Stewy leans back. "In Bob's dream world, there's never a memory of spilled drinks. There's only what's happening at the moment, as if everything was created seconds before you arrived."

I stand, walk to the kitchen and toss the can in the garbage, then rinse my thumb. "If it's true, how could Bob leave the bowl and these other things?"

Stewart shrugs. "Bob's a mystery, for sure."

I reach over and pick up the stick, inspect it and say, "It certainly is exotic."

When I get no comment, I go on. "What do you think Bob meant in the note?"

I study the wrapped wire. No one says a word. I look up to strained expressions on both Stewart's and Tazz's faces. "What's up?" I say and get no response.

Both men labor to speak. Their lips move, but they say nothing.

Stewart looks red in his face, like he isn't able to breathe. I watch with concern, while his face grows redder.

"You okay, Stew?"

He shakes his head in a panic and points at his face.

"What's wrong?"

Frantically he points at his mouth. I saw a man choke one time in a restaurant, and Stew has the same uncomprehending look.

"Are you choking?" I set the stick down and get up to give him the Heimlich maneuver.

Stew's words burst out in one long puke of run-on sentences. When he winds down, he says, "Man, what did you do?" His face shifts from beet-red to his biker tan.

"What the fuck happened?" Tazz says at the same time.

I look to see he's also returned to normal.

I'm confused. "What do you mean? I didn't do a thing."

Stewart says, "I couldn't talk."

"Me, neither," Tazz says.

"You couldn't talk? What the fuck does that mean?"

"I don't know," Stew says, "For a minute, I wasn't able to say a word, like my voice stopped working."

I look over as Tazz says, "Yeah, man, me too. What was that all about?"

Relieved to hear them speak again, I sit in my armchair while they talk in excited, one-sentence clips.

In the stir, the stick falls off the bowl. I set it back on the rim. The second I touch it, all excited chatter stops. I look up and drop the stick. When I release it, both men look at me and blurt out a string of sentences like they'd been forced to hold back their words.

"What?" I ask.

Stewart points. "You did it with the stick."

"What do you mean? I didn't do anything."

"When you picked up the stick, I couldn't speak."

I look at him, then at Tazz, whose head bobs in agreement. "The stick has something to do with it." Stew picks up the branch, and my voice is sealed, like I'm inside a soundproof room. My throat works to form the words, my mouth and lips do their normal talking movements, but I can't make a sound.

When he replaces the stick, all the words I wanted to say come forth at once.

"What happened?"

"See what I mean? This stick is weird."

Stewart gets an impish look on his face. "Man, what I could do with Renee around."

"What do you mean?" Tazz asks.

"Renee and I have been doing a lot of relationship stuff and things are better." His eyebrows rise and a smile crosses his lips. "Imagine, with this stick I could actually finish speaking before she interrupts."

I look toward the bedroom, then back at Stewart. In a whisper so Melinda can't hear, I say, "I got the same problem. When she gets excited, especially while we're discussing things, I can't get a word in edgewise. This stick could be a boon to all men."

Tazz grins.

I say, "I can't wait for Melinda to come out so I can try it on her. I mean, hell, it would be my luck if it only worked on guys."

Tazz reaches over to grab the feather that stands upright in the sand.

Stewart puts up his right hand. "I wouldn't do it yet, Tazz."

"What do you mean?"

"What are these other things for? It's obvious they're here for some reason. Maybe we want to be a little cautious. If this stick can shut down our voices, maybe that feather or those corks can make our dicks go limp."

Tazz looks at the feather, then at me. "Fuck, man, we got to know what they do sometime. I vote we get it over with." He reaches his scarecrow fingers out and grabs the feather gingerly by its quill. He picks it up and my throat constricts.

He jumps to his feet, stretches his arms sideways, pulls in a deep breath and launches into a long string of insane shouts and cusses at the extreme limit of his capacity to scream. His body vibrates. His face contorts, and he's focused on Stew. He gets angry enough that I'm afraid he'll throw something or punch Stewy. I'm ready to intervene before he turns Stew into hamburger. When he draws his right fist back, I spring to my feet. Although he doesn't move forward, he swings his arm and throws the feather at Stewart's face. The feather leaves his hand, shifts in the air, drops to one side and floats into Stew's lap.

I look at Tazz, whose narrow face returns from a hot lobster pink to its normal color. He steps back a pace and sits hard on the chair. His body relaxes.

"What happened?" I'm finally able to ask.

"Somebody get this feather off of me," Stewart mewls. "I don't want anything to do with it."

Tazz holds his head back, like he has a bloody nose. "Get some tweezers. Trust me, you don't want to pick it up."

I rise and walk into the kitchen. In the junk drawer, I find a pair of short tongs and toss them to Stew. "What happened?"

"I don't know," Tazz says, head still back in a blank stare at the ceiling. "The second I picked it up, I had an uncontrollable urge to scream at both of you and especially you, Stew. Actually, I wanted to kill both of you, but my body wouldn't respond. All I could do was scream. I was barely able to throw the feather away."

With the tongs, Stewart picks the feather up. Once it is back in an upright position in the sand, I breathe a sigh of relief.

"Man, that was too much," Stew says. "I don't know about you, but I'm not ready to experiment with anything else. I've had enough for one day."

Melinda opens the bedroom door and goes into the kitchen. She's dressed, hair brushed, she's even applied makeup. She opens the coffeemaker and pours in water. She puts coffee into the well, flips its switch and steps back into the living room. Her face looks puffy.

She asks in a calm, sleepy tone, "What're you guys up to in here? You're making enough noise for sixteen men."

"Bob left something for us." I point at the bowl and its articles of devastation.

She takes a step closer, studies the bowl and reaches for the beads.

"I wouldn't touch anything just yet," I say.

She looks at me with a defiant grimace and picks up the beads, studies them, then discards them in a haphazard manner, like they're children's plastic pop beads.

I look at Tazz, at Stewart, then back up at my puffy-faced woman. "Nothing happened?"

She flashes a glare at me, as if to say, "You got shit to pay when these guys are gone." She says with syrupy sarcasm, "Was something supposed to happen?"

Tazz reaches out and picks up the beads. "We don't know. Something happened with the stick and feather. We assumed--"

"Obviously you assumed wrong." She gives him a glare as the room drops into an abyss of feminine disgust. Although she hasn't picked up the stick, we men say nothing, and not because we can't. If we do, the price will be much greater than any of us wants to pay.

Tazz looks at me, then across at Stewart. "I gotta' go, Twig. I got things to do on the other side of town."

Stew chimes in. "Yeah, me too. Renee expects me to call."

Both men get up and start for the door. The air is thick enough to smear across the walls.

"Cowards," I say under my breath. I wish I could step out into the relatively breathable air, too.

The coffeepot stops its gurgles, and Melinda steps into the kitchen to pour a cup. She doesn't offer one to me or even look in my direction. She sits in the chair chicken-shit Tazz sat in. She takes a sip of brew, looks at the bowl, then at me.

The room is silent.

Her smile drives me crazy. I throw up my hands. "What?"

She takes another sip and says nothing.

I hate her "I'm-better-than-you" silent treatment. It will end soon enough, I just don't know when. The suspense drives me insane.

"Look, Melinda," I say. "It wasn't right to have sex in your excited state. I just can't--"

"You can't what, you bastard? You can't get it up any longer? You can't be bothered? You can't find time for me?" She continues with her line of thought and never runs out of words. I'm intimidated with her quick mind. I could never pretend to keep up with her. I sit wringing my hands while she sprints from one "can't" to another.

As she reaches what I hope is a peek, her voice, high in tone and louder, moves from subject to subject even faster. My temper rises ever closer to the breaking point. The last thing I want to do is burst all over her again. I feel it. I sit in silence while she pummels me with her "can't" list. In a desperate move to protect her and myself, I grab the stick. When I lift it off its perch, the sound of female intensity stops. The room is silent. She reaches up for her throat, mouths another string of words, but makes no sound.

"This is one of the tools Bob left," I say. "It's my turn to talk. When I'm done, you can have this stick, then it'll be your turn."

Although she continues to mouth a constant string of words, her silence is golden. I revel in the non-blaming, non-razor-sharp tongue and zero-shame, silence.

"I can't have sex with you anymore after we fight. Although I'll miss it, I don't think it's safe. Maybe it was never safe, but things are out of control now. I mean, look at us. I've got a fractured collarbone and countless bruises. You have cuts and a black eye."

She stops mouthing words. It looks like she's listening.

"This chaos won't work for either of us." I hold the stick between my hands.

I'm afraid to set the stick down. Abuse will fly when the gate opens. Hours of lectures are what I have to look forward to once she picks up the stick. But, I've said what I had to say, and I set the stick back onto its cradle. With a snap of sound, she blathers out a series of unintelligible sentences before the overflow runs down and she sits quietly, looking at me with a defiant glare. She reaches for the stick and when it's in her hand, my larynx constricts and I prepare for her diatribe.

"Something happened in the bedroom when you refused me." To my surprise, her voice is calm. It's her Melinda voice, instead of the harpy I expected.

"At first I was enraged, but when you left the room, I imagined my stepfather and mother when they used to fight. It was the same thing I saw in the Sattley Cash Store. They were having sex after another huge battle. I saw myself in the next room with an open door, because neither was coherent enough to remember I was there."

I shift on the couch and want to say something. My mouth works, but nothing comes out. I relax to let her continue. What choice do I have?

"I remember too many massive battles ending in bed or in the washroom or kitchen. Anywhere their fight ended was where sex took place.

"By the time I became a teenager, it happened so frequently, I thought it was how everyone had sex.

"My first boyfriend was astonished one day after an argument when I leapt upon him. That first experience set a precedent for the brand of sex I needed to feel excited. Hell, to feel alive."

She shifts position and drops back in her chair, rests her head against its soft back and stretches her hands out on the thick padded arms. "Having this experience twice in a twenty-four-hour period has sent the message home, but what do I do? I don't know any other way to have good sex."

After a thirty-second pause, she sets the stick back into its cradle.

Without picking up the stick, I say, "We have an opportunity to make some changes together."

"Yes, but what?"

"Some time ago, Bob showed me how to release my anger without hurting anyone."

"Oh really? Why haven't you used Bob's method with me?"

"Back then I was angry all the time, but I wasn't aware of my anger. I used the bat method every day for years, until my backlog of anger got vented. Once I was clear of it, I seldom needed the bat and tire."

"I'll ask again," she says. "Why don't you use it with me?"

I shift, cross one leg over another and put my right arm out across the couch. "Our anger is always such a surprise. I can never tell when it's going to show up. It looks like things are fine one second and the very next, I strike out at you or you at me. My old anger was the result of slow buildups, sometimes days, sometime hours, never seconds."

She leans forward and rests her forearms on her knees. "I never know when it's coming either. It happens and the next thing I know, we're cleaning up a mess."

She looks at me with an odd expression. "What can we do?"

"When Tazz picked up the feather, he went into a rage like I've never seen. Usually he's such a non-expressive guy. The feather turned him into a monster. One thing he said after releasing the feather was he wanted to kill Stewart, but his body wouldn't respond."

"You want me to use that little feather?"

"I want both of us to use it and see what happens."

"One at a time?"

"Until we get a second feather, it'll have to be one at a time."

"You go first," she says.

"No, I don't trust it yet. You go first, and if anything happens, I can stop you. If I go first, you won't be able to stop me."

"That's bullshit, Twig. You already know from Tazz's experience that you can't do anything physical. Why should I be your guinea pig?"

"Does the feather work the same on everyone? What if it works on Tazz one way and different on me? I can stop you, but you--"

She interrupts, "We already know what the feather does. We know why it's here. Why do you question it?"

"I don't question--"

She stomps her foot. "I'm not first and that's the end of it."

"But Melinda--"

"Melinda nothing, you wimpy bastard. Don't think your male logic is. . ." She launches into a long dissertation.

I feel wrath climb up from my gut to my throat. I hate being interrupted, yet she does it so smoothly, I usually don't even know it's happened until I've struck her. Never the victim, Melinda does not shrivel up and cringe in a corner when I strike. She vaults at me with her claws. It's not easy being with a woman of action.

I feel anger climb past my throat. She berates me, for what reason I don't know. Her razor tongue slashes at the restraining straps that hold old rage in place. Melinda won't quit until I come undone. It's like she's riling me on purpose.

My hand doubles into a fist. My arm readies for a swing. My last few threads of restraint are gnawed through by her sarcastic voice. My legs twitch. My feet shift into position. I'm ready to clobber her, anything to stop her constant yammering.

At the last split second before I jump into action, I grab the stick. The room falls into a needed silence. My pitbull anger relaxes. I don't move. I'm not being forced into action.

My body slackens, and I sit back.

Melinda is in an animated frenzy. Her hands fly, mouth a blur, strawberry hair tousles from side to side, but she can't make a sound. I can't think of a thing to say, but I don't want her to speak. I continue to hold the stick and feel relief in being able to turn off the fire hose of feminine upheaval.

She leaps out of her seat, and I put up my arm in defense. Instead of attacking me, she grabs the feather.

My throat constricts. My voice is silenced, though I still have the stick. What happened?

With feather in hand, she springs into the air, head back, hands outstretched and lets out a long, high-pitched wail. Her screech lasts for more than fifteen seconds. When she ends her unleashed wildness, she looks at me and starts into a long string of loud, unintelligible sentences. Although I want to hear what she's saying, I can't understand a word. She's louder than I've ever heard. I return the stick to its bowl and watch.

Two minutes go by while her body tries to wriggle out of some kind of restraint. Her arms are free to swing, fists clenched, head straining, but she can only swing into open air.

I sit in awe of Medusa. Her arms move so fast, I believe she has more than one set.

Her body and voice climax, and she tosses the feather in my direction.

When it leaves her fingers, she collapses into her chair, exhausted, unable to hold up even one hand.

The plume floats to the floor.

I pick up the tongs and grab the quill, work it back into the sand and look over at her. "What happened?"

Still breathing hard, her eyes closed, she says, "Oh my God, Twig, it was like. . .I was able to be violent without hurting anyone."

"Did you get it all out?"

"What's inside me is the size of Alaska. It would take a thousand sessions with that feather to get it all out."

I study her. "You look different, much calmer."

"I feel sexy, but I'm too exhausted to do anything about it."

"I'm frightened."

She opens her eyes and looks at me. "Why?"

"Because I guess I'm next, and I'm too big to do what you just did. I'm sure I'll break those invisible restraints and destroy everything."

"Take a chance, you pansy." Before she used the feather, her statement came from the bitch I know too well. These words, though they have lots of meaning, are given in a playful tone.

I smile. "I ain't no pansy."

I pick up the feather and spring to my feet. My rage meter jumps off the scale. I try to smash against Melinda. I can't move. The more I try, the more enraged I get. I scream, but I can't move. I want to smash the bowl, Melinda's face, the kitchen sink, the coffee table, anything, but I can't take any action. Quickly, my anger reaches a climax and like a raging bull, I stamp, ready to charge, but I'm glued to one spot. For a minute I've lost control and want to destroy everything. In a desperate attempt to rid myself of the feather, I throw it toward the bowl. I stand drained of a piece of my anger never before touched. I'm wiped out. All I can do is take one step back and drop, rock-like, onto the couch. My head falls back and rests against the wall. I feel dizzy, unnerved and ready to cry. I blink back the tears, but can't hold the dam. I'm embarrassed, yet relieved, while I dive into an abyss I've never experienced. My sobs turn to a howl. I gasp for air, hold myself and go into another long bout of sobs.

My feeling gate swings wide open for what seems like an hour, but probably is only five minutes. When it closes, I pull myself together and look at Melinda.

She studies me and says, "Wow! That was something."

"It's a place I never went before."

"How do you feel?"

"Like a new baby, just smacked on my butt, ready for life."

"Good description. I couldn't have said it better."

I lift my head and look over at her. "Now I feel sexy. What do you say?"

She gets a familiar look, stands, and pulls off her halter top, releasing her expressive breasts. She rounds the coffee table, unzips her blue skirt and lets it drop to the floor.

After an hour, we're complete, having had one another on the couch, the chair, the floor, in the kitchen and next to the front door. We end on our bed, sprawled from side to side asleep in each other's arms.

When I awake, she's looking at me. "Hey, you."

"Hi."

"That was a first."

I raise my eyebrows. "First for what?"

"The first time I had great sex without hurting anyone."

"Or getting hurt by someone."

"Yes, that too," she says.

I point at the bowl. "Maybe the feather might be the very tool we've looked for. If we can step into our violence without anyone getting hurt, then we may have something."

"It sure protects us from one another."

"It lets out my passion in a good way. All men like me need that feather."

"Maybe all men," she says.

"What do you mean?"

"If a guy like Stewart could pick up the feather, he could also experience a part of himself he's frightened to feel."

"You might have a point."

She swings one bare leg over mine and pulls closer. "Stewart could visit a wilder part of himself, maybe for the first time in his life."

"Maybe we need to get him to try it and see what happens."

She smiles. "It's my guess that he knows what the feather does, and he'll never consciously pick it up. Stewart's scared of his anger. He's buried it so long, it's become a chained monster in a deep dungeon."

"Better than a loose monster," I say.

"Maybe, but that monster also pulls his spontaneity down with it. He's doing a lot better than when I met him, but you must agree that he's misplaced his basic impulsive nature."

"Another good point." I untangle from her limbs and get off the bed.

"Where are you going?"

"Bathroom. Be back in a second."

She speaks loud enough for me to hear her over the sound of water splashing in the toilet. "This feather would be great for most women, too."

"A woman like you, for sure. We've already proven it."

"No, I mean all women."

I step out of the bathroom, walk to our bed and drop like a brick on my face. I slide up to her and re-establish the entanglement of limbs, her back facing me. We spoon close and I smell her hair rinse. I love her female smell.

"All women?" I ask. "I don't think all women need to get enraged. Most seem just fine."

"I don't think you get it. Most women have been trained from day one to be nice. Our culture keeps us under the tyranny of the status quo. Calm women are good and loud women are bad. Even you can see it, can't you?"

"See what? Most women are nice. It's in their genes."

She unwraps herself, turns and faces me. "I can't believe you said that. Maybe you don't know much about women."

"What do you mean?"

"Most women have been trained to be agreeable. The difference is, some don't wear nice so well and they rebel. They are women like me, who get called bitches and whatever other names society has come up with to shame women into being subservient.

"If a woman could shed her nice-girl act and get down to her core person, our world would be a much different place."

I sit up on the edge of our bed and put my hands on my forehead. "Melinda, please don't do it."

"Do what?"

"Don't pop my bubble. Until now, I believed most women were basically nice creatures, that they wanted to be gentle and kind."

She smiles and puts her hand on my forearm. "I wouldn't say they're not gentle and kind. What I'm saying is there's a wolf deep inside each of us, females included. This wolf wants to get out. It's a good reason why a woman will pack up and leave a man, sometimes after thirty years of marriage. Her wolf was suppressed inside a cloak of the gentle lamb. Whether she wants to or not, her wolf will destroy everything to run wild, or she'll go into a permanent depression and become part of the Prozac generation."

"You paint a bleak picture."

"It is bleak. Most women don't even know there is something wrong until it's too late. Most men don't know they're scared of the she-wolf, and they'll do everything possible to keep her wildness suppressed. Our entire culture is frightened of a woman's wild side."

She sits up and slides closer to me. "Wouldn't it be wonderful for women everywhere if we all had a feather to help us blow to bits the part of us that wants to make things nice? We all need help tapping into the devouring she-wolf. The feather does it without causing anyone harm."

"Is that what you feel inside?"

"Heaven's sakes, Twig, haven't you listened? Every woman has a she-wolf inside, including me. I'm different, though, because my wildness comes out in a destructive way. I hurt those I love: you, for instance."

Chapter 8

Stick It

"I don't know, Tazz," I say after we ride together over to Sally's Breakfast Nook; a favorite hangout. "I'd love to get that stick between Renee and me just once."

"I know what you mean, Stew. Women dominate most arguments. Maybe it's because they think faster than us."

After we walk in and find a table in a back corner, I say, "Faster or not, I'd like to finish one sentence sometime, before the end of my life, without interruptions from my wife."

"Good luck."

"Maybe I can borrow the stick next weekend when Renee comes to visit. What I wouldn't give to see the look on her face when she can't interrupt."

The waitress leaves two glasses of water and menus.

Tazz takes a sip of water. "She does it a lot?"

"You can't believe how much and in every situation. Bob's helped me to stand up to her, but it isn't easy. When I remember what I'm supposed to do, I stand up. Ten times will slip by with me asleep before I catch myself and stand up to her again. When I'm able to wake up, we get into a fight. It isn't easy being with a strong woman."

"Hey, compare yourself with Twig. I don't think you have as much to worry about. Melinda is one weight lifter of a strong babe."

The waitress bounds up to our table and we order. When she leaves, I say, "Yeah, remember she and I traveled together two years ago. Melinda is ten strong women rolled up into one, though Renee is still my main concern these days. I can't wait to use the stick with her."

"We all could use a dose of the stick with our women and with other people, too. Men interrupt one another just as often, but in different ways."

I take a sip of my water. "We could use one of those sticks all of the time."

He snickers. "No one would be able to talk."

"You're right. Some things are good only in moderation. Okay, just me."

He takes a sip of coffee. "What?"

"Only I would have one, then I could control the world."

"Stewy, you're weird."

"Yeah, but isn't it fun to think about?"

When our breakfast arrives, I grab the salt and pepper, shake liberal amounts of each on my eggs, then spread two blackberry jam packets on my toast.

Tazz forks a piece of his omelet. "You could use a dose of the feather, Stew."

I have my first bite to my mouth. "Feather? What feather?"

"You know what feather. The one in the bowl used for rage."

I swallow extra hard, and remember an old Bogart movie. "I don't need no stinking feather."

He gives me a wry grin and continues while chewing his food. "I know you don't think so, but from my point of view, it's the one tool you need the most."

"What do you mean?"

He washes down his food with a sip of coffee. "I've never seen you get angry."

"So?"

"Don't you think it's kind of strange that you never even get a little perturbed?"

"I'm a level-headed guy."

"Is it level-headed or frightened?"

I try to put the first bite into my mouth, but my hand shakes. "I'm level headed. I've got no problem with anger."

"Well shit, man, you got no problem, because unless Biker Bob is inside of you, you never get angry."

"I don't need to. My wife has enough anger for both of us."

"You still ain't got a clue, do you?"

"What?"

"Ever occur to you that Renee is doing your anger for you?"

"What do you mean?"

He takes another bite of eggs. "Maybe you're such a nice guy, you leave all your repressed animosity at her doorstep. If you refuse to do anger, she's forced to pick up the slack."

"She doesn't do a thing for me."

"She doesn't have to. I've watched you two. Trust me, Stewy, whether either of you knows it or not, she does anger for both of you."

"You may be right."

He puts his fork down. "Look at this very second, for instance."

"What do you mean?"

"I know you don't agree, but instead of standing up for yourself, you just gave in and let me have my way."

"I did?"

"Yes, and you did it again. Instead of declaring yourself, you gave in and let me push you around with my opinion."

"Really?"

"Really, man, and I'm getting pissed, because you continue to weasel out of your opinion and dump it on me."

I put my fork down and wipe my mouth on a napkin. "What am I supposed to do?"

"She-it, man, you did it again."

"What?"

"You gave yourself away by asking what you're supposed to do. I'm not your dad. I don't tell you what to do. If this is how you act with Renee, I see why she's so pissed."

I shrug.

"Declare yourself, dickhead. You gotta' assert yourself every minute of every day, or someone will be forced to pick up the slack."

I grab my cup of java and take a sip. "I don't get it."

He leans toward me. "Okay, good, you stood up for yourself. A weak one for sure, but hell, it can't happen all at once."

"Saying 'I don't get it' is standing up?"

"It's a start. You told me your opinion; in this case, you're confused."

"I am."

"You could've said what you usually say, 'Oh, I guess you're right,' or worse yet, 'How else should I act?' Don't you see how fucked up and wimpy that sounds? Can you see how much responsibility you put on me by saying it? Your statement, 'I don't get it' at least tells me how you feel."

"So, what you're saying is I shouldn't take the passenger's seat when some egomaniac like you tries to shove some vague concept down my throat with a never-ending lecture?"

Tazz looks up from buttering his toast and gives me a wide grin. "Did Bob take over just then?"

I flush with embarrassment. "I think so, but just for a second."

"Were you able to hear what he said?"

"I thought it was rude."

"Rude, yes, but isn't it what you really wanted to say?"

"I guess, but that kind of behavior doesn't need to--"

"Don't you get it? The thing is, I can feel you're pissed, but you sit there smiling and being nice. Right now I don't trust you and probably, neither does Renee when you do this to her. It may be rude, but it's honest. I trust honest."

I take a bite of my toast, and before I finish chewing, I say, "If I ever said anything like that to Renee, she'd go through the roof."

"She might, then you two would be off into another argument. Hell, man, if you don't get into an argument over that, you'll find something else to argue about. Pick your fights. Between you and Renee, asserting yourself is your best fight anytime."

"If I said stuff like that all of the time, Renee would leave me."

"She'd have a hard time controlling you, yes, but to tell you the truth, I think she'd be relieved to have someone who holds his own when the going gets rough."

"Does she control me?"

"Don't you weasel out on me now. I have no idea if she controls you or not. Stand up for yourself and tell me to fuck off or agree with me. Don't wimp out and ask if I'm right."

While I think about what Tazz said, we finish breakfast, pay the bill and walk outside to our bikes.

Tazz pulls out his keys and unlocks his machine. "I ain't got nothing to do today. You want to ride out to the bluffs and back?"

"Sure, Tazz, anything to get in the wind."

Because he has an older bike, sometimes hard starting, I relax in my saddle while he advances his distributor, primes the carburetor, and throws his weight onto the kick-start pedal eight times before his machine backfires and lumps into an idle.

When he readjusts his distributor, pulls his gloves on and looks over at me, I turn my ignition key with my left hand and push the starter button with my right. My bike comes to life and settles into the rhythm of Tazz's idling engine.

He folds his kickstand and pulls onto Main Street. I follow, thinking how it would feel to ride a chopped bike like his, how it would be to sit on his stylish, but minuscule seat. The lean, sleek lines of his bike are what everyone looks at when we go by: the brilliant chrome extended front end, kicked out another four inches beyond the manufacturer's original design. His slender twenty-one-inch front wheel has a slick disk brake the size of a forty-five record. Tazz has all the style, and my bike, in comparison, is a clunky Fat Boy, but he looks uncomfortable hanging on the edge of that rail.

We drive through town, stop at a supermarket for sandwiches, then head east on Highway 40. Once on open highway, we crank our bikes up to a hundred all the way to Newberry Springs, where a highway patrol is known to lurk behind a defunct gas station. Twenty miles later, we approach Ludlow and after another twenty, turn left toward the Granite Mountains in the Mojave National Preserve. After a forty-five minute ride north, we pass Kelso, a ghost town, then on to Kelso Peak, where we stop for lunch.

Tazz and I sit on a ledge looking out high above Devil's Playground, an especially desolate part of the desert. I sip on a bottle of spring water while he pulls deep swallows from a liter of Pepsi. We work our way through the sandwiches and two small bags of chips.

The day is warm. The overhead sun reflects off Devil's Playground. Its white sand looks like a lake of milk. Distant mountains might be a hundred miles to the west of us. The land is open and free, as we sit among a field of stunted creosote bushes at the pinnacle of the entire scene.

Tazz says, "I haven't seen Nick Brown around. He still at his shop in Barstow?"

I continue to look out over the open country and take another gulp of water. "I hear he might quit making bikes."

Tazz turns to me with a shocked expression. "Are you kidding?"

"Guess Bob told him to pack it in and go back to school."

"Back to school? What the hell for?"

"Of all things, he wants to study art."

"Art? What a funny thing to study."

I finish my bottle. "Maybe, but if you look carefully, the bikes he built, you know, the ones he put his heart and soul into, they're kinetic sculptures."

Tazz takes another long gulp of Pepsi, and looks out on the desert. "You might be right, but what'll we do when our bikes break?"

I look back at our bikes. "It'll be difficult to trust some other Harley jerkoff."

"My point."

I finish the last of my chips. "You got to admit his talents are wasted if he isn't happy."

"Hell, man, he's not happy?"

"He and I talked a number of times. He felt hemmed in by bikes. He wants to build monuments."

Tazz throws up his hands. "Monuments? What the hell for?"

"I don't know, maybe just because he wants to."

"He can't do something because he wants to. What about all the people he'll be fucking up in the process?"

"Come on, Tazz, don't you think you're being self-serving?"

"I don't give a shit. Nick's the best. When he's gone, who'll tune up my bike?"

"Twig's not bad at wrenching on bikes."

Tazz takes a last bite of his sandwich. "Yeah, but he's not Nick."

We sit in contemplative silence for five minutes until Tazz says, "What's Nick working on?"

"I hear he's making pottery."

He rolls his eyes. "Whatever makes him happy."

We sit for another hour in silence, then take a short hike back to our bikes. The ride north to Baker has a stark beauty, dotted with inactive baby volcanoes, some as tall as six hundred feet. Many times, the road makes gentle climbs to wide vistas, then drops into sloping valleys that cut into long beds of ancient onyx-colored lava flow. When the sun drops low in the sky, stringy clouds turn the expanse to brilliant violet and burgundy. We ride west, headed for home. Once we turn onto Highway 15, it's a fifty-mile ride back to Barstow.

I wave to Tazz when he turns off the main highway on the east side of town and heads for Victorville. I ride toward my little bungalow north of town.

When I turn off the highway and start up my dirt road, I see a light green compact parked in the cul-de-sac in front of my cabin. I idle the quarter mile of gravel, then turn into my driveway and up to the garage. When I get off my idling bike, I look around, then open the garage door. As expected, my old Chevy is parked inside nose out, tool bench against the back wall, with the defunct refrigerator standing in the corner that was here when I moved in.

I pull Blue around and back it in next to my car, then kill the engine. When I dismount, I turn toward the house. Through the darkness, on my little back porch I see a vague outline of a figure. I say in a cautious voice, "Hello?"

"Stewart Chance," a familiar female voice speaks out of the dark, "what the hell do you think you're doing?"

"Renee?"

I walk up my driveway and step onto the porch.

She has a hand on one hip. "Where have you been?"

I reach into my pants for my key and slide it into the dead bolt. When the door opens, I flip on a kitchen light. "What do you mean?"

She glares at me with angry green eyes. "I've tried to call you for three days. Have you been out riding with that Melinda woman again? Because if you have--"

I surprise myself when I say, "Renee, will you stop with the jealousy bullshit? I haven't been with Melinda, not in the way you think."

Her voice rises one octave. "You admit it then. You have been with her?"

"Renee, will you stop it? Melinda and Twig have been together for a long time. Even if I wanted her, which I don't, Melinda is not available for anyone except Twig."

We step into the kitchen, and I take a seat at my little table. This is sure to be a long one, but it's Saturday night, and we've got plenty of time.

"Why are you down here? I thought you were in Sacramento this weekend, with PTA."

She pulls back a lock of her long black hair. Lately a few strands of gray have been showing. "When I couldn't reach you, I got worried you were running around again, like you did last spring."

I take a deep breath. "First, it wasn't last spring, it was two years ago and second, I'm not interested in running around. I like being with you, though I'm not sure I like it right now."

So far, I'm doing pretty good.

She huffs, but doesn't speak.

I say, "You couldn't get through to me for a couple of hours, so you decided to fly down and check up on me?"

She paces the kitchen floor, rotating her sexy, slender hips at every turn. "I was afraid something had happened. You always call on Saturday, and when you didn't, I got worried."

"Saturday isn't over yet, Renee. You kind of jumped the gun a little, don't you think?"

"Who do you think you're talking to, some bimbo? It's Monday. I called your work and they hadn't seen you either. It's not like you to run off. After work, I took the first flight I could to see what happened. I got here an hour ago, and your bike was gone. I was getting ready to break in and call the police."

"It's Saturday, Renee."

She turns and points at the wall with one extended finger. "You better check your calendar, Bub. I don't know where you've been, but Sunday and Monday have slipped away while you were out riding around." She says her last two words with a sarcastic spit.

I look at my watch, and it says Saturday. I call Time Service and the recording says 10:05, April 23. I look at my little Tridine calendar she pointed at. April 23 falls on a Monday.

I feel dizzy. "How could it be Monday? Last night was Friday."

"I don't know, but you've been gone since Saturday. Check your messages." She points at my blinking machine.

I look at the machine. "Twenty-two calls. I've never had that many on a weekend."

"Like I've been trying to tell you, the weekend is over, Stewart. You've been gone three days, and I'd be interested to know where you've been."

She uses her dry you-better-tell-me-everything-right-now-or-else tone. I hate that pitch of her voice. Right now, I hate everything about her.

"Keep talking to me in that voice, and I'll ask you to go into town and rent a room. I'm not in the mood for a lecture."

I'm thinking, wow, that was a great response. I'm on tonight.

She crosses her slender arms high on her chest. "I don't have any tone, Stewart Chance."

"You do, and I won't continue until you change your attitude to something more constructive."

"Hey, screw you, buddy," she says and smacks her hand on the table.

This is the moment where we shift from two people attempting to communicate to our consistent, at least for the last few years, screaming match, where nothing gets done except causing each other pain with hurtful words. Either way, it takes time to heal from these sessions.

I remember Bob's stick and stop the all-too-familiar spiral into a screaming match. "Honey, what if there was a way for each of us to get our point across and be heard without any long drawn out battles?"

"That would be a relief," she snaps. "I'm tired of you're 'get to the point' jabs before I've finished my thoughts."

I smile. "We might have an answer. Would you be willing to stay over an extra day and try an experiment?"

"I don't know, Stewart. My sister is keeping an eye on the kids, and you know how neurotic she gets around teenagers."

"Can we put her off for an extra day? You might be surprised at how well the tool works."

"What is it?"

"I can't explain, but it's effective in making sure everyone gets a turn to talk."

She seems to relax slightly. "I can take an extra day off work, but what about you? Can you afford to miss work?"

"Tridine is in its slow season. I haven't had any days off for a year, and I have some time built up."

She takes two steps and sits across from me at the table. "What about your disappearance today?"

"I'm sure people filled in for me. I'll call in the morning and let 'em know. What do you think, you want to try it?"

She picks up my phone. With her manicured red nails, she carefully pushes keys. "I'll call home and see how Mary is."

In five minutes, after talking to her sister and the kids, she hangs up and looks at me with a familiar impish smile. "I'll stay, but only if you take me for a ride on your bike tomorrow."

I grin. "No problem. We'll need to ride over to Twig's anyhow, to get the tools."

Her smile turns to a grimace. Her crowsfeet crinkle. She leaps to her feet. "I won't go anywhere close to that bimbo."

"She'll be at work, Renee."

"I don't even want to go anywhere where she's been."

"It's been two years. Can't you let bygones be bygones?"

She paces my small kitchen again. "Not when it comes to some husband-stealing floozy."

I lock my hands and release a long sigh. "If this conversation goes three seconds further, it'll turn into a fight. I'm exhausted right now. How about we give this argument a rest and pick it up in the morning?"

During the thirty-second silence, I feel satisfied with my responses. It amazes me how much more I've been able to stand up to her lately. Tazz's talk this morning helped too.

She stops pacing and looks at me. "I guess I got frightened when I thought she took you away again."

I reach out and slip my fingers into her hand. She allows me to pull her to me. I turn her around and sit her on my lap. She leans against my chest and puts her face in the nape of my neck.

I reach one arm under her legs, the other behind her back, stand and carry her to the bedroom. She lies on the bed while I undress her and get her under the covers. When I climb in next to her, she pulls me close and wraps her body around everything she can possibly wrap herself around.

An hour later, we're asleep. I reach over when the seven-thirty alarm buzzes. My hand hits the off switch. I roll back over and remember my lost weekend, then connect it with the dream ride to Reno, to the Sattley store and the revelations from that experience.

I sit up on the edge of my bed. "Bob has something to do with my lost days."

"Bob again," she says sleepily.

"I think so." I walk into the kitchen, pick up the phone and call Twig.

***

I've lived with Twig for almost a year, and it's been pretty good. I mean, we've had nothing but trouble with our violent natures and all, but at least with Twig, there's a possibility of working things out. He's not as exciting as other men I've been with, but these last three years, after Nick pulled his disappearing act, I've been more inclined to look for stability and commitment. Twig is certainly committed.

We awake to the seven o'clock radio alarm and after a bit of scrambling and checking calendars, surprise, it's Tuesday. I know what I did on Monday, but whatever happened to Saturday and Sunday I have no idea.

I climb out of bed and turn on the coffeepot before I take a shower. When I get out of the bathroom, I shake Twig until he stirs. "You got to get up and go to work."

He grumbles about not working and rolls over.

"I don't know what happened, Twig, but it's Tuesday, and I don't even know if we still have jobs."

"Tuesday?"

I say, "We missed our first day of the work week."

He spins around and looks at the alarm, leaps out of bed and heads for the bathroom. "I'm probably fired. What happened to the weekend?"

"I don't know, but maybe Bob and the dream ride to Sattley had something to do with it."

"Was it a dream?"

"You got any other explanations?"

By the time he comes out, shaved and dressed, food is on the table.

"That bowl is still on the coffee table," I say as I slide three eggs onto his plate.

He looks over and shovels his first bite. "Is it?"

"I thought maybe it was a part of the dream, too."

"I guess not."

I pour him a cup of java.

He asks, "Does it still work like it did?"

"I'm not about to try the feather before I go to work, but I'll give the stick a go."

I walk into the living room and pick up the stick. "What do you think, Twig, can you still talk?"

The kitchen is silent.

"Twig," I say louder.

When I set the stick down, Twig speaks from the other room. "It still works."

The phone rings, and I reach across the counter. "Hello?"

Stewart has a frantic sound to his voice. "Melinda, you still got the bowl and that stick?"

"Yes, I was just trying it out."

"Does it still work?"

"Yes."

"Renee is here, and I've called in for a day off. Can we borrow it while you two are at work?"

"Let me give you to Twig," I say.

I hand the phone over and listen to a one-sided conversation while I pull a work dress over my head and apply makeup.

While Twig talks, he slides on a T-shirt. "You can come over and use it, but Bob told me to guard it. I can't let it leave the house for now."

"Yeah, sure, Stewy, no problem. The key is above the corner post on the front deck. You know where."

There's a short pause before Twig says, "Okay, fine. Consider using the feather too."

After another break, with a patient voice, Twig says, "Look, Stewy, you don't have to use it, just consider it."

After ten seconds of silence on his end, Twig says, "Okay, no problem. We'll be back around five."

When he hangs up, I ask, "Are Stew and Renee going to use the stick?"

Twig gives me a Cheshire smile and as he puts on the blue boxer shorts I gave him two months ago, he says, "It'll be interesting to see how things turn out with them."

***

After calling Twig I deal with the few letters and postcards that still dribble in addressed to Bob. It's been two years since that excruciating television marathon and people still write with questions.

As the sun breaks over the distant hills outside of Barstow, I lick my last envelope, place a stamp on it and go in to wake Renee.

I give her a kiss on her temple. "Renee, Honey?"

She doesn't answer.

I shake her again. "Renee, you still want to go for that ride?"

Her eyes flash open, and she gives me a sleepy grin. "Yes, a ride would be luscious, but first come back to bed for a minute."

I strip my T-shirt. "By the look on your face, I'd guess you have more than a minute in mind."

"What do you care? You're going to get laid and that's all that matters."

My shorts drop to the floor, and I dive into bed.

We move with each other, savoring each sensation, until we both have found our moment. The skies open, and it rains cottonballs.

We both fall back into a slumber, when I awake and kiss her ear. I say, "Are you ready to go for a ride?"

"You betcha."

She gets up and steps across my small bedroom into the bathroom. "Give me a minute to take a shower."

Water runs and steam folds out through the door before I slip my Levi's on and step out to the kitchen to brew a pot of coffee.

I've finished my eggs and toast and a second cup of coffee before she saunters out of the bedroom, pours a cup of mud and sits at my dinky kitchen table.

"Want some eggs?" I ask.

Renee pulls a comb through her wet hair. "Sure, make mine scrambled."

"You never have scrambled."

"You're right, but I've never had sex like that before, either."

"Scrambled it is."

As I fold her eggs into a sizzling pan, she butters a piece of toast and takes a bite. "By the way you've acted, I can only guess you have a surprise cooked up for me at Twig's, right? This stick thingy can't be all that good."

I smile.

"Why do you guys call him Twig, anyway? The guy's as big as a house."

"Bob came up with the name years ago and it stuck. I think it has something to do with what Twig's dad called him when he was a kid."

"What, does Bob come up with everything you guys do?"

"Not everything, but this next thing of Bob's will knock your socks off."

"Really?" she says. "Give me a hint."

"All I'll say is, it'll be good for both of us."

"Well, hell, Stewart, there's a lot of stuff good for both of us. That isn't much of a hint."

I smile.

Renee finishes her piece of toast. "You're not telling me, are you?"

I set the plate of scrambled eggs in front of her. "Nope! It's a surprise. Dig in, and let's get this show on the road."

She finishes off her eggs without another word, drops her fork onto the plate and goes into the bedroom. "I've got to put on some makeup," she says. "I'll be out in a second."

Five minutes later, she reemerges and announces, "I'm ready."

I finish washing the last dish and drop it in the drain rack, pull my T-shirt off and step into the shower. Two minutes later, I lean a foot on the kitchen chair and pull my Harley boots over yesterday's socks.

"Okay," I say, "let's get in the wind."

She follows me out of the back door and helps pull the garage door open. Blue awaits.

I check the oil and front tire pressure. The tire's been leaky; not enough to warrant a repair, but I check it every three or four days.

Renee stands in perfect female patience until I start to throw a short polish on the chrome side case.

"What the hell are you doing?"

"It's dirty, Honey," I say in a syrupy tone. "You wouldn't want to get grease on your riding pants, would you?"

She acquiesces, steps to the garage door and while her gaze drifts along my driveway, I throw a quick polish on a few other critical visual parts.

"Who's that?" she says.

I look up and see a familiar faded blue van parked at the end of my cul-de-sac. "They park overnight now and then."

"Who are they?"

"I never asked. It's always the same junky van. They don't bother anyone, so I don't say anything."

"They?"

"A guy and some woman. Sometimes I think I hear a small child fussing. It's hard to tell."

"Do you mean there's a family living in that little van?"

"I guess." I throw the rag on my bench, lift my right leg over Blue and sit. "You ready to go?"

"Stewart Chance."

I hate it when she uses that tone and says my whole name.

"Do you mean to tell me an entire family is out in that van, and you don't do anything to help?"

"I help by not calling the police, if that's what you mean."

"Of course you're not turning them in, but that's not helping them."

"What would you have me do?"

"I don't know, feed them. Maybe find them a place to stay."

Before I turn the ignition key and push the starter button, I say, "Jeez, Renee, what do you want from me?"

My engine comes to life and lumps along in a deep-throated rumble. The sound covers her response. I cup my hand to my ear like I can't hear, then point at the back seat.

She nods her head, steps to the back of me, puts her hand on my shoulder and mounts the bike.

I rev my engine, pull down the driveway and onto the gravel road.

I turn left toward the highway, and the same roundish guy with dreadlocks steps around the beat-up van. He looks at me. I nod. He returns the gesture, and I make my turn.

Renee speaks loud over the sound of my slow-running engine. "Stewart, you act like you know each other."

"Not exactly, but he's a neighbor of sorts."

"We've got to do something."

I shift into second. "What do you have in mind?"

"I don't know right now, but if he has a child in there, something must be done."

I want to drop the subject, because I know my wife. When she sets her mind on anything, she isn't satisfied until something is done.

When we reach the end of my rutted lane, I turn right onto asphalt and gun my way through the gears until we approach ninety.

I feel Renee grip tighter. I back off and relax my engine into a quiet sixty-five, the speed limit.

She squeezes me and yells in my right ear. "What do you think we should do?"

"About what?"

"The homeless people in the van."

I knew it. She won't let it go. I'm destined to have an endless conversation on the homeless situation. Maybe if I give a quick solution, we can enjoy the ride to Twig's.

"We'll check the guy out." I yell. "I might be able to get him on as a janitor at work."

I think the problem is solved, and I can put this subject behind us, but not with Renee.

"We've got to get them a home for the baby's sake."

I make a left on Lincoln, ride to the top of the hill and park before I can answer. Looking out over the city, I say, "I won't take them in."

She jabs my kidney. "Maybe we could find them a hotel room until you get him settled into a job."

I think for a minute before I answer. This is a critical question and it needs a lot of consideration, because I sense a number of pitfalls; I just can't see them. "Hotel rooms are expensive. I don't have any extra money."

The conversation goes for another ten minutes before I start my engine, drive to the bottom of the hill and pull out onto the freeway. I crank the throttle, and my bike jumps away from the onramp, leaving it far in the distance before I realize she hasn't said a word. Oops, maybe I said the wrong thing.

Blue smoothes out at a steady seventy. While the wind whips our faces, morning sun in our eyes, I turn my head and yell, "What?"

"Stewart Chance, what if it were me or one of our friends who was down and out? Would you say the same thing?"

"I don't think so," I yell, "but they aren't our friends."

"You self-centered. . ."

A gust of wind hits me in my right ear and I can't hear the rest of her sentence. I'm not sure I want to, anyhow.

We ride in silence to Twig's. I pull into the driveway, park, and see Twig's landlord, who lives downstairs. He comes out to greet us, leaning heavily on his cane.

When I turn my bike off, he says, "Hello, Mr. Stewart."

"Hello, Glen, how's your week been?"

"Oh, so-so. You know how it is to get old. Lots of creaky bones."

"Well, the desert is the place to be with creaky bones, huh?"

"Mr. Goreman and the redhead are at work," he says.

"Thomas left his key out for me. My wife and I are using his place for an hour or so."

He hobbles over to the porch swing. "Okay with me."

I climb the first rotted wooden stair and listen to it groan with the strain of my weight. I turn toward him. "See you later."

He sits hard in the swing and waves me on.

At the top of the steps, I unhook Twig's key from its nail on the end of a beam. When I open the door, Renee follows me in.

Once I'm in and close the door, she says, "So, what's your big surprise?"

I toss the key on the counter and step into the kitchen. "Have a seat on the couch. You want anything to drink? We may be here for a while."

"Glass of water," she says.

I hope she notices the bowl, but she's busy looking at a copy of a modern painting next to Twig's moose head. I step into the kitchen, grab two handfuls of ice from the freezer, and draw two glasses of water, then walk back into Twig's living room. When I set the glasses down, Renee picks up the stick. I feel my throat constrict, but don't let on that anything has changed. I want it to be a surprise.

"What's this stick for, Stewart?"

I can't answer, but I give her a mysterious smile and sit in the recliner across from her.

"Is it one of those secret men's things you've kept from me these last few years?"

My smile continues, as she studies the intricacies of the stick.

"Does it have some kind of special male mo-jo? Is that why you're not telling me?"

All I can do is smile.

Much to my relief, she tires of looking at the stick and sets it down. My constriction loosens, and before she picks up the feather, I say in a very nonchalant manner, "Have a drink of water, Honey, before we get started." If I say it in any other way, being the contrary person she is, she would pick it up.

"Have a drink of water yourself." She reaches for the feather. "I have no interest in water right now."

I say, almost shouting, "Don't touch that!"

She looks at me, then grabs the feather. When she leaps to a standing position, she screams about the homeless family and what I should do about it.

With confusion in her face, she swings her fist, stamps her feet, and pivots her body in a display of angry passion I've never witnessed from her.

I motion for her to throw the feather away, but she doesn't get my point.

After a minute, she looks spent. I reach up at a critical moment, snatch the feather from her hand, and let it drop to the floor.

For the first time in my life, and only for a second, I feel my unbridled anger. My rage leaps to the forefront and wants to take possession.

When the feather drops from my fingertips, my beast oozes back into the shadows. I felt him, and my heart races. My blood boils. I feel like passing out. I'm on my way back to the recliner before I return to my calm self. It was a split second, but plenty of time to give me a glimpse of what the beast looks like, and I want nothing to do with it.

By the time I land hard in the recliner and look over at my wife, she has also dropped, splayed on the couch. "What was that?"

I'm shaken enough to have a hard time forming any thoughts. I manage to expel two words. "The feather."

"You mean to tell me that feather did all this?"

I nod.

She covers her mouth. "There was more, but I'm glad you stopped me, because I'm exhausted."

I manage a smile, but I'm still shaken to the core. I feel like I just finished a tour of duty in a battle zone.

I just have time to gather myself before she begins her salvo of questions, few of which I can answer.

"Stewart," she says. "How could one small feather cause that much to come out of me?"

"Bob left it for us."

"Bob again," she says. "He's got one too many tricks up his sleeve."

"The feather isn't why I brought you here."

She looks at me with a question on her face.

"It's the stick." I pick up the stick. "Do you feel strange?"

She mouths words, but no sound comes.

"I promise to put it down in a moment, but first I want you to get a feel for it."

Her face turns pink, then red, before I set the stick down.

After a string of unintelligible words, she says, "What the hell did you do?"

"It's the stick." I go on to explain its abilities, then present my plan. "If each of us gets a turn with the stick, the other person can have a chance to talk. Does that sound fair to you?"

She grabs the stick, and my throat constricts. "Sounds fine to me," she says. "I'll go first."

She talks about the homeless family until she swings over to when I plan to move back to Sacramento. The subject takes a leap into the condition of our house and how much work needs to be done. She takes another jump into the realm of me messing with other women while I'm in Barstow. The theme continues to unravel for the longest thirty minutes I've ever experienced. She concludes with the speculation that the homeless people worry her because she's always been afraid that she'd end up a bag lady.

I'm flabbergasted at the ease with which she wanders through her chaos, weaving in and out of subjects, until she comes to her own conclusion.

With tears in her eyes, she looks at the stick, then at me. "This is the first time in my life you or any man has listened to me to the end. This is the first time I've really felt heard."

Through the entire monologue, I wanted to interject a defense. I wanted to protect myself from unfounded allegations. At the very least, I wanted to tell her she was wrong about a few points, but I couldn't. When she's finished, I have no comment. I've seen her transformation from blaming me for not caring for the homeless, to understanding the core of her concerns. I have no need to express a view. I would, however, like to have my voice back. I motion for her to replace the stick. The second she releases it, I burst forth with a bunch of nonsense.

My voice calms. I look at her and pick up the stick. I see her strain to speak.

"First," I say, "this may sound selfish, but I have too much on my plate at the moment to worry about a family of people living out of their van."

I look at her face, which turns three shades darker. I see how difficult it is for her to not be able to interject a comment.

"Second," I say, "every day they stay in my little cul-de-sac, I help those people by not turning them in."

She strains so hard I feel sorry for her and relinquish the stick. I've said all I have to say on that matter, anyhow. I never have much to say at any one given time.

The moment the stick leaves my fingertips, her opinions burst on me.

She doesn't reach for the stick, but batters me with her sharp-tongued beliefs about the unconscious human being that I am.

I take it for a minute or two, then remember I can stop the abuse. I pick up the stick. In an instant, the harpy screech ends. The room is quiet. My thoughts relax.

I don't even want to look at her, because I'll start to feel sorry for her again. I think fast to come up with a subject. I don't want to put the stick down.

"I might see about getting the guy on at work and I might not. If you're so fired up about helping them, I suggest you go out there and do something yourself. Just don't bring them into my house."

I don't want to stop talking, but I'm finished with my statement, the one I've thought about ever since the subject came up. I considered the pro's and con's of the subject and weighed how important it was to say what I said, knowing it would get me in five kinds of hot water. It was important, so there, I said it, and that, as they say, is that.

I take a deep breath and put the stick down.

She snatches it with the speed of a cougar attacking, and my larynx locks up.

Her tirade goes on for fourteen minutes. I keep track, using Twig's wall clock behind her. I hear some of what she says, but only the highlights. Something about how could I dare speak to her like that, and who do I think I am. Yada, yada, yada, yada, it goes on until she unwinds, and I see the core of her reaction. When she finishes, she bursts into tears and moans, "My brother always talked to me that way, and I hated him for it."

Before she puts her hands to her face, she sets the stick down. I want to talk, but because this is a tender moment, I remain silent. I'll have plenty of time.

This back and forth, taking turns, goes on until 2:30, when we're forced to stop to eat.

"Let's go out for lunch," I say. "It'll be good to take a break."

"Okay. Let me splash my face and put some lipstick on first. It'll only take a minute."

I sit on the couch, grab the tongs and replace the feather, then wonder what special powers the beads have. Melinda said they did nothing, though I can't believe Bob would present them to us for no reason.

While Renee is in the bathroom, I reach my index finger out and touch one bead. Nothing happens. I rub a single digit along the strand, still nothing.

Feeling bold, I slide my finger under the necklace and raise it half off the table. Nothing happens. I lift it. Although the strand is beautiful, it produces no reaction. I reach with my other hand and rotate the beads, fingering them one at a time like a rosary.

"Another minute, Honey," she yells from the bathroom. I don't answer. The beads have me mesmerized.

She steps into the room. "I'm starved. If you're ready, let's get out of here."

I put the beads back and we walk out of the apartment. I replace the key, then we step down Twig's rickety stairs. Once on

Blue, Renee holds me tighter than usual, but not the tightness of fear. She wants to be extra close.

"What's up?" I yell over my shoulder. We make a right turn onto the main highway and head south.

"I don't know," she says. "I feel extra lovey right now."

I feel her lips on my ear. She nibbles my lobe.

After five minutes, I make a turn into the driveway of Mary's Lunch Bar and park in the shade.

When I turn my engine off, Renee rubs her chest on my back and says, "Let's forget lunch and go back to our house."

"What for?" I say, though I know what she has in mind.

She giggles and gets off the bike. "Okay, buddy, remember you had an offer from a hot woman. Things like this don't come around every day."

"If I don't eat, I'll never make it through whatever kind of love feast you have in mind. I'll expire in the middle of it, and you'll be forced to finish without me."

"Long as you-know-what stays hard, I won't mind."

"Renee, that was a terrible thing to say."

"Right now, I feel pretty terrible."

We walk to the front door.

I say, "I don't see a smidgen of remorse."

She gives me a devilish smile. "I said nothing about remorse. I said terrible. I'm a terrible person. You should take advantage of me while you have the chance."

I open the door, and we step into the dark, cool room. A quiet afternoon crowd fills half of the tables. We're seated at a corner booth.

A waitress steps up and grabs a pencil trapped in her early sixties bouffant hairdo. "What'll ya have?"

Renee studies the menu, as I order a dipped hot roast beef sandwich with fries.

Renee looks at me.

The waitress turns to her. "And you?"

"I'll have the tuna salad, no onions, and could you put some of those little green olives on top? I love olives."

The woman brings her pencil down, points her eraser toward us, and swings it from me to Renee. "Anything to drink?"

"Water for me," I say.

"Do you have herb tea?" Renee asks.

"Lipton. Is that herb enough for you?"

"Nothing like chamomile or peppermint?"

"Just what you see. This is a steak house, Honey, not an herb shop."

Renee's hackles rise. I know, because I've been on the receiving end too many times over the last twenty years.

I reach over and grab her hand. "Water, Honey, will that be enough?"

"I guess, but--"

Before she can say another word, our waitress turns on one heel and like a drill sergeant, stomps toward the kitchen.

Except for serving our food, the woman pays little attention to us. I could have left without paying our bill, and I don't believe she would have noticed.

I pay the tab, then we're back on Blue. I snake through back streets and connecting roads until we reach Twig's. We dismount and climb his questionable stairs. The only reason I chance them at all is that Twig climbs them every day. I'm certain he outweighs Renee and me combined.

When we enter the apartment, Renee steps over to the coffee table, sits and grabs the beads. "What do these do?"

I shrug.

She gives me a nudge.

In a quick move, during an obvious playful moment, she loops the beads around both our heads and gives me a kiss.

Before I can remove them, before I can do anything except stand, or lie, or sit, I'm not sure what, both Renee and I find ourselves dropping into a vortex that sucks us and all of existence into a dark vacuum.

We travel light years away from Twig's house until we're spewed out of a black tunnel, like someone might spit out a mouthful of overcooked cabbage. We find ourselves lying, limbs askew, on broken pavement in front of a white building. I turn and look at the sign above the small porch. "Oh my."

"Where are we?" Renee asks.

She grabs for the beads. "How did we get here? I'm taking this necklace thing off before it gets any weirder."

"No, don't, Renee; not yet."

"Tell me one good reason."

"Because I know where we are. I was here the other day."

"What does that mean?" She points at the ten-foot-wide sign.

I say, "I don't know what it means, but I do know where we are. At least I think I know."

She reads three words aloud, "Sattley Cash Store."

"This is interesting."

"I'm not interested at all, Stewart Chance, I'm frightened."

"Oh, it's scary all right, but not in the way you might think."

"What do you mean?"

"We're meant to go inside the store."

She points at the front door. "It's closed."

I help her stand, then tug at the beads to coax her toward the building. "It was closed last time, but the door wasn't locked."

She halts. "I'm not going any closer to that building until I know what's going on."

I look at her. An unaccustomed fear washes over her pale face.

"It's okay, Renee, I was here a few days ago. In ten minutes of being here, I learned more about myself than I could've otherwise discovered in ten years. This is some kind of emotional feedback place."

"Emotional feedback? What the hell do you mean?"

I put my hands on her shoulders and look into her eyes. "It works better if you don't know what's about to happen. Trust me, Renee, I've been through this before, and there's not one thing here to hurt either of us."

"I don't think so, buddy. I'm taking the beads off. Things are way too weird for me."

"No, Renee, not yet. I want--"

She slips the strand over her head, and in an instant we're both back in Twig's living room next to the coffee table.

She stumbles backwards and sits hard on the couch. "What happened?"

I look at the beads. "It's another gift from Bob."

"A gift?"

"We should have gone inside the building."

"It was way too scary. I never want to see that store again."

When I hear someone lumber up the creaky steps, I look at my watch and realize that in the short five minutes we were gone, an hour and a half slipped by. When Twig opens the door and ushers Melinda in, Renee leaps to her feet. Not sure what will happen, I reach over and lace my fingers into my wife's hand.

Twig says, "You two are still here?"

I lift the beads. "We found out what these are for."

Melinda and Renee square off, but not in the way two guys would.

"Renee, you remember Melinda." I speak more in an awkward attempt to disarm the tension, than to be polite.

Twig bellows, "Sweet Jesus, girls, I won't have a blood bath in my house. Calm down, and let's be civil."

I pull at Renee's fingers and tug her back onto the couch. Twig puts his massive right arm around Melinda and coaxes her into the recliner across from Renee.

After another awkward moment, Twig breaks the ice. "What did you find out?"

"We tried the beads on together."

Melinda leans forward. "You mean like both of you put them over your heads at the same time?"

"Yup, and you can't believe where we went."

"Went?" Twig sits on the arm of Melinda's chair.

I look at him, then Melinda. "The Sattley Cash Store."

"No shit?" Twig says.

Melinda doesn't say anything at first, but her face color has changed. Her expression shifts from wary female to childlike exuberance. "Are you sure?"

"We were there, all right, if the place exists at all."

Renee makes a rectangle in the air with her forefingers. "The sign was long and white with a dinky post office on the right side."

Melinda looks at Renee. "Was anyone there?"

Renee says, "The place was deserted."

I say, "Same as when we were there the other day."

"You were there?" Renee asks. I feel a sense of wonder in her voice.

Melinda fingers the beads. "All of us were, but only three of us went into the store. Inside is where everything happened."

Renee glares at me.

"Nothing sexual happened, if that's what you're thinking."

Melinda snickers, "Heaven's sakes, Renee, don't worry about Stewart and me." She reaches up and slides her hand through Twig's tree limb of a forearm. "I'm with Twig, now." She gets a funny expression. "I never got the opportunity to apologize for what happened between Stewart and me. Back then, violence and sex were two uncontrollable factors in my life. If one happened, the other was sure to follow. I couldn't help myself. Stewart happened to be in the wrong place at the wrong time. I'm sorry."

Renee sits with a thoughtful scowl for a half-minute, then a smile cracks her hard-shelled exterior. "From what I know of Stewart, I'm sure he thinks he was in the right place."

Melinda gives Renee a smirk. "You know how guys are."

Renee rolls her eyes.

Melinda asks, "Did you go in the store?"

Renee leans back. "It was too eerie."

"Not eerie," Melinda says. "Downright frightening, but it's worth going in."

Renee asks, "What happened?"

"It's like all of the fucked up parts of me rose to the surface. I found myself rethinking all my childhood conclusions. They seemed appropriate at the time, but since I've become an adult, they no longer apply. Funny thing is, I still fall back on them in certain situations."

The two women go into an animated dialogue about the Sattley Cash Store.

I look at Twig and he shrugs. I point at the front door, and without the two women noticing, we get up and slip out, then go quietly down the stairs.

"Hey, Stewy, check out my new super 'G' carburetor."

"No kidding? How's it make your scooter run?"

"Not too much more power, but man, it's smooth. Acceleration isn't jagged like it was before, and it starts easier."

We step across the concrete driveway and open the garage side door. His landlord's '93 Toyota sits in one corner, and Twig's hawg is backed in up to a small workbench.

"Did you put it on yourself?"

"Yeah, it was easy. A couple of bolts, throttle cable, and I was done."

"That's easy for you to say," I say. "I wouldn't know what a bolt looked like."

We stand in the corner and gawk at his machine, then talk about bikes and adding custom parts. When the subject is exhausted, I say, "I think Melinda and Renee might hit it off."

"Looks like it to me. It's why I got out of there, so they could talk, you know, girl to girl."

"Renee doesn't have many girlfriends."

"You know Melinda. Most women have no idea how to handle her direct approach."

"My wife can handle just about anything."

Twig throws a leg over his bike and pulls it up off the kickstand. "There might be a chance."

"Who knows?"

He touches the starter, and his two cylinders come to life in a thunderous rhythm. "I'd take you for a ride, Stewy, but I'm sure Melinda will be down in a second. She'll want to be on the back."

I point up the stairs. "I'll go up and get 'em. We'll ride together."

He snaps his fingers. "Good one."

I take the stairs two at a time and grab the doorknob. I poke my head in. "You two want to go for a ride?"

I look around, and no one is in the room. I step into the apartment and look in the kitchen, the bathroom and bedroom. No one's here.

The engine of Twig's Harley dies as I step onto his porch and look down. "They're not here."

"What?"

"No one is in your house."

When a realization hits me, I rest my arms on the railing. "Maybe they went to Sattley?"

"No shit," he says and unfurls his kickstand. He leans his bike, gets off and walks up the steps. The stairs sag under his weight and the porch tugs downward.

"Jesus, Twig, these steps won't last much longer."

"Maybe someday they'll get fixed."

When he gets to the top, we go inside. Twig walks over to the coffee table. "The beads are gone all right."

I say, "What I can't believe is Renee went with a woman she's despised for over two years."

"Seems odd, but I never can figure out what Melinda will do next."

"That goes for Renee too."

Twig sits in his recliner and kicks its position back far enough for his legs to be supported. He gets a goofy grin on his face. "Well, hell, Stewy, this might be a perfect time."

I ask, "Perfect time for what?"

"Because we're stuck waiting for our women, and I'm certain Melinda wants me around when she returns, it's time for you to experiment with the feather."

"The feather? Why would I want to mess with that feather? I don't have any truck with anger. You're the ones who have anger problems."

"Your condition just isn't as apparent, but I've often wondered, where's your anger?"

"I don't have any. I don't know if you've noticed, Twig, but I'm a pretty easy going guy."

"Sure, and I got a bridge to sell you."

"What's that supposed to mean?"

"You're such a jive-ass, Stewart. You've talked yourself into thinking you're mellow."

"I am."

"Okay, what-ever."

After a pause, Twig says, "If you don't have any problem with anger, you should be able to pick up the feather without anything happening."

"I'm not picking up the feather, and that's that."

Twig snickers. "Wow, man, I didn't realize how scared you are of anger. Sorry I mentioned it."

That's it. He said the wrong thing. I swing my hand down and grab the feather. My I'm-not-scared-of-anything ego drives me and nothing else.

I'm on my feet. I swing my arms, yell and scream at him. Like a dam has released, I spill my vehemence over him with unrestrained fury. I want to take his stupid moose head and crash it into his face. I want to kill him, but I can't do a thing except yell.

Although I'm not enjoying the moment, it turns into five minutes. I'm so engrossed, I don't consider putting the feather down until it slips out of my hand. I collapse on the couch. My head back, I gasp for breath.

Twig says, "That was good, Stew."

"Was it?" I take a deep lung full of air. "It was my first."

"It was the first time you ever yelled like that?"

"Yeah, and I don't like it."

"It's good for you."

Melinda and Renee reappear while pulling the beads over their heads.

Before the women have a chance to adjust, Twig says to me, "We gotta' do it again some time."

I nod, but I've already decided to never touch the feather again. I grab the tongs, pick the feather up and replace it upright in the sand.

"How was it?" I ask, once the women untangle themselves and look in my direction.

"Frightening," Renee says. She sets the string of beads next to the bowl.

"What happened?"

She looks at Melinda, then at me. "We went to the store--"

"I already know what happened to you in Sattley," I interrupt. "I want to know what you came up with."

Renee glares at me. "Stewart Chance, I get to tell my story the way I want to tell it. Take your pushy male attitude and butt out." She turns, sits on the couch, and pulls Melinda down with her. The two women sigh, and Renee starts into a long monologue about what happened. Every little detail must be explored, and Melinda is enraptured. I bide my time until she comes to the revelation part, about fifteen minutes later.

Twig and I look at one another. He shrugs.

After ten minutes of Renee recalling long-forgotten memories and washing them clean with her tears, she turns to Melinda. "I never trusted women, but you're different."

Melinda smiles. "It may have something to do with going to Sattley together. Some kind of bond has been created that normally would take months or years to make."

Renee pats her face with a tissue, then looks at Melinda. "I think you're right."

Melinda says, "I liked you from the first day in the hospital."

Renee snickers. "Up until today, I hated your guts."

Twig and I witness the two most unlikely women open a door to friendship. Being the kind of straightforward women they are, their door is not cracked with tentative caution, but swung wide with honest appraisal and admittance.

When all is complete and the two women give each other a hug, Twig interjects, "We have an hour of daylight. We could still go for a ride, if you want."

In five minutes, our bikes are lumping down Twig's driveway. We pull onto the street and thunder toward a glorious sunset.

Within a half-hour, high on a rise above Victorville, overlooking a long stretch of untouched desert, we sit on dried grass and watch the sky turn mauve, then violet. It's another impeccable desert sunset.

I lean against the front wheel of my bike. Renee props her back against my chest. My arms wrap around her. In a dreamy voice, Renee says, "I'd consider moving here for the sunrises and sunsets alone, but the landscape is so ugly."

I say, "If you're serious, I'd look for a nicer area."

"Nicer than what? Summer will not be nice at all."

"I found a nice area next to the San Gabriel Mountains, very much like our valley back in Placerville. You could look at it sometime when you're visiting. It's a drive for me to get to work, but the country is beautiful, and it's cooler in summer."

"Could we look tomorrow?" she asks.

"I thought you had to go back to work."

"I do, but I'm here and in the mood, so maybe you better take advantage and show me. I'll call in and ask for another day. I've got tons of leave time saved up."

She drops her head back on my chest and speaks while looking at the changing sky. "I'm tired of being alone. Now that I like you more, I want you around."

I turn my attention left and catch Twig and Melinda gawking. I raise my eyebrows. We're all floored with Renee's shift in attitude.

What's left of daylight paints a fading magenta across a darkening sky. Clouds squeeze the last possible hint of violet from dusk, then it's dark. Without saying a word, we remount our bikes, drive off of the hill and roll out over the open desert. The dry air feels good on my face. The sounds of our two engines harmonize while we drive the remaining two miles to Twig's. This is one of those fleeting, exceptional moments. When I'm eighty, I'll remember every mile of this ride.

While the women are in the kitchen putting together something to eat, Twig and I sit across from one another, looking at the bowl. A long silence ensues, until he says, "What do you suppose the corks are for?"

"God save us," I say. "I forgot about the corks."

"If everything else has magical powers, I'm afraid to try the corks."

Twig snatches one from the north position and holds it up.

"What?" I ask.

He gets a funny look. "I don't think they do anything."

"Knowing Bob, they aren't here just for show. They must do something."

"Maybe it can't be seen or felt, because I feel nothing."

"Try another," I say. "Maybe each has a different kind of effect."

He grins. "You try."

Cautiously, I pick up the southern cork and lift it to eye level. "You're right, it doesn't do a thing."

Twig picks up the third, the western cork, and the last, the eastern one, then he reaches over and takes mine.

I look at him.

"Maybe all of them together do something?"

"Well?" I ask.

"Not a thing. This isn't like Bob. Everything he does has some kind of significance. I've never seen him do anything by accident."

"Then what are the corks all about?"

Twig replaces them into their original location, careful to position them upright and evenly spaced. "It's weird," he says, "Maybe we aren't supposed to know now. When the time is right, I'm sure Bob'll tell us."

Twig gives me one of his sly grins and shifts subjects on the spin of a dime. "What about the feather, Stewy? Why don't you give it another try?"

"What are you talking about? I wouldn't touch it again if you paid me a thousand dollars."

"I'm not paying you any money, Stew, because you know it's for your own good."

"Nothing like that can be for anyone's own good. If you're so hot on that feather, you use it."

"I'll go first, then you."

"No, damn it."

Dinner was good, but the company was better, and it's late in the evening before we say good-bye. Renee and I take a chilly ride home, but my wife presses hard against my back and I don't notice the cold.

In forty-five minutes we nestle into bed and make love. When finished, we fall asleep in each other's arms.

I'm on Blue and looking sideways at big teeth and an arresting smile. I nod as Bob returns the gesture. He pours on the gas and races ahead until his brake light illuminates the ink black night.

He turns left into a broken asphalt parking lot. When we get around back, I realize it's Nick Brown's mythical bike shop. Bob pulls up and parks under a massive oak. I'm close behind. When I turn my engine off, Bob is already standing next to Nick's big wooden front doors. I dismount and follow him in through a side door.

"What happened to the bikes?"

"You may have heard, Nick no longer wants to build bikes."

"I heard, but what are we supposed to do without him?"

He walks me through a humid room stacked with large clay bowls, tall vases, racks of cups, pitchers, and platters, all recently thrown and drying. A small electric potter's wheel sits in a back corner, with scattered wooden hand tools on a low bench next to the wheel. Splatters of gray clay speckle the wall and floor.

Bob says, "Right now Nick wants to throw pots, and from what I see, he's pretty good at it."

We walk through the workroom and into the back office. Nick sits at a minuscule table with mud-caked hands. He's eating a white bread and peanut butter sandwich.

"Expected you two," he says with a mouth full of bread. He swallows. "What took you so long?"

Bob reverses a torn, red leatherette and chrome chair, then straddles the back. He picks up and inspects one of Nick's finished vases. "Dreams take time."

Nick takes another bite from his sandwich and grabs a bottle of soda. Before he takes a swallow, mouth still full, he asks, "You tell him yet?"

"Not yet."

I look at Bob. "Tell me what?"

Bob sets Nick's vase on the table. "Sit down, Stewy. Want a sandwich?"

"If we are in a dream, a sandwich won't do me much good."

He smiles and motions for me to sit. "Let's talk about the bowl and its tools."

"I've been wondering when you were going to tell us."

He ignores my comment. "I left the bowl for you to get a feel for what each of the tools could do, not to play with."

"I haven't been playing, especially with that feather."

"It's your job to make sure each man and woman of the One on One bikers uses each tool at least once." He grabs a potato chip off Nick's plate and pops it into his mouth. "I forgot how good these taste."

"What happens after each person uses them?"

"The bowl and all of its goodies will disappear. You'll have to make your own."

I grab a chip. "I get a sneaking suspicion our's won't have the same abilities."

"Nope."

"What good are they?"

Nick chimes in. "Men and women are different. When it comes time to communicate with one another, other than the obvious sex stuff, neither of us has a clue how the other thinks."

"True, but what's it got to do with these objects?"

Bob grabs another chip. "The tools and bowl help create a place where men and women can feel safe enough to express their own brand of emotion."

Nick takes another bite. "Both men and women need to release anger. We live in a culture that doesn't allow anything stronger than a grumble without upsetting the entire apple cart."

I say, "If we expressed our anger, wouldn't a bunch of people get hurt?"

"Express anger," Bob says, "not act it out. The feather allows a person to let it all out and not harm themselves or anyone else. If people can get a reference for how it feels, they can learn to express anger without violence. The feather does that."

I give him a confused look. "You ask a lot from a violent society."

Nick takes another sip from his drink, then sets the bottle on the table. "Through repression of healthy anger, our culture has become addicted to violence. Like a heroin addict, our culture is in love with, and at the same time abhors violence."

"The feather," Bob says, "is a tool to introduce us to the depths of our emotion with safety. Anger is one emotion the feather can help with. For you, Stewy, it's a rage feather, but for someone else it might be a sadness feather, if they have a hard time feeling that emotion. Some may even find it to be a laughing feather."

"I don't get it. How does the feather do that?"

Nick takes a last bite. With his mouth full, he says, "It gets us used to and not separated from our emotions."

"You might have a point."

Bob smiles. "The feather is a very fragile ritual tool. It must be soft in nature, because once emotion is up, no one knows what will happen. We tried it for a while with a small stick, but after three or four uses, someone got so angry the stick was shattered against the wall. Things like that happen in a men's circle. The feather was adopted because it can't break, nor can it hurt anyone.

Bob looks at me with an intense glare. "This is a very important tool and one that should be approached carefully. It must be used in ritual space only, with lots of agreements. The practiced use of the tool gives a person the chance to find his or her true emotion the instant it comes up, not after it's been edited."

"What do you mean?" I ask.

"Most of the time we edit our emotion because the moment isn't right, or we are afraid that we might hurt someone either physically or emotionally. The problem is, once the emotion is edited, it's rationalized into something more user friendly, usually at the expense of the person feeling the emotion. The tool allows us to come unglued at the very instant the emotion comes forward; tears, joy, anger, frustration, rage."

Nick adds, "For most of us men, the 'killer ape' has been repressed for so long, we have no idea how to access him, let alone temper him. When we can't access the ape, some other spontaneous part of us suffers. "The feather gives us a chance to practice this kind of access in an appropriate setting, with lots of safety."

Bob says, "Feather work should first be done with the same gender, men with men, women with women, because it is too unpredictable. The same genders know the warning signs and can help keep the person safe. Feather work between men and women should only be done once both parties are well versed in the tools agreed upon limits, and with other people around as spotters."

"Limits?"

Bob holds up one finger. "No touching anyone or anything while doing feather work. The job is to let the emotion run its course without harming ourselves, anyone else, or destroying property."

"Okay, I get your point on the feather. What about the stick? How will the stick help?"

Bob leans forward. "Haven't you figured it out yet?"

Nick stands and pulls another piece of bread from the fridge. He sits and dips his hunting knife into the jar of peanut butter.

"Our biggest job is to learn how to go into conflict without hurting one another. What do you want most when you and Renee are into it?"

I have to think. "Whether I'm right or not, or no matter how long it takes for me to say something, I don't want to be interrupted."

"Exactly." Bob snitches another chip. He looks at Nick. "This brand is good." He flips the chip into his mouth, then turns back to me. "Ask Renee the same question sometime, and she'll tell you she wants to be heard. Pretty much the same thing."

"Oh, I see, the stick gives both people a chance to be heard."

"Correct-a-mundo," Bob says. "It's called a talking stick for good reason. There are no real guarantees that any one person will be heard, but at the very least each person gets a chance to talk with no one to rush them or interrupt."

"Talking stick, huh? It's more than I could ever expect when I deal with Renee. She'll take over halfway into my every sentence. Talking stick. It's a good name."

Nick gives me a wry smile. "Women think much faster. They have an ability to know what we'll say before we even get a single word out."

"I hate to be interrupted." I pick up a wooden spoon-like tool caked with dry mud, and nervously scrape clay off with my thumbnail. "The talking stick stops it, but without being forced to, I don't think she'll honor any talking stick agreement."

"Give her time," Bob says. "It's a new concept to let her man finish his thoughts without interruptions. It'll take some getting used to."

"The talking stick does one other thing," Nick says, and pops the last bite of bread into his mouth.

"What's that?"

"It gives her a chance to find her own answers without some dick trying to rush her."

I hold the paddle up and point it toward Nick. "It drives me crazy when she wanders around trying to figure out answers while she speaks. Why can't she cut to the chase?"

Bob grabs the last chip. "Because women don't problem-solve in the same way men do."

"What do you mean?"

Bob smiles. "Tell me if I'm wrong. If you have an issue with Renee, what do you do?"

This is a trick question. I'm careful with my answer. "I think about it."

"To be more precise, don't you think through all the possibilities before you present a problem to her?"

"I guess."

"In fact, don't you continue to consider it until you come up with an answer? When you finally say something, don't you have your problem and solution bundled in a nice little package for her?"

I put an elbow on the table and rest my head on my hand. "I guess. What's wrong with that?"

Bob stands, turns his back, grabs a bag of chips from the top of the fridge and pours a pile of them onto the table. He replaces the bag and sits. "I love these chips." He puts three in his mouth at one time. He crunches his way through them and reaches for another handful.

Before he puts more into his mouth, I ask again, "So, what's wrong with that?"

"Nothing, Stew. It's the way we guys do it, right, Nick?"

"You got it," Nick says. "It's how I do it."

I grab one of the chips and toss it into my mouth. "If there's nothing wrong with doing it that way, what's your point?"

Three more chips crunch away between Bob's large teeth. He smiles. "It's not how women do it."

"What?"

"Women don't problem solve the same way men do."

I look at Nick, and he nods. "Shit, Stewy, don't you get it? Women don't think about it even for one second. Often, whatever is going on in their heads finds its way to their lips before they think about what they want to say. They talk from their emotions and emotion is not something that can be thought about first."

My mouth drops open for a long time before I can speak. "When they don't think about it first, they can be hurtful. Renee's first few words are usually like razor blades."

Bob has another chip poised to shoot down his consuming machine. He looks at me. "Razor blades? That puts it kind of mildly, doesn't it? I'd say more like atomic cruise missiles."

I grin. "I was being conservative."

"My point is, most men believe linear problem solving is the right way."

"It makes more sense."

"To us guys, it makes perfect sense. Women don't see it that way. Our mistake is when we expect them to do it our way."

Being in the habit of feeding my face when I'm nervous, I pick up another chip, but throw it back onto the table. "Jeez, Bob, these chips are terrible."

"Yeah, but I love 'em."

Nick grins. "We must accept that the way women problem-solve is right, too."

"It isn't right. If the first thing out of her mouth is hurtful, how could that be right?"

"Because sometimes it's where a woman has to start, for her to get to any answers. If guys can only understand that whatever she says isn't really directed at us, we can simply witness her unraveling and watch her come up with her own answers. One difference between women and men is most men think it out, and most women talk it out. Unhampered by the other, we both find our own answers in our own way. Both ways are right."

Bob has another couple of chips in his hand, when he looks at Nick. "You got anything to drink?"

Nick stands, steps to the fridge, opens it and pulls out a can of soda. "How about a root beer?"

"Sure, anything after these salty chips."

I say, "Don't ever let Renee catch you eating junk like this; she'll ream you from here to kingdom come."

He opens the top, takes a long swallow, lets out a loud belch, and says, "What do we men do in the face of feminine intensity? How can we hold our own when in conflict with a woman?" He takes another long drink.

I look at him. "I hope you don't think I have any answers."

He belches again, this time quietly and courteously. I look around, expecting that a woman has walked in.

"Look, Stewy, none of us guys have ever been able to answer that question. It's one of those mysteries that's confounded man since day one."

Nick picks up a clay-spattered carving tool and holds it in the air. "This is where a talking stick comes into play."

"That's no talking stick."

"It is if you and I agree it is."

"What?"

"Shitfire, man, don't you get it? If a strong woman speaks her mind at the moment a problem arises, we must be prepared at all times. You can't have an official talking stick with you all the time."

"You propose that I carry around a clay tool?"

"No, dipshit, I suggest you and Renee grab anything available. Hell, an old kitchen sponge will do, but both of you must agree on its purpose."

My hand comes away from under my chin. I bang my finger on the table. "So, according to you, the stick helps me when Renee has something to say?"

Bob reaches out and pats my arm. "The stick helps slow your drama enough that it won't escalate or get sidetracked. If you can listen to her to the end of her verbal thought process, without interruption, she'll come up with her own conclusions."

Nick says, "If you really think about it, women do it the same way we do. The only difference is we think it out before we speak."

"It's a much better approach," I say.

"I'm not sure."

I drop back in my chair, feeling defeated. "What about me? If I'm supposed to listen to her to the end without comment, when do I get heard?"

Both Bob and Nick say the words simultaneously. "When she puts the talking stick down."

"Oh, right, like she'll honor some little inanimate object like a stick. She needs a sledge hammer or a roll of duct tape to slow her down."

Bob gives me a serious glare. "You can't even think like that, Stewart. It's the 'he said, she said' stuff that'll keep you from moving ahead in your relationship."

"You know what I mean."

"I know you're frustrated."

The three of us are quiet. Bob crushes his empty can and folds it in half. "The talking stick is not a cure-all and it'll take some time to get used to. If you both have intent, it will become an important tool to use during moments of misunderstanding."

I ask, "How long will it take before we learn to use it?"

"Hell, man, right away you'll feel a difference, even though at first both you and Renee will slip up and interrupt each other. In a year or so, you'll have it down."

"A year?"

He gives me a fatherly smile. "Things take time, Stewy. We all have to be patient."

"Why can't we keep using your stick?"

"Because you can't carry the damn thing around with you twenty four hours a day, and you gotta' find a way to express emotion on your own, without any magic crutch."

"It won't be easy."

"Don't you get it? Nothing is easy. If it were, what would be the point of being in a body?"

I raise my eyebrows. "What I hear you say is we must make our own tools and practice our agreements that make the tools work."

"Bingo!" Bob finishes crushing his can. "Instead of everyone getting in line to borrow the stick from Twig, each of you will have a stick whenever you need it."

"What you say is fine, if Renee will agree to it."

"She'll come around. You gotta' be persistent."

"I'd much rather wait in line knowing she'll be forced to agree."

Bob stands, puts a foot on the seat of his chair and leans his right arm on his knee. He studies me before he speaks. "You can't afford to wait."

"What?"

"Think about it. If you wait even five minutes to talk about something, chances are, because there's so much going on in life, you'll forget about it, especially the little things."

I say, "If they're small, there's no problem if I forget 'em."

"That's the insidious part. If you wait, then forget, issues don't disappear; they go underground."

"Underground?"

"They get buried someplace down here." He rubs his belly. "Once down here, it may lie dormant for a week or a month, until something reminds you. When it comes back up, it's disguised as some other issue. It could take hours or days to unravel the truth of what's really bothering you."

"You mean like Renee sometimes brings up things that happened last week, along with another issue from three months earlier and sometimes stuff from years ago?"

Bob smiles. "They're all unresolved issues, buried instead of being cleared up in the moment. Having a talking stick around all the time makes certain that issues don't get buried."

"I get your point. Getting Renee to agree might be another story."

Bob tosses his crushed can into a garbage bag next to Nick's fridge. "For someone who professes to be Mr. Mellow, you sure got a stick up your butt about your wife."

"She isn't that easy to live with."

"Look, pal, neither are you."

"I guess I'm a little perturbed."

Bob whispers, "Use the feather."

I flush.

After a moment of silence, Bob says, "You gotta' carry the message."

"What do you mean?"

"You not only have to convince Renee about this work, but also all of the One on One bikers, then the world. This is important stuff, and you're our point man."

"Not that again."

"You're the one, Stew."

I put both elbows on the table and drop my head in my palms. "Not television again."

Bob pats my shoulder. "Not this time."

I look at him and his face brightens. "Anger is your next step, Stew. Without anger, you're stuck in your perpetual nice-guy act."

I protest. "I've been pretty good these last few years."

"Pretty good, yes," Bob says, "but anger will help you break free. It's your nice-guy act that no one trusts. Ask Renee."

I lift my head and glare. "It's not an act. I'll have you know I'm pretty happy with my life."

He grabs another chip. "Compared to what you had when we met, I agree, things look pretty good, but you've got a long way to go. The feather is your next logical step."

"Oh, shit," I say.

Bob chomps down on a chip. "Pretty frightening, hey?"

"Bone chilling."

Bob stands, like he's getting ready to leave. "All the better reason to get started. Twig can help, and it looks like those two women have made friends. They can help, too. What're you waitin' for?"

My eyes open to a lazy dawn of ochre and sienna. I get up and go into the bathroom. When I come out, Renee is in the kitchen, making a pot of coffee.

I look out my window at a brightening sky, step out onto the front porch and sit on an aluminum-folding chair. I hear the warble of a meadowlark and the distant sound of a coyote paying its last respects to night.

When the door opens, Renee steps over and sits next to me.

She shivers. "It's cold."

"Look out there." I point toward the east.

"Wow, the colors are magic," she says. "There's so much sky in the desert."

I put my arm on the back of her chair and slide my fingers around her neck. "Bob came to me last night."

She looks over. "Me, too."

"He told me what the bowl and its tools are for."

"Yeah, me too."

"You already know?"

"Yes, and you're supposed to tell everyone."

I feel my body freeze. "I guess."

She says, "He also said for you to use the feather."

"Oh, that."

She turns to me. "This whole thing with Bob is so weird, but damn if he doesn't say just what I'm feeling. There are times when I know you're angry about something, but you don't show it. I can feel it, and it drives me crazy. It makes me want to scream when you deny your anger. I'll help, if you want."

"I've been hearing a similar refrain from the One on One guys. For now I'll work it out with my Thursday-night men's group. I need to do it around men to start."

"I understand," she says.

I feel guilty, for leaving her out.

"Maybe when I get a handle on it, I'll be able to express anger in front of you. For now, I don't think I can."

"At least now you know what you can and can't do. It wasn't too long ago that you were clueless. It's easier being with you these days, Stewart, because I don't have to second guess your every move."

"Trust me, Renee, it's easier for me, too."

She rises and goes into the house. A moment later, she brings out two cups of coffee and hands me one. She returns to her seat while blowing air across the steaming liquid. "Are we riding up into the hills today?"

"Yeah, I thought we'd cruise back roads on the bike and look for a house."

She frowns.

"Not that we're in the market right now, only to see possibilities."

"Okay, I'll do it, but no pressure."

"Renee, have I ever been known to pressure you?"

"Lately, yes."

"Well, maybe you're right, but I promise not to try to persuade you on any houses that might show up for sale."

***

I awake and look across the bed at his big lug of a face. His ex-cop, hard-ass bullshit haunts him and us, and sometimes he's a real pain, but I love him. What I love most is his willingness to stick it out. I know I'm no picnic. Why they ever called him Twig, I have no idea. He must weigh in at 250. Twig it is, and I guess Twig it will always be.

His soft snore permeates the room. I look out our window at a tangerine sky. I don't usually wake up early, but Bob came to me last night and told me about the bowl and its tools.

I'm relieved to know Twig and I might find a way past our violence, but taking responsibility for my actions leaves me shaky and unsure.

If I let him, he would sleep until two o'clock, but it's time to go to work. I'm no longer the high-pressured, low-paid sales representative I was two years ago and I'm better off for it, but I have to find more excitement than being a waitress at a local hash joint. Unfortunately, in this town there isn't much else.

He stirs, rolls onto his back and starts into a serious snore.

"Twig?" I shake his furry shoulder. "It's time to wake up."

It takes a minute before he says a coherent word. When he does, he says, "Bob came to me last night."

"Me too."

"He told me what the bowl was all about."

"Me too."

He drops one of his thick-as-a-log arms across my waist and looks at me. "I guess it's to help us with our violence."

"I think so."

"It's good, isn't it?"

I don't answer.

He rubs his eyes. "Can we use the tools the next time we get into a battle?"

I caress his forearm. "The scary part is we'll eventually have to make our own tools, without any of Bob's mo-jo."

He says, "I'm sure we can come to the same conclusions, but it would be much easier to let Bob's magic do the work."

I give him a kiss on his cheek. "I guess easy isn't exactly the point."

In a concerted effort to get up, he pulls the covers back. "We gotta' find a way to take responsibility instead of leaning on Bob. We're not kids, and he isn't our dad."

"Speaking about kids, do you ever want to have kids?"

"Jeez, Melinda, we're still trying to figure out how not to kill each other. Let's talk about kids after we get a handle on our violence."

"You're right, but I want everything to happen now."

Twig sits up in bed and towers over me. "Being together will be easier once we get the hang of it."

"I hope."

He turns his back to me and drops his legs over the edge of our bed. "For now, I'd better get to my shitty-assed job."

"It can't be all that bad."

"Look, Melinda, being a rent-a-cop for the Tangles Rubber Band Company is a far cry from being a Vegas police detective."

"You told me the cop job wasn't good for you."

"It wasn't, but this one is bad for my self-esteem."

I never know how it happens, or what stupid subject causes it. Within the time it takes for Twig to finish his shower and get dressed, we're into another argument and it looks like a big one.

My fists are up, and I'm ready to lay into him, when he runs into our tiny living room, comes back with the talking stick and puts it in front of me.

"Hey, fuck that stick," I scream. He's controlling the situation with his little grab-the-stick trick.

I run at him with my fist drawn, when, and I don't know how, the feather floats in on a gust of wind and stabs me between my first and middle fingers. The second it touches me, I come undone. I swing my arms and stamp my feet. "How dare you try to control me?" I scream, but I can no longer make any movements toward him. I unravel for an excruciating five minutes, until the feather falls from my clenched fist. I drop to my knees in exhaustion. My tears burst like a dam. I have my head on the floor, bent over howling at the crappy avocado carpet.

When I feel Twig's hand on my shoulder, I lift and lace my arms in his. "I'm sorry, Twig; I lost control again."

"It's okay, Honey, we're practicing."

I hold him tight and we rock one another.

Once I've calmed down, I lock my lips on his. We flounder and flop on the carpet in an attempt to rip each other's clothes off. I feel his black fur on my breast. I'm all over him, kissing him everywhere. He surprises me by mounting me in a single quick motion. I roll over on top of him, and we flail across the floor, up to the kitchen wall, until I scream and pull him against me, into me.

For an eternity of thirty seconds, I hear nothing, see nothing, only feel explosions of heat spread from my belly out to the extreme limits of my fingernails and hair follicles. I'm alive.

"Use the talking stick, Melinda." A bomb of a voice goes off inside my head, as I come back to consciousness.

"Don't yell," I say.

Under me, Twig, with a big-faced grin, all his worry lines erased, says, "I didn't say anything."

"You yelled in my ear."

"Not me, Melinda, I was too busy. What did you hear?"

I tell him and he looks at me with an all-knowing expression. "Sounds like Bob."

"Bob never said anything to me."

"Sure he did. The first time you and Stewart were in the desert."

"Oh, right, I remember."

"He wants you to use the stick and so do I."

"Heaven's sakes, is this some kind of male conspiracy to control me by getting me to use that frigging stick?"

He smiles and again all his worry lines disappear. "What's wrong with the stick?"

I stand and glare at him.

"Nothing. It's who is trying to get me to use it. I take no orders from any man, ever. If you want me to use the stick, don't go get it and try to hand it to me."

"Oh, really? What do you have in mind?"

I point my forefinger at him. "I've got to come to a decision on my own, especially in those situations.

"So," he says, "how do I help you come to a decision on your own? We both know the violent side of you wants to beat the crap out of everyone in sight and to hell with the stick."

"I guess you're right. Maybe you could say something like 'popcorn.' It's an unrelated word that reminds me that I want to use the stick without you directly forcing it on me."

"Popcorn? It's kind of trippy, but what the hell, if it'll work."

I say, "It's worth a try."

"I guess I better continue with the work I was doing with that guy from Cazadero. You know, the one who was helping me with my anger."

"Good idea.' I say. "Hey, when are we going to see him?"

"I got a flier from him about a weekend workshop he does at Harbin Hot Springs in the spring. 'Healing the Father Wound' is what he calls it.

Chapter 9

One Percent

After work, I'm back home and relaxing in my living room before I remember it's Thursday afternoon. Our weekly One Percent meeting happens tonight. I look forward to guy's night because, no matter how much I like Melinda, I still have gripes. I need to get help from men on how to deal with my woman. Not that they know much more than I do, but when we all put our heads together, I see progress. When it comes to understanding how the feminine works, especially with a powerful woman like Melinda, I need all the help I can get.

I want to ride my bike to the meeting, but I also need to take the bowl. After a quick sandwich and a number of attempts at putting the bowl in a box and strapping it to my back seat, I pour the sand into a jar, wrap the bowl and tools in a towel, and slide them into my saddlebag.

I get ready to start my engine as Melinda pulls up the driveway.

"Men's group tonight," I say. "See you later."

She reaches over, gives me a kiss and pats my shoulder. I start my engine. She grabs a bag of groceries and climbs the stairs.

I pull out onto our street, idle to the end of the lane, then turn left before I pour on any gas. Gotta' keep it calm for our neighbors. After a day of almost nothing to do as a guard, being in the wind makes me feel alive.

I go through the gears to fourth before I settle down into riding north. I lean into each turn with childlike delight. The drudgery of my job melts away while I roll past open meadows and fields of wild grain.

Halfway through the thirty-mile ride, I break into an old Beatles song. Life, at this moment, couldn't get much better and to top it off, I'm meeting with the One on One guys for an evening of camaraderie and soul searching.

It took us a while to let go of the regular guy talk about sports and bikes, but once we tasted the meaty flavor of "telling it like it is," we all jumped in. Hell, if someone even begins to wander into sports realms these days, he's likely to get a dozen guys down his throat.

The sun drops behind the hills, leaving stringy desert clouds, first in pale lavender, then deeper toward golden oranges. I pull off the highway through a rusted wrought iron gate hanging from one hinge, then drive for three hundred yards along a rutted path. At a decomposing abandoned barn, I turn right and drive past an old homestead that burned to the ground years ago. All that's left is a concrete foundation, with two rusted car bodies next to it. I turn right and drive along a narrow footpath to an old creek bed. Inside the wash, I maneuver my bike and continue to notice the darkening sky. Burgundy tips of clouds reflect an erotic flamingo pink on the ground. I follow the wandering gravel bottom for a quarter mile until it opens to face an ancient beaver dam. Because I'm first to arrive, I park my bike on hardpan, sit in silence, and look at what's left of the fading colors of the sky.

Ten minutes go by before I hear another bike lumber along the ravine. I walk to the old dam, find some pieces of wood and drag them over to a well-used fire pit. On my third journey from the dam, Tazz idles around the bend and pulls his long chrome machine next to mine. When he turns his engine off, I hear two other bikes finding their way down the ravine. In the distance, I hear one bike downshift on the highway.

"Hey, Tazz." I drag a six-inch thick log toward the pit.

"Twig, what's up?" He steps over to the dam and pulls an armful of sticks from a mass of branches.

"All the same shit." I retrieve a bow saw from my left saddlebag and cut the log into usable lengths of wood.

"You bring the bowl?"

"Damn straight. I wouldn't miss this night for anything."

He smiles, drops his wood on the growing pile and goes for more.

I've sawed ten foot-long logs before two more bikes find their way into the clearing and park.

Bucky and Nick step over and pull up the twenty-inch wide cedar rounds we brought in last year for seats.

After a standard greeting, I say to Nick, "Heard you stopped working on bikes."

After a hesitation, he says, "How'd you know?"

"In a dream, where else?"

His smile widens. "It's like living in a fish bowl.

Tazz pulls another log over and drops it in the pile. "Ain't that the truth."

Bucky has a scrunched face and his eyes are dark. I see no smile from the light, playful guy I've seen lately. I ask, "What's up, Buck?"

"I got shit to talk about tonight."

Tazz takes the saw and cuts a bone-dry three-inch-thick scrub oak branch. “This is the place.”

The brilliant colors of the sky have dwindled into a deep plum. With ten minutes of light left and the sound of a half-dozen bikes winding their way along the little wash, I grab some dried brush and twigs, put them into the three-foot-wide pit, and strike a match. I feed the fire with larger pieces until a small blaze dances.

After the six bikes park and the men settle around the fire, Stewart’s bike lumps around the last curve and drops into the parking line. When his engine is off, silence permeates our circle of men. We prepare for another night under the stars.

I walk over to my saddlebag and remove Bob’s bowl and its tools. Next to the fire, outside of the ring of rocks, I pull up a three-inch-thick sliver of an eighteen-inch round and set the bowl in the middle of it.

“What the hell is that?” Bucky asks.

“You’ll see,” I pour the sand into the bottom of the bowl and feel a tense curiosity when I take tongs, pick out the feather and set it upright in the sand.

When the beads are on a small round next to the bowl and the corks are in their four positions of the compass, I place the talking stick across the bowl in its two grooves.

I look up and the sky is ink black. Although sparks fly skyward, behind them I see billions of stars and the Milky Way galaxy.

Tonight is my turn to oversee. I grab a sprig of desert sage wrapped with cedar and pull a stick from the fire to light it. I pick up a well-used hawk feather and fan smoke into the face of each man. I feel safe because of our intent. Our night begins, and everyone falls silent. I speak aloud a short prayer to our ancestors. I bring in our fathers, our grandfathers, their grandfathers, and all beneficial spirits of masculinity to help us with the night. In any other context, it would sound corny, but when the men gather, the words set the stage for seriousness, and bring attention into our fire circle.

One at a time, I honor the four points of the compass, include the fifth, vertical direction and open the meeting with an invitation for each man to speak for a minute. Tazz talks first about Donna wanting to have another baby.

Bucky, who sits across the circle, speaks next about his new girlfriend, Bridgette. He looked her up in Riverside after our dream ride to Reno, and they've been seeing each other for the last week. He asks for time to work on his confusion.

After each man speaks, we start into a more intense part of the night. As leader for the evening, and the leadership changes weekly, I hand Bob's talking stick to Bucky. My throat freezes while he tells a longer version of his tale. At one point his anger rises, but in a flash, he stamps it into submission.

When he sets the stick down and everyone comments about not being able to talk, Stewart explains the stick's abilities.

Once the questions subside, I ask, "Buck, you want to try out another of Bob's tools and give us a demonstration of how it works?"

"Sure, Twig, but what for?"

"Pick up the feather." I point at the smaller seagull feather that stands upright in the sand.

He gives me a suspicious glare. "What's it going to do?"

"It'll help you with your anger."

He nods, gets to his feet and steps over to the bowl. Before he leans down, he points at the bowl. "What's all this about?"

"It appeared the day after our ride to Reno."

A murmur rolls around the circle. Bucky says, "Reno was a dream."

"I know," I say. "This time all of us were in it, but what happened to the weekend if it was just a dream?"

Buck smiles. "Hell, I almost got fired for not showing up on Monday."

Tazz speaks from my right. "Me, too."

I turn toward him. "We all nearly got fired because of Bob's bullshit."

Buck says, "Does he realize who he's fucking up?"

"I don't know, but here we are and there's the bowl. You picking up that feather or do we go on with our evening?"

In one smooth, quick movement, Bucky rips the feather from the sand, then starts into a long peal of passionate anger. He screams, waves his arms, but doesn't move from the center of the circle.

I look around at awe-struck faces, some with curiosity, some, like Stewart, with fear. Each man watches Buck's five-minute display.

When he releases the feather, he stumbles back, trips on an unburned log and falls butt first onto the sand. "What the fuck was that?"

"You tell me," I say. "All I know is Bob left some tools for us. When I used the feather, rage boiled out of me too."

"Shit, Twig, here isn't the place for this kind of bullshit."

"What better place? We're in a circle of men who can be our spotters."

He gets up and dusts his black riding leathers. "Spotters?"

"Like in gymnastics or weightlifting. Someone stands around and keeps an eye out while the person tries a difficult move."

"I didn't do anything difficult."

"You did, Buck. Since I've known you, you've been a raging dick and almost never let it out."

He sits on a wood stump. "Yeah, what's it prove? I'm a man. I don't need to let it out."

I say, "Whose voice is that, your father's or grandfather's? You've stepped over the line into new territory, Buck. You need someone around to watch for potential problems."

Stewart says. "We're all such jive-asses, we need other men who know us and can see through the bull."

Buck glares at Stew. "I wasn't bullshitting."

"Not this time," Stewart says, "but you and I know there have been times for both of us. We're here, like Twig said, to be spotters for one another. To keep us from diving for cover every time things get rough."

I shift position and put my arms on my knees. "Well said."

Stewart grins, then continues. "With real spotters, not only can't we get away with any bull, but we have someone around to help us through when we decide to take the leap into whatever is going on, maybe for the first time in our lives. We also need someone to check on us after."

Buck stares at the fire. "My new girlfriend said she would check on me."

Tazz glares at Buck. "Shit, man, don't you get it? It's not their job. Our women can't support us, because our emotions are too big and dangerous for them. They have no idea what it takes to be a man, and they don't know how to help. When a man goes down into the ashes, he must go with other men who understand."

"Ashes?" I ask.

Tazz turns and looks at me. The fire glistens off of his eyes. "Into our grief. Feel the sadness of life. We must go down into the underbelly of our lives to discover what drives us. If we refuse to pay attention to that part of life, we will forever be hobbled and never find the gift."

Stewart asks, "The gift?"

"It's the ah-ha's in life that can only come from looking deeply. It'll take every one of us in our circle to help stand up to our women without overpowering them or stomping on our own masculinity."

"Isn't that the truth," Buck says in a soft, introspective voice.

The circle is quiet. I let silence sink in before I stand and yell into the night. "I hate my job. I want something more meaningful."

After a moment of stunned silence, Tazz says, "What would that be, Twig?"

I turn toward him. "I don't know. Something that makes me want to get up every morning."

Tazz says, "You got anything in mind?"

"I don't know."

A discussion about career possibilities lasts for ten minutes.

When the last man speaks his mind on the subject, and every man has something to say, our circle falls again into silence.

Three other men do their work before the night is over. My last duty is to designate next week's leader, and I pick Stewart, then close the circle. In ten minutes, we bury the fire and disband. Much work has been done and there is still more to do. It's exciting to be with a group of men who are willing to do it.

I drive home with four of my companions in a tight formation. We weave along the two-lane, with harmonizing engines and the sliver of a moon over my right shoulder. I feel a sense of security.

Memories of my cop days sneak in, and I wonder how I was ever able to survive, alone and isolated in the sea of humanity called the Las Vegas Police Department. I don't remember one person I could trust, but maybe I wasn't that trustworthy myself in those days. The contrast of my lost cop days with this night of close male friendship continues to surprise me.

Tazz and Buck ride thirty feet ahead of the new guy and me. We float through gentle twists and turns of old Highway 66. I'm involved in thoughts of the evening and things men said that apply to my life. I always have a lot to think about after our meetings.

My mind snaps back. My eyes focus as Tazz swerves. His back wheel slips out from under him. At the last possible second, he guns his engine and pulls out of the slide. His bike is still up, and he rolls out of the turn unscathed. Whatever he hit; an oil slick, wet pavement, some dead animal, I'm too close behind him to avoid. I prepare for a crash. I strain to see what's on the road, but see nothing. I attempt to miss the hazard by leaning my bike, knowing any correction at all will be my undoing. I try anyhow. My front wheel loses grip. For a short three feet, the wheel runs sideways, then re-grabs the road. My bike's off balance. My front wheel finds purchase. The bike pulls out. My back wheel hits whatever is on the road. The rear of my bike is at a sudden right angle. I'm going down; the question is, how hard? I give my throttle a twist in a last-second attempt to pull out. The bike responds, but not enough. It's too far out of whack. I continue to drop. I'm on my way down. I take a quick glance out. Lucky there are no cliffs or brick walls. All I see is flat, open desert.

Sparks fly as metal scrapes pavement. As my bike drops on its side, I pull my right leg out from under the engine and slip onto the upward side of the bike. I was going sixty, and it'll take a long time for this ride to end.

My left hand still holds the grip. I move farther onto the bike while it spins with me sitting on top. I watch the new guy hit his brakes. He almost loses control. He's out of sight. I spin and see dark desert, Tazz comes into view, then Buck. The new guy regains control. He drops far behind me. I make another revolution. Desert, Tazz, Buck, open roadway, then the new guy. Back out to desert. The heat of my engine soaks through my pants. I readjust my position to rest on the cooler oil bag. I'm still spinning out of control. I imagine chrome and bike parts scattered across the road.

Somewhere in the darkness, a double yellow line passes under me. I spin across the road. Sparks fly out behind me. I see only blackness in my direction of travel. The edge of asphalt comes too fast. I haven't slowed enough. On the highway surface, I've been able to ride it out. When I hit the sand, I won't slide so easily. I'm ten feet from the sand. Shards of broken bottles and discarded litter reflect off my headlight. In a split-second my back is to the direction of travel. I continue to spin.

In ten feet, something grabs loose dirt and my bike comes to a dusty and abrupt halt. I try to hold on, but momentum pulls me away from the bike. I float through the air, wondering when this insane ride will end.

For a moment, all is silent while I careen through darkness, six feet above the desert floor.

My engine makes a sudden, throttle-wide-open, scream. I try to twist back to see if there's anything I can do. I hope Tazz can get to it before the thing blows up. Hell, I just rebuilt the engine last fall. I'd hate to go through that again. Pipes and other ruined parts will be expensive enough.

My hand hits something spiny in the dark. It brings me back to my problem. My butt smacks a branch. My foot crunches something solid. My face makes the first contact with sand. I tuck one shoulder and momentum spins me into a bush, which shatters. I roll. Will it ever end? In a sudden, bright flash of inspiration, I get a glimpse of what I want to do with my life. It all comes to me between the first contact with sand and smashing into the bush.

I come back from a dark unconsciousness to desert silence. I'm looking up at the Milky Way and see a sliver of the moon still on the horizon. I move my right arm and it's okay. I move my left. Although my collarbone hurts a little, it seems fine. I check one foot, then the other. They work.

Tazz yells from a distance, "Twig!"

I try to respond, but only a small voice is able to call out.

"Twig, where are you?"

I lift my right arm. Branches surround me. I try for another call, but little comes out.

I reach in my front pocket and pull out the lighter we used to strike our fire. Did Bob's bowl survive the crash? Did my bike survive? With the shit wages I make, I can't afford to fix the damn thing.

I lift my lighter in the air and strike it. A short flame bursts into the surrounding blackness.

"I got him!" Tazz yells and runs toward me.

I look around and see why I can't get up. I'm trapped in a web of branches in the middle of a giant creosote bush.

Footfalls come close, and Tazz drops to his knees. "Well, shit, Twig, how did you get in there?"

"I don't know," I whisper, my breath still short. "But I know what I want to do."

"Want to do?"

"I want to quit my fucked-up job and work on bikes."

"Twig, you almost died here and all you can talk about is what you want to do for work?"

"It came out of the blue while I was flying through the air."

Bucky and the new guy arrive. Together, they begin the process of breaking the bush apart to get to me.

When the last branch is removed and I can slip out, I slide on my back into the open night air and sit up.

"How's my bike?"

"I don't know," Buck says. "We were more worried about you."

"Do all of your parts work?" Tazz asks.

I wiggle my fingers and toes, then sit up. "I think so, but I got cactus spines all over me."

"I can imagine," Tazz says. "You were in the air until we couldn't see you any longer."

I attempt to stand, but don't make it.

Tazz grabs my right shoulder and pushes me down. "Hang in there, Twig. Let's take our time here. You went through a lot."

"I gotta' see how bad my bike is fucked up."

Tazz says, "We got plenty of time, so relax."

I sit on the sandy soil, then try to get up. "I'm all right. Let me get up to scope out my bike."

"Have a look at your helmet, Twig and you'll see why I'm concerned."

I unstrap it and inspect a long starburst of a crack starting at the crown. "Looks like I'll need a new helmet."

"Without it, you'd have needed a new head."

By the time I hobble over, Bucky and the new guy have already righted my bike. In the dark it looks unharmed, but I know better.

Buck says, "It don't look too bad. I'm sure it'll start. Your bike always starts. You want me to kick it for you?"

"Yeah, I'm kinda' sore. What did we hit, anyhow?"

Tazz says with a disgusted tone, "Looks like someone changed their oil in the middle of the road."

Bucky sits on my bike, adjusts the distributor to the start position and leaps. All of his weight is on the starter pedal. After three tries, my bike starts and drops into a slow idle. Buck gets off. "You able to ride home?"

"You've done the hard part," I say.

He smiles, walks over to his bike and goes through the same kicks before it comes to life. Once we're back on the road, I feel a pain in my right knee, an ache in my left wrist, and the ever-constant twinge in my collarbone that is still knitting. I don't think I broke anything new, but a lot was going on. Maybe I should have listened to the doc and not ridden my bike tonight.

In town, I wave to my fellow riders, then turn right, away from the pack. A hundred yards later, I make a quick left. The streets are quiet. I pull onto my street, speed up, kill the engine, do a well-rehearsed coast to my driveway and roll to a stop in the garage. I don't want to bug the neighbors. I park, turn on an overhead light and dig into my saddlebag to fish out Bob's bowl. The tools are still okay. I take a quick gander at my bike. One footpeg is worn to a nub; minor scrapes show on my front exhaust pipe; the throttle and grip are mangled and my seat has a small rip. Other than that and a layer of dust, everything else is untouched.

I climb the stairs quietly. It's late and Melinda's asleep. I step inside and set Bob's bowl and its contents on the table. I slip my boots off and undress in semi-darkness before I go to the bathroom. A hundred itchy cactus spines stab me, bruises are forming on my right knee and left elbow and the end of my little finger is raw. Not bad for what I went through.

I take a quick shower and check for any ragged cuts, but find only road burns and minor scratches. I open the bedroom door and slip into bed. She stirs, but doesn't awaken. I'm so tired I drift off instantly; itchy cactus spines and all.

Sometime during the night, I sit up in bed and try to remember why I'd left the lights on. When I look across the room, Bob flashes his big-toothed grin.

"What're you doing here?"

I look over at Melinda, who's still asleep, then get out of bed, dress and follow Bob to the living room. I close the door behind me and whisper, "Why are you here?"

"Hell, Twig, don't you remember, you asked me here.

"Not really." I drop into my recliner.

Bob sits across from me with the bowl between us. He unscrews the jar and pours the sand back into the bowl, then positions each tool in a careful configuration. "You did good tonight when you went down."

"I didn't do much of anything except try to survive."

"The difference is, you did survive. On my first time down, I was dead. You'll be more careful now."

"Shit, Bob, I was always careful. What's your problem?"

"Not always," he says.

"Okay, but more so once I met Melinda. Why are you here?"

Bob places the feather in the sand. "You know."

"It's about work?"

"Bingo."

"I gotta' do something besides guard rubber bands."

He puts into position three of the four corks while he speaks. "I couldn't agree more."

"During the wreck, I thought about working on bikes."

"Good direction, especially since Nick's giving it up. How will you accomplish it?"

"I don't know."

"You've already got the tools and skills. Rent a garage and start doing what you love to do."

He picks up the last cork. "You wondered about the corks?"

I nod.

"Without interrupting, it's to remind a person holding the talking stick to stop telling a story and get down to business. There's no time for stories in a circle."

"You got that right, but how would I do that? The stick doesn't allow anyone else to talk."

"Just pick up the cork and it reminds the speaker."

"Seems too simple."

"It is, but it's effective when you have someone jabbering on."

He puts the cork between his teeth and says, "Cork it."

I point at the bowl. "Two guys tonight dominated the evening with their same old boring story. I wish they could have heard themselves."

Bob puts the cork in the sand and looks at me. "The cork would have reminded them."

"Why four corks?"

"One guy picks up a cork, and maybe he's just getting tweaked by what the man is saying: not that important, especially if the cork-holder is prone to be impatient. If four guys pick up corks at the same time, the speaker has to get the point."

He picks up the beads. "You figured these out yet?"

"Yeah, sure. When two people use them at the same time, they go back to Sattley."

"Yes, it's the magical use, but there is a much more important, longer-term reason."

I lean forward in my chair. "I'm all ears."

"If things get aggressive and dangerous, and when men do work, at any moment, someone might feel threatened or uncomfortable. That person can put the beads on and everyone in the circle must act like he's not there. No one looks at or speaks to him until he feels safe enough to remove the beads. Does it make sense?"

"Perfect sense. Just last night three guys were on one man's case for being such a dick. As usual, he needed to be an idiot first to get to the real issues, but no one could be patient."

Bob leans back and laces his hands behind his head.

I say, "Because he's that way, some men in our group can't stand to let him go through his process, and they attack him every chance they get."

Bob raises one eyebrow. "Not physically, I hope."

"Our agreement is no physical contact during anger, but they gang up and attack verbally, and his safety is often compromised. Over the last year, he's felt so threatened, he left in the middle of two of our meetings."

Bob picks up the beads. "When he puts on the beads, he doesn't have to leave to feel safe. Like the concept?"

I nod.

"Oh yes, after he removes the beads, he can volunteer the reason, but no one can ask him why he put them on."

Bob smiles. "I'm glad you understand. These tools are there to create safety for a man to go into himself and dredge up the muck of his past. Take what I've told you back to your men. Practice the use of these concepts. Get a bowl, find a stick and feather, some beads and get your own corks. Make magic with them, because someday, this bowl and its contents will be gone."

"But, we can't create the same magic as these tools."

"You won't have to. Once everyone agrees to the use of the tools, a different kind of magic will emerge that you can use every day, especially with your women, magical creatures from the get-go."

My eyes open with the brightness of another desert dawn. I lie in bed deep in thought about Bob and his tools. I'm honored he came to me.

When I move, I feel more aches and pains from last night.

I lie for an hour before our alarm forces Melinda to reach up and wack the off button. She turns to me and snuggles into my arms.

"I dreamed of sex with the dishwasher at work," she says.

"You want to have sex with a dishwasher?"

"No," she says, "It was a dream. I like being monogamous with you."

"What is it with women and monogamy?" I ask.

"What do you mean?"

"Why is monogamy so important to a woman?"

"Heaven's sakes, Twig, where did you come up with a question like that?"

"It came up in my men's group last night and I'm curious."

She turns on the bed and stares at me. "Twig, what happened to your face?"

"Oh, nothing."

"Don't say 'nothing.' You've got a huge scrape across your cheek. You look like you had sex with a bobcat."

I tell her a shortened version of last night's adventure, and she pulls the covers back, inspects me and comments on every little scratch. I would never have considered paying so much attention to minor injuries. "Enough," I yell. "Stop mothering me."

The room is silent, so I ask about monogamy again.

"Why," she asks, "do you have some other woman you want to have sex with?"

I'm in a feisty mood and I snap back a quick response. "Hell Melinda, because we aren't having much sex these days, I've got about ten women I want to jump."

"Why you son of a bitch." She's ready to scratch my eyes out.

I try to finish my sentence, but she's off on a tirade, ranting about what dogs men are.

I leap out of bed, run into the living room and snatch up the talking stick. Thank God, the house goes silent.

In the bedroom, she sits where I left her. Her face is red. Her mouth moves, but she can't make a sound.

I sit across from her in the rocking chair she brought when she moved in. "If I could ever finish a sentence, you might understand what I want to say before you jump to conclusions."

She strains to say something. Blessedly, no sound emerges.

"I fantasize about jumping ten other women, but I want you. Because you have this monogamy issue and are adamant about your view, I choose not to have sex with other women. I do wish we could have sex more often."

Reluctantly, because I know the silence will be replaced by a high-pitched rant, I put the stick on the bed next to her. Ten seconds of unintelligible babble runs out of her mouth until her thoughts clear. When she gets through her verbal chaos, she looks at me and says, "I'm afraid if you have sex with another woman, you'll fall in love with her and leave me. When we do have sex, unless I get angry first, it's flat and never very good. Compared to other women, I feel inadequate."

"Melinda, I want to be with you. Sex has nothing to do with me wanting to be with you."

"What are you talking about? Sex has everything to do with love."

She spoke that dangerous four-letter word, and I try not to flinch.

She looks directly into my eyes. "In any normal situation, anger aside, I would never have sex unless I considered love first."

"What about with Stewart, two years ago?"

"Stewart was different. Bob had a plan, and he was guiding me."

"Do you always do what Bob says?"

"Don't you?"

I take a moment to think. "Okay, I'll give you that. Whatever Bob says, I pretty much do. You mean to tell me he wanted you to have sex with Stewart?"

"Yes and look what came of it."

"What's that?"

"Two things changed Stewart's approach to life; sex with another woman, and going into the fire to save Nick's mother. He's turning into a full-fledged man and not the mouse he was when we met him."

"You might be right," I say.

I want to go back to the first subject, though I know it's a bottomless pit. "Do you mean to tell me you would only have sex if love were a part of it? You'd never have sex for fun?"

"Never, and I don't know many women who would."

"Sweet Jesus," I moan, "I don't want to hear this."

"For heaven's sakes, Twig, why?"

"Because if I accept that few women have sex just for fun, I can never, with a clear conscience, ever have sex with another woman just for the fun of it."

She looks at me with a puzzled expression. "You never knew?"

"No, and I still don't believe you. I'll ask other women to get a consensus, before I can trust what you say. This is much too big. It's way too depressing."

"Depressing?"

"To know I can never have sex again with another woman for fun. To know they're serious, though they act like it's casual."

"You won't have sex with another woman, anyhow," she yells. "Not and stay with me."

Oops, I stepped into a big pile. "No, Melinda, though I don't agree with your monogamy rule, I--"

She reaches down and picks up the stick. My larynx freezes. "Look here, you even think about sex with another woman and you and I are done. I'll walk so fast your head will spin. You got that? I don't give a rat's ass if you don't agree with my monogamy rule, you step even one single toenail over the line and we're finished." She throws the stick on the bed and stands. "I have to go to work. I want you to think about this subject." She stomps off into the bathroom and turns on the shower.

I follow. "Melinda, if I could ever get a single sentence finished before you interrupt, you might hear my full intent."

She turns toward me in a warrior stance. "Okay, what were you saying?"

I look at her eye to eye. "Although I don't agree with your monogamy rule, I want to be with you, and I want to continue being with you. I'll abide by your archaic, possessive rule, but," I add the "but" quickly, because she's ready to interrupt again. "I need to understand why it's important to women. I don't have a clue."

She softens. Her face relaxes. "We need to talk about it more, because I too don't understand what makes men want to go elsewhere to dip their little wickets. Right now, I got to get ready for work. Let's put this conversation on hold." She gives me a full-lipped, mouth-watering kiss, turns, adjusts the shower temperature and steps in.

I'm left with my rising manhood. By the time she towels herself off, my immediacy has lessened, and I sit on the bed.

She steps to her dresser and pulls out her blue panties.

I love watching her dress.

Once I've showered, I see she's put on the yellow blouse and my favorite pedal pushers. She walks out of the bedroom, and asks, "What do you want for breakfast?"

I look at my scraggly beard in the mirror and yell, "Couple of eggs and toast would be all right." I pull my hand along one side of my face, stroke my beard into position and promise to trim it in a day or so.

Teeth brushed, hair combed, fresh clothes on, I step into the kitchen and sit for another delightful Melinda breakfast. She's not the best of cooks, but eggs and toast are pretty easy, and I appreciate her efforts, especially when she's busy getting ready for work.

We sit in an unaccustomed silence across from each other at the little wooden table. She sips her coffee and eats. I take the last few bites of toast and look at the clock.

"Hey, I got to get to work." I stand, walk over to her side of the table and kiss her cheek. "See you tonight."

She grabs my shirt, pulls me closer and gives me a lip-lock tongue-lash of a kiss; enough to get me through the day.

"See ya." She kisses me again on my cheek, then lets me go.

I walk out the front door, down my rickety stairs, into the garage and mount my bike.

Work is a blur. Nothing happens in a small town. The most excitement is when I check the ID of some big mucky-muck lard-butt, corporate bean counter. All he can do is make a negative comment about my long hair and beard.

I make it through the day and get on my bike, then roar out of that boring hellhole. All day I've thought about setting up a repair shop. I could do it, I know I could, but taking a leap of faith is frightening.

During the short fifteen minutes it takes to get home, I feel free again.

Melinda isn't around.

I get a chicken out of the refrigerator, cut it into sections and spread the pieces on the broiler pan. Sprinkling on some seasoning, I pop it into the oven.

While I get rice prepared to cook, she walks up the creaky stairs and opens the door.

She sets a bag of groceries on the counter and puts things away. I grab a mineral water and drop into a kitchen chair.

"How was your day?" I ask and we go into an extended back and forth, catching up on our boring days at work in a not-too-exciting town. It's a regular day in our lives. Nothing stands out, but the act of sharing brings us closer.

"Let's go for a long ride after dinner," she says.

Before I know it, we're floating along a wide-open road, rolling out the miles in a tunnel of light, with a billion stars overhead.

The hot night air whips at my beard while Melinda snuggles into my back, pressing herself to me. I look in my mirror for police, then crank the throttle wide open for twenty seconds, while my bike tops a hundred.

The broken lines blur into a single ribbon down the middle of the straight two-lane.

When I let off the gas and allow my bike to slow to normal cruising speed, I feel alive for the first time today. Maybe I cheated death again and that's being alive. Maybe it's the wind. Whatever it is, I'm left in awe of living for the twenty seconds it took to open up the bike.

"You drove way too fast for me," Melinda says. "It scares me."

I'm still in biker heaven and say nothing, but squeeze her thigh to acknowledge I've heard her.

We ride into a desert canyon, make long, sweeping leans into turns and slip between rock formations the size of small skyscrapers. The crescent moon reflecting off the boulders gives the iridescent landscape an eerie quality.

Melinda points out a strange formation called Indian Head Rock, and I marvel at the accuracy of the name, especially in the moonlight.

We reach the top of the canyon, and I turn my bike around to face an open desert. I pull to the shoulder and kill my engine.

While we sit listening to the cooling tick, tick of the bike, Melinda says, "It's quiet up here."

"Victorville's sounds don't reach this far out," I say.

"Is this what earth is supposed to sound like without the intrusion of humanity?"

"There aren't many places left," I say. "It makes you think, doesn't it?"

"About what?"

"How it would be to live in this kind of silence every day."

She hugs me. "It's nice, but it would drive me crazy."

"Why's that?"

"It's too quiet."

"Sorry to hear that, because some day I'd like to live in a silent environment like this and see what would happen to my nervousness."

She looks around my left shoulder at the side of my face. "You don't seem nervous to me."

"Maybe not on the outside, but my insides are a trembling mass of Jell-O. The only time my inner anxiety subsides is when I ride."

She drops back onto her seat. "I guess because we're in absolute quiet, I feel anxiety creep in. It's funny, but if we lose the trappings of civilization, we open up to the possibilities of feeling our fragile, desperate lives."

I don't answer, because she may have nailed my feeling. She sees and articulates in a minute what I've struggled to comprehend all the years I've come here.

I bask in silence for another fifteen minutes, look out over the distant lights of Victorville, then northeast toward Barstow.

When I reach over to fire up my bike, she puts her hand over mine and pulls it away from the ignition. "Let's stay a little longer. I'm getting used to it."

"Hell, Melinda, let's build a house here."

She pulls up closer to my back and nuzzles her nose up to my ear. "I'll make some extra tips at the restaurant, and you can take on another guard job."

"I'd do it for a place up here."

"You'd kill yourself in the process."

"Maybe I'll be a cop again. The pay's much better."

"Over my dead body." She gives me a playful squeeze.

"Well, actually I've been thinking about working on other people's bikes."

She slips her fingers inside my jacket, finds an opening in my shirt and slides in her chilly hand. "You are certainly good at it, and I know it makes you happy."

We look at the moon on the horizon and the city lights. She lays her head sideways on my back, pulls herself up closer and caresses my belly with a single digit. "I love you, Twig."

Oh, sweet Jesus, she said it. She said the "L" word for the first time. We've made it eight months without having to go there. The word is out, and I'm petrified.

I want to change the subject. I want to start my bike and drown the word out, obliterate it, shatter it.

It's been used too many times in my past, just before disaster happens, before the woman leaves with some other guy. Those are words of death.

"What's wrong, Twig?" she asks.

"Nothing."

"Something's wrong, because you've tensed up, and you're not breathing."

I let out a long breath I didn't know I'd held.

We go through five or six exchanges, I go deeper into my fear of abandonment and she attempts to reach me. Finally, I blurt out the words, "You said you love me."

"Yes and so?"

"You said words of disaster."

"It isn't a disaster to say I love you, Twig, because I do."

"Oh, shit," I say and reach for the ignition.

She dismounts the bike and steps around the front to face me.

I frown. "Whenever someone's said that to me, they've left."

"I'm not leaving you, Twig."

"That's what they all said."

She takes me in her arms and pulls me close. I feel weak and don't try to pull away. I rest my head on her shoulder.

"I had a feeling the word would frighten you. It's why I've refrained from using it. Hell, Twig, we've been together too long not to start talking about these kinds of things."

In a small voice I say, "You're going to leave?"

"I'm not going anywhere, Twig, because I have a surprise, but I've been afraid it might make you even more tense."

She pulls herself back, reaches under my chin and lifts my head until I'm forced to look her in the eyes. With a serious expression on her face, she says in a nervous teenage titter, "I went to the doctor last week, and he says I'm pregnant."

I feel woosy.

"We don't have to go through with it," she says. "Say you don't want to, and I'll take care of it."

When I can say something, it's with a schoolboy stutter. My words are hard to articulate and don't make much sense. All I can get out is, "Yes, I want to be pregnant."

"I'm pregnant, silly, not you."

"I. . .I. . .want you to be pregnant, but how did it happen?"

"You know, the ol' dick and pussy stuff or don't you remember?"

"Oh."

She pulls me close and my emotions bubble. In a burst of happy tears and kisses, I say, "You're not leaving me?"

"I love you, and since you want to have our baby, I'm not going anywhere."

"I guess I have to get a better job."

"Twig, relax. For now, let's just enjoy the moment."

My mind churns with the responsibility of bringing a child into the world: get him clothes, set up a college fund, get him a car and watch him go off with a woman of his own. I've got some kind of preparation to do, and I'd better start now.

"Earth to Twig," she says, in the distance. "Where are you?"

She's still in my arms on the hill over Victorville.

"I'm right here, Melinda."

"You're not. Your body might be here, but your mind went to the moon. What were you thinking?"

"We'd better get back to the house, Melinda, I've got things to do."

"Look, you big lug, we don't have to rush into having our baby. We have eight and a half months before she's due, and we can take a moment to be here together."

"She?" I say. "You said she."

"I don't know for sure yet, but I have a feeling."

A small cloud of disappointment fogs my euphoria. It doesn't matter. I just want a healthy baby. I'll miss the baseball games and teaching him to drive a hawg. But hell, with Melinda as her mom, she'll own a Harley shop and run for president.

I try to stay on the side of the hill, but my mind makes back flips with all of the things I need to do before our baby arrives. Eight months, I'll need eight years. If I start now, I might have enough time to prepare, but I'm not sure.

I hold Melinda, but say nothing. My head reels.

Chapter 10

Obsession

It's been a week and a half since my encounter with the bowl at Twig's apartment, and I can't get it out of my mind. I stayed with Stewart longer than I should have, and the week was half over before I caught a Wednesday flight back to Sacramento.

Once I got home, kids and life in general consumed my every moment. Sometimes I resent Stewart for hiding out in that little cabin while I'm caught up in family matters. I'd like to trade him, leave all the responsibility at work and come home to a silent house.

His offer of a home in the hills by Big Bear is intriguing, and the houses we looked at had merit, but it will be hard to pull up stakes again and start anew.

I sit in the kitchen and wait for the kids to come down for breakfast. I have a piece of toast partially-buttered when my phone rings.

"Hello," I say, in more of a sleepy voice than I'd like.

"Hi, Honey."

"Stewart, why are you calling this early?"

"I miss you."

"You do?"

"Yes, and I called to tell you I'll be home tonight after work."

"Stewart?"

"Yes?"

"I thought I'd come down there, if it's okay?"

"Sure, Honey, but isn't it my turn?"

"I'm beginning to like it down there, especially if we're looking for a place in the hills. I also want to have another look at Bob's bowl."

"The bowl? What for?"

"The feather brought up a lot of stuff, and I'd like to have another go at it."

"Well, okay. When will you come down?"

"Tonight. I got Mary to stay the weekend with the kids. I'll catch a flight after work."

"Call me with your flight number and time, and I'll meet you in San Bernardino."

He's about ready to hang up, so I slip in a few last words, "Stewart?"

"Yes?"

"I love you."

"I love you, too, Honey. I can't wait for you to get here."

"Me too."

"I have to get to work," he says, and the line goes dead.

After the kids are out the door and on the bus, I sit for a precious moment of silence and sip my second cup of coffee.

I won't miss our house. I never liked this cookie-cutter dump in the first place. The layout is all wrong, and it's too close to the road. I'll be more careful with our next house.

By six-thirty that night, I'm in the air, and an hour later I peck Stewart on his cheek.

"I'm starved," I say, while he loads my two bags in the trunk of his old rattle-trap car. "Can we stop somewhere to eat?"

"Sure, Hon, no problem. There's a good Asian place and it's less than a mile from here." He slams the trunk, bounces around to the driver's side and gets in before I can think to open my door. He's much too eager.

"What's up?" I ask when I'm in and he starts the engine.

"Buckle your belt, and I'll tell you."

I fish the two ends of the belt and snap them in place while he pulls into the airport traffic. I look at him. "What's up?"

"I found it."

"What do you mean?"

"Our new house. I can't wait until tomorrow to show you."

I'm tired and a bit cranky. I don't feel his exuberance. "You found a house without me? Stewart Chance, the last house you found without me, I hated. This time I'll be part of the decision. You got that?"

"The ultimate choice is yours," he says, "but you'll like this one. It's incredible."

He pulls through the green light and turns left, shifts through the gears and makes a right onto the freeway, headed toward Barstow. The car is up to speed and I say, "I thought we were going to eat."

"We are. The Restaurant is a half-mile off the next ramp."

In the relative quiet, I say, "What's it like?"

He looks over at me with a shine in his eyes. "Like nothing you've ever seen. An architect built it for his family in the sixties. It's very deco."

"Deco? I hate deco."

"I know," he says, "but you won't hate this place."

"We'll see," I say under my breath.

The food is on our table and I've slipped a bite in my mouth before I feel better. I want to be more civil. I say, "So, describe your dream house."

He perks up, inhales some Chow Mein and talks with his mouth full. “It sits a quarter mile from a back road on the north side of the mountain, and it overlooks a hundred miles of desert. The house rests under six massive valley oak trees, which will give us a lot of shade in summer.”

“Oaks in the desert?”

“They’re valley oaks, and the house is on the side of a mountain, at about three thousand feet. The best part is, it’s got a swimming pool for the kids.”

“I’m sure they’ll like the pool, but I’m not sure they’ll like the desert.”

“Three thousand feet is above the desert, Renee.”

He goes into more detail, but I barely listen. My thoughts are on the feather in Bob’s bowl. I haven’t been able to get it out of my mind since I picked it up. Now that I’m closer to it, my impressions are stronger and more insistent.

I interrupt his monologue. “Does Twig still have the bowl?”

“Sure he does, but what’s that got to do with the house?”

“Can we borrow it for an evening while I’m here?”

“Maybe.” He looks at me. “You okay, Renee?”

“Yeah, I’m all right. I wonder about the bowl is all.”

“A little obsessed about it, are we?”

“No, just curious.”

“Don’t worry about it. You’re not the only one who is tormented by that bowl and its tools these days. Half of the One Percent guys have lined up to use it with their wives and girlfriends.”

“We can use it, can’t we?”

“I don’t know. I’ll have to make some kind of deal to get it this weekend, but I think we can figure something out.”

I don’t hear much for the rest of our meal, and the drive to Stewart’s cabin is like a dream. Maybe I’m tired or maybe the feather is calling to me. The closer I get, the more intense it is.

I toss all night, unable to get much rest. In the morning, while sitting at breakfast, I bring up the subject of Bob's bowl again. Stewart smiles and grabs the phone.

When he hangs up and looks over, I pick at my cold eggs.

He grins. "You've got it bad, Renee. Maybe it's not a good idea to use the bowl this weekend."

"Don't mess with me, Stewart."

He smiles. "We'll have to go to Tazz and Donna's to get it."

I take a bite of toast. "I believe the feather is the key."

"For some people, yes, but for me it's the talking stick. The feather has no appeal."

"Well, of course not, Stewart."

"What do you mean?"

"You're frightened of anger."

"Not you, too." He gets up and puts another piece of bread in the toaster. "I'm not frightened of anger."

"Come on, Stewart, admit it; you're scared to death of that feather."

When he sits down, his face has gone two shades grayer. He takes a deep breath, then exhales. "Maybe everyone's right. Isn't it funny? I'm scared and you're obsessed."

I reach over and put my hand on his. "I guess we'll get the chance to do something about it tonight."

He makes an obvious attempt to change the subject. "Today we ride out and look at the house. I can't wait for you to see it."

I let the subject of the feather drop, and we talk about other things through breakfast.

The cruise up into the hills is heavenly. After a week of being cooped up in my office, I enjoy the freedom of a ride along the curvy back road. We overlook the valley, and I see a hundred-mile view onto open desert. When we get high enough, oak and scrub trees shade parts of the roadway.

Stewart slows his bike and turns left onto a gravel road. I comment on how perfect the hillside is, and how much it reminds me of our area above Sacramento.

The dirt road is flat for a quarter mile past five homesteads, until it ends at a modern, low-roofed house. The building has odd, but beautiful lines that remind me of an old automobile. Intricate lattice made from painted wood trim looks like the grille of a 1930's car. A large, half-round roof partially overhangs three semi-circular decks.

We pull up, and I see terraced gardens in the same round motif. They work their way down from the front deck in a fan pattern, all the way to the lower patio, on an open hillside three stories below. Everything overlooks the desert.

I get off the bike and walk over the lawn.

"What do you think?" he asks.

"It's something."

"The back decks are even better."

We walk across the front patio. A small semi-circle of textured concrete sweeps around the side of the house. I take a fast glance through double-pane glass into a bedroom.

"No one lives here?"

Stewart cups his hands on the glass to look past the glare into the bedroom. "The wife died eight months ago, and no one was left to care for the place. It was donated to some foundation."

"Donated?" I pull away from the glass and stroll down the walk.

Stewart follows. "Wait until you see the back side of this place. It's like living in a forest."

We move along a concrete patio, two steps up onto a redwood deck and walk over to the far rail. I gaze down a fifty-foot drop and into a wooded area with six huge oaks that not only shade the deck, but also half of the house.

I walk back to the sliding glass door and look through the open curtains. "Can we go inside?"

He looks at his watch. "I don't have a key, but the real estate woman is supposed to meet us in a few minutes."

Our look around is inspiring, all the way down to a half-moon shaped pool.

I stand on the far edge of the lower deck and look back at the house. "The half-circle shapes are a little odd, but whoever designed it did a great job."

Stewart says, "The architect designed it for his family. You can tell his heart was in the place."

"I don't know if I can get used to its shape repetitions."

"I know what you mean. I spent a whole day here last week, though, and it grows on you."

He grabs my hand, and with schoolboy exuberance, pulls me upstairs. "I want you to see this part."

When we get to the second level, he coaxes me over to a large bay window with curved glass like the old Victorian houses in San Francisco.

"Look in here." He points through the glass at a circular column of smoothed desert rocks, artistically mortared to surround a huge open firepit. "Smoke goes up the center," he says, "and it's accessible from three rooms."

I put my hands up to shade my eyes and lean against the glass. "It's very beautiful, but why would you need a fireplace in the desert?"

"Oh, it gets cold here, too, just not as often."

On a gentle breeze, I hear the crunch of tires on gravel.

Stewart grabs my hand. "Let's go meet her."

We cross the deck and climb a remaining flight of wooden stairs to the top level. A fire-engine-red Mercedes pulls into the circular driveway and parks next to Stewart's bike. When she gets out, she yells an over-enthusiastic greeting. "Hello, Mr. and Mrs. Chance. How are you today?"

In an over-exaggerated walk of self-assuredness, balanced on two-inch heels, she steps up and gives me a vise-grip of a handshake. "I'm Kay Albright."

With Pomeranian-like nervousness, she grabs a small ring of keys from her purse. "Did you look at the back decks?"

"Yes," Stewart says.

"Good. Let's have a look inside, shall we?"

She unlocks and opens one of two eight-foot-high, half-round solid black wooden doors.

"You've stepped onto imported Italian marble in this entry, Mrs. Chance, and this teak bench was carved in the Philippines." We walk past the bench and she points up. "Don't forget to look at the crystal chandelier. It. . ." Her constant narrative continues while we wander from room to room. The living room opens to the semi-circular wall of curved windows we saw from the deck. Enough tree branches were removed to give a long-range view of desert. The house may have been designed with a flair for style, but the kitchen was designed by someone who cooked: lots of room, with islands and a restaurant-style stove-and-oven combination.

We stand in the dream kitchen with the yappy woman nipping at our heels. I look at Stewart and whisper, "Can we afford this?"

His face breaks into a goofy grin. He reaches for my right hand and pulls it up to his lips, gives me a small peck on my palm, then looks at me. Between the woman's ceaseless descriptions, he says, "I haven't checked the numbers for sure, but I think we can."

I'm forced to follow the woman through every lower-level room and hear about faucets and toilet seats.

Forty-five minutes later, Stewart peels us away from her squeaky voice. He starts his bike and drowns out her attempts to describe the type of grass in the lawn. We drive away, and I look back. Her mouth is still working.

After we're back on pavement, Stewart idles downhill on the winding two-lane. He turns his head. "She was like that the first time I met her. The woman never quits. I'd love to use Bob's talking stick with her."

"Maybe next time," I laugh.

"Next time," he says. He pulls over, turns off the engine, then rotates toward me. "Does that mean you like it?"

"I don't know, but I'd like to have another look. How do you think we can afford it?"

"It'll be a stretch, but when we bring both households back together, payments will only be a little over two hundred dollars more a month than what we're paying now, if you account for our weekly travel expenses."

"Odd shapes, but the guy did a great job. I love the kitchen, and it has a view to die for."

"The kitchen? Renee, I haven't seen you in a kitchen more than ten minutes at a time since I can remember. Why would the kitchen be such a draw?"

"I'm not sure, it must a woman thing. A functioning kitchen, whether I use it or not, is high on my list and this one has the right stuff. I'd like to see it without the realtor around."

"Maybe we'd better look again tomorrow morning before you go back to Sacramento."

"Okay, how do we do it without her?"

"We'll bring the talking stick."

"Oh, my god, Stewart, you're serious."

He smiles, turns and starts his engine. When he pulls onto the pavement, I whisper in his ear, "I love you."

The bike leans into a gentle turn, and he reaches one hand back to pat my outer thigh.

After forty-five minutes of dodging tumbleweed and being buffeted by a brutal crosswind, we enter the first speed zone of Victorville. Once we've slowed, I say, "Maybe when we sell our house, we can take a little money and buy a small bike for me."

He turns with a surprised look. "Really?"

"I've thought about it, and I'd like to learn how to drive."

He cracks a wry expression and pulls off the road into a huge empty parking lot of an abandoned grocery store.

"What are we doing?" I ask.

He pulls to the middle of the lot and comes to a halt. With the engine idling, he turns to me. "You could take a first lesson now."

"Oh no, not now."

"Why not?"

"Because I want to start out on a smaller bike, like a Honda."

"It's not rocket science, Honey. A bike is a bike. The only difference is if you drop mine, it's harder to pick it up."

"It's way too big."

He turns his engine off, unfurls the kickstand and leans the bike into a park position. He gets off and crosses his arms in front of his belly. "Just sit in the driver's seat."

"I don't think so, and stop pushing."

"What's the harm in sitting in the driver's seat? You don't have to start the engine."

"Okay, okay." I slide forward and drop down three inches into a wide leather seat. I reach out for the handlebars.

He points at the seat. "This bike is slung low enough that even you could put your feet on the ground and lift it up to balance."

I give him a glare, but I've always been curious about what it would feel like to sit up front and how heavy the bike really is.

He steps back two feet. "Go ahead and lift it."

I put my feet on the ground and with less strain than I can believe, I lift it to balance. "It's not bad."

"It's in neutral." He says, "Turn the key and tap the starter button on the right handle bar." He steps forward and points at a small black button.

"I'll just sit for a moment, if you don't mind."

"It isn't any big deal, Honey. The bike won't go anywhere until you pull on the clutch." He points at the left handle bar, then moves his finger to a small foot lever. "This is the shifter."

Before I realize what he's doing, he snakes his hand over and rotates the key.

"I'm not starting the bike," he says. "I thought that because you're here and the bike is in position, it would be a logical next step to feel it idle under you. You don't have to go anywhere."

"Stop pushing, Stewart Chance. I'll go no further and that's that." I've said my firm no, but I sense curiosity slip under my resolve. How would it feel, anyhow?

Without thinking, my thumb touches the starter button. The bike comes alive.

"Holy shit," I scream. I want to turn it off, but I'm afraid to let go of the handlebars. "Turn it off, Stewart!"

Instead of helping out and grabbing the key, he steps back with a grin.

I feel flutters of fear creep up my throat, constricting my ability to speak. The engine idles, but the bike doesn't move. After a minute, I'm more used to it, especially since it isn't going anywhere.

He says, "Relax into it and sit on the seat."

"I am sitting."

"You're standing. Let that cute butt of yours drop down onto the seat."

I glare at him. "You keep my butt out of it." I drop down two inches, and the seat forms around my bottom.

"Relax, Honey. It isn't going anywhere until you tell it to."

"Okay, okay," I shout. "Stop badgering me."

The whole thing makes sense; the fit, the design of the bike itself and its rumbling engine. I have a desire to feel the thing move under me, but that's going a bit far. I sit motionless.

"Turn the throttle, Honey, it won't bite."

My hand twists the right handle grip like Stewart does, and the engine comes to life. "Oh Jesus," I scream and let go of the grip. The engine slips back to idle. "This is enough. I've had enough. Turn it off, Stewart."

"You can turn it off. Let go of the grip and turn the key. The bike isn't going anywhere."

"What if it falls?"

"It won't fall. You can do it. Just in case it gets away from you, I'm right here to help."

In a quick movement from right grip to key and back, I twist the ignition and, thank God, the engine dies.

"When you're done, put the bike back on its kickstand. It's already out. Lean to the left."

In a controlled dash for the pavement, the bike begins a short fall, then drops its weight against the kickstand, and for the first time in five minutes, I relax. "That was hair-raising."

He beams with his familiar childlike exuberance. "But it was cool, wasn't it?"

I feel flushed, out of breath, like I've just seen a dream dress in a shop window. "Yes, I guess it was."

He stands beside me while I relax on the seat. Something is special about the moment: a crystal-like clarity, like after my experience four years ago on the freeway. All of those cars slammed on their brakes and slid sideways. The breathlessness of watching them make contact. They spun around in slow motion. The smoke and crumpled metal. I sat in the middle of a fifteen-car pileup without one scratch. I couldn't move until the ambulances were gone and tow trucks hauled off the wreckage. The whole time, I was in some sort of twilight zone, an out-of-body experience. I feel the same way now, without the carnage.

"How was it?" he asks.

"Terrifying and wonderful at the same time."

"Sure you don't want to drive?"

"Not on your life. This was more than enough for now. I'm already on overload."

I slide to the back seat. "Let's go see Tazz and Donna."

He swings his leg over and settles onto the seat. After I've experienced sitting in the driver's seat, I have a different view of its magic. For the first time I watch carefully when Stewart starts the engine, pulls the clutch, and taps the shift lever with his foot. It makes sense.

When he lets the clutch out, the bike moves into a long wide circle until we face Main Street. He rolls out of the parking lot and makes a right.

"Watch out, world," yells Stewart, "Renee's on the loose with a Harley."

What a dork.

***

I almost got Renee to take the bike for a spin. I knew if I pushed further, she would have given in and tried it, but she was at her limit and it wouldn't have been a positive experience. It felt good to trust my instincts and nudge her along, though she kept saying no. In the past, I would never have pushed.

She might be the first woman in our group to want to learn how to drive a bike. It's the last thing I ever expected, but she's done a lot of unexpected things in the last two years. Hell, she wants to move down here, which is crazy enough.

We cruise along Main until I turn onto Fourth, then left on Maple and into Tazz and Donna's driveway. When I park, Tazz pokes his angular face out the back door. "What are you guys doing here?"

"Come to visit, like any self-respecting 'burb' dweller would do on a Saturday."

"Get outta' here."

We climb five concrete steps, and I bang fingertips with him while Donna greets Renee with a shy nod.

They lead us into the kitchen and Tazz offers a beer.

"Non-alcohol?" I ask.

"What other kind is there?" He opens his fridge and pulls out one of those fancy imports.

"Renee, you want one?" he asks.

"Sure."

"Donna?"

"No, Hon, go ahead."

Tazz gives Renee an open beer, hands one to me and sits in the remaining chair. "What brings you guys down here?"

"We heard you had Bob's bowl, and we thought we might borrow it tonight."

"Holy shit, that bowl is wild," Tazz says. "You get a chance to use it yet?"

"Not every part."

"Man, it's incredible. It helped Donna and me get through a big disaster we'd worked on since the dawn of time. When she picked up the feather, everything came clear and we could talk about it. Right, Babe?"

She glares at him as she crosses her thick arms over her wide chest. "We agreed you would quit calling me that name."

"Oh, I forgot."

Renee picks up the talking stick. My throat constricts. The only sounds are Tazz and Donna's two boys in the other room making fire-engine noises.

Renee says, "I find it hard to even pick the stick up. A big part of me feels like I don't deserve to have your attention." With her index finger, she bats the single animal tooth that hangs from the center of the stick.

Renee looks at me. "I've heard too little about your Thursday night meetings, and maybe I'm all right that it's some kind of guy secret, but it's high time we women were included in some portion of those so-called gatherings."

In a dramatic finish, Renee folds the tooth parallel to the stick and sets it down.

No one reaches for it, but Tazz finds his voice first. "Well, shit, Renee, this morning Donna and I talked about something right along those lines." He nods to his wife.

Donna pulls at a strand of dishwater blond hair and makes a half-hearted attempt to smooth it into her ponytail. "I thought more like only us women would meet, and screw you obnoxious guys."

"Babe, I'd like to include you--"

She reaches out and grabs the stick. Tazz is silent the second she picks it up. "Look, you asshole," she says. "You call me that name too many more times, and there won't be much left of your balls come morning. You get my point?"

When she sets the stick down, Tazz says, "You don't have to get graphic."

"Sometimes it takes a graphic threat to get through to you."

He puts his hands up. "Hell, you told me about your gripe just yesterday. I've called you 'Babe' for twelve years. It'll take a bit of getting used to."

She glares at him with her big brown eyes. "Don't get used to it, just do it."

I look at Renee and she at me. She speaks a short sentence in the second pause between their bickering. "A men/women thing might be what we all need."

We all look at her.

"Stewart and I go through the same struggles and it would be helpful to bounce them off other couples."

It's enough to break the standoff between Tazz and Donna.

As if to clear cobwebs, Tazz rubs one of his callused hands across his face. "What do you think, maybe we call the guys and see if the women could join us once in a while?"

Donna's desert tanned face crinkles. "It's better if we women talk to each other without you jerk-offs to muddy things up."

"Sounds good to me," I say. "You got phone numbers?"

"I got 'em," Tazz says.

"Okay, Donna, maybe you call the women and we guys'll stay out of it."

Donna puts one hand on her wide hip. "How about I call if I want, and you try your hardest not to direct me?"

Stewart raises his arms in an "I give" posture, but says nothing.

After another awkward silence, she says in a quiet voice, "It's my period. I get a little hypersensitive before my period."

Renee points at me, then to Tazz. "Don't apologize to anybody. These two don't have a clue. It's the time of the month when we women see things more clearly."

Tazz tries to say something, but Renee gives him a glare that would kill an elephant. He stops in the middle of his first word.

The women start into a two-sided conversation, and I whisper, "Hey, Tazz, how 'bout you show me your new oil bag?" The two women ignore us. We stand and slip out of the kitchen.

Once outside, Tazz throws up his hands. "Well, shit, I never know what to do when she acts like that."

"Me neither." I take a sip of my beer. "Bob told me not to take it personal, but she came at us with everything she had. How do you not take that personal?"

Tazz looks at me with a grimace. "Trust me, man, she didn't give everything. You saw the tip of the iceberg. With me, she gives it all."

We stroll over to his bike, and he pulls up two small stools, short enough to work on a low-slung bike like his. He throws me a soft rag, and we start to polish. He's at the front and I scrub his rear rim.

He says, "Not take it personal, how do you do that? When we're alone, the first thing out of her mouth is how I did or didn't do this or that. Like the other day, she started in about what a jerk I was for never doing the dishes. Hell, man, I'd done dishes the very night before."

"We're all jerks in their eyes."

He dabs chrome polish on his rag and hands the can over to me. "Well, I ain't no fucking jerk, especially with Donna. I bend over backwards to accommodate her."

"You guys use the talking stick? How'd it go?"

"It was great. For the first time in our twelve years, I finished a sentence without her butting in. It was heaven."

"What about her?"

He stops polishing the front wheel spokes and looks over at me. "It's when the dishes thing came up, not that it was our first time. A weird thing happened, and it drove me crazy. It drives me crazy on a regular basis, but she had the stick and there was nothing I could do."

He continues to work on the front wheel.

"What happened?"

"She started in about me being a jerk with the dishes. I knew I was in for it. Her monologue would last an hour, and I was stuck. I had to listen."

I dip polish on my rag and continue to work on his chrome swing arm, moving my way up the left shock.

He says, "I knew she'd wander through the bullshit, pick one subject, then another and another, until I was insane. Can't they get to the point?"

I look up. "Maybe they aren't wired to get to a point. Bob says that they're supposed to do a back-and-forth thing, because they find solutions differently than us guys."

"Yeah, whatever. I don't care, because it drives me crazy when she brings too many subjects up. I can't keep up with her."

"Me too." I dip more polish, set the can on the concrete, then work my rag between the chrome spring of the left shock. We sit in a moment of frustrated silence, with only the squeak of rags on metal.

"What happened?"

He grabs the polish. "I'm stuck listening. After twenty minutes, I want to run from the room, scream and pull my hair out, but I'm stuck. It wasn't easy."

"Been there."

"The weird thing is, after a half-hour, she starts to make some strange kind of sense. I couldn't keep up with her, but everything she talked about started to fall into place."

I smile because the same thing happens between Renee and me. He's telling the story, so I keep silent.

"It took thirty minutes, but once things started to line up, our whole problem came into focus. She burst into tears after blurting out about how her dad never did the dishes and always left them for her and her sister and what a jerk he was."

My smile widens. I keep rubbing, working my way to his new chromed oil bag. I pick up the polish, dip more and bring out the brilliant surface.

"The strangest thing happened," he says. "She got up, came over to my side of the table, that fucking talking stick still in hand, mind you, and puts her arms around my neck. She said it was the first time in her life a man actually listened to her all the way to the end. When she put the stick down, I didn't have anything to say. I was in awe of how she did it all on her own. What do you make of it?"

"I don't have a clue, but I think we're onto something with that talking stick. Not only do we get a chance to complete our sentences, but our women, in their strange female way, also feel like they've been heard."

He picks up the container, dabs a little and starts on a front fork. "If I keep talking, will you help me polish my whole bike?"

I give him a sneer. "If you can keep talking? This is the most I've ever heard you say at one time since I've known you."

"Well, this is big stuff, and I had to tell someone. Donna and I made a huge breakthrough with that stick and it's exciting."

I dip a little more polish. "That Bob's done it again."

"You got that right."

A moment passes with only the sound of squeaking polish. Another Harley drives by. We both look up, but it's no one we know. When its roar fades, Tazz says, "Twig went down the other night after our meeting."

I stop working on the oil tank. "Did he get hurt?"

"A little banged up when he got thrown into a bush, but he's okay."

"How's his bike?"

"Lucky son of a bitch got a coupla' scratches and a screwed-up foot peg."

I'm ready to say more, but a sound at the front door catches my attention. Both Tazz and I look up to see the two women coming toward us. Donna asks, "Is that all you guys can do is polish your bikes?"

It's a rhetorical question and neither of us answer. We stand and I drop my rag across the seat. I still don't know how Tazz rides his bike and doesn't have a ruined butt. The seat is too small. I asked him once and he said, "Who needs comfort when you got cool."

Renee steps over, hooks her arm in mine and pulls in close. I ask, "You girls have a good talk?"

Donna stands over Tazz and looks down at him. "I figured out why I'm touchy."

He doesn't say a word, but rises and sits sideways on his seat. He crosses his arms.

Donna gives Renee a shy look, then glares at Tazz. "When I speak, I get the feeling you never listen. You act like you're listening when people are around, but I never feel heard. It's like you're putting up with me. When I get really angry to get your attention, you disappear out here to your bike or turn to stone."

"What do you mean turn to stone?"

She points at his face. "Your eyes go blank, and I don't have anyone to work it out with. It feels like you give in."

"Shit, Donna, when you have some kind of issue, it's never one thing, its always thirty things. I can't fix everything."

Her voice rises. "You don't have to fix any of them, damnit. I just want to be heard."

"What about with the talking stick? You get heard with the talking stick."

"That's different, and we've only been using that for a day. I'm talking about the rest of our marriage. Most of the time I just blow it off, because it's too much trouble to get you to pay attention."

He flings out his hands in exasperation. "I try to--"

She raises her arms. "Stop."

A silence follows that can be cut with a knife.

She relaxes her arms and puts one thick hand back on her wide hip. "When my period comes, I can't hold back any longer. It's like for those five or six days, I have to tell the truth, and I'm pissed that I held back for three weeks."

Tazz opens his mouth to speak. She grabs a blue plastic clip out of her hair and holds it out to him. "This is the talking stick for now, do you agree?"

He nods.

She says, "You're always too quick to respond with your own bullshit when you do answer, and I never feel heard. I just want you to listen."

For five minutes she expounds on her gripes, then hands the clip to him.

His pencil-thin lips crack in an unaccustomed smile. He lifts the clip between them. "The talking stick answers the problem, right?"

She nods and shifts weight to her thick right leg.

"If I agree to abide by the stick, you'll feel more heard, right?"

She nods again.

He stands and gives the clip back to her. "Okay, case closed. Let's go riding."

She gives him a glare. Her forehead wrinkles and lips narrow. "See, this is what I'm talking about. You didn't hear a word I said."

"Sure I did, Babe, no, I mean Sweetheart." He repeats every word she said and gives her an accurate interpretation of the content.

She drops her hand from her hip. "You never listen."

"But I did listen, didn't I?"

There is another moment of silence until Tazz says, "Are we finished here?"

She looks at him with reluctant acceptance. "I'm not done, but I'll give you a break for the moment."

He stands and reaches for her hand. They lock index fingers, and he pulls her toward him. "I love you, Sweetie, and whatever it takes to fix this, I'll do it."

She lets herself be pulled into his arms. "You don't have to fix anything, you idiot, I just want to feel like I've been heard."

They hug, and he kisses her on the neck. "With the talking stick, I think we got it pretty much solved, don't you?"

She pulls back and looks at him. "That would be nice."

I reach for Renee's hand, and together we watch yet another successful communication between the sexes. Tazz and Donna hug again. It's all such a mystery.

After the romantic moment, Tazz pulls away and looks at her. "If we're done here, I'd like to go for a ride. Want to come?"

She looks at her watch. "Remember, my mom will be here in a half-hour, and I want you here."

"Oh, shit, I forgot."

He turns to me. "Well, hell, no ride today, but you came over for the bowl, didn't you?"

I nod.

"Twig put a box together so things wouldn't get fucked up. I'll be back in a minute."

He turns and walks toward the house.

I turn to Donna. "I'll return it tomorrow."

"No need," Tazz says over his shoulder and slips in the house. A moment later, he returns. "Donna and I came up with our own tools. We can pass these on."

Renee takes the box from Tazz. "I have one more part to experiment with, then I guess we'll pass them on. We'll have to get our own, tools too."

Good-byes are said. The women hug, while Tazz and I make a comical attempt at hugging. We're not very good at it yet. I climb on my bike, and Renee slips in behind me. When the engine starts, I kick it in gear, and we roll down the driveway, then out onto the street. I pull my clutch and give the engine a slight rev; a biker salutation. We drive out of the neighborhood and back onto the ever-famous Highway 66, north toward Barstow.

Chapter 11

Who are you?

It's been a long day, and by the time we get to bed, I'm exhausted. When the lights are out, I drift off with the sound of Stewart's soft snore. A north wind rolls in and charges the air.

I open my eyes and the lights are on. I sit up in bed and look about the small room. Stewart lies on his side, facing away from me. His cheap dresser against the wall seems more exotic, more here. I look around the room until I see the sofa-style chair that sits in a corner.

"Thought you'd never notice me," he says.

I pull my covers up. I'm frightened, no, more like startled. He smiles, and his infectious grin dissipates any fear that he might want to harm me.

"Who are you?"

He reaches up and strokes his thin salt-and-pepper goatee.

"Thought you'd guess by now."

"You're Bob?"

"Bingo."

"Why are you here?"

"We gotta' talk."

"You're a figment of everyone's imagination."

"I am and now for you, too."

It takes a moment for me to adjust. "What do we have to talk about? I thought you only came to Stewart to screw up his life. What're you doing here?"

"If I fucked up his life, why are you two getting along better?"

"Because we've worked very hard on our relationship. I don't think it has much to do with you."

He leans back in the chair, kicks one leg over the padded arm, laces his fingers and puts both hands behind his head. "Maybe it's more like Stewart has stood up for himself and taken some of the responsibility off of you."

He might have a point, but I'll be damned if I'll admit it.

"Look, Renee, I'm here to help you two over the next hump, and it'll be a big one."

"What's that?"

"You're going to live together as man and woman for the first time in your life, instead of you being the bitchy mother and he the lost child."

"We'll do just fine without your help."

He's silent for longer than feels comfortable, before I say, "Stewart and I are doing good. Don't fuck it up."

"If you're doing so well, why is it you feel like you're losing yourself to his emerging maleness? Why do you feel left out of his life, instead of how it was before, when you couldn't stand being around him?"

"How do you know? I haven't shared that with anyone."

"Some years ago I signed on as Stewart's guardian angel."

I snicker. "I'd say more like a guardian Hell's Angel."

"A guardian just the same, and when I took him on, I also took you. I haven't shown myself to you until now, but it's time we got to know each other."

"Okay, you've shown yourself. What do you have to say?"

"Listen, Renee, I don't have time for your petulance. I'm going to show you a very special place."

"I'm not going anywhere with you unless Stewart is with us."

In less than a second, the scene shifts and I stand in a large room with taupe wall-to-wall carpet. I was naked under the covers, so now I reach down to conceal myself.

"Don't worry," Bob says, "I brought your robe."

I look down and pull the robe tighter around my waist, grab the terry cloth tie and yank a slipknot into it. "What're we doing here?"

"Recognize this room?"

I look around, then back at Bob. "I have no idea."

"Look closer, there must be something you recognize."

I look at semicircular windows that make up the back wall. The glass is curved. I search to my left, and that dream kitchen comes into view. "It's the house Stewart and I looked at today."

"Bingo once again."

I look out the window, and a desert scene stretches out for a hundred miles into a vague distance.

"Why here, and why is it daylight out there?"

"Because it's the place you and Stewart will go to in the next stage of your relationship. This house will help you get to that place and beyond. You might spend the next forty years here."

"How do you know?"

"Call it ghost intuition."

Bob turns and gives me a wink. "As Stewart finds his emerging manhood, you're losing the keen edge that was a part of you for eighteen years."

"Where did you come up with that?"

"Let's just say for now I know. I also know you're worried that this edge is lost forever and won't come back."

"Yes."

"It's not lost, Renee, only misplaced."

He walks to a huge window and looks out. His back is to me. "Tell me your biggest fear, besides falling from a high building, of course."

"No one knows about my fear. How do--"

He clasps his hands behind his back and shouts, "Stop asking how, just answer my question."

I think for a moment, and say in an unsure tone, "My bitch will come out and take over again. I'm afraid she'll ruin the romantic period Stewart and I are going through."

He turns, walks over to a wooden barstool and pulls it out. When he sits, he crosses his arms in front of him, high across his chest in an exaggerated manner. "So, you'll keep your bitch under wraps, no matter what?"

"Yeah, I guess I'm afraid of what she might do."

"It's not all you, Renee. You carried Stewart's bitch for him all those years."

Bob slips his foot under a second barstool and slides it out toward me. "Take a seat, because what I'm about to say might knock you off your feet."

I pull it over, climb up, then rest my feet on a higher rung.

"Your bitch is completely appropriate, especially when dealing with Stewart. I like to think that bitch means Babe-In-Total-Control-of-Herself. B-I-T-C-H. I know the Babe part might bug you, but if you can remember that little acronym, you can let her out more often. If you attempt to hold her in, she'll jump out at the wrong times."

"What do I do about feeling closed down?"

"Do what Donna did today. Let her out. Isn't that why you're intrigued with the rage feather? It unleashes a part of you that's wanted out for a long time."

I lean my elbow on the counter. "Something happened after Stewart took his masculinity back. I felt weak and unimportant."

"A common experience when a hole appears in our psyches. When Stewart's masculinity reemerged, a hole formed in your subconscious because you no longer had to carry anger for him. You have to find something to fill the gap."

"I have no idea, especially because our kids are more independent lately. What'll I do?"

"Your little mousy-voiced real estate woman took up selling houses to fill in the gap. I don't advocate real estate sales, because it's more than a full-time occupation, and jobs bring up a whole other set of problems."

"What then?"

"It's for you to figure out. Some take up art, maybe write or act. You could help teenagers in trouble. The list is endless, but it must be something that resonates with your core wishes."

"I don't know."

"Yes, this is why we're talking. You'll need time to find your place in this new life and put it into action. I'm here to plant the seed. It's up to you to water the damn thing and get it to grow. One thing I will say in favor of changes, living in this house will help you and Stewart take your next step."

"You think we should buy it?"

Bob gets to his feet and walks over to the massive hearth. With a single beckoning finger he motions me to follow. When he kneels and points, I strain my neck to look up the flue. He touches a large brick hidden on the front inside wall. Under his pressure, the brick wiggles.

"Don't touch this brick until you've signed the ownership papers. Oh, yes, I thought you were all fired up to learn how to ride a Harley?"

My eyes open to a pitch-black room. I reach out and put my arm around my husband. Yes, Stewart is still here.

***

Twig and I spend Saturday catching up on our lives: laundry, grocery shopping, bill-paying, our list never ends. When Sunday comes, while we still loll in bed, I mention maybe Stewart and Renee might want to go to breakfast with us, then ride into the hills for the day.

Twig drops his feet over the edge of the bed. "Sounds like a good idea. Why don't you give her a call?"

"No, Twig, it's too soon. You call Stewart. It's better between you men."

He picks up the phone and dials the number. "Stew, what are you up to?"

After a moment of silence, he says, "Melinda wants to talk to Renee." He hands the phone over. I glare at him and mouth the word "bastard" while I wait for Renee.

After a tense few moments of awkward chit-chat, we agree to meet in an hour at Marie's Restaurant in Victorville. I say good-bye and hang up.

"That was the all-time shortest woman phone call ever."

"I told you it was too early for her and me to talk."

With his back to me, he says, "We could get in a fight over what happened and work all the angles for the rest of today or, if it's not too important, we could blow this one off and go have some breakfast with Stewart and Renee. What say we let this one slide and get on with our day?"

His words make sense, but I can't help myself. I have something to say and no logical man will talk me out of it. I start into what feels like it will be a long dissertation about respecting each other's wishes, when he leaps off the bed and rushes into the living room, only to reappear two seconds later with our own version of the talking stick. He sets the stick on the bed, not in front of me, but close enough that I can grab it. He says, "We use the stick or I'm not participating."

When he sits on the far edge of the bed, I grab the stick and start in on him like there's no tomorrow.

Our stick doesn't have magical powers like Bob's, but Twig sits there and says nothing while I rant my way through my side of our dilemma. In ten minutes, I've run out of words and set the stick down.

He picks it up. "I didn't know how important your timing was, and I apologize for forcing the phone on you."

When he sets the stick down, I have nothing else to say. I give him a big grin. "We did it."

He says nothing, scoots closer and holds out his arms.

I'm so delighted with our first successful argument that I'm in his arms, and we fall back on the bed.

"We've got twenty minutes," I say. "Let's make the best of it." I press my lips to his, and a fast-paced sexual union ends in some deep-breathing exercises and a crescendo of satisfaction.

Fifteen minutes later, we're both in the shower, but I want more. Knowing men, and Twig is no different, his interest level dropped the moment he came, at least for now. I'll bide my time and catch him later when he's re-primed.

He rinses soap from his hair while I stand aside. He says, "I don't know if you noticed, but we succeeded on two fronts."

"What do you mean?"

"We were successful at thwarting a huge battle with the talking stick, and we had great sex without dipping to violence."

With his hair rinsed and water dripping from his scrubbed body, he steps out of our little shower before I have a chance to answer. I'm soaping my breasts and belly when he opens the door a crack. "What do you think?"

We both giggle like school children.

By the time I have my makeup on and dress, Twig is doing his standard nervous pacing from the kitchen to the bedroom. He doesn't say anything, because he knows better. His peek through the door says more than enough.

"Go sit down, you big lug or I'll rain all over your parade."

He draws a deep breath, lets it out with a long sigh, turns, and leaves the room.

"I'd go faster if you left me alone," I say through the open door. I hear the front door close. Maybe he'll polish his bike. That'll keep him occupied.

Once we're on the bike, we ride three miles to the south end of town.

Twig backs his bike into a curb, and I dismount as Stewart and Renee drive up. I greet them with a nod, as they pull into position next to Twig's bike.

I tuck some loose hair up under my scarf while Renee dismounts. Stewart unfurls his kickstand and turns the engine off. When things are quiet, I greet her. "Good to see you again."

"You, too." She's reserved. I guess I am, too.

Stewart and Twig give one another awkward guy hugs, and we walk into the restaurant. We're seated at a front window, facing the bikes.

I guess I feel sensitive. I don't know how to break the ice with Renee. We sit in silence until the waitress brings water. Renee asks for lemon slices. After our waitress has scuttled off, Renee turns back to us. "Bob came to me last night."

"No kidding?" I say.

She takes a sip of water. "I always thought he was a figment of everyone's imagination, but he's real."

Twig picks up his menu and gives it a perfunctory glance, though I know from experience what he'll order; he's a creature of habit, if I ever saw one.

Renee looks at each of us, then back at Stewart. "He told me to buy the house up at Big Bear."

"No kidding?" I say. "I put a lot of stock in what Bob says."

She picks up a menu, but looks at Stewart. "It's a little more magic than I can live with, but he's very convincing. I guess I want to have another look."

Stewart sets his menu down. "That's great, Renee." He looks at us. "Maybe you two would like to see the place."

"What the fuck?" Twig says. "It should be fun."

Our waitress steps up with pencil and pad in hand. "What'll y'all have?" She has a slight Texas drawl.

Breakfast goes smoothly, and I warm up to Renee. I like her, but there's a she-cat kind of scratch-your-eyes-out-if-you-cross-me air about her that makes me cautious. Maybe she feels the same from me. All I know is my hackles are up around her.

By the end of the meal, we both have calmed. We have a small conversation aside from the guy talk of sports and bikes, two subjects never in short supply with our men around.

We pay and go out to the bikes. Stewart and Twig focus on the three ugly exhaust pipe scratches from Twig's wreck. They talk with a bit of that stupid macho bullshit about other accidents. I butt in. "Are we riding or will you guys just be standing around all day?"

Stewart looks from me to Twig. He points south. "It's up in the hills. You got enough gas?"

"Damn straight." Twig fishes in his Levi's for keys, then mounts the bike. When it starts, he motions for me to climb on. Stewart starts his and we're off, riding abreast, thundering down Main Street, going south out of town.

We take a long, slow climb into the barren hills, riding beside one another when the road allows. Our engines lump along in a lazy Sunday drive. In the hills, we lean into each turn with a grace that only comes from being on a Harley.

For the first time since we left Marie's, Stewart guns his engine and pulls out in front of us. A mile ahead, he makes a left onto a gravel road. Because of the dust, we creep along in first for the quarter-mile, until we empty onto a circular driveway and pull up to an odd, semicircular house.

A red Mercedes sits at the front walk, with a slender woman in a bright pink summer dress leaning against the front fender. She looks like she's stepped out of Sunday church.

When the engines are off, she greets us with a fidgety, high-pitched voice I immediately can't stand. What is more grating on my nerves is that I soon realize that she never stops talking. One run-on sentence piles headlong into another, with only a nano-second of a rest between.

I look over at the men while her yapping continues. She tells us about the type of grass, the windows and rain gutters. The front door is from Spain. When Stewart gets something from his saddlebag, the yammering of the frightened little woman ceases. Her face turns red, more from embarrassment than any attempt to speak. She looks relieved.

"Mrs. Albright," Stewart says in a business-like voice I've never before heard from him. "I mean no dis-respect, but my wife and I need to discuss the aspects of this house. We'll need quiet." He nods and continues, "Thanks for accommodating us."

The woman is beside herself in an attempt to talk.

Stewart turns to me. "Melinda, check out these terraced gardens and what about the decks?" He leads us outside, then down redwood steps to the lower levels.

"What do you think?" He points out at the open view of desert. A single road, probably Highway 395, cuts a long band from the north and disappears behind the mountain.

Renee grabs Stewart's hand and pulls him toward the house and through a sliding glass door. We follow. She takes the stick from Stew and turns to us. "Bob brought me here last night in my dream. He said Stewart and I will spend the next forty years in this place."

I go around Twig and take the stick back from Renee. "I don't know about you, but Bob's suggestions always seem to work out. If you can afford it, I'd do it. Heaven's sakes Stewart, how much is this place, anyhow?" I hand Stew the stick.

"Seven forty-five and change. It's got twenty acres."

Twig takes the stick. "That's a lot."

Stew grabs the stick. "We'll get some big money for our house in Diamond Springs, and I still have money from the talk show stuff two years ago. Renee has a small retirement from her job, and I just got another raise at Tridine. With all of those together, we can trim our payments down to bite size." He hands the stick back to Twig.

Twig says, "You've got to pay somebody to live somewhere, so why not pay yourself and have a nest egg for later?"

The real estate woman steps through the door, trying to say something. She gets a pad of paper and writes a note.

"Something happened to my voice," she writes. "I'm going to the hospital. I'll have to lock up before I go."

Stewart gives her a grin. "There's nothing wrong with your voice this stick can't cure." He holds it up. "I'll set it down, but first go upstairs. When everything's flooded out, you must agree not to talk while we make up our minds. We're ready to make an offer, but you must be quiet while we decide. Is it a promise?"

She nods.

"Go up to the master bedroom. By the time you get there, you'll be able to talk again."

She turns and leaves the room. When we hear her traipse up the steps and close the bedroom door, Stewart walks over and sets Bob's stick on the fireplace mantel.

Chapter 12

Trust

From upstairs, I hear a profusion of squeaky verbiage. I walk over to Stewart and slip my hand into his. "We need to go home and crunch some numbers."

He looks down at me. "What changed your mind?"

"I told you, Bob came to me last night. If you guys put this much stock in what he says, I guess I'd better pay attention when he comes around."

I let go of Stewart's hand and turn toward Melinda. "Come with me and see the view from the lower deck."

I lead her through the door, and we walk out to the southern edge of the huge deck. We rest against the railing and look out. After a moment of silence, I say, "I guess I'm afraid of you."

"Me? Heaven's sakes, Renee, what for?"

"Probably because you're young and beautiful, and those days are fading fast for me."

She giggles. "Renee, you're only ten years older than me, and still a knockout. Ask anyone, they'll all agree."

"Thanks, but I'm not sure I'd believe anyone. I know what I look like."

We gaze out to the horizon. She says, "There must be more to it than me being younger."

I look at her. "I've never trusted another woman. I guess it's some old mother stuff."

"Are you asking if you can trust me?"

I flush. "I guess I am."

She turns away from the view and leans her back against the rail. "I would take to my grave anything you said to me in secrecy, but you have to tell me how secret it has to be first, so I can decide whether I want to be trustworthy with it or not. If you don't tell me first, I might blab it all over town, or at the very least, tell Twig."

"That's fair."

She crosses her arms in front of her. "What do you have, and how secret is it?"

"Big. Don't tell anyone."

"Okay, it's forever locked in me. Shoot."

I gulp and make three false starts before I finally let it out. "I had sex with a guy at work two months ago."

She flushes. "Oh, that is big. Have you done it since?"

"No, I'm afraid to. I liked it too much."

"This is huge. Do you love the guy?"

I stare at her and nervously rub one hand on the railing. "It was just one of those things. A few drinks at an office party, some conversation, then I was in bed with him, and I loved it. It made me feel young and sexy again."

"You telling Stewart?"

"I have to, but I'm scared. I don't know what he'll say. We've been getting along, and I don't want to wreck it."

She leans both elbows on the rail and looks toward the house. "Not telling him will eventually wreck it more."

"I know you're right, but. . ." My voice drifts when the two men step onto the porch.

"We'll talk more soon," Melinda says, then moves in close. She whispers, "I'll tell you something quick. I'm pregnant."

I look at her. "Oh, my god."

"I haven't told anyone except Twig yet. Don't say anything."

I nod and turn to greet Stewart and Twig.

The real estate agent walks down the steps and comes over to us. "What did you do? It felt different. I couldn't--"

Stewart butts in. "Mrs. Albright, you agreed not to talk until we were done."

"Oh, you're right. I'm sorry, I just--"

"Mrs. Albright."

"Oh yes." She makes a gesture of closing her mouth, takes an imaginary key out of her blouse pocket and locks her lips.

Stewart takes my hand. "What do you think, Honey?"

I say, "Let's go home and see what the numbers look like."

"Good idea." He turns to the delicate real estate woman and puts out his hand. She grabs his hand and gives him three solid yanks.

"We'll call you later tonight. If we decide, we may want to make a written offer tomorrow before Renee flies back to Sacramento."

The woman makes an exaggerated gesture of not talking and nods.

"Good," Stewart says. "We'll give you a call later. He turns to us. "Is everyone done here?"

Twig says, "Get the stick and let's get back in the wind."

Stewart drops the stick in a paper bag and we walk along the south side of the house. We climb three flights of steps to get back to our bikes.

Melinda and I hang back. I whisper, "Can I call you later?"

"Yes, for sure. I'll take our portable phone and go outside so Twig can't hear."

"Thanks."

"Don't mention it."

She gets an embarrassed look. "It's good to get to know you. I liked you from the start, but our circumstances were more than odd."

We catch up to the guys getting their bikes off kickstands.

The real estate woman runs up.

"Where did you get that stick?" she asks.

Twig shrugs.

"I guess. . .I mean. . .Well, could I borrow it sometime? My husband never lets me talk."

Twig looks at her with a thunderstruck expression. "I'll think about it and get back with you in a day or two."

"Thank you," she says. "I never knew I talked that much until I was forced to be quiet."

Stew puts the stick in his saddlebag and the engines start. We pull off the gravel onto pavement and roll downhill toward the flatlands.

An afternoon wind has kicked up, and getting home is more difficult than the pleasant ride earlier. Stewart and I are buffeted by desert gusts between Victorville and Barstow. When we get home at dusk, I'm exhausted.

We walk through the front door and I say, "All I want to do is soak in a bath."

Stewart tosses his keys on the counter. "I thought you and I were crunching numbers?"

I collapse on his dinky sofa and look at him. "How 'bout we eat in the tub and crunch numbers after?"

He smiles. "You take a bath and I'll cook dinner, then we do the number thing."

"You know, you're really okay, as husbands go."

"Don't get used to it. I feel generous tonight."

I drag myself into the bathroom and start a tub of water, turn and look in the mirror. My wrinkles are more prevalent each day. Aging is not easy. After two minutes of studying my physical decline, I drop my clothes on the floor, sit in six inches of hot water and close my eyes while the tub fills. I'm in heaven. The only thing to cap this off would be a good meal, which, after twenty minutes, I detect with my aging nostrils. God, I'm feeling pathetic. Maybe I'm coming upon my cycle?

Dinner is over, and I relax on the sofa while Stewart washes dishes. Normally, we bicker over cleanup, but there are times when he's extra considerate. I'm tired enough to take him up on his gesture tonight. I suspect it might have something to do with my decision about the house. He wants me in a good mood.

By eight o'clock, we've put together the numbers, considered many possibilities, added columns of assets and subtracted liabilities. On paper, everything looks feasible.

I lean back on the sofa for the first time in an hour. "What the hell, if Bob says to do it, we could give it a try."

Stewart's face lights up. "Are you serious?"

"I'm tired of living alone, but I warn you, I may not like the desert once I'm here. The building is strange, but it's a well-done kind of strange, and I love the view."

Stewart gets up and walks into the kitchen. "So, how much do we offer?"

I lean forward to see him through the door. "How long has it been on the market?"

He opens the refrigerator. "Mrs. Albright said eight months."

"Not a hot item. How about we offer a hundred thousand less than asking?"

Stewart turns with a shocked expression. "A hundred? Aren't we being a little bold?"

"Oh, what the hell, let's be bold. They can always counter."

Stewart picks up the phone and punches in a number from memory.

"Hello, Mrs. Albright; it's Stewart Chance." He rolls his eyes and waits a minute without a word. He's halfway into the second minute, when I grab the phone and bust in on her monologue. I speak fast without pauses. "We want to make an offer. If you'll stop talking, we can work out some details."

The line is silent. I think she's hung up. "Are you there?"

"Yes." A mousy voice comes over the line. I get a strong feeling she's about to cry.

"We want you to take an offer of six hundred thousand to the sellers."

The line is still silent.

"Did you get that?"

"Yes," she says.

"Will you call Stewart at work when you hear from them?"

Her lost puppy voice comes on. "It's the San Bernardino Save The Dirt Bike Foundation. It was willed to them last year when Mrs. Freedman died."

I look at Stewart and almost spit the words. "Dirt bikes?"

She says, "It may take a few days to get a decision from the board."

"Call when you hear something." I hang up the phone and look at Stewart.

He gapes at me. "Six hundred's over a hundred fifty less."

"What the hell; it's been on the market a while. It's worth a try. At six hundred, we'll have room to breathe.

I pick up the phone, and while dialing Melinda's number say, "Can you believe it? The damn thing was donated to the Desert Dirt Bike foundation."

***

I drive Renee to the San Bernardino airport early and get back to work just in time to show my face at nine.

Because of my last promotion, I have a free hand, though I still have to show good faith by being there every day and getting something done. After Layton's ineptness, I don't need to do much to keep everyone happy.

I settle into my day's grind and find myself enjoying morning phone calls, orders, and best of all a scheduled lunch with Steve Sinder. Last month he got promoted to head of production.

After lunch, I step into my office and see a note. "Call Kay Albright." Under her name is a phone number.

Her squeaky voice comes on the line, and I pull the receiver away to protect my ear from damage.

"They accepted," she says. "They didn't dicker, didn't want to counter, nothing. They simply accepted. If you come to my office, we can sign the official offer, then they will okay it."

"I'm sorry, Mrs. Albright, I can't go to Victorville right now. Can you have a courier bring it to me? I'll sign and send the completed offer back with him."

She says, "You'll have to put three percent into an escrow account to make the offer binding."

"Give me the account number, and I'll have my bank transfer funds. Of course the sale is contingent upon building inspections and what the title company comes up with."

"Of course, Mr. Chance. It's already in our contract."

"Great, send your courier over and let's get started."

I hang up the phone, and call Renee in Sacramento. She's out of her office. I leave a message there and at home in Diamond Springs.

By the end of the week, Renee and the kids fly down and we have a final look at the house to get our kids' opinions. Shortly after we park, Sheila meets a girl her age at the end of the drive and Mel loves the swimming pool. We get a reluctant okay from the kids, though they don't want to leave their friends up north.

Renee is so anxious to make the deal, she promises Mel one of those hated dirt bikes and Sheila a new stereo. Bribery, whatever it takes.

After I go north to oversee some needed repairs, the Diamond Springs house goes on the market and sells in a week. Our sixty-day escrow comes quicker than I can believe.

I fly back north and rent a huge moving truck. We pack before I realize we'll need two trips.

"It's okay, Honey," Renee says while we stand at the back of the loaded truck, barely able to close its door. "We still have a month to vacate. We'll come back next weekend and finish."

"I didn't realize the stuff we'd accumulated in seven years."

"It does pile up."

I reach up, grab the nylon strap and pull the door closed.

In the morning, we lock our old house, and I drive the truck while Renee follows in her car.

My son, Mel, rides with me to the first pit stop in Fresno. After a lot of arguing over who goes where, the kids switch.

It isn't five minutes after we're back on the freeway, when Sheila says, "Don't take it personally, Dad, but the truck is too noisy and bumpy. Can I get back in the car now?"

I pull over on the freeway, and she gives me a kiss on the cheek. "I'll send Mel back."

"He doesn't have to if it's more comfortable in the car."

She climbs out of the truck and returns in a minute. "He wants to stay in the car. Sorry, Dad."

"I don't mind. I've got things to think about, anyhow."

She closes the door, and we're off again in a roll of pavement and white lines.

At dusk I pull over in the town of Mojave and stop at the same motel I stayed at during my first desert trip over two years ago. We get an extra adjoining room for the kids, then after a late dinner and a long hot shower, I fall into an exhausted sleep.

Something startles me awake. I look at the edge of my bed and see Bob with a toothpick in his fingers, seriously mining the crevices of his teeth.

I sit up in bed. "If you're a spirit, you shouldn't have to pick your teeth."

"Habit," he says, then changes the subject. "You did it."

"What did I do?"

"You bought the house and brought your family back together. I'm proud of you."

"It took some years, but thanks to you and the One Percent guys, Renee and I are finally growing up."

He waves me off like it was no big deal. "Things are pretty smooth right now, but prepare yourself for changes."

My stomach churns. Last time Bob said changes, my whole life was turned inside out. "What do you mean?"

"Don't get your panties in a twist. The changes won't be too harsh, but be prepared, there'll be more than a few."

"Got any clues?"

He gives me his big-toothed smile. "It has a lot to do with the bike your wife's getting."

"Which bike?"

"Oh, she hasn't told you?"

"Told me what?"

"Renee's been taking riding lessons in Sacramento and she's getting pretty good. She'll want to buy a bike, but stall her for a month."

"Why a month?"

"It'll take a while for her to remember."

"Remember what?"

"Hell, Stewy, there isn't any fun in telling everything. Where is your sense of mystery?"

"With you around, I don't need any. My whole life is one big mystery."

His smile widens. He twirls the toothpick on his tongue. "Don't let on that you know about her riding lessons. She wants to surprise you."

A train passes our hotel room, blows its horn, and I awake. Although our room is far from quiet, it is dark, and Bob is no longer around. I listen to morning traffic and think about Bob's prediction. What surprises does he have in store now?

By noon, we've made the long haul up the hill, and I turn onto our gravel roadway. A neighbor trimming her roses looks up and waves while I lumber along in first gear.

When I pull up to the house, a row of six bikes stand to the side. Twig steps off the deck and guides my truck into place.

I turn the engine off and climb down. "Hey, Twig, what are you doing?"

"We came to help you move in, except I can't get anyone out from around your pool."

With this many hands, unloading takes less than three hours. Renee and Donna go out for pizzas and soft drinks while I finish sweeping out the truck. We sit around the pool, eating and cracking biker jokes. It's my kind of evening.

Renee and the girls are in the house. I hear laughter.

It's a night to remember, but too soon they're gone, and I drop into bed.

Monday comes much too fast, and I make my first commute to work on my Harley. It's fun on a bike, but the helmet crushes my hair, and I look like a disaster all day. In the future, I'll keep some clothes at work and take a shower in the little gym next to the child care center at the far end of the building.

By that night, Renee and Donna have reassembled the house, and things look comfortable.

"Do you like it here?" I ask Renee while we get ready for bed.

"I'm welcomed into your crowd, and they are kind people. I like it here for that reason alone."

"Good, because I like being back together with you and the kids."

"Yes, me too." She puts her toothbrush back in the special little jar she's had since we first got together. She rinses her mouth and stares at me through the mirror. "I guess I have something to say." She looks around and picks up her toothbrush again. "I want this to be a talking stick for now, okay?"

I look down at her hand. "Okay."

"I don't know how it happened, but I had sex with some guy at work four months ago, and. . ."

I don't hear anything else she says. My head reels. My entire life flashes before my eyes. When she puts her talking stick-tooth brush on the counter, I'm reluctant to pick it up. I don't know what to say. I hold it for a minute, then set it down. Is this what Bob meant when he talked about changes?

My mind grapples to hold onto something reasonable. She moved down here. She must still want to be with me. "Do you love him?" I ask. It's a logical question.

Her face contorts into a worried mass of wrinkles. "Didn't you listen? It was a one-time thing, and it happened months ago. I love you. I want to be with you."

I stumble back out of our new bathroom and flop hunchback into a sitting position on our bed. She follows and sits next to me. She grabs my hand, but I don't feel her touch me.

"Stewart, are you okay?"

I try for some words, but none come. I look at her with my mouth open. I'm neither angry, nor do I even feel upset. I'm numb. I feel nothing.

In my haze of nothingness, she lightly slaps my face. I look sideways and surprise, there she is, my wife. She takes my face in both of her hands. I feel blackness surround me. I want to go to sleep. I want to get away. Her insistent talking keeps bringing me back.

***

His color is too pale. I want to call 911, but I'll hold off for a while. I expected him to get mad, to rant around, like I did when he had sex with Melinda. It was lucky he was in the desert then, because I might have done some damage.

He's hyperventilating, and I'm sure he's going to pass out.

I lay him back on the bed and slide him over, hoping to get some blood to his head. I pull his left knee up, and his heavy breathing relaxes, then starts into a familiar soft snore.

His color returns and, thank God, my 911 scenario is out.

I make an attempt to pull him farther up on the bed, but only succeed in twisting him into an ungodly position. I'm much too winded and exhausted to continue.

With him still fully clothed, but back to normal color, I pick up the phone and dial. "Melinda, I told him and he passed out."

She spends ten minutes talking me out of my anxiety, then, with nothing else to do, I turn out the lights and climb into bed next to him. I lie awake for hours listening to him snore.

***

In a dream, Bob and I stroll around my new pool, looking over the desert. "Okay, man, she told you. What's the big deal?"

He stops and turns to me. "Remember, I'm not one of your buddies. I know what you're thinking."

"Okay," I say in more of an exasperated tone than I expect. "I'm kind of pissed."

"That's good. Give me more. Why are you pissed?"

We continue to walk around the far end of the pool, toward the half-round bench that overlooks the valley. I can't come up with any more. "I'm pissed, isn't that enough?"

"It's enough when guys talk. If you want to work it out with Renee, you'll have to come up with more."

We reach the bench and Bob sits. I stand because I'm concentrating. "I'm pissed because. . .because she violated our sacred trust."

"Okay, man, good start. If she violated your trust, you two are even."

I find a seat and look at him. "What do you mean?"

"I remember you and a certain redhead romping in desert sand a few years ago."

"Oh, Melinda. I guess you have a point, but Melinda forced me."

He laughs, then says with a sarcastic whine to his voice, "Oh, right, Melinda forced you; one time in the desert; once in a hotel room and a final wild fling on your bike."

I stare at ripples in the pool.

"You never came clean about your last two escapades."

"I didn't want to cause more trouble."

"In reality, if you two want to be even, Renee needs to go out and get laid two more times."

Fear constricts my throat. I speak with a scratchy voice. "I couldn't handle it."

"Why couldn't you handle it?"

I blurt, "Because she can't go fucking some other guy with my pussy."

Bob's smile widens. He pats my arm in a fatherly gesture. "Good job, Stew."

"I didn't mean to say--"

"Stop!" he shouts.

I'm startled into silence.

"It isn't the most politically correct thing to say, but you and I both know it's how you feel."

Bob rests his elbows on his knees. "We've got a lot of work to do."

"What do you mean?"

"Most men rail against woman's need for monogamy. Our entire being wants to spread our seed, pollinate all of the little plants. It's a natural mandate to perpetuate our species. If we didn't want to screw every woman we saw, how could the gene pool widen?"

"I see where you're going."

"What most of us guys don't realize is we're more monogamous than women and for all the wrong reasons. What's happened to you is a perfect example.

"Renee wants you to be faithful because she's scared you'll find someone else to love. You, on the other hand, want her to stay true, because you think you own her little sweet triangle of fluff."

"She has no right to--"

"Stewart," he interrupts. "She has every right to do whatever she wants with her body, especially if it pleases her. You, on the other hand, also have all of the same rights. The problem lies in your neurosis about one another. She's fearful about you leaving, while you suffer from pure, unmitigated possessiveness."

I sit and lean forward on my knees. I look at the pale moonlight shining on the valley below. "Everything is confusing."

"That ain't the half of it."

"What do I do?"

"The job between a couple is to let go of being politically correct. Intimacy comes from showing our jerky, possessive sides, without acting on the feeling."

"I don't understand."

"Talk to her about your possessiveness, but don't act on it. No way you could do anything about it, anyhow, especially with a woman like Renee. You got a tiger by the tail, buddy, and count yourself lucky."

"Lucky?"

"In the last few years, she's told you everything about herself, while you've been hiding out in your men's group, using some archaic secrecy clause to avoid filling her in on what's going on."

I pick up a spiny oak leaf and fold until it cracks. "Now you've got me confused."

"The men-and-women idea you've been playing with?"

"Yes?"

"Do it. Now that Renee lives here, get everyone together and sit down with both genders. It won't be easy at first, but it's where men and women need to go to figure out how to communicate."

I say, "It's the most frightening thing I can think of. It would be like being in relationship with five women at one time without the advantage of sex. I don't know if I could handle it."

"You can handle it, Stewy. It's your logical next step."

That said, he puffs out of existence, and I open my eyes to a gray dawn.

I turn and slide up to Renee. "Honey," I shake her shoulder.

When she comes to, I feel her stiffen.

"What?"

"I'm confused about how to deal with what you told me."

She's silent.

With nothing to add to my statement, I fall back on an old standard. "But, I love you."

She reaches back and grabs my right butt cheek. She gives me a pat. "We going to be all right?" she asks in a sleepy voice.

I kiss the back of her neck, settle my head down on the pillow and fall back to sleep.

An hour later, my buzzer goes off, and I'm blasted into another day. While Renee continues to sleep, I shower and shave, then go down our new stairs to our new kitchen and get something together for breakfast.

I'm eating my two eggs and toast, when Mel bounds out of his room at the far end of the house and says, "Hey, Dad, this is a cool house."

"Glad you like it, son. "Are you about ready for school?"

"Another ten minutes. Could you heat me up a Pop Tart?"

I smile and take a last bite of my toast.

"You know your mom doesn't allow--"

"Just joking, Dad. Mom would have a fit if one of those evil things came within five hundred yards of our house."

"You got that right. I'll make you eggs and some toast."

"How about just the toast, Dad; I'm running late."

I've learned not to push, especially with my son or he'll leave with nothing. I plop two pieces of bread into the toaster. I get peanut butter and some jam.

I leave early and take a leisurely early morning ride to work. After Twig tuned my bike up last week, it runs at peak performance. The cool air feels good. I bank into turns while coming off the hill. A feeling of freedom, even though I'm on my way to work, makes me happy and carefree.

On the flats, I crank my bike up to seventy and roll off miles in motorcycle bliss, passing slower cars without effort. I draw near Barstow and cut my speed, then ride through the town in a slow rumble of twin cylinders. Two other Harley riders, bound in the opposite direction, give me a high sign.

I nod to Brian, the guard, pass through security and park in my private space. My back tire is against the building, bike faced out for a quick escape. When I dismount, I kiss my fingers and touch the tank of Blue for luck, then go into the building. Inside, I walk to the far end to a small gym Tridine built for employees last year. After a quick shower and a fast change into a sport jacket and tie, I stroll down the halls and give everyone a morning greeting. It's a good day.

After work, I take a wind-whipped, thunderous ride back home, I pull my Harley into my new garage, and Renee comes out to greet me.

She gives me a kiss on the cheek. "The wives called me today, and we decided Tuesday nights are best for us, starting after next weekend."

Over the ticking of my cooling bike, I ask, "What about the guys? Don't we get a say in this matter?"

"Well, no, silly. It's the wives' schedules that count. You men just go to work and come home to watch football. We got kids and household schedules."

I lean the bike on its kickstand and dismount. "It's baseball this time of year."

"Football, baseball, you know what I mean."

She has a point, but I don't want to admit it.

"So, next Tuesday, in the evening, I suppose."

"Seven."

She looks at me with a sheepish grin.

"What?"

"Can I take your bike for a spin?"

My mouth drops.

"I finished riding school before we left Sacramento, and I think I can ride your Harley without any problems."

I feign surprise. "Riding school?"

"How else would I learn?"

Chapter 13

It's all new

We've been in our new house two weeks, and I'm still not unpacked. Last weekend Stewart flew back to Sacramento and got the final load.

I gathered enough courage to tell him about my infidelity with the computer hunk. After the first shock, he took it in stride. I'm sure Bob had something to do with his acceptance.

We've talked about our commitment to one another, and I assured him it was a one-time thing. There's a piece of me that still wants to run wild, but I didn't tell Stewart. It's probably just a stage I'm going through.

I open the last stupid box of junk and find a place for each item, when I run across a framed picture of the family before Stewart met Bob. God, we looked pinched. I'm not sure I want it to be out, but I take it to the fireplace mantel and position it. I can always put it away later. When I set it up, it slips and topples to the slate hearth. In the silent room, the breaking glass startles me. I grab the broom to sweep the shards. When I reach into the fireplace to pull up a quarter size piece of glass, I remember my dream with Bob. What's it been, three months?

I rest one hand on the hearth floor and twist my body to look up the chimney. With my left hand I reach up and push against each brick until one actually moves. It's much too big to handle with one hand. I get some newspaper, lay it out and sit inside the hearth facing the room. I reach high, grab the brick with my fingernails, slip it first to one side, then the other, until I get a grip. It's an extra-large brick. I carefully slide it out until it drops. It's too heavy, and I can only slow its descent. I push it away from me and wince when it clunks hard against the fireplace floor.

I look at the empty space, which is the size of a shoebox, but I'm not about to reach in there without being able to see. It takes a while, but I find a flashlight, crawl back into the pit and shine a light into the cavity. I see nothing. Why would Bob want me to look? I get on my knees and lift myself up into the chimney, direct my light and see a silver reflection. I reach for the glint, feel nothing and point the light again.

There is a bright reflection, but I can't grab it. Okay, I'm serious. I go to the bedroom, grab a bath towel and put it over my head. I climb inside and stand. Bent over, I'm eye level with the hidden shelf. I shine my light on the object, reach in and feel it, but I can't loosen it from the shelf.

In a second, I'm back from the kitchen with a butter knife. I stand inside the pit and direct my light, slip the knife under the glint and twist. With a twang, the object pops loose, ricochets off the back wall, and tinkles onto the pit floor. When it stops on the carpet, I see it's a key.

I crawl out, set the knife down remove the towel and dust soot off my shoulders. I pick up the key and study its inscription. The word "Master" in raised letters covers the top of the handle. Under the brand name, in careful print, probably done with an engraving tool, are the words Reseda Storage. Under the inscription is an address and phone number, with a five-digit number below it.

I put the key on the kitchen counter and try to replace the brick, but I can't lift it. I'll leave that part for Stewart.

When I've washed and settled on a barstool, I pick the key up again and grab my phone.

"Reseda Storage," a gruff masculine voice says.

"Can you tell me if I owe rent on unit number five-thirty-four?"

"Give me a minute," he says, and drops the phone hard enough that I think my eardrum has split. I listen to a minute of a scratchy version of a whiny country song. "No, Mrs. Freedman, you're paid in full." He pauses. "It looks like you rented the unit when we opened, and you're set through next year."

"Are you still located at," I read an address from the key.

"Yup. Been in business eight years. Don't think we could move if we wanted."

"Thank you very much," I say and hang up.

For the rest of the day, each time I pass the kitchen, I stop and pick the key up, study it, then go on with my chores.

When the kids get home at three, I say nothing. When Stewart pulls down the driveway after work, I can't wait to show him.

He walks in the house, opens the fridge the way he always does, grabs an O'Doul's, sits on a kitchen chair and drapes one leg across a corner of the table. I pick up my key and hand it to him.

He studies it. "What's this?"

"I found it today."

"Okay?"

I tell him every detail, but he isn't too impressed until I explain my dream about Bob.

"Bob told you about this key?"

"He told me to look behind the brick. I hadn't remembered until I broke the picture."

"You called the storage place?"

"The unit is paid up for the next year."

"No kidding?"

I shrug.

He studies the key. "Maybe Saturday we'll take a drive to Reseda and have a look-see."

"On the bike?"

He smiles. "You've really got a lust for bikes, haven't you?"

I step over to him, and he makes a place in his lap where I sit. I put my arm around his neck and give him a kiss.

***

At the men's group, the first thing on our agenda is meeting with the women.

Tazz stands. "I don't mind getting together with the women, but I resent the fuck out of them setting up times and places."

"Maybe it's time they were leading for a while," Buck says. "I don't mind."

"You don't have a woman who tries to direct you in the first place. I'm in constant battle with Donna, trying to get her to back off."

"Me, too," I say. "Renee has always been the leader in our house. In the last few years I've succeeded in wrestling some of my manhood back from her, but it's a constant struggle."

"If we want them in on this meeting," Shorty says, "maybe we better let them have this one. You got to choose your fights."

"Ain't that fucking right." Tazz sits down, and we go on with our evening. Each man speaks and three do some deeper work. All in all, it's a good evening, working with men I trust and making headway in dealing with the world in general and our women in particular.

During the ride home, I always have lots to think about.

Friday flies by like a blur. Saturday morning, Renee asks the kids what they're up to. Mel responds with a non-committal, "Not much." Sheila and the girl down the street have a haircutting appointment together.

Renee says, "We're going to Reseda for the morning. Anybody want to come along?"

I turn away with a grin before the kids can see. Renee is a sly fox. Let's not present it as something too interesting. They'll want to stay home so we can take the bike.

True to form, neither kid wants to spend time with dear old Dad and Mom. Within an hour we're cruising down the highway, except this time I'm on back, and more than a little nervous.

The ride out Highway 18 is beautiful, and soon we're moving down California 15 in motorcycle bliss. Saturday morning traffic is slow and congested. Renee surprises me with her ability to maneuver in traffic. Guess Bob was right again.

An hour later, we motor off the freeway and come to a stop on a side road. Renee turns right and drives three or four miles east, parallel to the freeway, then turns up and over a small hill into an industrial park. We wind through a maze of roads and find Hepler Street and finally Reseda Storage. At the gate, Renee punches in a code inscribed on her key and the gate opens. She drives down three sterile alleys before we find the right unit. When we dismount, my legs vibrate.

Renee takes her helmet off and pulls the key from her pocket. She turns to me. "Who legally owns it?"

I say, "The whole thing was donated to the Save The Dirt Bike Foundation."

"I'm sure they'll build more dirt bike parks with the money."

I remove my helmet. "Sure, like dirt riders ever stay inside park borders. Someone ought to spend money for truckloads of upholstery tacks and spread them over the entire desert. It would give the landscape a rest. In a hundred years or so, maybe the natural landscape will start to come back."

"I don't know how you can say that, Stewart. You're a biker. Isn't riding the same, no matter what kind of bike?"

"It is, but I have a problem with trashing natural terrain. I don't know if you noticed, but we stay on the pavement."

She flips the key into the air like a fifty-cent piece and catches it. "We have to, don't we?"

"Okay, I'm finished ranting."

"Thank God." She holds the key between us. "I'd say what's in this unit is part of the purchase of the house. The only record of its existence is this key which was hidden in our fireplace. Bob led me to it. The previous owners of the house are dead. I'm not about to donate one more nickel to some dirt-bike conservancy. This storage unit is ours." She inserts the key in a heavy chrome lock.

I stop her. "I still have a problem."

"Let's work problems out later. For now, I want to open 'er up and have a look."

"What if something really good is inside, like an old car or something else that needs to be registered? Then what?"

"I don't care. Let's open it and play it by ear."

"There are too many legal implications."

"Stewart, stop it. I'm opening this door and that is that!"

"Okay, okay, but remember, I warned you."

The lock snaps, and she pulls the hasp back. I step over to the door and yank up on its handle. It squeaks in protest, but rolls up and out of the way.

Renee gasps before I have a chance to look. When I do, my mouth drops open. Boxes are piled to the ceiling along each wall. A dusty upright piano rests against the back. Some household objects show: an old washing machine, two box fans, a tattered ironing board, two sets of ancient wood skis. One thing stands alone centered in the room under a rotted old green army tarp. Renee is frozen. I walk over to the tarp and lift it. I run one finger over a milky pearl color and wipe a layer of dust. I notice an envelope taped to the wide leather seat. I pick it up, fold back the flap, and pull out its contents, then study ownership papers to a 1956 Indian Chief motorcycle.

Renee touches the machine like it's some kind of mirage. "It's beautiful," she says.

I unfold a second piece of paper. It's a handwritten letter in tight, careful architectural script. I read it aloud. "To whom it may concern; My name is Archibald Freedman, and if you are reading my letter, I bequeath the contents of this storage unit to you. For more legal information, please contact my attorney, Samual Hertzog."

"What else?" she asks.

I continue. "You might ask why the gift and why in such an odd manner. I can only tell you this motorcycle was one of two owned by my older brother, Robert Freedman, who died at a tender age of thirty-six, in 1959.

"Because he and I lived together at the time of his demise, I inherited his machines. I had no idea what to do with them, so they sat in my garage. When I was about to sell them, he came to me in a dream and instructed me to start the good one periodically and give everything away in this manner."

"Oh my God," she says.

"That's an understatement."

We both stand slack-jawed and look at either a perfectly restored motorcycle or one that has hardly ever been ridden since it came off the showroom floor.

I finish the last few lines.

"In some of the boxes are spare parts for what is left of the motorcycle he was riding when he was hit by a turnip truck in Pacheco Pass. In the remaining boxes you will find his personal items.

I look up from the letter.

"What a strange way to give something away," Renee says.

She dusts off the seat with her arm and unscrews the oil bag cap. "It's full," she says. She lifts a leg over the bike. "Oh, God, it fits me like a glove.

It looks about twice too big for her, but I say nothing.

She rotates a key, looks to her left, twists the gas petcock and looks for a starter button.

"Older bikes don't have electric starts," I say. "I don't expect it to start, but you can try. The starter is right there." I point at a pedal on the right side.

Renee rotates the pedal out and gets in position to kick.

"Wait." I rotate the distributor to the left.

"What are you doing?"

"It's necessary when starting these old machines. A backfire could easily dislocate a knee or send you flying."

"Okay," she says, "stand back, and let's see if it'll run."

It's an eighty-cubic-inch engine. Petite Renee, who might weigh a hundred-twenty pounds soaking wet, won't be able to start it. Even if she knew how to throw her weight into the kick, I'm certain she wouldn't be able to move the pedal even one inch toward the pavement.

She leaps into the air like a pro and puts her full weight onto the pedal. A cylinder pops, the engine rotates and dies. She leaps into the air again and throws everything she has into her kick. The machine comes alive. Although it runs rough, Renee is able to keep an idle when she feathers the throttle.

The garage fills with fumes, so she lifts the heavy idling machine to a standing position like she'd been doing it all her life, then rolls it outside in neutral.

When she reaches down and rotates the distributor back, the bike settles into a deep-throated, smooth idle.

I stand back and admire the scene. My wife, who hated motorcycles two years ago, sits on this massive machine experimenting with levers and buttons. Without any warning, because had I known, I would have cautioned her against it, she pulls the clutch, slips the bike into first gear and drives away in a roar. She races to the end of our aisle and turns left. The engine thunders on the next row behind me. When she's made a full circle, she rolls the bike up and stops next to me. Over the loud idle of the engine, I sign for her to turn it off. She gives it one last rev and rotates the key.

When the bike dies, in the relative silence, she says, "That was great. Let's take it home."

"Oh, God, Renee, we can't ride this thing just like that."

"Why not?"

"No insurance, for one. No current registration and the oil must be changed before we go anywhere. It's probably been in the engine since 1959. The bike would eat itself up by the time we got home."

"Let's get some oil."

I reach out and put my right hand on the chrome teardrop headlight. "What about insurance?"

"We call Mr. Feldstein and leave a message if he's not there. Once we leave a message, our insurance automatically kicks in."

"Not with an unregistered bike."

"No, but we don't have to live by rules all the time. Come on, Stewart, take a walk on the wild side."

"Holy shit, Renee."

She gives me a wild look. "Let's do it. I'll drive this one."

"It hasn't been driven for a long time. We've gotta' go slow."

"No problem. Let's take back roads."

I help her roll the bike into the garage. She closes and locks the door. We drive off on my bike and look for an auto parts store.

Once the oil is changed and we grease its chain, she pulls the bike back outside, closes the garage door, puts her helmet on, and mounts the machine. "Let's go."

I get on my bike while she starts hers. After a trip to the gas station, we drive in tandem on back roads. I have to admit that it's exciting riding next to my wife.

Chapter 14

Men/Women

"Tonight is the night," I say to Twig as I walk down the rickety stairs. He's in the driveway, on his knees, polishing an engine case. He looks up while his thumb pushes a cloth across the bright metal. "What do you mean, Melinda?"

"The men and women get together for a sit down at Stewart and Renee's."

"I'll be home from work at five," he says. "Maybe we could grab a bite at Marie's."

"I'm not sure she's open on Tuesday nights."

He squeezes a small dab from a tube of Semi-Chrome and works on another section of polished aluminum. "She's closed on Wednesdays."

I walk over to my car, open the door, get in, and roll the window down. "I'll meet you here and we'll ride together to eat, then go over to Stew and Renee's?"

"Sounds good."

I start my engine, back down the driveway and wind my way through town to work.

By evening, I'm tired. Too many lonely desert rats and no-tip honky-tonk cowboys for my taste. On the way home I think about when I worked sales in corporate America. Slinging hash in a small town is much better for my soul. At least I don't have to constantly watch my back.

Dinner at Marie's is rejuvenating, and the ride to Stewart's recharges my batteries. A slight nip in the evening air brings my senses alive. When we climb a hill, the temperature drops, which reminds me of autumns in Philadelphia. I miss fall colors, but I'm glad I don't live there any more.

As we idle along a gravel drive, I'm excited and at the same time anxious about what might happen when men and women work together.

In Stewart's driveway, we park next to the other bikes that belong to Tazz and Donna; Bucky and his new girlfriend; Bill Sanders and his wife Sylvia; and Stewart's blue Fat Boy. I also see a new pearl-white machine I don't recognize.

When Twig turns his engine off, I point at the bike. "Whose bike is that?"

He shrugs and pulls off his cracked helmet. "I haven't got a clue, but it's a beauty."

Renee greets us at her front door and leads us into their huge living room. A crackling fire makes it feel warm and comfortable.

"Whose bike?" I whisper to Stewart.

He gives me a Cheshire grin, shrugs and moves toward the door to let more people in.

Everyone is seated in a large circle of chairs, sofas and a love seat. Twig takes his new bowl out of its box and sets it centered on the coffee table. He removes the cap from a jar and pours sand in the bowl, then places a votive candle in the center of the sand. He positions four corks around the candle and hands slips of printed paper to four people around the circle. Before he arranges the silence beads, another bike rolls up the driveway and goes silent.

Stewart shrugs.

I look at Renee. She puts her hands out, palms up. "I'm not expecting anyone else."

A knock at the front door makes us all look toward the foyer. Renee opens the door. Nick Brown and a leggy blond in her late twenties walk in.

Keys and chains rattle as Nick walks in with Blondie in tow. "This is Carolyn."

She lets out an apprehensive giggle and flushes.

Stewart comes in with two kitchen chairs, and the furniture is moved back to open our circle.

When everyone is seated, Twig continues to arrange the tools. The beads lie beside the bowl. A new talking stick Twig built last week, with a long, slender crystal hanging from its center, gets ceremoniously placed across the bowl. Last, he pulls out a single gray gull feather, not big by any normal feather standard, but from my point of view, it's the biggest tool.

Stewart asks, "What happened to Bob's tools?"

Twig reaches for a sprig of desert sage. "They disappeared last week. It's time we all work with our own tools, anyhow."

"Disappeared?" Nick asks.

"Bob told me he would take them back when everyone had a chance to use 'em."

Twig strikes a match and lights the small candle. Questions cease. Twig speaks in a loud, somber tone. "This flame symbolizes an opening for community."

With a second, larger, black feather, he goes around the circle, wafts sweet sage smoke and smudges each person. When I was first smudged years ago, I thought the hocus-pocus stuff was pure dork, but it didn't take long to see the validity in creating a separation to leave behind the daily world and help us to be in the present. What better way to open the circle than with burning sage?

When finished with the smudging, he begins by explaining the use of each tool, like everyone doesn't already know. Only Nick's Blondie might not be aware.

Twig says, "The bowl is a sacred circle and holds the intention of each person here. The four corks are placed in position to honor the four compass directions. Let us honor the four directions."

He looks at Stewart who sits in the north position. Stew reads from a slip of paper. "I honor North, which symbolizes the element Earth. North brings us winter, silence and death. It rules body, growth, nature, fear, shock, stress, worry, chasms, caves and standing stones. The colors of North are blue and black. I honor North."

When he's finished, Twig nods to Donna, who sits in the eastern position. She gives him a tense look and reads the message with a nervous voice. "I want to honor East, symbolizing the element air and the season spring. East brings us birth, breath and the rising sun. It rules mind, intuitive knowledge, abstract learning, anger, shouting, walking, grief, windswept hills and high mountain peaks. The colors of East are blue and green. I honor the East."

Twig signals Bill Sanders, who reads in his deep voice, "I honor the South, which symbolizes the season summer and element fire. South brings us the noonday sun, warm tropical air, life force and joy. It rules energy, spirit, healing, flame, blood, and destruction. It's ruled by maturity, bitterness, watching, laughter, deserts and volcanoes. Its color is red. I honor South."

Renee, who sits in the western seat, picks up where Bill left off. In her strongest voice, she reads. "I'll honor West, which signifies the element water and season autumn. It brings us sunsets, the Ocean, emotions and courage. West rules feelings, love, sorrow, weeping, fertility and the unconscious mind. It symbolizes skin, hair, lakes, rivers, streams, pools and springs. Its color is white. I honor West."

Twig speaks again. "The candle represents a fifth direction. I honor the vertical that grounds us to the center of earth. It's the direction of going into ashes of grief, while smoke from the flame reaches to far galaxies to which we all aspire."

He stands, grabs the talking stick and holds it high. "Let us honor each person here and create a safe place, respecting each person's chronicle. I ask, with the opening of our circle, that it becomes a container and that our focus be here. I also ask that all outside business stay outside until we close."

He looks around to each person to get a nod of agreement, then continues. "We want to bring in the spirits of our fathers and mothers and the spirits of our grandfathers and grandmothers and their grandparents to create an appropriate place for us, our sons and daughters and our children's children.

"Do we agree that we have a safe and sacred space and nothing said inside this circle will be spoken in the outside world?"

Instant nods from the men, who are used to his question. The women agree, but with trepidation.

"Take a moment to tell us in a single sentence what is going on. Later we'll open with a few minute check-in for each person. Please, no cross-talk during check-in and no questions."

He raises the stick farther, then with a flair, repositions it on the bowl and sits.

Tazz stands, steps forward and picks up the stick. He lifts it high and twirls the crystal while he talks. "Donna and I had a good day today and it's a relief, because we've spent a bunch of days not doing well with each other."

He repositions the stick and returns to his seat.

Renee doesn't pick it up, but simply touches her index finger to the stick. "Stewart and I are doing well, but I'm nervous about what's next for us."

When she releases her finger, murmurs arise. As agreed, no one questions her statement.

Bill gets up and follows with a one-sentence statement about his job.

Sylvia, Bill's wife, doesn't touch the stick. In a one-sentence burst of energy, she says, "I always wondered what happened at these meetings, and I'm so nervous I can't sit still." The stick goes around until everyone has spoken a single sentence.

Twig completes his opening statement with a mini rendition of how relieved he is we've found a way to have good sex without violence. I'm embarrassed.

Twig picks up the stick, and so far, everyone has respected the agreement of the stick. He takes us into the next phase. "Each person who wants can have five minutes for a more in-depth check-in." He sets the stick down, and the evening continues with Bill, who leans forward, grabs the stick and sits back. "My boss is such a jerk. . ." Bill dives into a full five-minute bitch about work. I want to tell him to quit the fucking job, but I hold my tongue during check-in.

The stick continues to be picked up and put down in a random, whenever-a-person-feels-like-talking, kind of way. Finally, it's again left to Twig. He picks it up and sits, then hands the watch to Stewart to keep time. Twig goes into a longer version of what happened with our violence and sex. When he's finished, he puts the stick down and takes the watch back. He asks the circle if anyone has any pressing issues and would like to schedule any of the remaining time.

Nick speaks out. "I'll need fifteen minutes."

As usual, Bill wants time. After a long silence, I stand. "I'd like to be first, and what I have to say will only take a second, but it may take longer for each person to discuss it."

Because Twig is leader tonight, he nods, and I speak without picking up the stick. I turn to him. He already knows what I'm about to say and tries to hide a stupid smirk. I turn back to our family, our true circle of friends. "I'm pregnant."

Murmurs of reluctant praise come from the men. I already know their first thoughts are of fear, responsibility and commitment. Twig and I went through it already, now all he can do is grin. The women, on the other hand, have lots of oohs and ahhs for me, followed by regular girlish questions about when it's due and whether it's a boy or girl.

When I'm finished, when all of the women are finished, I sit, and the meeting goes on.

Tazz snatches the stick from its resting place, and the room drops back into silence. "If we're speaking truth, then I. . ." and he goes on about his fear about a woman getting pregnant, the responsibilities of children and how unfair it is for him to take the financial burden while Donna stays home and takes care of the kids.

Donna leaps to her feet and yells, "I work much harder than you. You get to come home and relax at night, while I work twenty-four hours a day."

Twig puts his hand on her arm and points at the stick.

She fumes, but Tazz still holds the stick. She sits back in her place with a huff of indignation.

"I can't work hard enough to afford another child," he says. "I'm already over-stressed and she wants another. I believe it's because she's afraid to get out in the real world."

He turns to Donna and points the stick at her. "Our kids are old enough. Why can't you go to work and help me? I'm tired."

I look over at Donna, and she sits on the edge of her seat. Her face is red with the effort of holding herself back. I don't look forward to her response.

Typical for a man, Tazz has said his statement and can't think of another thing to say. Reluctant to let go of the stick, he sits without putting the stick down.

Donna leaps to her feet, snatches the feather from its vertical position in the sand and unleashes a string of verbiage at him. She uses key words like jerk, bastard and irresponsible. The tirade goes on for three minutes. She doesn't go over to Tazz's side of the room, doesn't try to touch him, only throws threats and insults at him like a pitching machine. They come fast, curved, slow, drop like a rock, then go fast again. The only thing they don't do is stop until she's wound down to an exhausted mass of flesh. She throws the feather toward the bowl, stumbles back to her position on the couch, collapses and tilts her head back like she has a bloody nose.

I grin, because it's the first time I've seen the feather used outside of Twig and me. It's frightening and yet beautiful.

With Donna's head back, we all look at Tazz, who still holds the stick. He's nervous and who wouldn't be? He went through the fire of feminine fury.

He looks over at Donna. His voice carries genuine appreciation. "That was good." He sets the talking stick into its position on the bowl.

I look around to see who wants to go next. When no one speaks, as leader for the night, Twig picks the next person and points at Bill. "You're on."

Bill snatches the stick and returns to his seat. "Last September I went on the ride with you guys and . . ."

And nothing. . .I think, but Bill goes into a long explanation about the Reno ride, then proceeds to catch us up on day-to-day events. I'm bored to tears before he's said five sentences. I can take it no longer. The guy loves to hear his own voice. Bill is still yammering away when I grab a cork and show it to him. At the same moment, Renee grabs one. Bucky snatches one, too, and holds it up.

Bill would be happy to ramble for the next fifteen minutes, but three corks cannot be ignored. He stops. "What?"

Twig motions him to put the stick down, but he refuses to relinquish it. The room remains quiet. "Why does everyone let Donna rant on, but when it comes to me telling my truth, no one wants to give me any time?"

We're silent, because he still has the stick.

"Why won't anyone listen to what I say?"

Silence, but he likes silence.

When he puts the stick back in its cradle, Twig says, "You got corked, because you put the person who picked it up to sleep. Remember, Bill, the cork is only a reminder for you to see if you're revealing yourself or merely telling a story."

"But it's such a good story."

"Yes, and you're a good storyteller, only this is not the place to tell it. We have a limited time together. Our job is to keep on track or turn the floor over to someone who needs the time."

He sulks. "I just want to participate."

"Wait until something comes up before you jump in."

Bill's sulk drops a notch deeper and he goes silent. I want Twig to continue trying to get through to him. I know from experience that, other than for a rare few seconds when something sinks in, Bill will forever be a human sponge, soaking up energy in every room he is in.

He and his wife Sylvia are good people, though. They're a part of our family, and most times his stories are funny and playful.

I look over at her, and she sits without saying a word. "Bill's the talker in our family," I heard her say once. "All we need is one."

The circle is silent, filled with expectation about who will go next and what they'll say. Twig nods at Nick. Nick stands. His wallet chain and keys rattle. Before he speaks, he spins and looks at me with piercing eyes, then one at a time at each person in the room. When he does, it's with an air of finality, like someone died and it's his job to break the news. "I've made a decision," he says, "though it's not one I came to alone." He swings the stick high in the air. "Bob helped and Carolyn, too." He points the stick at her and smiles.

"It's been a long time coming. I've been stuck in a role I wanted at first, but that's worn thin over time. I no longer find it exciting or even interesting to build Harleys. My heart's not in it anymore. Maybe I'm bored or maybe I'm ready to expand into things other than Harleys, I don't know."

He turns and speaks, making eye contact with each person randomly. "For this reason, I won't touch another Harley for a few years and maybe never again."

There is a constrained rustling in the room. When he continues, it's with a defiant tone. "I'm pulling up stakes and moving north to study sculpture at a community college in San Francisco." He looks around as if he expects comment. He has the stick and our uninterrupted attention. "There's only one thing I'll miss about this crappy town; it's all of you." He sets the stick in its cradle.

I ask, though I'm still bowled over with shock, "How long will you be gone?"

He turns to me. "Maybe forever. I want a new life and this is a critical moment."

Although I've hardly said a word to him in the last two years, I ask, "When are you leaving?"

Nick glares at me. "Tomorrow."

I leap to my feet and grab the stick. "We have some stuff to complete before you leave. I've waited for you to come to me, but I guess you're too much of a weenie, so we better do it tonight."

Nick shrugs, opens one hand palm up and extends it; a signal for me to go on.

I know what's coming. It's developed for a long time. I only hope I can control the part of me that wants to scratch his eyes out. Twig and I have worked the violence thing for months, I hope I can apply it. "You left me in Vegas, you bastard, and you never said boo about why. I need to know."

I set the stick down and remain standing.

Nick picks up the stick and looks at me. With his eyes glassed up and a catch to his voice, he says, "Fuck, Melinda, I wanted to love you, I truly did, but I didn't know what to do with your violence. I tried to work with you, only I'd end up with black eyes and bloody noses. I'd hoped therapy would help, but we ran out of time. I had to survive, and the only way to do it was to disappear. I was afraid that you'd stalk me if I moved and left a forwarding address."

We look eye to eye. He gets his familiar guilty look. "I was addicted to our sex-violence scenario. The only way for me to disengage from my drug of choice, you, was to go cold turkey and disappear. I was terrified that if I didn't leave, at some point I would match your violence. By the time I made my decision, I was enraged. I wasn't sure I could stop once I started, sex or no sex."

His eyes glaze. "I was afraid for my life, Melinda, and I wasn't about to die waiting for you to get a handle on your violence."

He shifts his weight, turns, looks at Twig and back at me. "I couldn't tell anyone what was going on, because I was too embarrassed to be the victim. I mean, hell, you're a woman, but I was the one with black eyes and broken noses. We'd end up in the emergency room on a regular basis, and all they could ask was why I was so clumsy."

He points the stick at Twig. "It's all worked out in the long run. You met your match with Twig, and together the both of you are working this one out. I couldn't have done that, because I didn't understand what drove you."

I snatch the feather. I don't touch Nick or throw anything at him, but go into a scream about what a jerk he is.

When I wind down to a whisper, I drop the feather, glare at Nick, then step back to my seat and sit. I wipe my eyes in an attempt to focus. His face melts into glimpses of all the men I've ever been violent with. I see fear in their eyes. Incredibly, I see love and sadness as well. I feel raw and exposed in front of everyone. For the first time, my gut wrenches with the pain I have caused. The last face is a baby, laughing and gurgling. I break down and weep. God, how can I even think of being a mother? I feel the touch of someone's hand on my shoulder and look up into Nick's face. I know he means well, but I can't face him or anyone. I push his touch away, lean to the bowl, grab the silence beads and turn my back to the group. When I put them on, I relieved to know that no one will look at me or try to make contact until I remove them. Ten minutes later, when I calm and remove the beads, as agreed, no one asks about why I needed the beads.

When there is a pause, I pick up the talking stick. The room tenses. I clear my throat and look at Nick. "Something happened just now. Maybe it was Bob, or maybe I finally woke up. I always blamed men for leaving me, because the sex wasn't any good unless I was violent. Tonight I felt your pain and the pain of all the men I've ever hit. The truth is, men left me because I hurt them."

I turn and one at a time, look at everyone in the room. "I'm getting better, but it's obvious that the cells of my body only feel alive after I've had a violent episode."

I look again at Nick. "Thank you for being honest and courageous." I sit and place my hands over my belly, "I'm complete for now."

Twig glances at his watch. "It's five to nine. Is there any more unfinished business?"

No one speaks.

He says, "It's time to choose a new leader for next week and decide who will host the evening. Any volunteers?"

I hear more than a bit of mumbling and see lots of reluctant faces. After a minute, he performs the last duty of the leader for the evening. "If no one volunteers, I choose Donna."

Donna looks at Twig. Her mouth works up some words of protest. Eventually she doesn't speak, but reluctantly accepts the role.

Twig says, "I have a quick statement, then I'll officially declare the meeting closed." He looks about the room. "This morning I rented a garage on Fifth Street. I'm going to quit that fucked up job at the rubber band company and fix Harleys."

The room is silent until Twig says, "Okay, I want to release all spirits who have helped us this evening, and I declare this evening's meeting closed for--".

Renee leaps to her feet and grabs the stick. It's obvious she's tense. Her hands shake. She turns and looks around the room at each one of us, then speaks. "Bob came to me in a dream two months ago. He told me to look in a certain secret place in this house, once we bought it. I found a key, which led Stewart and me to a storage unit in Reseda. Inside the garage was the pearl Indian that sits out front." She turns and looks at me. "Robert Freedman owned that bike in the fifties. After a lot of checking, I'm almost positive Robert Freedman is Biker Bob."

A gasp fills the room. No one speaks. She turns to Stewart, stick still in hand and continues. "Bob came to me again last night, Stew. He told me to get the bike looked over and he wants me to go on an extended journey with it."

It's obvious Stewart wants to say something, but he keeps silent.

She gets down on one knee and comes closer to his pale face. "How long I'll be gone, Bob didn't say."

Stewart's face is a mass of confusion, maybe even a rare hint of anger. Since Renee holds the stick, he remains silent.

Renee pauses and looks around the circle, then rests her gaze on Stewart's face. "I know, we finally move back together, we even have friends that support both of us, and now I'm going off on my own. It doesn't make any sense, but I too need to find out who I am and what I really want. From what I've seen so far, this Bob character knows more about me than I do.

Stewart nervously clinches his fist. His breath is shallow.

Renee takes one of his hands and gently caresses it. "Like you did two years ago, Stewart, I'm following Bob's lead.

"I want to be with you in my strength, and I need to explore those parts of myself that have nothing to do with being a mom or a wife. If I don't do it now, I'm afraid I'll leave forever one day and never know why.

Available soon

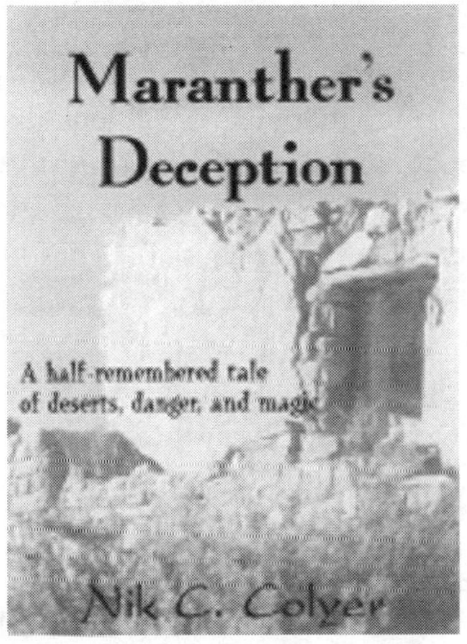

Nik C. Colyer's
third novel

Maranther's Deception

Martin and Leigha's vacation to the Sonora desert becomes a journey into their past, the future, and the ever-growing awareness that nothing is as it appears, especially the mysterious medicine woman, Maranther.

Excerpt from
Maranther's Deception

With nothing else to do, I consider our predicament; the blessing of finding these adobe buildings, how much walking we've done, and how much we must still do. I contemplate our car, buried in the sand, and what it will look like once we get it out. I think about our lack of water in this barren desert environment. I consider many things before I hear Leigha stir. Once she's awake, I ask, "What about the ghost thing?"

Her pallor returns. "I thought I'd dreamt it." There's a long pause before she continues with a shaky voice, "An old woman walked through the door with an armful of wood. She didn't open the door, simply walked right through."

I point toward the hearth. "Someone left wood stacked next to the fireplace. I assume that same person left this." I hold up the pendant.

Leigha takes the pendant, looks at it, then slips it in her top shirt pocket.

"Hey, that's not yours."

"What?"

"The pendant I handed you."

"What pendant?"

"The one in your pocket."

"Of course it is, silly. I've had this pendant forever."

"I've never seen it before I picked it up by the fire."

"Are you kidding me? My lucky pendant has been with me for as long as I can recall. Last year, we had to take it in and have a new leather strap made."

"We did nothing of the sort. I've never seen it."

"I can't believe you don't remember."

After an awkward silence, she breaks the tension by changing the subject. "The old woman walked through the tent, you know like in all the ghost movies we've ever seen. I felt something when she walked back through to go out the door. I'm not sure how to describe it, like a shiver of bitter cold had settled into my bones."

I listen to her, but I need time to digest the meaning. I need to distract myself from the insane evidence that some kind of spirit visited Leigha. I never gave credence to ghosts, but the pile of dark firewood and the pendant mean something. Someone came bearing gifts.

While I was battling the shrieking wind, Leigha certainly had time to pull such a prank, but I know her. A joke would be the last thing she'd be capable of. I can't remember one single time when my wife ever thought of spoofing me, much less doing it on such a grand scale. Even if she wanted to, there would have been no way she could have found fresh-cut wood in the middle of this desolate landscape, especially in this wind. And, what about her claim that the pendant was hers all along?

I don't want to frighten her, so I try to remain calm, but a new fear adds to the ongoing anxiety about being stranded in the middle of this desert, and it howls at the edge of my awareness. Me and my stupid desert holiday. What have I gotten us into?

Channeling Biker Bob 2 Lover's Embrace

-Reading Group Guide-

1. During the first part of the book, is Thomas Goreman's anger the only emotion he expresses?
2. What events led Goreman to hit his wife; and what was the emotion driving him during that time?
3. What was Goreman's emotional response to his loss of control during the bust, at the bar and at home? What did he mean when he said he hated feeling small?
4. Who did Goreman blame for his troubles? Why was it important that he accept responsibility for his actions?
5. What part did the baseball bat and tire play in Goreman's transformation? Why was it crucial for him to learn how to express his anger without hurting anyone?
6. Why was it necessary for Goreman to get sober?
7. What part did Bob play in Goreman's metamorphosis into Twig?
8. Was it important for him to hear from the dream-Georgina, about why she was leaving him?
9. Could Gorman have made changes without the help of the One Percent guys? Why was it so hard for him to reach out? Do men and women have an equally difficult time asking for help?
10. What did Bob mean when he said that Twig didn't feel like he deserved any help?
11. What did the roses represent?
12. How did the dream-world men's gatherings change Goreman and what did they do for Twig?

13. What did going into the Sattley Cash Store do for Melinda, Twig and Stewart?
14. Though it was abusive and inappropriate, what was Twig's dad trying to teach him? How did it affect the rest of his life?
15. How did Melinda play out her addiction to violence? What past experience tied her to the violence/sex scenario?
16. Bob said that men and women problem solve differently. Does that make sense to you?
17. If men shame women by saying "get to the point", and women discount men by interrupting and finishing their sentences for them, is it possible that a tool such as the "talking stick" could enable both genders to be heard? Would you be willing to try it?
18. What did Donna mean when she told Tazz that she needed him to listen to her and not fix anything?
19. Did it resonate with you when Melinda said that women are trained to be nice, to go along with the status quo; those women that refuse, the ones who speak out are called "bitches"?
20. Does Bob's statement, "unshed tears turn us into enraged and violent men", sound reasonable to you? Since sadness is acceptable territory for a woman, what might unexpressed anger do to her?
21. Have you ever felt like Renee when she told Stewart that it made her feel crazy when she could sense his anger but he denied it?
22. Why did Nick feel humiliated with Melinda's violence? What step did Melinda finally take in the circle?
23. What about Renee leaving? Can you understand her need to discover herself outside of being a mother or a wife? If you had the opportunity, what would your journey look like?